Prospect For Murder

GoodReads
Being a resident of Hawaii, I could not pass up a murder mystery based in Honolulu. It was thrilling while at the same time oddly relaxing to read a story with so many local references to places, food, culture, and traits... The writing was insightful, observant, emotive, and intelligent. Each scene, task, and event was highly detailed and meticulously described.... I savored the sense of familiarity as well as the intriguing storyline.

AudioBook Reviewer
(Audiobook narrated by Jeanne Burrows-Johnson)
Highly recommended... The Narrator, also the author, Jeanne Burrows-Johnson did an excellent job of reading the book. The enunciation and clearness of her speech as well as the passion was not over the top or fake...Her voice was soothing and calming.

Joe Kilgore, U. S. Review of Books
In this debut whodunit, Burrows-Johnson displays a fine eye for detail, a sharp ear for dialogue, and a commendable commitment to tie up loose ends. One suspects this is only the beginning of Natalie's adventures.

Murder on Mokulua Drive

Kirkus Reviews
A semiretired journalist in Hawaii who experiences visions tries to solve a neighbor's murder in this second installment of a mystery series.... the protagonist is first-rate...The plot offers a couple of impressive twists. A diverting tale led by a smashing amateur detective whose dexterity far exceeds her paranormal gift.

Jordan Landsman, The US Review of Books
This author knows her genre, and she skillfully blends familiar ingredients that faithful cozy mystery readers will appreciate....Natalie's dreams are downright prescient, bringing a mystical quality to the crime-solving activities.

Murders of Conveyance

Kirkus Reviews

In this third entry of a mystery series, a woman's latest vision seems to be an unsolved, decades-old murder that links to a present-day homicide... Burrows-Johnson's protagonist, as in preceding novels, is an accomplished sleuth...The author's bountiful details explore Hawaii's history and culture, as scavenger hunt clues direct Natalie and Keoni to historical landmarks and the inquiry includes Chinatown in Honolulu. A Whodunit as smart and engrossing as the unlikely gumshoe.

Tamara Benson, San Francisco Book Review

There are many reasons to recommend this novel. The descriptions of each destination and the players' race during the scavenger hunt are well done and leave the reader ready to book travel plans to see the sights first-hand... The relationships between the neighbors are wonderful and something that really makes the characters likable. And, of course, any murder mystery that involves a cat is a winner from the start!

THE NATALIE SEACHRIST HAWAIIAN MYSTERIES
Yen For Murder
Murders of Conveyance
Murder on Mokulua Drive
Prospect for Murder

OTHER WORKS
Co-Author, *Under Sonoran Skies, Prose and Poetry from the High Desert*

YEN FOR MURDER

A Natalie Seachrist Hawaiian Mystery

By

Jeanne Burrows-Johnson

Artemesia
Publishing

ISBN: 978-1-951122-85-0 (paperback)
ISBN: 978-1-951122-86-7 (ebook)
LCCN: 2024933270

Artemesia Publishing, LLC
9 Mockingbird Hill Rd
Tijeras, New Mexico 87059
info@artemesiapublishing.com
www.apbooks.net

I am grateful that in spite of the tragic losses from the Maui wild fires of 2023, the survival of the Lahaina banyan tree (planted on April, 24 1873) has brought a revival of the spirit of the people of Maui and all of Hawai'i.

It is the dim haze of mystery that adds enchantment to pursuit.
Antoine Rivarol [1753 - 1801]

ISLAND OF OʻAHU

N W E S

Kahuku Point
Kaleuila Point
Turtle Bay
Kawela Bay
Kahuku
Lāʻie

'Ilima
Flower of Oʻahu

Waimea Bay
Pūpūkea
Polynesian Cultural Center
Kawailoa
Haleʻiwa
Mokulēʻia

Hauʻula
Punaluʻu
Kahana Bay

83

Kaʻaʻawa

Kaʻena Point
Dillingham Air Field
930

KOʻOLAU MOUNTAINS

Kāneana Cave
Waialua
99
Dole Plantation
Mokoliʻi Island
Waikāne
Kāneʻohe

Mākua
Wahiawā
803

WAIʻANAE MOUNTAINS

Mt. Kaʻala
H-2

Kahaluʻu
Byōdō-in Temple
Kāneʻohe Bay
Marine Corps Base

93

Mililani

Mākaha
Plantation Village
90

Waiʻanae
Waipahu
Pearl City
ʻAiea

Kailua
Lanikai
Nā Mokulua Islets

Likelike Hwy.
65

Māʻili

61

Waimānalo
Mānana Island
Sea Life Park

Nānākuli
Pearl Harbor
Bishop Museum
52

Pali Hwy.
Pali Lookout

72

Makapuʻu Beach
Sandy Beach
Hālona Blowhole

H-1
29
Joint Base Pearl Harbor-Hickam
80
Punchbowl
61

Mānoa Valley
University of Hawaiʻi

Koʻolina
USS Arizona Memorial
Kewalo Basin
Aloha Tower

Hawaiʻi Kai

Hanauma Bay

Kapolei
ʻEwa Beach
Honolulu Airport
Waikīkī Beach
Honolulu

Diamond Head

ʻAina Haina
Kāhala
Koko Head

OVERVIEW OF THE HAWAIIAN LANGUAGE

The Hawaiian language was unwritten until 1826, when Christian missionaries transcribed the sounds of the language into a thirteen-letter alphabet. Hawaiian consonants are pronounced as in standard American English. They include H, K, L, M, N, P, W, and the ʻokina [ʻ]. Often, the "W" is pronounced like an English "V." As there is no "S" in the Hawaiian language, plurals are determined by the preceding article. Each vowel is sounded in Hawaiian; they are similar in pronunciation to those in Spanish, and other Latin-based European languages:

A = *Ah*, as in above
E = *Eh*, as in let
I = *Ee*, as in eel
O = *Oh*, as in open
U = *Oo*, as in soon

~ Diphthongs are expressed as common English sounds. The "au" transliteration is pronounced as "ow" in "How."

~ Diacritical marks indicate emphasis and syllable separation. A *kahakō* [-] placed over vowels indicates an elongated vowel requiring the speaker to hold the vowel sound slightly longer, as seen in the "a" in the word "card." The *ʻokina* [ʻ] is both a consonant and a diacritical mark [phonetic glottal stop], employed to produce a break, as in "oh-oh."

~ The Hawaiian language does not have verb conjugation.

~ There is no "S" in the Hawaiian language; plurals are determined by the preceding article. However, in accordance with standard publishing practices, foreign words included in this work are subject to the grammatical rules of English, including pluralization and possessives. I should note that the interviewee often used an "S" for possessives and to pluralize Hawaiian vocabulary.

CAST OF CHARACTERS

Anthony Brennan Retired detective, Honolulu Police Department

Esmeralda [Izzy] Cruz Neighbor of Natalie Seachrist; one of The Ladies

John [JD] Dias Lieutenant, Honolulu Police Department

Akira Duncan Master chef; owner of a restaurant and culinary school

Ayameko Kōha Fujimoto A minister of Jōdo Shinshū Buddhism, deceased

Adriana Gonzalez Consulting physician, Hale Malolo Shelter

Nathan Harriman Twin brother of Natalie Seachrist; psychologist

Keoʻni Hewitt Boyfriend of Natalie Seachrist; retired homicide detective

Alena Horita Detective, Honolulu Police Department

Nori Horita Father of Alena Horita; Japanese linguist

ʻIlima Feline companion of The Ladies

Hitomu Kiyohara Patriarch of the Kiyohara family, deceased

Koji Kiyohara Chief Executive Officer, Nippon Antiquities

Tommy [Yasuhiro] Kiyohara Brother of Hitomu Kiyohara; Nippon Antiquities auctioneer

Kūlia Canine companion of Nathan Harriman

Harry Longhorn Publisher and chief editor, *Windward Oʻahu Journeys*

Leonard Makani Captain, Honolulu Police Department

Miss Una Feline companion of Natalie Seachrist

Lori Mitchum Intern, State of Hawaiʻi Coroner's Office

Akita Okumura Crime scene specialist, Honolulu Police Department

Natalie Seachrist Semi-retired journalist

Manny Salazar Undercover detective, Honolulu Police Department

Bō Shen Commercial realtor

Larry and Lulu Smith Neighbors of Natalie Seachrist

Martin Soli Assistant coroner, State of Hawaiʻi Coroner's Office

Evelyn and Jim Souza Neighbors of Nathan Harriman

Joe Swan Evidence specialist, the Central Intelligence Agency

Samantha Turner Neighbor of Natalie Seachrist; one of The Ladies

Joanne Walther Neighbor of Natalie Seachrist; one of The Ladies

Pearl Wong Natalie Seachrist's friend; apartment complex owner

PROLOGUE

Death never takes the wise man by surprise, he is always ready to go.
Jean de La Fontaine [1621 - 1695]

I sit at the back of a darkened theatre-like space, listening to incantation by voices male and female. The word "OM" whispers unceasingly across the large room, as though the chanters take no breath between their intonations of the repeated sound. I inhale and exhale, nearly able to join in with the prolonged nasal baritone range of the prayerful.

At the front of the rows of pews are plum-colored silk drapes that fall from an unseen ceiling. Framing this tableau are the sepia-toned edges one expects to see on a vintage photograph. Abruptly, the drapes sweep open and rise slowly before disappearing. A wide shrine area is revealed. In the center of its black floor is an altar with a golden standing Buddha, flanked by two attendant statuettes. On the far left is another smaller altar with the statue of a Buddha in seated position. To the right and left edges of the space are podiums from which the ministers of the temple address their congregation.

Between the podiums, white pedestals of varying height support a variety of sacred statues. With the images of revered figures from numerous Asian religions, this scene is clearly an altered presentation of reality. Despite the profusion of mixed faiths, I recognize where I am. It is an exaggerated representation of a Japanese Jōdo Shin Buddhist temple I have visited and written about on numerous occasions. While I hear the soft murmuring of voices, I know I am alone. And although I am surrounded by rich fragrances, there are no lit candles or incense on the altar.

My reverie is broken by the reverberations of a large bell. As if on cue, the unrealistic elements of the scene evaporate, and the true sanctuary of the temple is revealed. A middle-aged minister now enters from a door upstage left. Her hair is cut short, providing an attractive frame to her face. Although she wears no makeup, her skin glows with an inner joy. She wears black rimmed glasses and I cannot clearly see her eyes. Unlike many of her male counterparts, who wear suits under their robes, she is dressed traditionally, even to the black getas on her feet. On top of the layered clothes hangs a plum-colored surplice embroidered with a gold wisteria flower.

As the minister walks serenely across the wide stage, she pauses to bow to honor the spirit that each of the four statues represent. Afterwards, she turns and glides to the central altar, where she stands in contemplation before the standing Amida Buddha for a moment. She lights the candles and joss sticks of incense before her and steps back a couple of paces. As I breathe in the room's intensifying scent, I hear the faint clicking of her prayer beads. I marvel at the peace and joy I feel, as though united with the woman who stands in front of me.

At that point everything freezes. A profound silence descends. Like my surroundings, I am transfixed without movement of eye or breath. And then, amidst the idyllic scene, a single sharp sound explodes through my consciousness. I watch, horrified as the gentle woman falls to the floor and the sepia tones of my recurring visions envelop all of the room.

CHAPTER 1

Silken words, delivered gently.
Baltazar Gracián [1601 - 1658]

"Natalie. Wake up, honey. You're okay," said the love of my life soothingly.

"Mmhm."

"You're home with me, Natalie."

"I was dreaming. It was a terrible dream. Terrible."

"Back at the mall in Haifa in 1988? Or that Nairobi cab in 1998?"

I licked my dry lips and shook my head. "No. I was here. In Honolulu. At a Buddhist temple."

"Mm," murmured Keʻoni, rubbing my shoulder.

"At first it was so beautiful…The incense, the statues, the chanting. And then…then she died."

"Who died?" he asked, concentrating on rubbing my arm.

"A woman."

"What woman?" he asked, pausing.

"I've no idea. I don't think she was anyone I've seen in person. In fact, there were many things about the scene that differed from the temple I used to go to occasionally for special events. It was like a theatrical version of a Buddhist sanctuary…with statues from many faiths scattered around," I said.

"Let me get you some water, and then you can tell me more," said Keʻoni reassuringly.

In a couple of moments, he returned with a glass of cool water. I sat up, sighed, and took a long drink.

"Better?" he asked, staring at me intently with his glittering blue eyes.

"Much. Don't worry. It probably wasn't a vision. At least, I don't think it was. It was pretty much in real time and full color. Maybe I had the dream because of all the antique catalogues we've been looking at. You know. With stunning figurines, oversized candelabras, and other beautiful altar pieces."

Keʻoni continued to give me an appraising look for another moment and then invited me into our steam shower. The soothing water, and the presence of my beloved, was exactly what I needed to shake off my disturbing dream. After settling in for a few hours of peaceful sleep, I was ready to face another day.

With my flexible calendar as a semi-retired freelance journalist, I could remain at home that Wednesday. Anticipating a casual day, I threw on an old swimsuit and pulled my mid-length hair back in a scrunchie. In contrast, since Ke'oni was meeting with clients, he had dressed in chino trousers and another of his classic mid-twentieth century aloha shirts.

When I arrived in the kitchen, I was still feeling a little out of kilter. Luckily, Ke'oni had brewed coffee from syrup made in the French coffee press he had given me as a gift in hopes that I would take a giant step forward in my culinary efforts. My contribution was to pull out a couple of bowls from the cupboard, clean soup spoons from the dishwasher, and a selection of fruit from the refrigerator. We're fortunate to always have fresh diced pineapple from our local deli and papaya from the trees of the cottage that had been my Auntie Carrie's. There were also strawberries from the women living behind us whom we have designated The Ladies. With fresh malasadas from Agnes's Bakery, we were ready for a lovely breakfast on the back *lānai*.

Although I am the new owner of White Sands Cottage, I always think of it as my auntie's home. When she passed, Ke'oni and I had just become a committed couple and were glad to take on remodeling her bungalow. After an investment of six months of our lives—and frequent infusions of cash from redeeming many of our savings bonds—we moved into the cottage with Miss Una, my feline companion named for the tortoise shell her coat resembles.

My Auntie Carrie's passing is not the only death that has occurred in recent years. In fact, it was the death of my grandniece Ariel that brought Ke'oni Hewitt and me together. Since then, death has been our companion on more than a few occasions. That is not to say I have been having tea with my auntie's ghost. But I can picture her flitting about each of the home's many rooms, especially on holidays, which she lived to the fullest.

I shall always miss her...and even her neighbor, whom we had barely gotten to know when she was murdered shortly after we moved into the neighborhood. Fortunately, we enjoy the company of her former housemates. Our over-the-fence friends include housekeeper-turned-roommate Izzy Cruz, Joanne Walther, a retired schoolteacher, and their last short-term housekeeper, Samantha Turner.

Samantha is a lovely woman whose husband decided he would not honor her desire for freedom. Now that she is permanently rid of him, she has returned to college for a degree in international business. With a class schedule that precludes her having a full-time job, Samantha happily accepts assignments from both Ke'oni and me. For despite our relaxed beachside home, our post-retirement careers have grown larger than we expected.

After joining forces with a national security firm, Ke'oni now busily analyzes the needs of local businessmen and wealthy homeowners who appreciate having the eye and mind of a former police detective at their disposal. Since he can no longer handle every detail of his clients' needs personally, Samantha eases his schedule by inputting data and acting as a courier for Hewitt Investigations. In addition, she performs occasional research for me. With a new monthly magazine column on food, drink, and entertainment, I am always on the alert for locales to feature. Once I have an idea for an article, background research is of paramount importance, and I am delighted to have Samantha's assistance.

As I watched Ke'oni stare across our yard, I again thanked the universe for the life I am experiencing. Despite the murder and mayhem that have periodically intruded, everything surrounding us today glows with a peace-filled light. Even when we are apart, our adventures provide the basis for delightful sharing when we come together at the end of our days.

After Ke'oni left to meet his client, I decided to go for a walk. With my sometimes-valiant feline at my side, I walked toward Lanikai Beach. As expected, when we arrived at the roadway, Miss Una decided to return to our neighbors' backyard, where I knew she would soon be frolicking with 'Ilima, the kitten she has been mentoring for several months.

Strolling along the sand for a while, I sat down in front of a large rock with an indentation that made an ideal backrest. I leaned back and thought about how nice it was to live just a block and a half from one of the most beautiful beaches in Hawai'i. The water seemed to sparkle especially brightly, as I raised my sunglasses to rub them on the edge of my towel. For a while I simply enjoyed watching the antics of gulls flying above Nā Mokulua, the two islets sitting three-quarters of a mile offshore.

I was glad to have shrugged off the lingering discomfort of my dream-vision and eventually sank into a blissful sleep in the warmth of the morning sun. I awoke feeling a refreshing breeze brush across my face and neck. I stretched my legs, stood up, and reversed my steps to White Sands Cottage.

After a quick shower to wash off the sand and sea salt, I wandered into the kitchen for something to eat. Since I needed to spend the early afternoon researching a few new ideas for my column, I decided that a glass of sun tea with peach juice and cinnamon would provide the ideal pickup...as would soaking my feet in the spa. I headed out the door for a few more minutes of leisure time with a plate of leftover ham, cheese, and water crackers.

There were no surprises when I re-entered the office. Clearly Miss Una had not arrived at the garden window above the sink that serves as her highway to the world and rampaged through the office. The same back issues of *Honolulu Magazine* and a stack of feature articles from the *Honolulu Star-Advertiser* were sitting on my desk. Although I have a *carte blanche* directive from Harry Longhorn, my publisher at *Windward Oʻahu Journeys*, I did not want to address a topic covered recently by another writer—especially if it was a good piece. I would have preferred to spend the day reading a mystery, or playing with Miss Una and little ʻIlima, but I knew I needed to buckle down and act like the professional I am.

For a couple of hours, I diligently read through the materials Samantha and I had assembled and contemplated relevant articles I had written previously. Finally, I looked at a website with an interactive map of Oʻahu displaying island entertainment venues that attract both local and overseas visitors. After a long career as a journalist and sometimes presenter in the leisure and travel industry, I am glad I now control my assignments. I am also pleased that I no longer have to work alone since Harry has suggested that Keʻoni join me in sampling the delights I write about.

Despite having written pieces for several issues, I am still refining the tone of my column. While it is presented from my viewpoint, I try to introduce each locale in a way that allows readers to gain a sense of what their own experience might be. Since Keʻoni and I sometimes differ on our appraisal of a featured business, I have experimented with layout options to highlight our contrasting views. One element I am employing is colored side bars in addition to he-said-she-said asides. This feature allows room to highlight recipes and the culinary techniques of restaurant chefs, as well as the micro-farmers who supply unique foodstuffs.

Although they may not generate sufficient crops to be considered commercial farmers in the traditional sense, their additions to the menus of farm-to-table establishments have brightened the overall dining experience for restaurants of every type. I have been amazed at the excitement their endeavors generate. The chefs and restaurateurs with whom they work are so pleased to offer their clientele high-quality food, that they willingly pay a premium to do so. As to the patrons who consume the end product, many of us are becoming outright foodies.

Recently, Harry offered Chef Akira Duncan a column of his own. I had introduced the men during the launch of my renewed career with an article featuring this chef's approach to Pacific Rim cuisine and his windward Oʻahu culinary school. After partaking of Chef Duncan's delicious food at his popular Honolulu restaurant, Harry was delighted to discover the man is as gifted with a pen as he is with cutlery. The focus of Chef Duncan's seasonal column will be meal planning, as well as distinctive recipes for holidays and special occasions. Harry anticipates that the two of us will offer the magazine's readers a plethora of food and entertaining ideas.

In addition to my new career in sampling some of the most interesting food on Oʻahu, I am in the process of enhancing my own abilities in the kitchen. My self-improvement program is undercover for the time being. It will remain so until I can produce several meals with predictable success. Considering my reputation for burning even a pan with water, I have decided to limit knowledge of my current endeavors to The Ladies in order to avoid being openly ridiculed by the men in my life.

Joanne provides unending supplies of fresh fruits and vegetables from her garden for my experimentation. Izzy gives me impromptu cooking lessons when I indicate a particular interest in her unending culinary triumphs. Despite the limitations of her rheumatoid arthritis, she continues to amaze us all with her varied baked goods and mealtime staples. Fortunately, with the hands of two housemates, and even me, she generates nearly the same volume of tasty treats that she did years ago.

The primary source of my increasing culinary skill is Chef Duncan's school. There I am about to undertake a course in meals centered on classic soups. After surviving the course in kitchen basics, I needed to take a break in my studies to launch my column. When I initially undertook an appetizer course, I failed to complete a couple of assignments and had to retake the final classes. So, while many of my original classmates are zooming through the school's curriculum like advanced placement students dying to get out of high school, I am trailing behind on a much slower track.

The next morning, I was running a little late and was glad that the opening day of my new cooking class focused on the course outline and materials we need to provide. By the time I had asked my instructor a couple of questions, I was late leaving for an appointment at my hairdresser's. I exited the building without removing my pinafore apron, lost in contemplation of recipes for the soups I would soon be mastering. I unlocked the trunk of my Kia Optima and prepared to drop in my basket of cutlery and cooking utensils. Just then I heard a voice.

"Playing Little Red Riding Hood, Sis?" called a voice from behind me.

Only one person would call me *Sis* and he has not done that since we were kids.

"Guilty as charged," I replied turning to face my twin, Nathan. "But why are you calling me *Sis*, little brother? I thought we agreed we were too old for nicknames when we entered high school."

"Hey, stop referring to me as your *little brother*. I don't think a few minutes head start in the delivery room qualifies you as my *older sister*. And when you look like you've just come from seventh grade home economics class, what should I call you? So, what are you doing at Chef Duncan's school? And don't say you're writing a follow-up article for your column."

After removing my apron, I turned away to drop it into my basket.

"Nathan, I'll admit my crime *if* you can keep this little secret between us—at least for the time being."

"All right, but your story had better be good," he said with a gleeful smile.

"You know how you've never allowed me bring anything edible to your parties—except bottles of wine—and now, Ke'oni's sun tea concoctions?"

He nodded. "God forbid I should ever need to take another guest to the hospital to have their stomach pumped—like that time you brought a crab dip that was so old you couldn't even read the sell date on its label."

"Okay. I'll admit to that one grievous error. But that's the only time I've made a mistake like that."

"Thank God that's true, Natalie. So, let's consider your attempts at baking. It didn't matter whether Mother or Auntie Carrie provided the recipe—let alone the lesson. You managed to burn every batch of cookies you baked as a kid."

"Okay, I'll admit I've never been any good at baking. But I thought that after all these decades, I should finally learn to use the pots, pans, and knives Bill's mother gave me when we got married."

"Gee, it's great you've thought this out so carefully. No reason to rush into anything rashly—what with your having been a widow for nearly forty years and your mother-in-law's being gone for at least two decades. But why plunge into a course of self-improvement now?"

"Well, until *now* I really never had a reason. After all, I was on the road for so long. I was never anywhere long enough to need to cook anything. And besides, there was always Mom or you and Sandy to handle holidays and other special occasions during the few times I was here."

"And now?"

"You know how wonderful Ke'oni has been about beautifying Auntie Carrie's cottage. I feel the least I can do is offer more than salad and pizza when he's been working hard. Now that I'm writing an entertainment column, Ke'oni and I are being treated to a lot of great meals. But that doesn't do much for our day-to-day nutritional needs. I've already taken the culinary basics course and one on appetizers. And I've just started one on classic soup recipes. After I complete that, I was planning to invite you and Adriana over for a wine tasting with heavy *pūpūs*. So, please help me by keeping my secret for a few more weeks."

"All right. That's a reward worthy of my silence. If only for the fun of watching you pull it off. It's just too bad Mom and Sandy aren't here to appreciate these advances in your culinary life."

That last remark was bittersweet for its truth. There are so many regrets in life for which no one can compensate. Mom and Nathan's wife had celebrated food and holidays as much as Auntie Carrie. How wonderful that the rest of us had been privileged to sample their delightful efforts! As Nathan and I parted, I made a promise to go through my cupboards and closets for items to donate for an upcoming fundraiser being held by the Hale Malolo Women's and Children's Shelter. Perhaps I was finally ready to part with reminders of both of these strong women.

The concept for the Yours, Mine, and Ours Fair is unique. After the donations of new and gently used items have been organized in an empty warehouse, the families being helped by Hale Malolo may select items to enhance their daily living. Then, members of the public pay twenty-five dollars to race through the facility for fifteen minutes with a grocery cart they can fill with anything they desire. Other features include: Selling bulky items for flat fees; offering a few high-priced items in silent and live auctions; and a raffle with tickets sold at ten dollars each.

Nathan is a semi-retired psychologist who has served on the non-profit's board of directors several times and I am always glad to help the program. While his private practice precludes a high commitment of time to the shelter, he helped design the fair. I think it is wonderful that so many people are involved in it. Not only does this event garner necessary operating funds, but the shelter's women and children benefit directly by receiving needed clothing and household items. In addition, the generosity of businessmen and women is rewarded with tax benefits and members of our community (especially the young) see the tangible benefits of recycling and helping those in need.

Luckily, my hairdresser was a bit behind schedule. With my hair barely touching my shoulders, it did not take long for her to even my cut, touch up the blonde highlights, and apply a protein pack to offset the effects of the sun-filled days in Hawai'i. After bouncing from the salon to my car, it took only a couple of turns to reach the Kalapawai Café.

There I purchased Mandarin orange and chicken salad. I also got crostinis of toasted Italian bread, a bruschetta of chopped tomato marinated with olive oil and fresh basil, and chevre goat cheese with herbs. Knowing the Bernardus Monterey County Sauvignon Blanc I had chilling would pair well with the chicken and cheese, I considered the issue of my kitchen duties complete.

When I got home, I had just enough time to wash and put my cutlery back in place before Ke'oni arrived. Keeping my cooking classes secret from Ke'oni was only one of the reasons I was rushing home. During the early supper I planned for that night, we would map out our social plans for the next several months. As I had told Nathan, I wanted to host a wine tasting party for my twin, his new girlfriend Adriana, and a few neighbors...although I was not sharing the underlying reason with my sweetheart. As newer homeowners at this end of Lanikai, Ke'oni and I also wanted to find an annual occasion for opening White Sands Cottage to our neighbors.

As I was putting our salads, Italian bread, and the bruschetta onto small platters, Miss Una arrived. She hopped from the garden window onto the counter, and then per her training, onto the floor. Then she crossed to the kitchen table. Against our rules, she promptly jumped onto the table and began pawing through the pile of mail I had set out to sort.

"What on earth are you doing?" I asked, sweeping her into my arms. "You know that's a no-no."

She looked at me with her amber eyes shining brightly.

"Don't play the innocent with me," I said concluding my disciplining. After I set her on the floor, she looked toward the table but seemed to take my instructions to heart. However, she had a few wishes of her own. She moved swiftly to her empty food bowl and turned to give me an accusatory look.

"All right. We're having a good dinner. I guess you deserve one too. How about shrimp casserole?" I asked.

As though to encourage immediate action, she mewed and remained sitting tall and alert.

Ke'oni came into the kitchen from the garage a couple of minutes later while I was rinsing out the cat food can for recycling. After kissing me, he headed for the back of the house to drop his tablet in the office and take a quick shower. A few minutes later, he arrived in the kitchen looking at ease in his swimsuit and an old University of Hawai'i T-shirt. He was hungry as I had expected and delighted that I had our meal ready.

"How about we eat dinner in the dining room and then go out to the spa for our powwow?" I asked. "Do you want a glass of Sauvignon blanc or tea to begin the meal?"

After concurring on a romantic meal beneath the dining room's sparkling chandelier, he suggested we save the wine for a barbecued dinner later in the week. He prepared large glasses of nutmeg infused sun tea in its place. After placing our plates, silverware, and glasses down on my auntie's beautiful *koa* table, Ke'oni pulled out my chair with a flourish and squeezed my shoulder as I sat down.

"It must be telepathy...again. There I was, sitting in traffic and wishing I could just blink, pull into the driveway, and find dinner awaiting me. Thank you, thank you," he said enthusiastically.

I smiled and we turned to enjoying our food. After clearing the dishes a half hour later, Ke'oni poured glasses of the port Izzy had brought us after a recent trip to visit her family in Portugal. We then went outside. Ke'oni immediately got into the hot tub, while I sat down on the rattan *papasan* chair on the side. With my notebook and pen in hand, we were ready for a serious conversation. Even Miss Una knew there was something exciting in the air. She generally dislikes being near any container of water larger than her new hand-blown glass goldfish fountain. But tonight, she honored us with her presence, perched on a footstool positioned dangerously close to the spa.

Leaning back, I considered upcoming events. Our involvement in Hale Malolo's forthcoming fair would be minimal. I knew that Nathan and Adriana would not be overly involved until the final week of preparations. This meant we should be able to schedule the wine tasting I wanted to hold. My only concern was whether I had learned enough in my cooking classes to be able to add some interesting morsels to the sampling menu.

There was also the question of pinpointing an annual event that would appeal to all of our neighbors. Each month, our neighborhood held a potluck hosted by each family in rotation. Fall was approaching and that meant the onset of additional celebrations. What could we add to the mix?

Ke'oni looked over at me. "After a day on the road, there's nothing better than coming home to you...and the spa."

"I'm glad you've got your priorities straight," I quipped.

"Have no doubt about that, Natalie. You are the love of my life and I'm grateful for every day and night we have together."

I reached down to clink glasses with him and nearly got pulled into the water. "Come on, sweetheart. It's time to take charge of our calendars. Now that we have Samantha to help with our daily tasks, it's time to plan a few special occasions with our friends."

"Well, the biggy next year could be that trip to Japan—to join Stan Carrington and his girlfriend Tamiko at the Sapporo Snow Festival," remarked Ke'oni.

"I could hardly forget anything as major as that, honey. But we have a few months before we have to organize for that potentiality. I've been looking over our upcoming social calendar. It looks like celebrations for most of the holidays have been claimed by one neighbor or another. The only gap seems to be Auntie Carrie's favorite—Halloween. I'd love to do something in honor of her, so I think that's the ideal time for us plan a neighborhood bash."

"I hope you don't intend to revive the Halloween horror of having kids bob for sticky caramel apples that had been stewing in a vat of molten water all afternoon. I've never been able to get that image out of my mind since you first mentioned the fiasco."

"You and the rest of the neighborhood! But setting that unfortunate incident aside, I think there are other Halloween memories for us to build upon. Like her insisting that everyone wears costumes. And don't forget the great food she served the year you came."

"Your idea sounds good! Several of our neighbors—like Larry and Lulu Smith—have said they don't want to hand out candy anymore. I'm sure they'd be glad to have somewhere to go for the evening."

I pictured decorating the house and yard in keeping with Auntie Carries love of all things sparkling and colorful. "I do think it would be nice for everyone to wear costumes. But I don't know that I'll be able to fit into Auntie Carrie's witch's costume."

"You could just wear her hat," proposed Ke'oni with an inviting leer.

On that humorous note, I slipped into the warm water and enjoyed some extended aquatic playtime.

CHAPTER 2

*Death lies on her, like an untimely frost upon
the sweetest flower of all the field.*
William Shakespeare [1564 - 1616]

When I got up on Friday, I found that Miss Una had been playing with the mail lying on top of the kitchen table again. Perhaps the bright colors of the antique auction brochures had attracted her interest. Nevertheless, we were going to have to have a talk about the rules of etiquette she was supposed to follow in the kitchen.

Since Ke'oni and I were about to take a walk at the beach, I grabbed a couple of yogurt cups from the refrigerator and poured some coffee to hold us until we could eat something more substantial. I walked back into the bedroom carrying a tray with our food. There I found my human partner playing with the wayward Miss Una on our bed.

"So that's where she's been. If it's not food or forbidden items for play she's looking for, it's attention—especially from you."

I set the tray on the nightstand and invited Ke'oni to partake of our small meal. "Look what just came in the mail," I said, offering him a peek at a glossy catalog with a beautiful Phoenix and Dragon pendant in gold and silver on the cover.

"Looks great, Natalie. But you may have to step up your wardrobe if you're going to start wearing this caliber of bling."

I swatted at him with the catalog and laughed at the idea of posing for a picture with the incredible bauble hanging on a heavy gold chain to complete an outfit of a shorty *mu'umu'u* and my red gel sandals.

"I'll admit my day-to-day wardrobe doesn't quite match the opulence of this necklace, but wouldn't it look lovely with my long black and gold *mu'umu'u*. Say for the next gubernatorial ball, when you bring out your tuxedo for a periodic airing?"

"Talk about an elegant pairing, that's a great idea," he replied. "But why is a catalog of jewelry here in the first place?"

"You mean aside from the fact that we live in a high-income ZIP Code? I'll have you know that it features every delightful thing you could want for your body or your home!"

"Well, there is the minor detail of our high-rent neighborhood," he said. "I'll have to admit I've enjoyed the mailings we've gotten about boats and travel opportunities."

"And then there's the bonus of being a loyal customer of the Memories Antique Shop. You know...where we bought Bàozhǐ Shēn's old desk? The shop's been sending us catalogues about fabulous antique auctions ever since we made that purchase. Speaking of which, I have an idea for that desk. What do you think of putting something special in the desk's hidden compartment?"

"I don't think we can compete with the original Chinese scrolls and a riddle leading to the hidden treasure we found during our investigation of the man's death. But maybe we can think of something that will make an interesting find for future generations. What about a family time capsule, since you're planning to leave everything to Brianna since her twin Ariel has passed?"

"That's a lovely idea, Ke'oni. Brianna's email after her semi-finals said she loves what we've done with White Sands Cottage. I think she'll end up living here. And, since she likes mahogany wood, I'm pretty certain the desk will remain here for a very long time."

"Your twin may have other ideas—with his home being on the shore of Kāne'ohe Bay."

I sighed. "I think you know that Nathan and I thought we had it all planned out. One of his granddaughters was to have his home and the other would take Auntie Carrie's. But since Ariel and Auntie Carrie are both dead, you and I have ended up here. Once you and Nathan and I are gone, Brianna can live in whichever home she wishes, or simply sell them both."

"She might decide to live in one and use the other for rental income," he said.

"Well, honey, that's all a long way off. Who knows how long any of us will live? Brianna may have kids who'll also be thrilled to have a couple of homes to choose from."

"Back to the matter of the desk. It's a classic piece and goes with a lot of your Auntie Carrie's furniture. So, I think you're right that Brianna will want to keep it," he said.

"And in case she doesn't...we could put a note in the secret compartment to identify the hidden objects as being intended for Brianna Harriman," I suggested.

"Or her family. We could include sufficient detail for anyone to find her, or her offspring, even if her surname has changed," said Ke'oni.

I realized how lucky I was to be with such a wonderful man. Neither of us had children, but that did not mean we were without family. Some of my friends complain that their life partner does not connect with their family. But, Ke'oni has befriended Nathan and the time he has spent with Brianna has grown the bond between them.

"So how do you want to go about this project? The space isn't that big. We'll have to select things carefully," said Keʻoni somewhat serious-ly. "How about we set up a small box in the office and drop things in until it's full. Then you can go through everything to choose the most appropriate items, show them to Nathan, and invite him to add a few objects of his own."

"Oh Keʻoni, that's sounds perfect. It'll be fun for us to do and how lovely to envision someone discovering the niche one day!"

We drank our coffee and I picked up a pen and notepad that I keep on my nightstand for just such occasions and then I jotted down a few notes regarding items that might be appropriate. My first thought was to create a new small photo album. The last time I had reviewed family pictures and scrapbooks was at the time of Ariel's passing. During the first days after my vision of her unlikely death, I had poured over all of the pages of pictures and keepsakes that recorded our familial history. I also noted a reminder to add a picture of Keʻoni and me at the front of Auntie Carrie's cottage.

As at the time of Ariel's abrupt passing, I now felt regret. It was not only for the loss of my lovely young grandniece. It was for all the years I had spent so far from everyone who should have been at the fore of my mind and activity. Having been a widow in my twenties, it may have been understandable that I had reached out to a new existence. That al-lowed me to avoid being constantly reminded of what I had lost because I had chosen to place my work above my personal life for decades.

By the time I was ready to redirect my life, several of my closest loved ones were dead or on the brink of passing. Sadly, there is no way to reach into the past and correct our errors. We can only move forward with a conviction to do better in the years to follow. And that was what I was attempting to do: to live each day connected to those I care about! On that note, Keʻoni and I sauntered down to the beach for a while, *sans* the accompaniment of our four-legged roommate.

Along the way, we chatted about elements we might include in our celebration of Halloween. When we returned home, I began making calls to our neighbors regarding our plans for the future party. I also solicited them for immediate donations to Hale Malolo's fair. That event served as a nudge for many of us to examine, sort, and let go of belongings that were not truly useful...or sadly, had belonged to loved ones who were no longer with us.

Within a couple of days, I received calls announcing the assemblage of donations of housewares, furniture, and clothing. Keʻoni found a gap in his schedule and spent several hours loading his truck and delivering the collections to the warehouse that was serving as the fair's headquar-ters.

Miriam's Ladies were among those who provided items for the fundraiser. I felt concern about asking them to open their friend's bed-room closets for what would probably be a final time. Despite everything else they had disposed of in the house, there were many odds and ends. On the personal side were clothing, jewelry, and towels with the initials of Miriam and her husband Henri. There were also a couple of mismatched chairs and small tables, as well as odds and ends of china, glass, and cutlery.

When I went over to pick up a couple of battered suitcases filled with donations, I found Izzy sitting in Miriam's old room. She was looking out one of the windows flanking the bookcases that had held her deceased friend's journals. For a moment I reflected on the innermost thoughts and professional history of Miriam's life as a champion of the rights of women, children, and the underprivileged of the world.

With a faint smile, Izzy got up and came to greet me. We hugged, and she drew me into the room. "Do you remember the day when Miss Una came scooting into the house from the upstairs *lānai*? We chased her, and she ran up right up the stepstool to the top of Miriam's wardrobe closet and hid until you came to pick her up."

"I do. I was mortified that I'd barely met you when my cat invaded your home."

"I have to tell you how much that day meant to Miriam. It was the most excitement this cottage had seen since Joanne and I moved in as her roommates after Henri died."

"Miriam, and all of you, certainly made Ke'oni and me—not to mention Miss Una—feel welcome in our new home. And you should know that Miss Una always watched Mokulua Hale every night from our back *lānai*. It was almost as if she knew something dreadful was about to happen in your cottage."

We paused for a moment, and then looked around the room. "So, all of you are comfortable about these donations?" I asked.

"Oh, yes. Miriam would be delighted. She didn't want anything wasted. She always looked forward, never backward, in life."

Each of us carried a suitcase downstairs and out the Dutch door into the garden. Ke'oni came through the gate to greet us. He smiled and took the cases from us to put in his truck. As I turned to wave goodbye to Izzy, I caught a whiff of the lilacs growing beneath Miriam's bedroom window. In the flower bed, I saw Miss Una playing with 'Ilima, whose orange and white fur contrasted with the purple flowers she was batting with her paws.

After Ke'oni collected the furniture sitting on The Ladies' *lānai*, he departed to drop off a final load of donations. Later, we enjoyed a patio dinner of barbecued pork chops, skewered vegetables, and the last of an order of bagels we ship in regularly from Noah's New York Bagels in San Francisco. The night was beautiful and the scent of plumerias floated in the air. As clouds crossed the moon and the stars became masked, I lit some citronella candles.

"The water is really warm tonight after a solid day of sun. Why don't you hop in?" invited Ke'oni, who was already in the spa.

"Oh, honey. I don't have my suit on, and I'd hate to ruin our sterling reputation in the neighborhood."

"I think the 'hood' can handle you in your lingerie, or even your birthday suit. Do you think the Mings have never gone skinny-dipping in that fantasy pool of theirs?"

"I guess you're right, dear," I conceded. Moving back behind the spa, I blew out a couple of candles. Looking around, I pulled my sun dress over my head, and hopped in the spa. Sliding next to Ke'oni, I took the hand he extended and began massaging his fingers.

"When you're through with that hand, I have another that is also tired from that long drive today," he said with a sigh.

After a while, the clouds separated from the moon, and we lay back to enjoy the heavy sprinkling of stars in the night sky. I finally suggested we go inside when my fingers felt wrinkled and nearly numb. After rinsing off briefly, we fell asleep entwined. I do not know how long I slept. Sometime in the night I awoke to the tick-tock of Miss Una's tail tickling my nose. I stepped out of bed quietly to avoid waking Ke'oni. I ran to the bathroom and then went into the kitchen for a cup of warm tea. Not hot, not cold. Sometimes a tepid cup of tea reminds me of the end of events shared with women around a pot of tea. For the cooling temperature of the final drops from the teapot is often the *dénouement* of a joyous occasion.

With Miss Una perched on my wingback recliner, I sat in the happy solitude of my Auntie Carrie's living room sipping my tea. After a while, I picked up the antique catalogue thinking of the many happy times I had shared with her. What a shame that she was not there to enjoy the wonderful offerings I was perusing. Leaning back, the catalogue slipped to my side. Taking that as an invitation, Miss Una hopped down onto my lap. Stroking her soft fur, I sighed and sank down in the chair. After a few moments I start to fall asleep and soon sink into that space between waking and dreaming.

I hear a rustling of air as though I am out of doors. From a distance there is a soft murmuring of intoned chanting. Soon the repeating sound of "OM" stirs me. In the space between my inhalations, I hear a mellow throb of a drum. It sounds like the stretched deer skin of a small shime daiko *drum being lightly tapped by the musician's hands, instead of the usual drumsticks. I sigh and open my eyes.*

I look to the left and then to the right. I sit alone in a room with pews that are banked slightly as the seats in a theatre. I am again in the Buddhist temple I envisioned previously—in its normal form. Suddenly, I am moved from a back pew to a seat in the front row. I look down and see a red book in my lap. I run my hand over the emblem of a gold circle of en-

twined wisteria blossoms stamped on its cover. Having attended weddings and other celebratory occasions here, I know it is the family crest of Shinran Shonin, *the founder of* Jōdo Shin Buddhism.

For many decades, I have driven past the temple's gleaming outer walls, stupas, and grand staircase. In disquieting moments in the lives of friends, I have joined its congregants in the cadenced toning of sacred sounds believed to bring comfort. As I watch, the hymnal opens by unseen hands to the Nembutsu, *the Mantra of Amida. It is a simple expression of gratitude to the* Amida Buddha *for his gift of boundless wisdom and compassion. Upon the facing pages, the tones for chanting are presented in treble clef musical notation. Below are the repeating words, "Namu Amida Butsu," I take refuge in the Amida Buddha.*

I rest my hands with palms up on the edges of the open book and listen as the mantra is repeated slowly, syllable by syllable. The harmonious chant reflects the humility and dedication of these practitioners of Buddhism. After a while, punctuation from the chiming of finger bells is added to the experience. When the sound eventually recedes, the notation in the hymnal fades to plain white and then the entire book fragments into confetti that falls to the floor. Again, I am surrounded by the intoning of the single sound of "OM." I sigh and inhale the heady scent of incense.

Atop the stage is a single podium fashioned from fine grained koa *wood on downstage left. Behind that is the altar I know. It features a standing Amida Buddha in burnished gold. I remember being told that the revered figures flanking him are the sect's founder* Shinran Shonin *and abbot* Rennyo Shonin. *To the far left is another statue of the Buddha. This one is seated. Covering the edge of its base are gemstones. Beautiful gemstones that I remember from the antique catalogue I was just reading. To the sides and in front of these statues is an array of candles and joss sticks in polished brass holders. On the far sides are vases with fragrant flowers from the garden I know lies beyond this sacred space.*

Silence descends. After a while, a rustling of air and the flutter of wings reaches my ears. I am reminded of a dharma *message I heard in this temple many years earlier. It may have been on Mother's Day, for there were many flowers and balloons in the sanctuary and the women seemed especially lively. Whatever the occasion, the day focused on honoring love in all its expressions.*

That day, the talk was delivered by a small gentle priest who told the story of the unending love of a flying insect. During a home's renovation, this tiny creature's mate was impaled by a nail against a wall. Immobilized, the insect would have died if not for the food its partner provided consistently. When further remodeling was begun, the walls of the building were re-opened, and the plight of the creature discovered. And while a tradesman carefully worked to free it, its mate remained hovering until they could both fly away. I smile at the emotion the memory stirs.

Suddenly, I hear the booming sound of a lotus-shaped bonshō *bell* whose heavy reverberations are generated by a wooden beam. Clearly, this is another aspect of my mental movie's reinterpretation of truth. The actual temple has a kanshō, a small bell rung with a mallet. The ringing in my ears vibrates the core of my being. I slow my breathing and close my eyes, trying to calm my inner self in preparation for what I know is to come despite my desire to prevent its happening.

When I reopen my eyes, the sanctuary looks normal. I watch the minister from my original vision enter from stage left—to my right. As before, she is attired in multi-layered garb. Beneath her black silk robe is an edge of white showing from her hangesa. Over this is a purple surplice with a gold embroidered wisteria crest. Today I notice that pristinely white split-toe tabis cover her feet and hear the soft tapping as she walks across the wooden floor on her black lacquer getas.

She moves to each icon with graceful movement where she bows at each and silently offers a prayer. This is not idol worship as some Westerners think; it is a token of honor for the aspect of enlightenment represented by each of the four statues. After reaching the far edge of the stage, the minister reverses herself and glides back to the central altar with the Amida Buddha. She lights the altar's candles and joss sticks and then stands in silent repose.

I feel as though I am joined with the woman standing before me. I feel her slow measured breathing within my breast. With an exaggerated sense of hearing, I listen to the clicking of her prayer beads and watch a faint glow of light envelop her from the crown of her head to her feet.

A profound sense of peace envelops me. I am transfixed without movement of eye or even breath, unified with all that is and all that one day might be. The tranquil moment lengthens, and I entertain the hope that the end of this vison will be changed from the previous.

But that is not to be. The door through which the minister entered opens and I watch a hand reach in. I sit in sickened disbelief as a gunshot slices through my consciousness, halting the incantation and dissipating the fragrance of incense. The figure of the one ringed in light straightens and turns toward me before crumpling to the floor. I stare with a horror that throbs throughout my being...and yet I see a smile upon her serene and seamless face.

At that point everything around me freezes.

In silent, slow motion, two men enter the scene. They wear navy blue coveralls with the logo of a moving company that I know has been out of business for more than a decade. They glance to verify that their victim is out of the way and push a metal trolley toward the far left altar. With his back to me, a tall, slim man guides the cart from its side. A shorter, stocky man pushes from the rear. When they are aligned with the statue of the seated Buddha, the tall man locks the trolley's wheels. He then removes a folding ladder from a shelf on the cart. The short man helps his collaborator position it securely along the top edge of the altar.

Next, the taller man pulls out a blanket from the cart's top shelf. As he places it over the ladder, I see flashes of gold and silver on his hands. Carefully, the pair maneuver the statue forward onto the ladder, then slowly down onto the trolley. After the sacred artifact is covered with another blanket, the short man takes a long strap off the bar at the back of the trolley and uses it to secure the statue. Once the ladder is replaced on the cart, the men turn and move the loaded trolley from the sanctuary.

As the images of this chilling vignette fade to the sepia tones I know too well, I release the breath I have been holding.

A soft voice called out to me. "Natalie, where are you?"

I murmured, "Mmhm." But I could not pull myself back from the abyss of fear that seemed to be swallowing me. I looked down at the catalogue lying open on my lap and gulped.

"You're here, honey. At home. What's wrong?"

I struggled to rouse myself. Directly in front of me is Miss Una, perched on the desk I would always consider the property of Bàozhǐ Shēn. Slightly behind her, staring in from the hallway was Ke'oni.

"I, I was trying to let you sleep, dear," I said after clearing my throat.

"That's a nice idea, but when I woke up and you hadn't returned to bed, I decided to come looking for you. Are you all right?"

I licked my lips. "Uh-huh. I guess."

"That's not exactly a resounding affirmation of wellness."

"Well, you know that nightmare I had about a Buddhist temple?"

"Yesss," he said cautiously.

"I just experienced the sequel...well, actually a re-run, with a few details that didn't appear in showing number one."

With each breath, I was regaining my strength...and my anger about the violent murder.

"Do you want to talk about it?" asked Ke'oni, helping me to stand.

Picking up the catalogue, I rose and said, "Let's have some tea."

A few minutes later, I was seated at Mom's old Formica table in the kitchen. With a single *meow*, Miss Una jumped up onto the counter beside the sink. But instead of exiting through the garden window, she turned around. Staring at me with shining eyes, she looked as though she was ready to hear what I had to say.

"I guess the family is gathered," I declared with a nod in her direction. Ke'oni handed me a mug of mint tea and sat down.

I began my revelation by confirming that what I had seen was definitely a vision, not merely a dream. I realized that I was still holding the catalogue with my right index finger inserted in the page displaying the statue of the Shākyamui Buddha. I opened the catalogue and stared at it for inspiration.

"The vision was in a Buddhist temple in which I've sat for numerous events. But there are a lot of differences between reality and the details of my visions. The actual temple has six pillars reaching up to the ceiling. Two of them frame a central altar, which has three standing statues. In my vision, a second altar to the left has a seated, Buddha. I see only one podium on the stage, and chairs for the ministers and special guests in front of that far left altar. Outside the real sanctuary is a small *kansho* bell.

"In this vision, there was the sound of a *bonshō* bell. You know. The huge kind that's rung with a big swinging log—like the one at the Byōdō-in Temple in Kahaluʻu."

I stopped for a sip of tea. There was silence for a moment as Keʻoni glanced across at the upside-down image of the Buddha. He then pulled the catalogue toward him and turned it around.

Under his breath, he said, "I know this statue...And I know the temple you're referring to. The real one. On the town side of the Nuʻuanu tunnels. Right?"

"Yes."

"And that's where you saw a female minister shot. In front of the central altar?"

"Yes."

"Did you see anything else? Any*one* else?"

"Yes. After the shot was fired that killed the minister, two men in navy blue moving company uniforms entered the sanctuary. They brought in a large metal trolley and pushed it up to the altar on the left and slid the seated Buddha onto the cart. Then they exited. They just left the woman dead. Where she fell. They didn't even look at her, except to make sure she was out of their way. It was so horrible."

"Yes, I know it was," he said reaching to cover my hands with his.

"What do you mean—*you know it was*?" I asked. He did not respond for a moment, and I knew there was something he had not told me previously. I hoped that if I remained silent, he would reveal himself more fully.

CHAPTER 3

*Twenty years from now you will be more disappointed by the things
you didn't do than by the ones you did.*
Mark Twain [Samuel Langhorne Clemens 1835 – 1910]

Ke'oni replied softly, "It was one of the worst crimes I ever dealt
with on the job."

After taking a sip of tea, he continued. "Not in terms of gore. The single gunshot that killed the Reverend Ayameko Kōha Fujimoto lodged in her cranium. She died almost immediately. But the aftermath of her demise was tremendous. Not only was she beloved, but the Buddha that was stolen has never been found...at least not until you saw it in your visions and now in this brochure. The theft was of a statue of an antique Shākyamuni Buddha given by a temple from another Buddhist sect in Japan...to signify their unity with members of the Jōdo Shin temple in Honolulu whose families came from the same area of Japan."

I sniffled and took the napkin Ke'oni extended. "How do you know all this?" I asked, fingering the catalogue.

"Because what you've envisioned is a case that haunted me long after my retirement. In fact, it has given me more sleepless nights than the shot that ended my career. At least *that* incident resulted in nearly complete recovery and early retirement. I don't think the members of the Honolulu temple have ever recovered from the loss of either their minister or the Buddha."

"So, what do you think this vision means?"

"I'm not sure anyone could give you a clear-cut answer, Natalie. The larger question is, why are you having this vision *now*? Actually, having it twice, with expanding details? What else might you learn in a future vision? There's also the question of how these visions fit into my memories of the case, as well as seeing the Buddha when I attended a friend's wedding in the temple."

We sat in silence for a while. When I looked up at Ke'oni, he had a blank look on his face.

"So, what are you thinking about?" I asked.

"A lot of things," he said, looking down for a moment. "You know I've never questioned the validity of your visions, Natalie."

I nodded slowly.

"One of the reasons for that is that I actually had one of my own… quite a long time ago. But I didn't make the connection until now, when you revealed the new elements from your second vision."

Remaining calm I asked, "The connection?" I did not want to shut down Ke'oni's desire to tell me something that was clearly important to him.

"Mmhm. To my own dream. Or, as I now realize, *my vision*. You see, I had one of those dream-visions about this case. Nocturnal, like most of yours. But it was merely a short flash in the middle of the night. At the center was her corpse…lying in front of the central altar with that unbelievably serene look on her face. And to my right, I saw the back of a man in a navy-blue jump suit pushing a cart out the door. That was it.

"After that incident, I'd have an occasional nightmare in which I saw the exterior of the temple and felt like something horrible was about to occur. Once I even saw myself running through the parking lot toward the temple, but rather than getting to the entrance, I seemed to be moving slower and slower. Sometimes the dreams have occurred on a night after I'd been on the Pali Highway and passed the temple. Other times they arrive without any stimulus."

At that point I was speechless.

"You were probably overseas in the nineties. I think you've said you were reporting from the Mediterranean, making travelogues, and writing that magazine column you had for so long."

"That's right. I was gone for much of the eighties, nineties and the start of the new millennium. I didn't even get home for most holidays."

"You've mentioned that you weren't reporting hard news during most of those years. So, you might not have been aware of the rash of grand thefts from churches, temples, and synagogues that were taking place around the world. A few of the crimes involved murder and other mayhem, often depending on the religion and the politics of the region.

"The stolen goods included antiques in gold and silver—some with jewels imbedded. There were also objects that were more valuable for their age and cultural significance, than their materials…like manuscripts, scrolls, Bibles, paintings and statues—like the Buddha in this case."

"Actually, I've heard of those cases. I remember some of the thefts involved considerable violence. Sometimes, the fact that the items were missing went undiscovered for unknown periods of time and that meant there was no active crime scene for the authorities to investigate in real time."

After a moment of silence, I asked "What should we do about my vision and your…mm, memories?"

"I think we begin with JD. He'll know where to go next. But there is one thing I'd like to ask of you, Natalie."

"Anything, dear."

"This may sound odd...even unfair. But I'd appreciate you not mentioning my little revelation to anyone."

"Okay."

"It's one thing for JD to accept *your* special gift, but I'm not sure how he'd feel about my having had a vision, no matter how brief."

"I understand how you feel. I've faced the question of *to-tell-or-not-to-tell* repeatedly. I think you know I've never told Margie O'Hara about my dreams and visions, and I've known her most of my adult life."

This was a unique moment. One I had seldom experienced with anyone. It was one I had never expected to share with Ke'oni. No wonder he had been so accepting of my revelation of my initial vision of Ariel's death. Not even my brother Nathan is comfortable with my crossings beyond the here and now. The unspoken link I shared with my twin in childhood disappeared for the most part at puberty. The most we share now are dream elements related to our individual lives, or members of our family. If only the visions I experience always had a direct link to me, it would be easier to put them into some kind of context I could understand.

"I didn't want to interrupt your...revelation...but there's something that will confirm all of your thoughts on this matter." With those words, I set down the catalogue, opened to the page showing the statue of the *Shākyamuni* Buddha.

For several moments we sat in silence.

After rinsing our cups and closing the window to keep Miss Una in the house, Ke'oni and I returned to bed. Later that day, Ke'oni called John and told him about my latest vision...and his belief that it is linked to his recognition of an antique statue of a Buddha in an auction catalogue. Afterward, he told me that we would be meeting John the next day at the yacht club that we had come to regard as our in-town office. In preparation for our meeting, Ke'oni did some research on the forthcoming auction.

We met with John as planned. With a seared *'ahi* Caesar salad in front of me, and the men enjoying *kiawe* broiled steak sandwiches, we settled down for a rather enjoyable working lunch. If only there had not been a review of a decades-old murder on the agenda. Again, I wondered why it seems that young or old, those who are brutally murdered are so often the best of humanity. Our waiter poured another round of mango tea. Then I gave a summary of my two visions and Ke'oni launched into a recap of his investigation of Minister Ayameko Kōha Fujimoto's murder.

"As you can see in this listing catalogue for the upcoming auction, the artifact I am talking about is substantial in both size and value," Ke'oni said. "It's hardly the kind of thing a small-time hood could easily swipe. I'm pretty sure the amount of the minimum opening bid will disqualify many potential bidders. I also wonder how much of the backstory of the statue is known to the Nippon Antiquities' staff participating in the auction."

"Well, since we have no idea of those responsible for the theft—or the murder—we can't go around asking too many blunt questions," said John.

"You're right about that," Ke'oni concurred.

"That's going to make it difficult to learn where that Buddha has been through the years. In a potential trial, I'll bet the prosecutor will need to cite the *provenance*, the chain of ownership. Many people could have had possession of it without knowing the truth about its history," I observed.

"According to its description, the Buddha has been in the Kiyohara family's possession for a long time," said Ke'oni.

Looking at the catalogue, John asked, "Do you think the Kiyohara family was responsible for the theft from the temple?"

"There's no way of knowing, JD. I was just telling Natalie that at the time the crime went down, there were a lot of contracted thefts of religious objects occurring across the world. If members of the Kiyohara family *were* involved in the theft of the Buddha, they may not have been involved with the murder of the minister. Even if they were uninvolved in the killing, they would hardly have come forward to confess connection to grand larceny. Thanks to television and movies, most of the public knows that such a person would be charged for a murder that occurred during a crime to which they *were* connected," Ke'oni responded.

"Aside from all of that, the guy who's now selling the piece may not have any personal regard for, let alone personal connection to, the Buddha. To him, it may simply be an asset that can generate the cash to buy a something that's more in keeping with his style," speculated John.

"I saw a picture of the current owner of Nippon Antiquities Company; he doesn't look old enough to have ordered the theft," I added.

"Maybe not. But he's not a kid either. Since the time of the theft, someone could have told him the whole sordid story," stated Ke'oni with a firm nod.

"Or maybe he heard a deathbed confession and does care about what happened. Maybe that's what inspired him to sell it," said John. "Regardless of what the current owner might know, we don't want to tip our hand and announce that we…you…have recognized the piece from a years-old crime. I'll run the story up the chain of command and see what the higher-ups want to do."

"Okay, JD."

"By the way, you haven't said who you were partnered with on the case," said John looking at his nails.

"I think you can do the math. For a brief three months, I was teamed up with Detective Anthony Brennan."

"Oh, yeah" responded John, staring steadily at Ke'oni.

"Am I missing something?" I asked, after a pregnant pause in our conversation.

"Not a lot. That was after my year of partnering with Tim Akuna, who abruptly retired. Before JD and I entered our long-term marriage. Right, ole buddy?"

What followed was a constrained discussion hinting at the questionable behavior of Ke'oni's former partner. There was no way for me to determine if my presence was responsible for the strained atmosphere. Clearly, both Ke'oni and John were being cautious about any vocal condemnation of Detective Brennan. It made me remember a parallel conversation I overheard between Ke'oni and another of his colleagues.

They were discussing another detective who moved from O'ahu to one of the neighboring islands. While the names and circumstances were different, both situations included an unspoken hint that the ethics of the person under consideration were questionable.

"Did you catch the call from the temple yourself?" asked John.

"I did." Looking at me, he continued. "In those days, a crime in a place like that usually went to senior teams. At the time, we were all stretched beyond our normal hours. The main reason Tony and I got the case was that he was already in the area."

Returning his attention to John, he said, "I don't remember why he was up on Lusitana Street, but he said a guy blew through a stop sign and nearly hit a pedestrian who was walking her dog. Since the first directive of HPD is public safety, he said he stopped to render assistance to the woman who was very shaken by the experience. Just as Tony was ready to leave that incident, he got the radio call to join me at the temple. Because he was so close, he arrived at the scene at about the same time I did."

"So, how'd the on-site investigation go?" John inquired.

"The usual. The crime scene unit took lots of photos. And in those days, we carried throw away cameras to take a few quick shots of our own. Tony and I did a once-over together. We checked the interior of the altar area, sanctuary, and the rest of the building. That included all the entrances and even the exit-only doors. After that, we walked through the grounds. That took a while since it's a pretty large property. And even though there weren't a lot of people present, crowd control was a bit of a problem—especially when the ME removed the body.

John and I nodded and remained silent to encourage Ke'oni to continue his report.

"There was really nothing in the way of leads. The scene was almost as spotless as if a clean-up crew had processed the property. There was little blood spatter, and except for the victim—and the vacant space that had held the statue—there was no evidence of a crime in the sanctuary. That was because temple staff and volunteers had cleaned and polished everything the night before.

"With today's technology, the CSIs would probably have turned up something. But we found no prints, hairs, threads or other forensic evidence at the crime scene. There was nothing in the rear corridors, doorways, or either parking lot. There were smudged fingerprints on the main double door to the parking lot in the back. We figure that's how the team that hit the place entered and exited. The few prints we were able to lift belonged to the head minister who had gone into the temple earlier that morning with his wife for a short time of prayer. And, the victim, who probably entered that way, since she lived in a small cottage adjacent to that back parking lot.

"We were able to rule out the front parking lot as a means of departure since there was a bus of tourists taking pictures at the time. I'm sure someone would have noticed the Buddha being rolled out to a van or truck if the perpetrators had exited that way. That leaves the back parking lot. As there were no activities scheduled that morning, the few members of the clergy who were on the grounds saw nothing and heard nothing. The last issue speaks to a silencer being used for the single gunshot that was fired. Does this fit what you saw in your vision, Natalie?"

"Not exactly. I heard a shot ring out. But with so many interwoven deviations from reality, I can't be sure about which aspects of my vision were real."

"What about the guys you saw, Natalie," wondered John. "You've ID'd their uniforms as coming from the Menehune Transfer Company. It had been out of business for a while by the time the crime went down. Can you think of anything else that's distinctive about the men themselves? Size. Build. Skin color, if not ethnicity. Length of hair. Tattoos, scars, birth marks. Jewelry. Undershirts. Belts. Shoes. Socks. Close your eyes for a minute. I know you were stunned by the murder. But try to picture the men as they enter the sanctuary."

At that point, Ke'oni took over directing the replay of my vision. "They're coming in the door at the back of the room, to your right. They're moving forward with the cart. They're facing you, before they turn into the altar area. Can you freeze the scene for a moment?

"Uh, okay. I'm trying to put the scene on pause. Before the murder of the minister, the first thing I saw was a man's arm reaching through the door with a gun. I see the dark blue edge of his uniform as he aims and fires the shot that kills the minister. Then he pulls his arm back out of sight. I don't know which man it was. A couple of moments later, the two men are wheeling the cart into the room."

"Are the men struggling with what you first called a *trolley*?" asked John.

"No, everything moves easily."

"Okay. Now they're in the sanctuary."

"Mmhm. There are two men and a trolley. I'm looking at the first guy. He's walking sideways. I see a flash of the company logo on a patch on the arm of his jumpsuit. Hmm. I realize that he must have been wearing someone else's uniform. The pant legs of the jumpsuit are short. I can see the cuffs of gray slacks below. He's wearing black socks and black shoes. And, I see a flash of gold. Maybe he's wearing a watch. And he may be wearing a ring."

"Could it be a wedding ring?" asked Ke'oni.

I was getting tired. As the scene replayed in my mind's eye, I felt as though I was losing track of some details. "I don't know. I didn't notice which hand it was. I should note that I'm assuming that what I saw was a *watch*. It looked like a gold metal band. If it was a watch, it was turned to the inside of his wrist. Like Ariel, who did that with *her* watch because of her playing tennis games on the spur of the moment...when she didn't have time to change clothes or remove her jewelry. It kept the crystal safe from being broken. Of course, I could be completely wrong and instead of seeing a watch, the man could have been wearing some kind of bracelet.

"And his face?"

"Well, that's the funny thing. I only saw his profile. He was glancing down as they turned the cart, and he kept watching the floor in front of the altars. But I'm pretty sure he was a *haole* because his arms and hands are lighter than the second man, what you guys call a co-conspirator."

"What about that man?" Ke'oni inquired.

"He moves more easily than the first guy. Maybe that's because he's at the back of the cart and it's easier to push than pull. He's not very tall. He's wide. No offense, John, but he's got a middle that's a bit larger than yours. I can tell you he's got huge arms, so pushing the cart doesn't seem to be a struggle.

"What about his facial features?" inquired John.

"Well, he's a *hapa haole*."

"*Hapa* of what?" John asked, seeking more detail.

"I'm not sure of the exact ethnicity. Slightly dark and swarthy. Maybe Portuguese. Of course, he could be suntanned. Almond shaped eyes. Probably part Asian."

"That's good, Natalie. Sounds like you might be able to ID him, if he hasn't changed too much. Now, think carefully about what he's wearing."

"Well, there's the long-sleeved dark blue jumpsuit. It has a patch with the company logo of a Menehune carrying a big box on his shoulder. I didn't notice any jewelry. He turns toward the altar and shifts periodically to maneuver the cart. I can tell he's wearing a V-necked T-shirt. And on his feet are scruffy, old-fashioned, white high-top gym shoes without socks.

"Anything else?" questioned John.

I paused for a moment. "No."

"Can you think of anything else about the overall scene, or the

Buddha?" inquired John.

"I think I've covered everything I saw. I never paid much attention to the statue in the actual temple, so I can't really say that the one I saw in my vision is identical to it."

"That's what you say *now*. But sometimes when you revisit a vision, you've seen new details," Ke'oni noted. "I only wish I'd had the opportunity to learn more about what happened to the Reverend Fujimoto. Even when I attended her funeral to check out the attendees, I saw nothing but harmony. In short, nothing came of any of the investigation...at least until now."

Feeling almost as drained as after having a vision, I was glad that our meeting concluded almost immediately. On our way home, Ke'oni recognized my exhaustion and suggested we stop off at Kalapawai Market for another take-out supper. Inspired by my lunch, he chose blackened 'ahi, a cobb salad and a loaf of sourdough bread. Since I fell asleep after a short soak in the spa, this proved to be a good idea. By the time I awoke that evening, Ke'oni and Miss Una had enjoyed most of the 'ahi. Luckily, there was plenty of salad and bread to satiate my hunger.

John had said that it would take him a day or two to access the old records about the murder of Reverend Fujimoto. On Monday we turned to playing catch up with several aspects of life. Even before the issue of Ke'oni's old case arose, the short-term plans for our Halloween party and the growing list of questions about our trip to Japan were crowding our minds, if not our calendars.

Considering current uncertainties, it seemed appropriate for him to take Samantha on rounds to meet clients who might call on her when he is unavailable. Fortunately, many Island businesses have staff with Asian language abilities, so Ke'oni has found those skills readily available. What he sometimes needs is someone with passable skills in European languages. Therefore, he is pleased that Samantha's conversational Spanish is quite good, that she is progressing in French, and beginning to learn German.

The next day they dropped off another load of donations for the Hale Malolo fair and then embarked on visits to a couple of clients. Meanwhile, I turned my attention to my column. Having recently discovered an innovative free-range poultry farm in Waimānalo, I called to arrange a tour the following week. With a single photo which I could shoot myself, I thought the details of the family-run enterprise would be ideal for one of my side bar snippets on O'ahu's farm-to table industry.

I then considered columns that would focus on locations where individuals, families, and organizations like to hold special events. Sometimes the occasion would be celebratory and center on a birthday, anniversary, or annual potluck. At other times, commemoration of the passing of a family member might be the focus of such a gathering.

Whenever the magazine launches a new feature, publisher Harry Longhorn likes to focus on a landmark that will grab his readers' attention. I was certain he would like my idea of highlighting a Royal Hawaiian Band concert at 'Iolani Palace. Held nearly every Friday afternoon, the performances have been well attended for decades. Sitting beneath *koa*, banyan, and royal palm trees, audience members enjoy our balmy weather as well as some of the best music Hawai'i offers residents and visitors alike.

Since the atmosphere at the Palace is subdued compared to the free-for-all environment of a beach park, the concerts on the grounds of 'Iolani Palace are often chosen for intimate gatherings. I remember planning a rendezvous with friends one year when I was preparing to go abroad for an extended assignment. I had spread out a large blanket to provide comfortable seating for an indeterminant number of people. I set out packages of sandwiches, fruit, cookies, and a large dispenser of Auntie Carrie's special *luaū* punch. My friends and I had a wonderful time, although a couple of people misunderstood my directions and ended up on the opposite side of the bandstand.

For the article I am now envisioning, I thought it would be ideal to write about a specific gathering of people. Perhaps I should focus on downtown workers, as a new demographic to address in *Windward O'ahu Journeys*. As I scrolled through my business contact folder, I speculated about several of the professionals I already know.

Within a couple of minutes, I had determined that one of my newer acquaintances would be an ideal subject for my current article. Bō Shēn was a commercial realtor I had met during my involvement with two unusual murders. The first was that of Bō's granduncle Bàozhǐ, who was believed to have disappeared on a trip to China several decades earlier. The second was a man I had met personally when helping to solve the murder of a neighbor.

I was pleased to reach Bō on my first call. He was happy to hear from me. His personal news was that he would be sending an invitation to his wedding scheduled for May. When I relayed my reason for calling, he said he would be delighted to be the focus of my planned article. His office of realtors already attended the 'Iolani Palace concerts on a monthly basis, he thought it would be a great form of publicity for his expanding enterprise. That is what I call a win-win! Now all I had to do was to coordinate everyone's schedule...and do some reconnoitering of the venue.

While the public may think a magazine writer sits at a keyboard and generates wonderful copy, there is actually a great deal of preparation that goes into each article. In this case, I would need to review the history of the Palace, as well as the Royal Hawaiian Band's current director and performance schedule. I also needed to scout the area around the bandstand to determine appropriate background images. That way, the magazine's chief photographer, Andy Berger, can take some shots ahead of time. Finally, I needed to think about coordinating wardrobe selections for Ke'oni and me, since we would be featured in a couple of pictures.

CHAPTER 4

The world is all gates, all opportunities.
Ralph Waldo Emerson [1803 - 1882]

By the time John called that night, I had completed research for my article on the Royal Hawaiian Band's concerts at 'Iolani Palace. While I was doing that, Ke'oni had finished his day by beefing up Samantha's training with a session at a shooting range. Despite her occasional nervousness, she proved to be a good shot, at least with a small revolver. I was glad that that was a skill I would never seek to master.

Having worked over the weekend, John decided to enjoy some golf at the Mid-Pacific Country Club early on Tuesday morning. After that he wanted to drop by the cottage to summarize the results of his presentation of the case of murder and grand larceny to his superiors. Therefore, after a quick morning swim, Ke'oni tidied the back *lānai* and I prepared a simple brunch of scrambled eggs with chorizo and bagels...plus mimosas.

Gleeful about his win, John was tired and hungry by the time he arrived and grateful for the simple meal. As usual, we delayed discussing business until our appetites had been satiated. Eventually he sat back on one of the lānai rocking chairs and deeply inhaled the scent of plumeria and pīkake blossoms. "Anyone who says beer is the only drink that quenches thirst has never had your mimosas, Natalie," he said with a sigh of pleasure.

"We are delighted to serve the needs of one of our finest first responders," I replied, gesturing toward the Meyers lemon tree that provides my secret ingredient for most beverages.

Since we did not want to be overheard discussing police matters, we moved into the kitchen. A couple of minutes later we were seated at my Mom's old table with a fresh round of drinks. For once John did not need any notes, but he did pull out a calendar.

"Things went pretty well with Captain Makani. He's interested in our cold case especially since he's already had a call from the Feds about the auction. It seems there are a couple of items of interest to law enforcement in the catalogue you showed me. Consequently, the Feds are looking into the company, its owners, and their questionable inventory.

We've got just a week and a half to put together a small team to monitor the setup and conduct of the auction. While we're doing that, a forensic team will be reviewing the paltry amount of evidence from the crime scene and the autopsy with Marty Soli at the ME's office. Afterwards, the Captain will want to meet with you for a briefing, for which he's hoping you might have some private notes, Ke'oni.

"Yes, I have my notes from the original investigation...and a few I've made over the years since then. What about Tony? Is *he* being included in the re-examination of the case?" inquired Ke'oni.

"No, there's no reason to involve him at this point. For that, and other reasons, Makani thinks it might be good to meet away from the office. So, do you want to stay with the yacht club as our office away from the office?" John said with a twinkle in his eye.

"Why not?" I agreed. "Unless I'm not included in the invitation..."

"Oh, no, Natalie. I didn't mean to leave you out of anything. The Captain is very interested in meeting you."

After glancing at his smart phone, Ke'oni turned to John. "Why don't you check on his schedule and set up a meeting for any day after two o'clock. That way there'll be fewer people to hear what we're talking about, and we can ask for a large table to spread out any papers we bring along."

John nodded. "As usual, we'll refrain from mentioning Natalie's visions. You two stick with the simple truth. You'd finished remodeling your auntie's cottage and were looking through some antique brochures. You didn't pay much attention when you first saw the Buddha, Ke'oni. But when Natalie expressed interest in going to the auction, you visited the Nippon Gallery website. There you saw detailed photos and read the full description of the piece. That's when it all clicked. How does that sound?"

We both nodded our approval.

"So, what's next?" Ke'oni asked.

"Well, you know that small team I mentioned? One of the other players will be someone you both know. Alena Horita. She's just completed a degree in Interior Design at Chaminade University and is beginning a masters' program in art history at the University of Hawai'i. She's been promoted to detective and with her background, we think she'll be perfect as your companion in your quest for some artistic touches for your home, Natalie."

John called later that night to announce he had been unable to set up a meeting with Captain Makani. However, he had scheduled a late lunch with Detective Alena Horita the next day. In the morning Ke'oni and I made some phone calls to clear the decks for a concentrated time of togetherness with HPD. I was grateful that my culinary class had been postponed for a week.

When we arrived at the yacht club for lunch, John and Alena were waiting for us. John was such a regular, that the club waived the rule about members like me and Ke'oni needing to sign in their guests. Of course, John's badge might have had something to do with the warmth with which he was greeted by the *maître d'*. To simplify our meal, we all chose to have the luncheon buffet which featured freshly caught *ukupalu* served as *sashimi*. I was amazed at the amount of food that the svelte Detective Horita managed to consume.

"I'm just a grad student and fledgling detective. I can't believe I'm going to be at an auction with *objets d'art* valued at hundreds of thousands of dollars. The closest I ever thought I'd come to such art would be on a world tour—which isn't likely to happen anytime soon."

"Congratulations on completing your bachelor's degree. How are you enjoying life as a grad student?" I asked.

Without pause she said, "I love it. I never thought I'd complete my BA. I was at Chaminade for what seemed like forever. I'd switched majors a couple of times, but couldn't decide what I really wanted to do, until I learned about the master's degree in art history at the University of Hawai'i. One good thing about the program is that the staff is understanding about the complexity of my job. And they even accepted a few of my credits in interior design."

"You certainly put in your time on the street. Congrats on making it out of uniform!" Ke'oni said to the beautiful young woman.

"Thanks. It's been quite a change."

"I think you'll find the changes will keep happening for quite a while," added John.

"Why is that?" I asked.

"Because with her language skills in both written and oral Japanese, and her growing knowledge of art and design, the department's going to be moving her from case to case and division to division, as she's needed. I think it's safe to say that Alena won't be getting bored any time soon," affirmed John.

"So, has a game plan been laid out, JD?" Ke'oni inquired.

"Yep. I think it's all coming together quite nicely. Alena's already started going over descriptions of the auction on the Internet. For us, there's nothing of interest other than the Buddha, so far? Right?" said John.

"Right, Boss. I've compared the pieces on offer with photos of items being sought by the FBI's National Stolen Art File, as well as Interpol, Europol, and the Royal Canadian Mounted Police. I haven't found anything else that connects directly to our case. But I understand there are some pieces that Europol and Interpol are looking into. As to the Buddha, there's nothing but the description provided by Nippon Antiquities.

"The details they've offered are far more exact than the description in the case file—or the bill of lading that came with the Buddha when it arrived in the Islands in 1965. In fact, the copies of the bill of lading and shipping records offered by the temple were too faded to be of much use. Since the statue was shipped from one religious group to another, with no commercial aspect to the transfer of ownership, no one paid much attention to the lack of information."

At that point, the young officer produced printouts of Nippon Antiquities' specifications on the statue. Since I am not very good at dealing with the technical aspects of three-dimensional objects, I skimmed the numbers and contemplated the historic, artistic, and financial aspects of the piece.

To aid our review, Alena noted, "As you'll see, the company is fairly complete in their description. However, it's rather light in the area of *provenance*. It's like the Buddha was created in antiquity and just materialized in the vaults of the firm. Careful to avoid raising a red flag, I asked a friend at a high-end gallery to call Nippon Antiquities and pretend to have a client interested in bidding on the Buddha.

"All he learned was that World War II blurred the sequence of ownership. When the company was reorganized after the war, the statue was added to the family's personal art collection. Despite the vagueness of the timeline of possession, I did learn one thing of interest. Their art experts were able to define the probable age of the piece and a guestimate of the notable family of artisans who created it."

For the next few minutes, our conversation was put on hold as we read the information on the Shākyamuni Buddha.

The gilt bronze statue dates from the late sixth or early seventh century Common Era in the Asuka period of Japanese history. With its traces of bright pigment, it is believed to have been produced in the workshop of the renowned Buddhist sculptor Tori Busshi of Nara Prefecture. The artist's patrons included Prince Shōtoku and Empress Suiko of the imperial family. Unlike the realism of Grecco-Buddhist sculpture, the work of many Asuka period artists features front-facing, triangular geometric shapes in the design style of the Wei Kingdom of China in late fourth to sixth centuries.

This weighty figure is seated upright on an inverted lotus blossom with crossed legs. The elongated head features curled hair and a tranquil face with slitted eyes and nostrils. It is framed by a flaming halo displaying the images of previous incarnations of the Buddhas known as the *Seven Buddhas of the Past*. The robe drapes the body in the carefully defined folds of Wei era art. The raised right hand faces outward... Resting on the left leg, the left hand's palm is up, offering guidance to the end of the believer's suffering. The halo garnets and lapis lazuli around the lotus blossom on the base may reflect the patron's admiration of previous creations of the Tori Busshi studio. The ruby embedded in the third eye and silver inlay along the tops of garment folds indicate creative experimentation within the studio.

"So, did you learn anything new or surprising?" asked John, directing his question to Alena.

"Well, the picture displays most of what's contained in the narrative. It isn't surprising that there's no clear identification of the artist. In antiquity, pieces of art generated by a particular studio were valued for their overall artistry—not because of the stature of the person responsible for individual aspects of its design and execution. There is one thing that surprises me about the statue. Perhaps I should say, about its *presence* in Hawai'i. You see, while it's not surprising that a major Japanese temple of the *Tendai* School of Buddhism would have such a piece in its collection of revered art, it *is* surprising that they sent it to a *Jōdo shin* temple in Honolulu.

"So?" John asked.

"Varied images of the Buddha are revered by the different Buddhist schools, or sects. This statue of the *Shākyamuni* Buddha represents the historical man who would *become* a Buddha. Its Greco-Buddhist style was brought to Japan in the mid-sixth century. That's roughly the time when *Tendai* Buddhism was established. The Honolulu temple where our crimes took place, is of the Jōdo shin, or Pure Land, tradition that dates from the late Twelfth Century. The image of the Buddha *they* revere is called the *Amida Buddha*, referring to the one who has *become* the Enlightened Buddha."

Alena sighed and shook her head. "I'm sure this is more information than you ever wanted to hear. But, without the *provenance*, the record of this piece's origin and ownership, we're just guessing about how the statue ended up here...and what the motive was for someone to steal it, beyond its monetary value."

"Could the rivalries between these schools of Buddhism be a reason for the theft?" Ke'oni asked.

"I think that's a stretch," Alena said.

"I would think that the statue would be revered by any Buddhist," added Natalie. Alena nodded her agreement.

"Wow. That *is* a lot to absorb," said John with a frown.

Alena quickly responded. "The bottom line is that despite the historical differences between these two sects, the gift of an image of the *historical* Buddha to the Honolulu temple *might* have been appropriate."

Seldom concerned with the finer details of philosophy, John said, "Okay. I'm trying to take it all in. All that matters is that *you* know what you're looking at. The key points are that it's old, it's valuable, and lots of people might want to own it. One thing's clear, even to me: I don't think it would have been profitable to sell the jewels in the statue separately. As far as we know the ruby for the third eye has never been removed, or the garnets and lapis lazuli around the base.

"That makes me think the gems aren't that valuable by themselves. And I'm sure that no one could remove enough of the gold leaf overlay to reap much profit. In short, the Buddha is worth more intact than broken apart," he concluded.

Ke'oni looked up from his smart phone. "We've got about a week until the auction. That doesn't give us much time to prepare for it."

"That's true. But I've been through your old case files, and I think that if we review the main points together, we'll both be up to speed," said John looking around the table.

"What do you want me to do?" I asked.

"Now that's where the fun begins," said John, turning from me to Alena. "We've worked out a pretty simple plotline. Ke'oni and Natalie play themselves. They've recently inherited the family home and are in the market for a few pieces of art to complete their remodel. You're their designer, Alena. Between now and next Thursday, I want you to take Natalie around to galleries and shops to establish your backstory in the Honolulu antique community. Sound okay to you?"

"Sure boss. I think it's good that you're keeping things as close to the truth as possible. With Natalie writing a popular magazine column, she could easily be identified."

I looked at my designer for a moment. "You look quite young Alena. We could say you're a friend of my grandniece Brianna and I'm helping you fulfill a college requirement."

"Good idea. Anyone checking on Alena will find she *is* an art student. And she's about the right age to be a friend of Brianna. Another point in our favor is that she's had a very low profile while on the street, so I think we're safe," mused John.

"What about me?" Ke'oni asked. "Are you sure I won't be an obvious plant?"

"Naw. I think we're cool. You've been described as a private investigator in her magazine articles. Anyone checking up on you will not be surprised to learn you're a retired cop. Besides, you've been off the force for several years and I don't think you were cited in the media coverage of the minister's death."

"You're right on that point. I didn't have much seniority at the time the case went down and had no interest in the media. I passed off anything newsworthy to those who wanted the attention. Tony and I were only partnered for a short time and only two of our cases got any serious coverage. I let glory hound Tony take the lead with anyone who had a press pass."

John made a wry face. "Well, I think that covers everything for now. You ladies synchronize your schedules and figure out how you're going to check out the art market. While you're making the rounds, be sure to introduce yourselves and *talk story* with everyone you can. That way, on the day of the big event, there are bound to be one or two people who'll recognize you and back up your cover story.

"Oh, before I forget it, we've already followed up on the mailer you received and have confirmed your attendance of the auction—with two companions. Your tickets will be waiting at the door. We've also managed to place a person inside Nippon Antiquities and he's putting together a list of people who've registered as bidders."

"I can say that I've decided to invest in a few pieces of art. I saw there'll be a few items in at least the silent auction that aren't too costly. I should be able to make a few bids that will make me look legitimate," I said hopefully.

"Good thinking, honey. No one's going to buy into a story of my bankrolling this game," said Ke'oni shaking his head.

"Oh, I can picture you pulling out bundles of money from a steel briefcase—for baseball memorabilia," John chuckled.

"With all the places we'll be visiting, Natalie, I'm sure you'll pick up some talking points that will strengthen your image as an eager new collector," agreed our fledgling detective.

I smiled at the memory of the young man who had encouraged my course selection in my sophomore year in college. "And I'll have to admit I actually took a couple of classes in art history and the philosophies of noteworthy artists. Maybe the hours I spent memorizing color symbolism through the centuries will prove useful in our current undertaking," I said.

"Despite the short lead time, I think we've got a good overall plan. There should be plenty of security—a couple of undercover cops and at least one federal agent. In addition to that support, the hotel's chief of security knows what's coming down and he's alerting his team to be responsive to our needs. And remember, I'll be in a nearby room with electronic coverage of all of you," declared John.

"Ke'oni, your main assignment is to watch for anyone you recognize from the original case—or someone known to be involved in moving stolen goods. You just be yourself, Natalie. Just go with the flow regarding anything Alena or Ke'oni do or say. They'll both be plugged into me and can notify you if anything changes from our end. You can let me know later if you notice anything unusual," said John with a seldom heard authority in his voice.

With the way he stared at me, I knew he was hinting at my remaining alert for anything or anyone I recognized from my vision. That made me feel more comfortable, but I was glad Alena did not seem to catch his unspoken signal.

"So, are we good for the next few days, girls and boy?" teased John on a lighter note.

The rest of us looked around the table and nodded in rhythm.

"With the auction preview scheduled for a week from Saturday, the installation of the collection has to be completed by Friday. That means the HPD techs will have checked the hotel's electronic surveillance equipment on Wednesday and Thursday. It would be great to have a dry run with everyone, but we can't control who might be accessing the rooms.

"We can't afford to have any of you seen ahead of the big event—especially in the company of police personnel. Therefore, we'll position you three in a surveillance van somewhere on the premises next Thursday night. I'll meander around the show rooms to show you how things are laid out. With you three watching and listening from nearby, and me making a few comments under my breath, we'll be able to share information in virtual real time. If there are any lingering questions, we can address them on Friday.

"On Friday, we'll put you in the observation room one floor above the auction rooms while the HPD security team that's covering the high value event will perform an official walk-through. It won't surprise anyone that a few cops are checking the layout in advance. In fact, the auction personnel would find it unusual if we didn't."

We all began gathering our various papers. Alena and I compared calendars and found we were both available to launch our adventures in interior design the next day. That would give me a few hours to tidy the house...including some of my accumulated filing. John and Ke'oni agreed to confer on the old case files by phone, unless a major issue arose.

Alena and I were beginning our new relationship with a tour of Auntie Carrie's cottage. That way she would have sound knowledgeable about both the property and its furnishings. By the time she arrived, Ke'oni and I had already had a brisk walk and he had departed to check on things at his bungalow in Mānoa. To simplify the day's work, I had clip boards with lined paper for taking notes on potential items for me to bid on at both the silent and live auctions.

While the cottage is an Island style bungalow, its furnishings are a bit eclectic. Most of the mahogany furniture had been my aunt's, while the classic *koa* furniture came from my parents' home. Ke'oni had added a couple of modern *koa* pieces, including a prized rocker that has eased his back since the time of the injury that ended his career with HPD—and the leg he injured in taking down my grandniece's murderer.

Nathan prefers modern lines and finishes and did not mind my keeping the old *koa* items. However, he had asked that we share the paintings our parents and Auntie Carrie had accumulated through the years. I have added a number of small pieces of art from my years of traveling overseas to the mix of family art. As we wandered from room to room, Alena commented on the way the rich colors and patterns of art complimented the depth of the finely grained wood pieces.

The tour reminded me of the occasions on which I had acquired many things. The brassware had come from South Korea, where I had travelled to write an article on U.S. military families stationed in Asia. Vases of china, porcelain, and silver were obtained at every stop I made across the globe. Varied figurines and carvings came from varying locations including the Black Forest of Germany and the tip of South Africa.

There was even a small painting of a Chinese temple I had purchased during my first short trip to Hong Kong where I learned my husband, a naval officer, had died at sea.

Alena was particularly interested in items my father had brought home during his career in the U.S. Navy. In addition to a large collection of dolls, there were lengths of silk in rainbow colors, (some with gold threads), and primitive beads strung on leather thongs, woven thread, and silver and gold wire. Several postcards revealed images of exotic places I could not identify, except by the countries of origin of their stamps.

"Some of the cards were sent from my mother to her sister Carrie when she traveled overseas to join my father on spur-of-the-moment holidays. My twin Nathan wasn't particularly interested in them. But he and I have shared my Dad's collection of paper and coin currency, stamps, and military buttons dating back to the time of Napoleon," I said.

"You have so many beautiful things. You could place a selection of the smaller ones—like some of the buttons, beaded necklaces, and post-cards in display boxes," suggested Alena. "And a couple of the canes and rain sticks could be hung horizontally, maybe above the *koa* sofa in the family room."

"I love those ideas. What about the currency, coins and stamps? Do you think I should display them? Or would that just be inviting theft?"

"Well, several of my superiors have warned me, never go looking for trouble. And the problem with displaying money is that it might encourage someone to wonder how valuable those pieces are...and to speculate about what else you possess that isn't so visible."

"Good point. I'm sure Ke'oni would agree that keeping them in their protective sleeves in the safe is the best idea."

"Speaking of Ke'oni, does he realize how valuable his vintage charcoal sketches of the Pacific are?" asked Alena.

"I'm pretty sure he does. He may buy classic aloha shirts on a whim, but I think he's pretty prudent about his artistic purchases."

We laughed and finalized our list of small art galleries, antique and pawn shops, and dealers in unique furniture. Many of the antiquities dealers required appointments made in advance of visits to their premises. There was one positive aspect to these businesses: I could easily introduce my backstory, thereby ensuring I was leaving my mark on the collectables industry. We decided to bypass Nippon Antiquities, since an undercover officer was already embedded on the premises and there was the potential that someone might recognize Alena from her true profession.

CHAPTER 5

It is a bad plan that admits of no modification.
Publilius Syrus [1st Century CE]

After consideration of the cottage's furniture and accents, we stopped at Heritage Antiques which is one of my favorite shops in Kailua. I have known the family that runs the business for many years and have always relied on their honesty and forthrightness. Without revealing the underlying purpose of our visit, the smartly clad detective at my side steered the conversation toward our cover story.

Being familiar with my art, furniture, and collectibles, she smoothly mentioned the several types of wood and other finishes in my home to the young salesman. As he guided us through the appropriate pieces the store had to offer, Alena conveyed my interest in cloisonné vases and Chinese porcelain panels. I was glad that the only *cloisonné* the store had were vases sized for a mansion.

Next, we tag-teamed our way into downtown Honolulu. Alena parked her car for our eventual parting in the afternoon and hopped into mine to simplify our visits to a few more antique and vintage stores. One of the first stops on our list was Memories Antiques where I had bought the mahogany desk of a murder victim several months earlier for my living room. Although they only have a few high-end pieces at any one time, there was a chance that someone from their management might be planning to attend the auction. Seeing a poster for the event by the cash register, I added to my biography by expressing my enthusiasm for expanding my doll collection.

Since we would have to make appointments to visit some of the exclusive galleries, we decided to spend the rest of our day at the Honolulu Art Museum. Their open-air Pavilion Café afforded us an ideal spot to review our current work. Faced with a variety of delicious sandwiches and salads, we decided to share one sandwich of filet mignon and another of portobello mushrooms.

"Did you know that despite being somewhat small, this is one of the finest art museums in the country?" said Alena proudly.

"I know that it has some fine European paintings, in addition to Pacific and Asian art. I used to come here whenever I was in town because

I found it so peaceful. Just walking up under the shade trees on a hot summer day gave me a wonderful sense of tranquility, especially after my husband died," I responded.

"I didn't know you'd been married," said the young police officer.

"It was a long time ago. Bill Seachrist was a young naval lieutenant. We married after I graduated from Lewis and Clark College in Portland, Oregon. We had recently moved to Honolulu for him to assume the position of communications officer on a ship that was preparing to go on a six-month deployment at sea."

"You mean at Westpac?" asked Alena.

"That's right. He had been gone a few weeks, and I was to meet him in Hong Kong for a romantic rendezvous. I traveled there with a group of officers' wives and girlfriends. We were scheduled to arrive a couple of days ahead of the ship. This was good since I was working on my first magazine article and needed to scout locations for photos to accompany my text. Of course, we didn't know the exact day the men would arrive. For security reasons, the United States Navy did not announce its schedule like a cruise line.

"When we arrived at our hotel a bit late, I discovered my room lacked a view, so I abruptly changed hotels. The next day, when the Navy tried to reach me, the other women in our party didn't know where I was. The situation was soon resolved, but the delay didn't change the message the casualty officer delivered: My husband was dead from encephalitis. After I was notified, my life became a blur as I returned home, arranged the funeral, and tried to realign my life."

"I'm so sorry. I had no idea," said my companion.

"In the midst of it all, I managed to complete my article, and before I knew it, I had begun my career as a leisure and travel journalist. My parents had retired here, so I continued to visit Hawai'i. In fact, Nathan and I actually lived here as children a couple of times when our Dad was overseas. But I never resided here full time until my official retirement a couple of years ago."

"You've had an amazing life," said Alena between sips of tea.

"It certainly doesn't seem like it. I just blinked, and the decades rolled by. Speaking of which, Ke'oni and I were comparing notes about our lives during the late twentieth century. I realized I wasn't here at the time of the murder we're re-examining. What about you? You would have been a young girl at the time. Were you aware of the case?"

"I was. You see, my dad is a Japanese linguist who's involved with many aspects of Japanese culture in our local community. He's a professor at the University of Hawai'i and also teaches after-school Japanese language classes to high school students at the Mo'ili'ili Community Center in Kaimuki. During summer breaks, he takes students and their families on tours of Japan. And then there's his part-time job that directly impacted my own career choice.

"You see, when HPD has a sensitive case involving Japanese language and culture, they call him in for translation and clarification. One such occasion was the murder of Reverend Fujimoto. At the time, there were several Japanese visitors to the temple and my dad was called in to help the police interview them. That helped spread news of the case across the local Buddhist communities."

"On the day of the incident, I'd forgotten my homework, so my mom brought it to me. When I was called out of class, I found my mom, the secretaries, and several teachers crowded into the principal's office. I moved quietly up to the doorway, but everything became quiet when they saw me. Seeing me, Mom hurried out and closed the door behind her.

"I remember sitting on a hard, wooden chair in the reception area. Mom was quite upset. Silently, she handed me my book report. She looked from my hands to my face. I watched as a single tear slid down her cheek. She quickly assured me that Dad was okay. Then Mom told me that something terrible had happened at the temple. She simply said that Minister Fujimoto had died. Nothing more. Since I was young, she may have thought I wouldn't watch the news that night...that maybe it would be another day before I learned the details of the *sensei's* demise.

"In truth, no matter how old a child is, their parents should know that someone, somehow, will tell your kid about anything bad that happens. When my English class was over, my friends and I went into the lunchroom. Everyone seemed to know everything about the case except the name of the perp. Whoever had done the deed had eluded the police and continued to do so until the story slid off the front page of the newspaper and from the nightly news broadcasts.

"Of course. That didn't take CNN into consideration. Even though students couldn't access the news, they heard faculty members sharing the news stories they'd heard in their lounge between classes."

Alena went on to describe how the death impacted her family. "My parents didn't say much that night. We sat in the living room watching the nightly news, picking at our dinners on lap trays. In the days that followed, my father and mother had quiet conversations that ended when my brother or I entered the room. I overheard my dad say he was glad she didn't suffer...that her death was instantaneous. He also mentioned that he was horrified by the theft of the Buddha.

"There isn't much else I recall. Although, after one rather gruesome news report, I remember my dad questioning how anyone could attempt to sell something as recognizable as that statue. My mom said the thief must be someone who was going to put it into a hidden collection. Time passed, but the case never faded for the temple community. Some people have never recovered from it...we just grew silent about our sorrow."

I shook my head in recognition of her continuing distress about the case. I was glad that as we wandered through the museum's collections of European, Asian, and Pacific art, Alena grew increasingly excited about working in her new area of expertise. She explained how the world of art struggles at every level, from the artists to the institutions that strive to present their works to the public.

"Fortunately, there are many streams of income for museums. On some days a museum may even sell copies of fine art and the work of local artists on commission."

"I've enjoyed visiting some of the finest museums in the world, but I never thought about the business of operating one. Lately, I've noticed a severe cutback in art classes in public schools and the reduction of good art in public buildings," I said.

"That's something that irritates me about our country. I'm not that old, but it was different when I was in public elementary school. All of the students had the opportunity to take art classes, and music, and sometimes even dance. Now these programs are only available to the kids whose families are rich enough to send them to private schools."

"You're right. I always vote in support of the arts. And I highlight the musicians who perform in the restaurants and entertainment venues I cover. Perhaps I could mention the artwork they feature on their walls. Maybe if there's enough buzz in the community, a few businesses will feel compelled to offer more visual features. In a small way, that could stimulate the public to demand more art."

"What a great idea. That's why this museum has a tearoom and offers art classes, hoping they can get the public to linger a while. I doubt that the public cares that the business of art is costly. Even though the art sold to museums is often lower in price than pieces sold through galleries, it still takes a lot of money to acquire great art. And when an individual collector, or a family, makes a donation, they don't realize their gift will be a real financial burden."

"What do you mean? Isn't that one way that a museum makes money...by having more items on display to encourage the public to visit?"

"You'd think so. But every piece has to be cared for. Even when they arrive in great shape, they have to be maintained. Think of the archival preservation and special program staff that's required. Then there's electricity, insurance, and display supplies. And there's periodic expansion of facilities. Some institutions have gotten quite creative in their fundraising. Beyond offering their property for weddings and other social events, sometimes they rent out pieces in their collections."

"Thanks for sharing your knowledge, Alena. You've given me a fresh perspective on the world of art," I said, as we parted on the first day of our adventure.

While Ke'oni shared his operational methods with Samantha, Alena and I continued our hunt through O'ahu's shops and galleries on Friday and Saturday. My ability to converse about art and collectables with some degree of believability increased. This allowed me to play my role proficiently and to enjoy my time with Alena more fully. Along the way, I picked up a few frames, two shadow boxes, and some stands for plates and vases. Best of all, I got a pair of new intricately beaded dolls from Southern Africa. Previously, most of the dolls in my collection had been gifts from my father when he was on assignment in Asia. My new additions were a divergence, but I felt it was time to expand my horizons beyond the Pacific.

We found my new pieces in a small mom and pop shop owned and operated by former employees of the United Nations. A portion of each sale was donated to the international organization, including *Linga Koba* dolls made by the Ndebele women of Africa. Like the art and crafts of women in many cultures, these dolls are treasured and often handed down through generations of women.

Although we barely had a week in which to visit all of Honolulu's antique and collectible community, Alena and I established our cover stories satisfactorily. Since many shops would be closed on Sunday, we decided to spend the morning dropping in at windward O'ahu yard sales, while Ke'oni was performing some maintenance on his truck.

For the most part, I was continuing to keep my culinary education under wraps. Since I would not be available for any of our explorations on Thursday, I knew I had to divulge a little secret to Alena.

"I may be known as a foodie in my personal tastes and career, but that can hardly be said for my skills in the kitchen. But since remodeling my Auntie Carrie's kitchen, I've embarked on a program of culinary self-improvement." I told her about my article on Chef Duncan and the classes I was taking. To my surprise, she expressed interest, so I said I would get permission for her to join my class the following week.

When I returned home, Ke'oni and I embarked on a serious round of vacuuming and dusting. Motivated by my new acquisitions, I even spent a couple of hours cleaning the dolls in my collection and reorganizing their displays. At sunset, we were sitting on the swing on the back *lānai* enjoying a bottle of Hula O Maui sparkling pineapple wine from the Tedeschi Vineyards on Maui that a client had given Ke'oni. That wine might not be appropriate with every menu, but we paired it successfully with a loaf of fresh Italian bread and the last of a French Dream cheese round from the Surfing Goat Dairy.

Soon after, John called. Although the men had said they did not require a face-to-face consultation prior to our meeting at the hotel, John had worked through the weekend again and decided to take Monday off. Since he would be in our neighborhood for another golf game at Mid-Pacific Country Club early in the morning, he suggested having another roundtable meeting in our kitchen. I was delighted when our favorite detective said he would be bringing a surprise brunch.

When he arrived, one hand carried his briefcase and the other held a large carryall. With smiles of greetings all around, we quickly moved into the kitchen to discover what the day's feast would be. Aside from the expected Martini and Rossi Prosecco, he brought a variety of breads, cheeses, fruits, and sliced rare beef, from his cousin's deli.

"What a treat!" exclaimed Ke'oni, inhaling the fragrance of the fresh crab.

"I was disappointed to learn that Kona crabs are out of season, but the *kuahonu* variety aren't a bad second," said John. "The only thing disappointing about take-out from the market as opposed to eating in the café, is that we don't get that huge bed of fresh watercress underneath the salad."

"Well, that may disappoint you, but the salad alone is great. And with a meal like this, I'm thrilled there will be few dishes to wash," I added with glee.

To simplify both preparation and cleanup, I brought out plastic champagne flutes and sturdy plastic dishes and flatware. After opening and spreading out the many containers of the delicate fare, we began helping ourselves to an excellent meal.

"I have a contribution to make to this lovely occasion," I said with a broad smile.

Both men looked up from their plates with identical looks of doubt on their faces.

"Don't worry, it's not one of my experimentations. It's a delicious blackberry and strawberry dessert from Izzy that warrants china bowls and fresh vanilla ice cream."

They smiled in anticipation and returned to consuming their food.

The focus of this confab was the overall approach to the original investigation. As the men spoke, I realized why the case had gone cold rather quickly, despite the expressed concern of the community and the best efforts of the Honolulu Police Department.

It had been a simple formula for failure—little forensic evidence and no witnesses. No wonder it was a case that had troubled Ke'oni through the years. With the temple being such a large institution, it was amazing that no one had seen anything out of the ordinary—least of all the removal of the statue. It was hard to imagine how someone could get in and out of a popular tourist spot without being seen.

It was clear that John had done his homework before he arrived at our door. He opened his notebook and began adding his own research to the old reports in the case file.

"We've confirmed there was a bus of tourists visiting the temple on the morning of the murder. In addition to tourists from Asia, there were American and Canadian converts to Buddhism who were visiting. Whether they came to the Islands specifically to see the statues in the sanctuary, or were simply on vacation, a visit to the temple would have been easy to fit in.

"Although the stop was scheduled, that party of tourists had specifically stipulated that they were renting the bus for the day and didn't want to be on a set timeline. The tour bus company's records are rather vague. Obviously, the caper demanded more preparation than for lifting a pair of altar candlesticks. One thing is clear: that statue isn't exactly something you could slip into your pocket as a tourist or a thief."

"So, you're saying that aside from the pair of criminals being fairly strong, at least one of the perpetrators had a head for planning," I said.

"That's right," John continued. "Our guys killed the woman and pulled the statue from the altar onto a trolley. Then they rolled it out of the sanctuary, the building, and then loaded everything into a vehicle. All in quick order, without being seen."

"After that, they transported the Buddha to someone who must have paid them a hefty fee for their efforts," chimed in Ke'oni. "We don't know if that person ordered the theft for him- or herself. They may have been serving as a middleman for an unknown buyer. Maybe the whole thing was set up for a black-market auction. Of course, as we've already said, that was before there was the internet as we know it today—let alone commercial auctions on the dark web."

"And don't forget that at the time, many art thefts were being committed on demand. It was almost like calling a real estate agent and saying you'd like a Victorian mansion of 20,000 square feet, with a specific list of amenities," added John.

"Grand theft to order?" I offered with a laugh.

"That's about it. Actually, we might say grand larceny to order. So, now we fly ahead more than a decade and you have to wonder why the piece is back on the open market," said Ke'oni, musing.

"Maybe something happened to the person who originally bought it. It might not have been the Kiyohara patriarch who just died. He, or she, may not be a member of the family at all. That family may not know anything about the Buddha's history and are innocently dissolving part of their private collection. If they've known about the theft and murder, how could they have been so dumb as to think there isn't a government agency or insurance company that's monitoring the international market?" I asked.

"Sometimes when you've got that kind of money, you think you're safe from legal retribution," declared John.

"Based on your visions, Natalie, we know there were two perpetrators in the temple's sanctuary. There could also have been a third man in the getaway vehicle. You can bet the delivery happened sooner than later, if the perps were waiting to be paid," observed Ke'oni.

"Don't forget, we're talking murder here—not just the lifting of an antique statue," responded John.

I poured another round of bubbly and tried to ignore the review of the autopsy.

"COD was a single small caliber GSW that lodged in her cranium.

There wasn't much splatter or pooling of blood," commented Ke'oni. "It also helped that the gun shot was on the right, and the victim's body fell to the left."

John shifted through some of the papers he had brought out from his briefcase. "I didn't find anything of use when I looked over the evidence. Is there some forensic detail, or maybe someone's suspicion that I'm not seeing in the reports? Was there anything about the crime scene that bothered you, Ke'oni? Or maybe something about the vic that you wondered about?"

"Because of the heist—and the absence of red flags in our initial look at the victim's background—we didn't examine her life any further," said Ke'oni. "I've recently looked into her life. The facts are pretty simple. She came from a family of priests in Japan. She was single. She was a virtuoso on the *koto*—that's a Japanese stringed instrument. In her youth, she had attended summer school at the University of Hawai'i. While she was here, she performed several times in the Islands. She left her career in music after returning to Japan and soon became a Jōdo shin Buddhist minister. Her work brought her back to the Islands eventually. She maintained a vow of celibacy throughout her life. Her social as well as work life revolved around the temple."

"The bio you've just related rings more than one bell," I said. "I remember her as a young performer. And later, as a newly arrived female priest at the temple, when she received a fair amount of media coverage. With her youthful energy and bi-lingual skills, it was hoped she would inspire a renewal spiritual consciousness in the Buddhist youth of Hawai'i."

I continued reminiscing about my personal awareness of the deceased, as John began repacking his briefcase.

"She was a magnificent musician as a young woman. Her talent for playing the *koto* was recognized across Asia. I watched her perform at the International Festival of the Pacific. It's an annual event sponsored by the Hilo Japanese Chamber of Commerce. You see, *kumu hula* Dottie Horita—no relationship to Alena's family—booked the entertainers. She had many connections from extending her teaching of *hula* to Japan and was delighted to learn about the girl. When Mrs. Horita learned that Ayameko Fujimoto would be in Hawai'i for the summer, she was quickly added to the program.

"The reason I remember so much about the time is that I was a young widow and my parents insisted on taking me on a vacation while I was between writing assignments. We were relaxing at a resort in Kailua-Kona when my father saw a brochure for the festival. I think that's where he found mention of the arrival of the *Nippon Maru*, a sailing ship of the Japanese National Institute for Sea Training.

"I recall those ships visiting Honolulu," John said. "Their arrivals created quite a stir. It was quite a sight for both tourists and locals. The people around me talked about how it was like the old Boat Days when ocean liners arrived. Everyone flocked to the port for the music and *hula* girls, and kids diving into the water for coins."

"Now don't put that down," retorted Ke'oni. "I was one of those boys who dove in for the coins a couple of times. It was cold and dirty, but a great story to tell at school. I even got a few silver dollars that I still have."

CHAPTER 6

If you need to take action, only do what is necessary.
The Tao Te Ching [Third Century BCE]

Being a retired naval officer, my father was always eager to see a unique ship. He was especially eager to take a tour of the *Nippon Maru*. We were quayside as she sailed into port. It was a scene from an earlier century. Everything about the sleek vessel glistened in white. From the sails of her foremast to her hull and fixtures...especially the cadets in their crisp dress uniforms.

"Despite your saying you dislike everything that floats on water, it sounds like you had a good time," noted Ke'oni with a smirk.

"You're right. But there were a lot of things I enjoyed more than looking at that ship. My parents and I ended up spending more than a week on the Big Island. The Festival kept us busy every day. There were artists and craftsmen plying their talents and the most delicious international foods to sample. There was even a formal Japanese tea ceremony.

"We also visited orchid farms and hiked through the Pana'ewa Rainforest. One day we left the Hilo area and toured Parker Ranch in Waimea. That's not far from the Kūka'iau Ranch where you got those delicious steaks for our first dinner together...and I think it may be where Auntie Carrie got her holiday roasts. Like you said, those two ranches produce the best beef in the Islands—due to their clean air and water and the rich volcanic grassland.

"That's a great reminder. Why don't we order some of their steaks, honey? Then you can bring Lori over for a barbecue, John," suggested Ke'oni. "She spends too long in the morgue."

"She's been working hard during her internship because there's a chance she might get hired here permanently. But I think the pressure's been getting to her lately. She's complaining we only get together over work. I'm sure she'd love a day out of the city. We'll bring the wine and a loaf of fresh bread," offered John.

"We'll look forward to the occasion," said Ke'oni. Turning to me he asked, "So, what else did you and your folks do on the Big Island?"

"Since we were nearby, we dropped in at the Kamuela Museum. It was amazing. At the time of my visit, the collection was so eclectic that everywhere I turned there was a new category of treasure. My favorite piece was a round Chinese table covered with the most exquisite mother of pearl inlay. There were also a few pieces of furniture originally from 'Iolani Palace. They're worth millions of dollars. I think the Palace finally negotiated their return."

"I sure like the way you tell a story, Natalie," commented John. "I can see what you're describing as if I was there with you."

"Thanks for the compliment. Some images just stick in my mind. The highlight of our vacation was an evening of performances by out-standing musicians and dancers representing many cultures. Even the Japanese cadets participated. I remember them marching down the aisle and smiling broadly as they sang a medley of songs. It was obvious they were truly pleased by the welcome they received so far from their home port.

"In the midst of the show, I was wooed by the haunting tones of the *koto* played by a young Japanese woman. I made a point of closely read-ing her bio in the program. I learned a lot about her distinguished family and discovered why the sounds of the instrument can be so complex.

"Isn't a *koto* like a zither?" inquired John.

"Yes...with bridges. The first of the instruments were imported from China around the eighth century and exclusively played by blind men. The traditional instrument is made of *Paulownia* wood and features ivo-ry bridges and thirteen silk strings. Ayameko Fujimoto played a variant. It had seventeen strings, which yields a broader range of music. After her performance, a member of the Chamber of Commerce informed me that her performance in Hilo provided an opportunity to reunite with her brother who was a midshipman aboard the Japanese ship."

"That fits with what we were told about her in our interviews," said Ke'oni, as he cleared our dishes. "It's too bad her moving personal story didn't generate any new information from the public. Except for the re-appearance of the Buddha, we're sitting here with the same absence of evidence. As Sir Arthur Conan Doyle observed, *it is a capital mistake to theorize before one has data.* We just need to continue probing until we obtain enough pieces to figure out this puzzle."

On that note, our *tête-à-tête* concluded. For the next couple of days, we all continued our individual preparations for the auction. Although my sweetheart was not expected to display much knowledge of the world of art and antiques, we realized it was important for each of us to master as much specialized information as possible. Doing so meant we were more likely to recognize the significance of whatever might mate-rialize at the two-day event.

I had the easier job, since I was only expected to find items on which to bid and write a check if I won a bid. Except for Wednesday and Thurs-day, Alena and I did more telephone conferring than idea shopping at galleries and stores. In each of our conversations, I learned more about the auction business…and some of the finer points of international theft and smuggling. During subsequent pillow talk, I was able to express my appreciation of Ke'oni's former profession.

He has been publicly recognized as my boyfriend for a while. A few people also know him as the craftsman who has done much of the refurbishing of the Lanikai cottage. These facts alone justify his attendance at the auction. But as the retired cop who first investigated a murder and grand larceny, his actual role is to help the authorities look for anything or anyone even peripherally connected to the case.

This makes it all the more important for him to comprehend the intricacies of the auction process and to know the biographies of expected attendees. Luckily, HPD, the FBI, and several international agencies have provided a substantial amount of information for him to study. It is a balancing act, for Ke'oni needs to avoid tipping his hand and alarming any criminals who might be present. As to our personal lives, I feel any increase in our knowledge of art and antiques will eventually be put to good use.

In the midst of our preparations, there were a few adjustments to my personal work schedule. I pushed back a visit to the Waimānalo poultry farm since I couldn't be sure about any follow-up activity that might result from the auction. Soon after I received a call from Bō Shēn apologizing that a business trip would preclude his company's participating in the event at 'Iolani Palace. That meant I had to find other subjects to showcase in my article. The change of focus was resolved by a TV news story that highlighted chefs who have been instructors at Kapi'olani Community College.

Although I had known about the school's culinary program for a long time, I became intimately aware of it in my scrutiny of Ariel's death. The apartment complex where she died was owned by two elderly Hawaiian-Chinese sisters from Shànghǎi. Pearl Wong had a stepson who was the epitome of the perennial student, attending classes forever without earning a degree. I never did learn whether the middle-aged man had any talent in the kitchen. Tools of one type or another seemed to be a constant preoccupation of his.

I was not facing a publishing crisis, since I always have an article in reserve. Harry had already suggested that we occasionally run a piece that has nothing to do with Hawai'i. So, I was happy to ask him to be prepared to run a back-up piece I had written about my experiences with South American river cruises. This would allow me to forestall the 'Iolani Palace project if necessary.

With everything shipshape in the home and even the office, I was glad to return to my education in art and antiques with Alena on Wednesday. We wandered around Chinatown part of the time. It was delightful to duck in and out of shops peeking at whatever specialties the owners have to offer serious local customers. Alena surprised me by being somewhat conversant in the Yue dialect of southern China. This time it was her turn to land a lucky purchase…a beautiful small Kuan Yĭn carved in ivory-colored jade.

We remained on the windward side of Oʻahu the next day. First, we visited a couple of small second-hand stores. Next, I suggested we drop in at a home noted for year-round yard sales. I seldom find anything I really need, but it's fun to see recycling being enjoyed by so many people. Our final stop before my culinary class was the gift shop at the beautiful Byōdō-in Temple in Valley of the Temples Memorial Park. It is a smaller version of a temple built in Uji, Japan, nearly a thousand years ago. The exquisitely maintained grounds, bass toned *bonshō* bell, crying peacocks and golden Amida Buddha statue always brings a smile that remains on my face for hours.

I could not have picked a more appropriate culinary class for Alena to attend. During the session, the featured recipe was classic *miso* soup. Alena watched respectfully from the sidelines as the students worked their way through each step. Then she happily participated in our sampling and recipe analysis as the instructor insisted. She described how her grandmother from Kagoshima, Japan, had always added a sprinkling of local seaweed as she served her *miso* soup.

After the class ended, we went to Windward Mall to drop in at an art gallery. I fell in love with a small Delores Kirby seascape that glowed with a realism that presented the beauty of the Islands as it might have been seen a hundred years ago. Sadly, the price tag was a bit over my limit since I needed to keep enough funds in my bank account to bid on a few of the upcoming auction's tempting offerings. With a sigh, I closed my mind to the chance to own even a small Delores Kirby original painting.

It would have been useful to meet with John's boss prior to the auction. Unfortunately, Captain Leonard Makani needed to extend his testimony at a high-profile trial. This meant that many of HPD's onsite preparations had been pushed to Thursday evening. When I arrived home from my class, there was not much time until we needed to leave for our preview session at the hotel. It was good that I had stopped at our favorite market for roasted chicken and a broccoli and raisin salad. This ensured that Keʻoni and I had eaten enough to last through what might be a very late night.

Since he was returning from downtown, Keʻoni did not show up for another half hour. To ensure our anonymity, he was borrowing an old Citroen from his Mānoa neighbor Ben Faktorr. The vintage vehicle is one of his dearest possessions and we assured him there would be no police action. After a quick break to eat, change clothes, and pack our electronic toys for the evening we were ready to depart.

We minimized the number of cars associated with HPD's surveillance post by picking up Alena at her Nuʻuanu apartment. We followed

John's directions and drove into a parking lot designated for deliveries and special event vehicles. Despite HPD wanting to keep a low profile, someone had chosen a bus that looked like a country singer's home on the road. However, it was surrounded by non-descript cars and vans. With its darkened windows, I doubted that anyone would question its being there, much less accidently open its door.

Ke'oni dropped Alena and me near the bus and pulled back to park the Citroen. With little space between the wall of the hotel and the bus's door, no one could get near the vehicle without being seen from within. Alena entered first. I watched as she flashed her badge at a man in the driver's seat. We turned to look at the layout of the bus and saw two men viewing a variety of electronic equipment. They were dressed in shorts and logo-laden T-shirts and might have been tourists, if it were not for their deep tans and regimental haircuts. Their focus was on an array of monitors displaying a ballroom, hotel suites, hallways, and restrooms.

They never looked up, but the man standing behind them smiled at Alena and nodded at me. He was wearing a pale green and ivory aloha shirt and dark gray slacks. In his hand was the stub of a well-chewed cigar. Even though it was not lit, the close air of the bus carried the unwelcome smell to my nostrils. I tried to be subtle in my response. He quickly took out a handkerchief, wrapped up his cigar, and placed it in a tin box on the table in front of an L-shaped banquette.

"Natalie Seachrist. Nice to meet you. I'm Leonard Makani. I've read your work through the years. Really like your new column."

"Thank you. We're still refining the format," I said with gratitude.

"What do you think of our temporary home?" asked the Captain, gesturing with his arm. "After a large stash of heroin was found in the luggage compartment, this little baby became our newest asset."

"Don't you usually sell assets that are confiscated?" I asked.

"You're right. But in this case, the powers that be determined that changes in paint and decals will ensure this will be a gift that keeps on giving for years."

At that point Ke'oni climbed aboard our stationary chariot. After a round of handshaking, we formed a semi-circle behind the officers monitoring the scenes from the hotel. We watched for a moment as uniformed hotel personnel pushed supply carts along the hallways. Persons without uniforms or insignia carried large packages into the suites in which we were especially interested.

"As planned, we're observing things from here tonight. John's upstairs in the observation room we've set up. He'll soon check in with us as he tours the auction rooms," explained Capt. Makani. "Tomorrow night was to have been our official walk-through, since the installation of the collection has to be completed for Saturday's preview. The problem with that scenario is a wedding that's scheduled in two sections of the grand ballroom tomorrow. Since the bride's related to the Governor, their nuptials couldn't be changed.

"That means the layout for the auction preview can't be finalized until about midnight tomorrow. It's not a complete catastrophe because much of the setup for both activities is the same. Even the storage and staging area for the live auction won't be affected by the wedding, since it's hidden by a curtain behind the stage. As to the stage itself, that's worked out rather well. Since the band for the wedding knocks off at ten, the only things to be removed are their chairs and music stands. The podium and mic just have to be moved to the center of the stage. And, you could say the wedding is providing us with an audio rehearsal. As you can imagine, tomorrow is going to be a long day and night, but we'll have everything prepped for Saturday's eleven a.m. preview".

Our trio nodded.

"In terms of your participation, forget the schedule we gave you. I'll leave the timing of your private peek at the setup to you. You can stay up really late tomorrow night and float in any time you want on Saturday, or show up for the beginning of the preview.

He looked at me and smirked. "I guess the time will depend on how early you want to enter bids in the silent auction. As to you, Ke'oni, between Saturday's preview and Sunday's live and silent auctions, we're hoping you'll see something significant. That's why I'm asking you to be present for as many hours as possible."

"No problem, Captain," answered Ke'oni.

"Good. There's no telling who might saunter in this weekend. If we're lucky, there'll be at least one person you recognize from the time of the heist. That could give us a new starting point, even if they don't seem connected to the case directly."

Nodding at Alena and me, he said "As to you ladies, your covers are great. On Saturday, you're going to wander around looking at everything in the preview. Then you'll take a break and have lunch somewhere in the hotel. Of course, you need to look at everyone wherever you go. Once you've eaten, return to the preview for a second look and then head upstairs for a little confab. The room we've got for on-site surveillance is next to members of the wedding party—but they should have cleared out by about eleven o'clock on Saturday.

"You'll be wired, Alena. Anything that you and Natalie notice can be mentioned aloud, and we'll immediately know what's going on. Although you'll have a small revolver in your purse, I don't want you to use it unless someone's life is in danger. Keep your eyes and ears open but remain in character and try to stay out of trouble."

"Yes, sir," responded Alena happily. I knew she was delighted with her first major assignment as a detective. Ke'oni and I had watched her career blossom for a couple of years. I knew that her formal education, proficiency in Japanese, and experience as an officer on the street, made her an excellent addition to the Criminal Investigation Division.

Another positive aspect of our investigation was that for days HPD had worked with hotel security. Surveillance cameras had been positioned to maximize coverage of areas that hotel, auction staff, and attendees might access. As we waited for the tour to begin, the Captain passed out diagrams of the layout of spaces allocated to the auction. Ke'oni snapped a picture of it with his smartphone so we would not be caught looking at hardcopy during the event.

It showed the main ballroom used for both the wedding and the auction. Within it, a large area was allocated to seating. In front of that was the stage on which auction items would be displayed by lot number, plus a podium where the auctioneer would hold court. Behind that were movable walls with a holding area being filled with tables and lockable containers to be used to store items up for auction before and after the bidding process. Luckily, the wedding reception and post nuptial dinner were being held in a smaller room in a separate part of the hotel.

To the right was another large space designated for the preview and silent auction. Items scheduled for the live auction were being placed along the left and rear walls since they were adjacent to the live auction storage space. An exception was the statue of the Shākyamuni Buddha that was being placed on a large round table in the center of the room. Smaller tables with items being offered in the silent auction surrounded it. The far-right wall featured the larger items in the silent auction.

In a few minutes, John and Benny Tang (the hotel's chief of security) arrived in camera range at the doors of the ballroom. Since Benny was participating fully in the investigation, the two men kept a running dialogue allowing us to catch the nuances of what we were seeing. Although they were alone most of the time, there was no way to control who might abruptly enter the scene—especially the Nippon Antiquities' Auction Porter, who was there to ensure that everything was done correctly. Therefore, it was good we were able to speak to John directly from the trailer and he could steer their open dialogue to address our expressed concerns.

Not knowing which items would prove of interest in the investigation, the men walked at a leisurely pace during their tour. This allowed us to see the edges and corners of the rooms as well as their centers. Personally, I found the entire process of assembling the displays of antiques fascinating to observe. Nothing was allowed to detract from the exquisite qualities of each piece. Each item was placed to maximize its visibility. The use of round tables allowed one to examine all sides of the smaller artifacts. There was a graceful flow to the overall aesthetic of the layout. With a team of such professionals, it was no wonder that the promotional photos had been so beautiful.

The supervisor of the endeavor was a slight middle-aged Japanese man. Assisting him were two teams of personnel. The first positioned the artifacts; the second focused lighting on each. Per his direction, the movement of heavy objects was accomplished by two muscular Samoan men who resembled successful wrestlers. Two elderly Japanese women placed small items in front of, or on, black and ivory textile backgrounds. Mirrors and clear acrylic stands were used to heighten the effect of some displays.

Lighting was handled by a man and woman who followed behind the first team. Their assignment was placing and adjusting focal lights to justify the high selling prices being demanded. A man wearing a hotel maintenance uniform was charged with moving a tall ladder on wheels to adjust overhead spotlights. After everyone else completed their work, the supervisor moved from table to table and case to case with a cart full of many objects. He placed some items on pressure security pads and covered others with acrylic cubes and replaced bulbs in several of the small light fixtures. When he was through, pure white light made each display radiate as though the item was indeed priceless in value.

Listening to the bantering conversation between John and Benny was interesting. Their detailed conversation addressed many technical issues. Distances between cameras, their angles, the type of devices recording the data and playback equipment were all itemized. It reminded me of the times I have seen John make such observations during investigations he has undertaken with Ke'oni and me.

"Well, Benny it looks like you've made quite a few modifications in the last day," commented John.

"You're right, Lieutenant. One thing we had to do was install polarized camera lenses since the pin-point lighting could affect the quality of footage we'll be recording during the event. Otherwise, about all you'd be able to see is screaming white light. Of course, being responsible for millions of dollars of antiques makes you examine every detail. Nippon Antiquities is responsible for their own event insurance. But we want to discourage anyone from thinking about theft, let alone grand larceny."

The image being shot by the camera on John's glasses bobbed as he observed, "Mmhm. Smart decision to place the bid sheets on stands outside the roped areas in front of the silent auction items. That should keep everyone but a bratty kid out of the way."

"You must be joking. With the price tags on even the smallest things being so high, there shouldn't be a kid in sight."

At that moment, the men sped up as they approached the end of the room. "Hey John," I called out loudly, forgetting he would hear even a whisper in his ear. "Can you back up a bit? Even though I'm officially attending the live auction, I think I want to bid on one of the enameled eggs you just passed, or maybe that collection of pill boxes."

To accommodate me, John touched his companion's sleeve. "You know, it's amazing how many *tchotchkes* a person can cram into a home. I'm thinking my girlfriend would love this enameled egg."

"How much was your last pay increase? You must be getting paid a hell of a lot more than when I was on the job," joked Benny.

John tapped the edge of his glasses and Benny indicated his understanding that one of their listeners was the one interested in the ornately enameled eggs. He then leaned toward the pieces that seemed like poor cousins of the gem-encrusted art fabricated by Peter Carl Fabergé for the doomed Russian monarchy. Seeing the sparkle of gemstones, I was sure that even these eggs were undoubtedly beyond my budget.

After a couple of moments, John moved on to a trio of *cloisonné* pillboxes dating to the 1920s. The first was round, with a silver bottom and a top that looked like black jade set on ivory. The second box was covered in gold and topped with a bouquet of gems. The third was the most likely candidate for my pocketbook. The simple rectangular box appeared to be silver with a vein of mother of pearl running horizontally across its lid.

I did not know whether I would actually bid on these fragile beauties. However, I knew they would fill my dreams with fancy-dress events in the ballrooms of European aristocracy. They were lovely images of past generations. Of course, I knew the only way *my* ancestors would have been part of such scenarios would have been as seamstresses and footmen waiting upon the lords and ladies in elegant carriages drawn by festooned horses.

The men completed their walkabout by striding through the spaces surrounding the ballroom: Exits and entrances; hallways; restrooms; and nearby suites assigned to the event. The Captain had certainly planned things well. It was almost as if we had been walking through the spaces in person.

CHAPTER 7

*The real voyage of discovery is not in seeking new landscapes
but in having new eyes.*
Marcel Proust [1871 - 1922]

Some weeks seem destined to reach a high climax at their conclusion. That was now the case for both Keʻoni and me. We had
planned to be present at the late Friday night setup for the auction, but
several things prevented our doing so. We had awakened early and began the day enjoying a quick meal of fresh pineapple, yogurt, and coffee.
Sans cat, we arrived at the beach at half past seven. We walked briskly
for a while, seeking any unusual shells or coral that might present themselves. We then sat blissfully staring at the sparkling turquoise waters
of Kailua Bay.

With empty pockets, we returned home to check voice messages
and emails. Keʻoni had received a frantic call necessitating his taking the
long drive out to Ewa Beach to examine the remains of a break-in at a
client's home. Then I got a call from Nathan that required adjusting my
schedule. One of his colleagues had unexpectedly canceled his shift at
Hale Malolo and my brother asked if I could go to his Kāneʻohe home to
care for his dog. Kūlia had been injured in an attack by a stray dog and
required a sequence of medications throughout the day. The little guy is
a mix of beagle and cocker spaniel. He has a wonderful disposition since
Miss Una taught him that cats are not for romping after and is now a
delightful companion to kitties large and small.

Nathan's closest neighbors were on vacation and the dog's condition prevented him from accompanying my brother to the women's
shelter. Therefore, I became the designated caregiver. Initially it appeared that I would be home with sufficient hours for Keʻoni and me to
eat, review our notes, and arrive in Waikīkī in a timely fashion. Unfortunately, Nathan's return was delayed when an irate husband of one of the
shelter's women arrived in a drunken state. He was soon calmed down
and left the premises. But just after Nathan called to assure me that he
was on his way home, the troubled man returned with a gun.

Police and SWAT officers were called and several hours of hostage
negotiations ensued after the subject barricaded himself in a bedroom

with his hysterical wife and young son. Nathan was involved in relocating women and children who had been playing in the yard. The chief negotiator was a former colleague of Nathan, and he called on Nathan to remain at the scene to help hostages as they were released.

I made a quick call to Ke'oni regarding the situation. After feeding Miss Una, he picked up his touch screen tablet and everything else we might need for the evening. Since there was no way of knowing when Nathan might return, Ke'oni arrived with a takeout dinner from Whole Foods Market. He found me distraught about the situation at Hale Malolo.

"There's nothing either of us can do, Natalie," he said, giving me a long hug. "Nathan's the psychologist on duty and I know there'll be a police negotiator on scene. Anyone who's not needed will have been removed and the property cordoned off to keep the neighborhood as safe as possible. There will also be plain clothed officers to help keep everything calm. If everyone (including the media) follows the directions given by the authorities, it should all work out peacefully."

I took the bottle of tea Ke'oni had brought from home and walked into the kitchen. Inspired by our DIY projects, Nathan had enlarged and updated the space. He had added a new bay window that accommodated a large rattan dinette set and the room was now quite lovely. I set the tea down near the sink and opened a cupboard for glasses and dishes. Since I remained silent, Ke'oni knew I was not satisfied by his canned speech on hostage-taking protocols.

He turned me gently by the shoulders. His bright blue eyes staring into my green ones, now clouded by doubt. "You know I've been through a lot of these situations. Most of them turn out fine—especially for the police and other experts trying to resolve the situation. If anyone is going to be injured, it's likely to be the perpetrator, or his hostages."

"My mind knows you're right Ke'oni. But my heart is aching...and not just for Nathan. You remember when Miriam died, and Samantha was trying to help with the arrangements for her funeral? Her primary friend at the shelter was Abby. She's the esthetician who offered to do makeup for Miriam. Well, that's the target of this crazed guy. Abby's been in and out of Hale Malolo several times. Just last week she told Samantha that she'd had enough and was getting ready to move to the mainland to live with her sister."

"I'm sorry, honey. I know you're agitated, but there's nothing we can do. Nathan's aware of how concerned you are. I'm sure he'll check in as soon as he can. Why don't you put together a couple of plates of food for us while I call John and Captain Makani to let them know what's happened. They may have heard about the situation, but they won't necessarily connect it to your family."

Soon, we were seated at the table eating a delicious meal that was not diminished by the occasion. The herbs on the chicken were perfectly balanced and the crunchy broccoli salad had the ideal proportion of raisins, bacon, and candied cashews. I could not decide if I was eating a healthy salad, or a slightly less than naughty dessert.

Referring to the auction, Ke'oni said, "We've already seen all of the layout. Captain Makani said we shouldn't worry about missing tonight. It's too bad I didn't bring a bottle of wine, but not knowing what would develop at the shelter, let alone at the set up for the auction, I thought it would be best to forego the alcohol."

"Smart call, dear. Maybe we can all enjoy a glass of something stronger than tea when Nathan returns."

An hour later my brother arrived home.

"There are leftovers in the refrigerator," I announced. "I hesitated to fix you a plate until you walked through the door."

"That was smart. A kind neighbor brought pizza for those of us on watch during the hostage ordeal. I'm more tired than anything," he replied.

"Why don't you throw on a pair of shorts and I'll fix a tray of snacks and beer for you guys?"

"Thanks, Sis. There's some Weasel Boy ale and a bottle of Barefoot Moscato wine in the cooler for you. It's sweet and almost sparkling; I use it in fruit salad dressing. Well, I've sweated so much today, I think I'll quickly rinse off."

As the men greeted each other, I turned to prowling the refrigerator and cupboards. I was pleased to find pretzels, crackers, and a wedge of brie cheese. I only wished there were some Muscat Blanc grapes to pair with the cheese, but you cannot expect to have everything on a night of crisis. At least there were beer steins in the freezer! With everything arranged on my mother's old *monkey pod* tray, I walked into the family room as Nathan was pulling a sun-faded T-shirt over his head.

"What a day," he declared, picking up a chilled beer stein and a bottle of ale.

"Hardly what any of us had planned," rejoined Ke'oni.

"I'm sure glad you were able to help me, Natalie. On any other day I could've run Kūlia back to the vet. But when everything fell apart at the shelter, I couldn't leave."

"Thank goodness it all worked out," I said.

Ke'oni then filled Nathan in on our case. "Captain Makani said we really weren't needed at the hotel tonight. We'll be there early tomorrow and can check out any changes that have been made in the layout or operational plans."

"I know you'll be in the public rooms of a hotel, but please call to let me know when everything is over and you're safely out of the way of any nefarious characters," requested Nathan.

"Yes, Daddy. I'll give you a ring when the preview is over. But remember, the main event is on Sunday."

Although I had not done anything strenuous physically, I was exhausted by the time we reached Lanikai. Thankfully, Miss Una has 'Ilima and The Ladies to keep her occupied when Ke'oni and I are gone very long. Aside from refreshing her food and water, she didn't demand much attention. Soon we were all nestled down for a late summer night's rest.

Anticipating a long day, we bypassed our usual morning walk to the beach and simplified breakfast by having protein-infused piña colada smoothies. I was not watching my diet so much as anticipating an excellent lunch with Alena.

With so many uncertainties regarding our activities that weekend, I opted to draw on my usual wardrobe of Hawaiian attire for both days. Saturday's preview was a casual affair, so I wore a mid-calf cotton *mu'umu'u*. My hips had been feeling fairly good lately, but I bypassed my array of slip-on gel sandals and chose a pair with straps that offered the stability I would require if I needed to move quickly.

I completed my outfits with earrings, a broach, and a pair of glasses whose inner workings were as unique as Alena's. Our glasses connected us audibly to our team of handlers; the broach allowed them to view what we were seeing.

Ke'oni also made concessions in the wardrobe department. While he wears shorts most days, his need to carry a gun today necessitated wearing slacks with deep pockets. His Class G firearm license allows him to carry concealed weapons throughout the state of Hawai'i. As a courtesy to law enforcement, he usually checks in with local agencies if he's on a case on a neighboring island. Since he is now part of an official investigation, there is no need for him to mention his Smith and Wesson .357 five-shot revolver to anyone.

For safety as well as style, I am glad he has found a line of menswear with waistband flexibility and a stretch fabric that allows him to hide a few items. His weak left ankle requires extra support during active days. I am glad that he has shoes that feature dressy leather uppers and composite soles that ease the need for occasional sprinting.

Shortly after ten, we picked up Alena. After a few minutes of techie talk with Ke'oni, she turned to me.

"Do I look like an aspiring designer?" she inquired hopefully.

"I think you look like the wonderful young professional you are. Your gray slacks are perfect with the navy jacket. Your pink silk blouse is very elegant. And I love seeing that you're wearing your Chaminade class ring," I returned.

"Few people in my class ordered rings. Those that do often order a custom design. The jacket was a graduation gift from my parents. Knowing I was becoming a detective, they ordered the custom-tailored pantsuit with deep pockets to carry anything I might need. I've got room for my badge, Glock, and wallet, and a couple of electronic toys the Captain issued to me for the weekend."

As we neared the hotel, she pulled out a pair of black rimmed glasses with clear lenses. I knew they had both audio and visual features. "What do you think?" she asked gleefully.

"They make you look very serious...a designer who will go to all means necessary to make sure her client's needs are met."

With all our gadgets, we could easily communicate with one another and Central Command in the upstairs observation room. Unless there was a real emergency, Alena would remain at my side. This would leave Ke'oni free to roam and connect with Captain Makani and John as necessary.

The main assignment for all of us was to maintain our cover stories. I might be recognized from my work as a journalist and Ke'oni from his years with HPD. Since John and Ke'oni are known to have partnered for several years, it would be normal for them to be friendly with one another—provided it does not look as though they were currently working together.

The unknowable factor in our role-playing was Alena. Unless someone knew her date of graduation, her tale of continuing studies while launching a career in interior design should remain viable as long as she does not run into anyone who knows she is a police officer.

We dropped her at a side door of the hotel since she needed to check in at the surveillance post. I called John while Ke'oni parked the car. He said that registration for the preview had begun. He and Benny were completing their first sweep of the rooms designated for the auction.

By the time Ke'oni and I entered the hotel, I was so excited about my forthcoming adventure that I needed to use the ladies' room. I left my personal detective standing at a large window overlooking a tropical garden planted with many varieties of ginger plants, including white and red shell, yellow rattlesnake, and white crepe. I could also see the bright bracts of Maya gold heliconias and lavender anthuriums growing among ferns and zebra plants. My favorite was the faddishly popular *medinilla* houseplant, whose pink flowers stream downward from upright stems.

Alone in the restroom, I took a minute to pull out my phone and study the layout of this wing of the hotel that Ke'oni had loaded for me. I was just putting it back in my purse when Alena came in. Before speaking, she looked around carefully...even below the stall doors.

"Any news?" I asked.

"Op is a go. Everything is on schedule. We'll do our first walkthrough and then have lunch," she declared.

Just then an elderly Hawaiian woman entered with several young girls who each wore a matching *mu'umu'u* and *haku lei*. I wondered if they were part of the wedding party or members of a *hula hālau* performing somewhere in the hotel. Alena and I smiled at them and exited to join Keʻoni. Our trio moved casually toward our destination, quietly discussing details of the forthcoming event. "There are several ways this high-end auction deviates from the norm," said Alena, moving into a teaching mode. "The first thing I noticed is that there aren't any private showings. It looks like the company's cutting a lot of corners generally. I noticed that there's no mention of their providing standard services like financing, insurance, or shipping. And, although they're holding this preview, there's not a presale day. Maybe this is the result of the family patriarch's death in Kyōto and Nippon Antiquities having lost their lease at Ala Moana Shopping Center.

"Of course, none of that impacts our case. According to the company's records, the Shākyamuni Buddha has been in the Kiyohara family's possession since at least the Second World War. We can't be sure if that's true since we have no definitive proof of its provenance. Setting that issue aside, our first concern is proving that it is the one that was stolen from the Hawaiian temple. The fact that the investigation is moving forward may indicate that art historians have confirmed its provenance already."

We ceased our conversation as we approached the line to register. I noticed that everyone connected with the auction wore navy blue blazers with Nippon Antiquities logos on their breast pockets. We were issued badges that allowed us to enter all the events planned for the weekend. However, we would not receive our numbered catalogues for the live auction until we checked in the next day. I had not realized there would be a party following the live auction. It would be held at the gallery in Ala Moana Shopping Center...probably as a farewell to the clients that Nippon Antiquities has served in the Islands through the decades.

Moving on, we had a choice of where to focus our attention. Keʻoni was especially eager to view the Buddha that had started phase two of his unfinished investigation. Accordingly, we began by looking at several of the more valuable artifacts destined for the live auction.

As we entered the area displaying those pieces, the porter charged with caring for the collection walked forward to greet us. He was an elderly Japanese gentleman who seemed to know many of the people who were coming to view his treasures. He smiled and nodded to everyone. I wondered how he could look so happy if the Honolulu gallery was about to close and he was losing his job. Perhaps he was not concerned because he was retiring.

Alena must have noticed the interest I showed toward the man. "His job is extremely important. He's not just responsible for supervising the preview. He sometimes acts as the bidder for absent clients of the auction house."

I might not understand the organization of an auction like this, but I was looking forward to all of its parts. In this silent auction, the taller pieces were set at the back of the room, making it easy to see everything at a glance. The two-dimensional images of the sale catalog now came to life vibrantly. Although the promotional photos of the collection were superb, the beauty before me was overwhelming.

As I walked past the displays, I envisioned the homes of the people in the upper one percent of society who would be bidding on these unique treasures. Their elegant dwellings were unlikely to be places I would ever be invited to visit. The thought that I would never see these pieces again made the tour especially meaningful. The free art shows and minimally priced trips to museums I have enjoyed throughout my life now seemed all the more significant.

Moving forward, I saw that several of the tables held magnificent collections of silver. Some were items that would have come from the *boudoirs* of wealthy women living in ages that featured dressing tables topped by all manner of beauty aids. There were perfume atomizers, bottles, and jars in faceted crystal and fine porcelain adorned with silver. Looking at the large and heavy combs, brushes, and mirrors, I could not imagine lifting them, let alone wielding them to produce an upswept hairdo.

Other displays had intricately carved wood chests with serving pieces and flatware services for twenty-four in gold trimmed sterling. Some items were so unique that I could only guess at the foods with which they would be used. There was a late nineteenth century "Japanese style" teapot, creamer and sugar bowl from Tiffany and Company. It featured motifs of butterflies and insects flitting across combinations of metals including silver, copper, gold, platinum, and *niello*. There was even an Imperial Russian tea *samovar* in sterling and gold flanked on each side by two Meissen porcelain teacups and saucers.

"Although this massive samovar will bring in tens of thousands of dollars, its value is nowhere near that of the cups and saucers," noted my designer. "Dating from the early eighteenth century, that "half-figure" pattern is one of the most sought after by collectors. A few years ago, a tea set with just eight pieces was sold at auction for more than a half-million dollars."

"I certainly picked the wrong career," observed Ke'oni. "At these rates, I don't think I could afford to bid on anything in even the silent auction."

Alena continued her instructions. "Professional bidders have to do their homework. There are no returns, or even cries of foul play, unless proof of criminal activity can be verified."

She leaned into me and almost whispered. "That's why my being with you as your designer is a no-brainer. Some bidders bring their own appraisers to a preview. I think the term *cash and carry* pretty much describes this event. The buyer is responsible for paying for everything up front: the closing bid; sales commissions; fees for photographs, or evaluations. Then there are the Hawai'i and Honolulu sales tax, not to mention the VAT—value added tax—on the few items from the European Union. And, have I mentioned storage, insurance, shipping, and delivery?"

That did it. I was too overwhelmed with the logistical and financial details to take in anything else. Thankfully, Alena seemed to have run out of steam and we continued to wander around the room. Each of us grew silent as we immersed ourselves in our private moments of awe.

For Ke'oni, there was the wide array of samurai armor and swords. Most unique were the full suits of armor dating back as far as the sixteenth century. They were made of unusual combinations of metal, leather, and fabric, with some featuring clan crests on the breast plate.

The swords were finely crafted and varying in size, type, fabrication, and adornment. Most were exhibited with their scabbards and many rested upon stands. I was amazed that informational plaques stated that each item had a certificate of authenticity. With the number of technical terms included in the descriptions, I knew Ke'oni would be busy for some time.

Alena and I continued toward the back wall that offered Asian furniture. My attention was captured by a large Chinese floor screen. It was a folding screen of four mahogany wood panels with porcelain plaques. The auction book stated that a Ming Dynasty official had commissioned it for his residence hall. The carving made me think of the two chairs my friend Pearl Wong has in her family crypt. Each of the inset porcelain plaques had a cobalt blue under glaze and featured a coastal scene and calligraphic poems in the upper corners.

"It's so beautiful," I said with a sigh. "I have absolutely no place for such a thing, even if I could afford it."

My companion laughed. "You've got great taste Natalie. This is one of the finest examples of Ming furniture I've seen. There's no metal; it's all mortise and tenon joinery. That's so the piece could be easily disassembled if the official was moved to a new assignment. Often times, the art on such a screen depicted a scene from a diplomat's home.

"The carved dragon may indicate that the screen was created during the latter period of the dynasty, a sign that the more ornate Qing Dynasty was approaching. Depending on the artists or studio that produced the frame and painted the fine details of the scenes in the porcelain, I wouldn't be surprised if it fetches $150,000 or more.

"In the early days of Imperial furniture making, pear wood as well as mahogany was used. While sources for mahogany continued to be found, those for pear wood became depleted. Eventually sandalwood was substituted, imported from as far away as here in Hawai'i."

"I remember learning about the exporting of sandalwood from Hawai'i beginning in the late eighteenth century," I commented. "It's always amazed me that whether or not you like capitalism, international trade has connected peoples from around the world since before recorded history. What's your favorite piece so far, Alena?"

"Personally, I'm drooling over the pink and white wedding *kimono* I see at the end of this row of furniture. Can you imagine wearing such a thing? For a single day? And that's just the outer gown. With her ornamental wig and elaborate makeup, the bride would have been a rare beauty."

Just then Ke'oni caught up with us. Giving a small nod toward the center of the room, he cheerfully said, "I hope you ladies have been enjoying yourselves. I've certainly had an excellent reminder of why you would never want to take a samurai by surprise."

I was glad Ke'oni did not elaborate on the exquisitely brutal ways in which samurai swordplay was once utilized in Japan. Following his lead, Alena and I strolled toward the center of the room. We spotted our destination by the small crowd standing in front of the statue of the Buddha, which was set on a round table in the center of the room. The display was beautiful, with fresh flowers, candles, and burning incense. Nearby stood a smiling Buddhist priest. Almost simultaneously, Ke'oni and I opened our catalogues to compare the picture with the actual piece.

"You know, this is the first time I've seen it up close, Natalie. I've seen photos of course. Most of them were casual shots taken by parishioners. The only time I saw the statue in person was when the daughter of a colleague got married. Not only was I seated in the back, but there was no reason to think I'd ever need to remember anything from that brief time in the temple."

"I saw it years ago. Sitting in the third pew, I was actually fairly close to it. But there's nothing like being this close to an artifact to appreciate what has made it so memorable to both art *aficionados* and believers in the faith," I said softly.

Ke'oni glanced around casually. "Regardless of your beliefs, this statue is beautiful and inspiring, like any good piece of art. I wonder how many people have been injured or died to keep it safe in all the years since it was created."

"Maybe that's one of the tests of a truly sacred artifact," Alena commented. "That people are willing to put themselves in great danger to ensure it will be available to those who come after them."

Although it was not a sacred object of faith, Alena's words reminded me of Pearl Wong's beautiful *Taijitu* necklace. Representing the elements of *yin* in silver for the moon and *yang* in gold for the sun, it was originally designed as a two-section pendant for the mother of Pearl and her sister Jade. Even Miss Una had been attracted to the bright Yang half of the symbol, as she swung her paw at it.

CHAPTER 8

Plunge boldly into the thick of life, and seize it where you will,
it is always interesting.
Johann Wolfgang Von Goethe [1749 - 1832]

W e were all drained by the time we intensely studied the statue
that was the impetus for this sojourn among priceless beauties of the past. We finished looking at the room's contents and decided
to take our lunch break before moving on to the pieces contained in the
silent auction. We paused in the corridor for Ke'oni to give John a call
to verify their "accidental" rendezvous at the bar attached to the grill
where Alena and I were eating.

I gave him a hug at the entrance to the bar and a few moments later,
my designer and I were seated and enjoying glasses of iced tea flavored
with pineapple juice. The choices on the hotel's grill menu were delicious to contemplate. Nevertheless, we kept things simple and chose the
salad bar that was intended to tempt us back for a rich evening repast.
Bountiful greens, marinated baby Japanese eggplant, delicate slices
of 'ahi sashimi, chilled lemon shrimp, and Hawaiian sweet bread rolls
were the centerpieces of our caloric fortification for the remainder of
our workday.

"I'm so thrilled to be involved in this auction," I said. "It's a wonderful show that doesn't cost anything to attend. The few bids I'll make will
be for items I can actually afford and will put to use. That means most of
my bidding will be in the silent auction. There's so much variety that I'm
wondering if all of the pieces are owned by the Kiyoharas themselves?"

"That's one of the biggest questions about this event," Alena responded. "The company has been in existence for several hundred years.
Of course, they were closed during the two world wars...and they've
only been in Hawai'i since the early 1950s. The text in the listing catalogue, and on their website, says that the Buddha and other remarkable
items have been in the family for a very long time.

"That makes me wonder why there aren't members of the family
who want to keep them? Why is any of it being put up for auction? I
don't know that it's significant, but some of the younger members of
the family have dual citizenship and must feel linked to their esteemed

heritage. Maybe there's been some major upheaval in the family that no one's talking about openly."

We were just finishing our meal when Ke'oni joined us. Looking around as he sat down, I could tell he was glad that no one was seated near us.

"I see the buffet gave up a large number of their classic lemon shrimp," he said stuffing the last one on my plate into his mouth as he sat down.

"You're lucky I am too full to fight you for that, mister," I said with false bravado. "In addition to the sublime look of pleasure from your theft of my food, I sense you have something to share with us."

Speaking quietly, Ke'oni said, "You're right. It seems that Nippon Antiquities is pretty *akamai* when it comes to marketing. This morning they sent out an email blast updating the description of each of the major items being auctioned tomorrow. That gave us a chance to do a bit more fact checking before the sales begin tomorrow.

"After a quick look-see, the team of Feds performing this round of research noticed a few inconsistencies with records released previously. I don't know if the Buddha's included in that finding. If it is, that may point to a conspiracy involving the Kiyohara family. No matter what I've thought before, it's possible the person who ordered the theft was the deceased patriarch. Those details would allow us to present a clearer picture to jury members hearing the potential case against the men who actually committed the crimes—if *they're* still alive."

"I've studied cold cases that were eventually solved," said Alena. "One thing has caught my attention. Although a detective may think there's proof of how a crime was committed, there's no guarantee a jury will find that the prosecution's argument passes the test of reasonable doubt. It seems to me that the trials of old cases that fail to bring convictions often have witnesses who've aged poorly, or simply don't do well on the witness stand."

Ke'oni snorted. "While that's often true, the officials involved in this case either left strong depositions on file or are young enough that their mental faculties are still in good shape. As I see it, there are two problems in this case. The first is proving without doubt that this statue of the Shākyamuni Buddha is the one stolen from the temple where the minister was murdered. Even if that can be proven, there's the matter of the chain of possession.

"If it *is* the same piece, there's no clear proof of where it's been between the time it left the temple and its going on the auction block. As noted, Nippon Antiquities says it's been in the hands of the Kiyohara family since at least the end of World War II. That means everything may come down to the testimony of forensic specialists. And there's no assurance that the prosecutor's experts will be found superior to those representing a defendant—at least in the minds of jury members."

As we returned to the preview, I thought about the fact that most important events in Hawai'i take place in one of three places: a government building; a religious site; or the ballroom of a hotel. And that did not factor in beaches and parks. At the moment, we were in a hotel space that contained so many religious icons that it almost felt like a church or temple. They came from across the globe and featured symbols from myriad faiths...most of which I could identify Many—like crowns, capes, and scepters—had obvious ceremonial purposes.

As I stared at the richness of items surrounding us, I thought about the men and women who had utilized these vestments and objects in their religious vocations. From the historical pieces I have researched, I knew that often sacred materials are dispersed when a religious leader has an epiphany that altered the direction of the institution they serve. On a more mundane level, the divesting of items sometimes happens when a new figurehead presents a change in waistline...or the bureaucracy simply decides to update the trappings of their sect's religious practice.

I wondered how many of such institutional paraphernalia have ended up in the trunks or attics of older practitioners unwilling to part with the symbols of their past. How many had simply been repurposed—or sold—by greedy persons making the most of their access to such pieces. I remembered when the scion of a prominent Island family passed. Since the old man had been declared incompetent, mainland relatives arrived to *care for his needs*—and to liquidate the family's estate.

That couple wasted no time in initiating the sale of everything they did not deem worth keeping. Gates that been locked for decades were suddenly opened for the *hoi polloi* to enter and gaze upon the prized possessions of a man they had only known through the media coverage of high society. I had been privileged to join the masses that poured into that exclusive enclave. I even bought a Little Orphan Annie themed mug that matched ones my Mother and Auntie Carrie had as children.

For a few moments, I considered how that estate sale had been conducted. I realized that the wealthy, as well as the poor, can execute an amazing number of cash transactions—without the IRS or any other governmental agency being the wiser. The transactions are finalized quickly in such sales. The items are removed immediately from the premises. At least with a formal auction, there should be an electronic trail to follow.

I turned to my companions and said, "You know, looking at this estate sale has made me think of one I attended on Diamond Head. The way they were snatching money from people and casually packing up the goods has made me realize something. I think it's highly probable that most members of the Kiyohara family really have no knowledge of the source of the statue they're selling."

In a near whisper, I finished my thought. "Otherwise, they could have conducted a private sale that would never have brought the statue to the attention of the authorities."

Neither Ke'oni nor Alena responded, but I could tell they had absorbed what I said. I was about to continue my reflections when a small dinner bell chimed. Immediately, people began walking toward the entrance to the silent auction room. There was something about the pace of their steps that reminded me of the response of dogs conditioned by physiologist Dr. Ivan Pavlov in his famous experiments using bells as a stimulus.

Within moments, our team was standing in the middle of a foyer filled with other preview attendees helping themselves to their beverages of choice. Since Alena, and even Ke'oni, were officially on duty, they had to accept glasses of iced tea. I, on the other hand, was a totally free agent. Given my history, it would have looked downright peculiar had I not partaken of the bubbly wine being poured.

After finishing our beverages, we joined the flow of people entering the silent auction preview. Across the room I saw a familiar face. Evelyn Souza, one of my twin's neighbors, was waving a large notepad at me. Shortly, she and her husband Jim were standing beside us.

"Isn't this exciting," she said. "I know we're supposed to have finished decorating the house years ago, but as I always tell Jim, there's nothing wrong with a little freshening of things from time to time. Don't you agree?"

Ke'oni kept a straight face as he shook hands with Jim. Smiling at Evelyn he asked, "So what's on *your* can't live-without-it list?"

Jim rolled his eyes upward. "Please don't egg her on. And I mean that literally."

"Now, Jim. Your mother came from St. Petersburg, and I'd think you'd want to have a reminder of your family's homeland," responded Evelyn.

"If that were the source of those little baubles you're looking at, I might not feel so negative about them. But to buy something that's promoted as merely being in the *style* of a Fabergé egg is laughable. Don't you agree, Ke'oni?"

If there is one skillset that Ke'oni has in abundance, it is a combined sense of time, place, and diplomacy. "I'm not about to get in the middle of this conversation. I've seen far too many domestic disputes in my professional life to take one on during my years of semi-retirement."

At this point Alena, who had been standing politely between Ke'oni and me, spoke up. "Well, it's not like they're being advertised as original Fabergé eggs. Although they pay artistic homage to Fabergé, they're valuable pieces in their own right, representing a category of collectibles that many people are pleased to own."

Thinking of both my manners and the purpose of our presence at the event, I introduced Alena. "I'm so fortunate to have her assistance on this final phase of redecorating Auntie Carrie's home. You know, I have some Northern European ancestors myself, and have been eyeing those eggs. But the only ones I can afford are the simple enameled ones without any gems."

After a little more chit chat, Ke'oni and I promised to have cocktails with the Souzas and our group returned to examining the room's offerings. Standing beside some of the wealthiest people in Hawai'i, I was reminded that our Lanikai address had qualified Ke'oni and me to receive one of the glossy catalogs. However, the chief reason we were sipping wine with these esteemed citizens of the Islands was that Ke'oni had reported his suspicion that a least one of the featured pieces was more than it was purported to be.

While I might be thrilled with all the tantalizing items, Ke'oni seemed less impressed. Signaling that he needed to place a phone call, he walked toward the hallway. My designer gave me a quick nod and I knew she was confirming what I already thought; he was checking in with Captain Makani. Earlier I had wondered why Alena was not doing the same, but she had explained she was instructed to remain in character and not to report in unless she had specific news that had to be transmitted in a timely fashion.

Since John Dias had already walked us through there, I knew what I wanted to purchase. Left to my own role as a redecorating diva, I zeroed in on the table displaying numerous elegant evening bags and decorative pill boxes. The first box that had caught my eye on Thursday night was round and had a sterling silver casing with a top of black and white jade. It reminded me of a dress my mother had worn on the night she and my father had celebrated their anniversary, a couple of months before their untimely deaths.

I had been readying myself for a three-month visit to several locations in the Pacific. Since they were having dinner at the Halekulani Hotel in Waikīkī, I had suggested they join me for cocktails prior to their night on the town. As with the death of my husband Bill, I had had no premonition that I would never see them again in person.

The second box I desired was fashioned of fourteen carat gold. Its lid was a floral pattern in semiprecious stones. The bright bouquet made me think of Auntie Carrie. Its splash of color would have delighted her free spirit...and coordinated with many of her favorite mu'umu'us. The last of my desires was rectangular in shape. It was made of sterling silver and had a vein of mother of pearl running horizontally across its top. Its simplicity in both design and fabrication reminded me of the clean lines of Ariel's wardrobe and accessories.

Most of the other offerings were exquisite silk garments and small paintings. I took a final look at the silent auction catalogue and considered the items on which I would bid. In fine print on the back page was a note promising that a few new pieces were going to be added on the day of the auction. Perhaps there would be something else I could afford that might slide past the attention of other bidders!

As the preview drew to a close, we toured the silent auction space once again and then went into the hotel lobby to compare our findings. None of us had seen anything unusual, but Alena needed to report her overall impressions of the event and its attendees. John or another officer would take her home. Since Keʻoni and I were free to leave, we decided to drop in at the yacht club for some refreshment. There was always the chance that our companions in sleuthing might be able to join us after their briefings. Being off-site would mean that we could compare our perspectives on the next day's grand finale freely.

I realized how warm the day was as we walked out into the afternoon sunshine. By the time we arrived at my Optima, I was completely drained and ready to have Keʻoni play the role of chauffeur. Even Keʻoni was glad for the air-cooled seats the car featured and I enjoyed resting in my reclining seat during the short trip to the harbor. Once we were settled at our table at the yacht club, I was grateful for the misters along the eaves that provide relief to patrons enjoying outside seating.

I do not usually partake of sweet drinks designed for the tourist market. But that evening, a Mai Tai—invented by that restaurateur extraordinaire Victor Bergeron of Trader Vic's—seemed on target. Regardless of whether we would be joined by anyone, I wanted to stay for the night's prime rib special. It featured a salad bar with fresh Italian bread, French onion soup topped by goat cheese, roasted beef carved to taste, garlic riced potatoes, and chocolate mousse. Even though it was a buffet, I knew I would be allowed to take Miss Una a small treat to compensate for our being absent for so long.

With the many complications that can arise during a large event, Keʻoni and I ended up dining by ourselves that night. Being a weekend evening with a superb meal on offer, the club was rather crowded. I was so tired that the buzz of conversation surrounding us seemed like white noise. Keʻoni is always sensitive to my well-being and insisted on serving me. I had the feeling he would have offered to cut my meat if we were at home.

I fell asleep on the ride home but awoke when we pulled into the garage. Once we were in the kitchen, I saw that Miss Una's dishes were not empty. I assumed she had been sharing in the tasty tidbits Izzy was serving little ʻIlima next door. I again thanked the Universe for the kindness of my neighbors. I checked my voicemail and was pleased that except for my publisher's reminder of a deadline, there was nothing that required any attention until the following week.

Since becoming a chronicler of people and places connected to Oʻahu's food and entertainment venues, I have increased my personal delight in dining opportunities like this evening. Professionally, I love featuring locales and products that are good for the environment. If I get the chance to take my column to neighboring islands, I would love to highlight Surfing Goat Dairy located on the leeward side of Mount Haleakalā. In the meantime, I enjoy their products whenever I find them.

Despite my half-hour nap, I was over-stimulated mentally and still had aching legs from having been on my feet for so many hours. How wonderful that both conditions could be eased by something as simple as warm moving water. As if reading my mind, Keʻoni led me to the bedroom and pulled out a couple of swimsuits from our dresser. The spa was the perfect temperature and the jets were set ideally to reach my back, legs, and feet. After a couple of minutes, I pulled up my feet and planted them across Keʻoni's lap.

"Am I to take that as a hint, my love?" he inquired, flexing his fingers.

I smiled and sighed in anticipation. I am always grateful about his giving my feet and legs gentle massages, especially as I know most men are not keen on that activity.

"You may indeed."

For a while we remained silent. The stars winked at us between wisps of cirrus clouds that crossed the sky. Even Miss Una seemed inspired as she entered our yard from The Ladies' garden. Uncharacteristically, she ignored the bubbling water and perched beside the towels I had set on the table between the spa and the French doors to the bedroom. After giving me a stare that I was sure was a reminder that I had neglected her social if not dietary needs, she moved to the top of the towels and began washing her face.

Later, I addressed her nightly need for food and water before taking a brief shower. It had been a long day. I was not surprised that Keʻoni was also tired after our day's stroll through antiquities spanning a thousand years of human activity. He kissed me good night and turned to fall asleep immediately. I, on the other hand, revisited a vivid dream I sometimes experience after driving across the Pali Highway.

Initially I felt myself floating on a cloud near one of the uphill flowing waterfalls that sometimes materialize when there has been considerable rain. Basking in warm sunlight softened by a gentle breeze, I inhaled the scent of greenery on the mountain slopes. Then I stretched out on my back and played a game of discovering magical shapes within the changing patterns of clouds above me. Prominent was an image of *Kuan Yīn* who sometimes visits my dreams.

Covered by a hooded robe, the Goddess of Mercy stood beneath a pear tree with her two acolytes. On her right was Shancai, the Golden Youth who brings gradual enlightenment; to her left was Lóngnü, the Jade Maiden, credited with conveying rapid enlightenment. The clouds shifted and I watched Kuan Yīn extend her hand to her filial white parrot. Dipping her face toward that of the bird, she looked up at the striking of a bonshō temple bell. Startled, I realize that I have slipped from dreaming into visioning.

Once again, I am at the temple where Reverend Ayameko Kōha Fujimoto will experience her final moments. I stand outside the temple doors, watching a woman move down the grand staircase to greet a small Japanese man of indeterminate age standing near a car in the parking lot. Although her back is to me, I know she is Minister Fujimoto because of her garb.

She wears her black silk *okesa* with gentle dignity. Her *hangesa* displays the perfect band of white. On her plum-colored *okesa*, I note fine gold threads outlining the wisteria emblem of her sect of Buddhism. Unlike in the temple, she wears sensible leather sandals allowing her to walk easily across the black top.

The man and woman near one another and bow deeply in respect. Seeing the smiles on their faces, continuing nods, and gestures, I can tell the pair often converse in this warm and polite manner. Soon the man gets in his car and drives off. Reverend Fujimoto waves and retraces her steps up the grand staircase and around the side of the building.

I sense her joyous appreciation of life, but am saddened because I know too well what is to follow. I close my eyes for a moment as that scene fades. When I reopen them, I am again sitting alone in the front pew of the sanctuary. The soft murmuring of intoned chanting of "OM" clashes with my rapid heartbeat. I am riveted on the unfolding tableau. As before, the minister enters from a door on stage left. She wears the black lacquer *getas* I have seen in each repetition of the scene. Again, I hear a soft tapping on the floor as she moves along the altars to pay respect to each of their iconic statues.

She again lights candles and sticks of joss in front of the burnished gold statue of the Amida Buddha. As she stands in silent repose, I inhale the heady fragrance of incense and listen to the clicking of her prayer beads. The faint light I have envisioned before envelops her from the crown of her head to her feet.

Soon the mellow throbbing of a drum is punctuated by a chiming of finger bells. Syllable by elongated syllable, I hear the chanting of Namu Amida Butsu. As expected, the sound of a shot slices through the air. I stare in horror as the gentle woman crumples to the ground, her black rimmed glasses lying beside her. A smile of beatific tranquility rests upon her unlined face.

Everything around me freezes, then proceeds at the pace of real time. The two perpetrators of this heinous crime enter the sanctuary as before. I study each detail with closer scrutiny. The taller man toward the front of the trolley walks sideways. He is turned away from me, watching the space between the trolley and the altars. He steers the cart with his left hand on the bar at the front of the cart and his right hand on the side bar to the front of him. I note that he is slim in build, displaying charcoal gray slacks beneath the navy-blue movers' coveralls that are clearly too short for him. He wears black dress shoes with tassels.

The second man walks forward. Both of his hands are holding the bar on the back at the cart. He is short in stature, burly, and has thick strong arms. He walks with a slight limp. His uniform is too long for him. His pant legs are rolled up. He is not wearing any distinctive jewelry, just a steel-banded watch on his right wrist. Unlike my last vision, they are not silent. Unfortunately, I cannot hear their conversation clearly. The lead man has the voice of a mid-Westerner; the second talks in short phrases voiced in a local rhythm.

I watch as the killers steer the trolley around their victim. They position themselves in front of the altar on the far left. The slim man locks the cart's wheels and reaches down to lift a folding ladder from a shelf on the cart. His collaborator walks forward to help extend the ladder and set it securely on the edge of the altar. Again, the front man bends down and pulls out a padded blanket for moving furniture.

Once the blanket is spread out along the ladder, the men carefully maneuver the Buddha onto the ladder and then down onto the top of the trolley. The leading man again pulls another blanket from the cart and carefully drapes the Buddha. With a long strap his partner hands him from the bar on the back of the cart, he secures the statue to the cart. As he moves his arms, I see he is wearing a wristwatch on his left arm...a gold wristwatch of obvious value. On his right hand I see a silver toned ring. It features a deep blue stone with a carved insignia with something that sparkles at the top. At the bottom of the design is silver toned lettering.

The men then reverse their positions and exit the sanctuary. They move toward the door at a slower pace than I remember in my last vision. I note the bottoms of the slim man's black shoes have the same type of composite soles as Ke'oni's.

If I had not watched the cavalier murder of the minister, I would have thought this was a normal workday for an average commercial transfer company.

CHAPTER 9

No one is so brave that he is not disturbed by something unexpected.
Julius Caesar [100 BCE - 44 BCE]

The day had arrived. At ten o'clock *Ante Meridian* Ke'oni and I were to arrive at the auction venue ready to spend some of the inheritance I had been touting around town. Knowing how well-groomed most of the women at the action would be, I spent quite a while on my hair and makeup. I do not normally invest much time on this since I no longer need to be concerned about making videos or being broadcast live. In keeping with my character for the day, I had purchased new lipstick and eyeshadow. I was glad that although my hair is getting thinner, it has developed a wavy texture that makes styling easier.

As I would play no role in any policing action that might arise, I wore a long dressy *mu'umu'u*. Instead of a vintage favorite, I chose a recent purchase from the Princess Kaiulani line. The ruffling around the shoulders and neckline was fussier than I normally wear. But the turquoise dress highlights Auntie Carrie's black coral and gold jewelry beautifully.

In his usual short preparation time, Ke'oni looked debonair in khaki slacks, a light blue shirt, and navy jacket. His homage to style was a blue paisley silk pocket square. He completed the look with a polished black leather pair of his composite soled shoes so he was prepared for any sprinting that might be required. Because our "designer" would be taking notes, he left his tablet at home and merely carried a large smart phone with him.

There was no way of knowing what might occur during the long day. Since Alena needed to arrive at the hotel earlier than Ke'oni or I did, she was driving her small Fiat which could zip in and out of tight parking spaces and heavy traffic. I drove into town so he could call John. The initial call was cut short because of a meeting with the HPD and Federal officers who would be monitoring the day's activities. By the time our favorite lieutenant called back, we were across the hills and approaching Waikīkī. I was pleased that Ke'oni turned on the speaker feature so I could follow the game plan for the day.

"There's really nothing to report," John's deep voice declared. "No new info on the Kiyoharas or their colleagues. We're still awaiting the finer points of the autopsy on Hitomu Kiyohara from the Kyōto authorities. Given his age, there's probably no foul play involved but we're checking every detail we can."

"Anything new on the international front on other pieces in the collection?" questioned Ke'oni.

"Naw. But hope springs eternal. Especially for the geeks who are doing the research on Nippon Antiquities and the little baubles they're offering the public today."

I mentioned the few new clues from my latest vision. I did not think the voices I had heard would lead us to any firm evidence. However, the details on the man's ring might indicate that it was a class or special event commemorative ring. As we completed our Sunday morning sojourn toward the water, I was already regretting the lack of a large breakfast. At the minimum there should be coffee, tea, and cookies to fortify us. Although the hotel would have a large contingent of public safety experts on its grounds, Ke'oni wanted to be assured that we could depart quickly if the need arose. As we pulled into the open parking lot reserved for special event organizers, we were fortunate to find an empty stall mid-way between the gate and the side entrance to the hotel.

"I see the police caravan is still in place," I noted.

"No reason to pull it. It's streaming images from throughout the building. And although we have access to the same views in the observation room above the ballroom, the van's wireless equipment serves as a backup in case of a power outage. Also, it makes shifting policing teams in and out of the premises a little easier since there's less movement in the hallways to draw unwanted attention."

"Do we need to check in with the Captain upstairs?" I asked.

"No. We've already touched base with John. If something comes up, I'll duck out for a moment and make a short call. I know the back stairs and corridors well enough that I can always run upstairs if there's a need."

True to our actual relationship, we held hands during the brief walk into the hotel. I again visited the ladies room, knowing my opportunities to take a break would be few. Reminded of that fact, I resolved to minimize my consumption of tea. I moved down the hallway with conflicted feelings about the day. I really *was* grateful to be attending the auction, but I felt sad about the true reason for our participation.

Everything was operating smoothly when we entered the foyer where participants were lined up for the daily check-in procedure. This was a closed auction. This meant the salesroom assistants re-verified our identification and contact information and that we had received our badges for the weekend. Buyers were expected to pay for their purchases immediately after the auction, so I had to provide a credit card before being issued a numbered bidding paddle. A leftover from my days on the road, the platinum card precluded a need to verify my credit limit. At the end of the registration table, I picked up a final addendum to the catalogue and a short procedural note highlighting auction etiquette.

Beyond the greeters and registrars was a continental breakfast bar. Clearly someone who understood the impact of refreshments on an interactive event had influenced the menu. With a variety of fruits and breads, the numerous food choices offered something for most everyone's taste. Unless someone was overly affected by caffeine, there should be relative calm.

At the back of the space was a large screen on which images of each lot of goods destined for the live auction were being projected. It was a good way to entertain attendees. One of the more interesting lots showed a variety of Asian coins dating from the seventeenth century. I was tempted by the spread of food and beverages, but I wanted to put in bids at the silent auction. Surprisingly, it would continue for an hour after the live one had concluded. I assumed that the organizers' strategy was that people who had lost out on the higher value pieces in the live auction should have something else to consider purchasing.

Walking through the silent auction room was like seeing the family holiday tree and presents on Christmas morning. Everything sparkled from the finishing touches that had been performed overnight. My primary interests remained the art deco pillboxes from the 1920s and one of the less valuable enameled eggs. Keeping pace at my side, Ke'oni looked over the instructions for bidding at the live auction.

"I think you already know that when you're making a bid, you're supposed to nod your head or raise your paddle," he declared.

"Mmhm," I said, while upping a previous bid on a set of pillboxes by fifty dollars.

"You know those old movies you love to watch? Well, unlike what they show, pulling your ear or scratching your nose doesn't count as an official bid."

Although I chuckled at the references to behavior we have all seen in classic movies, I was determined to avoid any confusion about the few times I would be joining in the live bidding process. Just then, Alena appeared beside us.

"Good morning," she said with a broad smile for the public. "Are you ready to find something special for your living room?"

"Oh, yes. I've been waiting more than a week for this opportunity," I replied.

"I'm so glad you could join us this morning, Ke'oni," she cooed. "It's lovely when a couple has the chance to complete a project together."

"That's so true, Alena," he said with a twinkle in in his eye. "Has anything been added to the collection that we should know about?"

"No, everything's about the same as the last time we spoke, although there was another email blast about some items from the Kiyohara family being offered at another event," she said. "As to the procedure today, you'll note there's sort of a bell-curve to the sequencing of the lots up for bid. That way the anticipation builds."

"Do you ladies want to complete a tour of this room? Or, have a bite to eat and watch the video preview of the live auction?" our handsome escort asked.

"The latter idea is a great start to our day. I can hardly stand here and try to scare off other bidders from the items I want," I remarked.

"We can watch the looping video while we eat. Then we can return here so you can check on your bids before the big event," suggested Alena.

The beverage table included orange juice, coffee and tea, milk and cream. Our food choices were considerable: peach turnovers, bite-sized pecan pies, croissants, miniature bagels, butter, cream cheese, and a spiced tangelo and *liliko‘i* marmalade offered smidgens of protein and a lot of sugar. It was most inviting, but obviously the caterer had not been tasked with providing the balanced menu recommended by nutritionists.

After I checked my silent auction bids, we moved on to the live auction room where I noticed two luncheon size tables along the right side of the room. Seated behind them were men and women with headsets sitting in front of laptops. That meant telephone bidding would take place. I knew that was a concern to Captain Makani and the international policing organizations monitoring the event. The anonymity of buyers made it difficult to track the movement of objects whose ownership might be in question. From the day's program I saw that the items that permitted telephone bids were high-end. Therefore, I would not be facing much competition for the low-value things on which I might bid.

I was glad to be seated in the fifth row to the left of the aisle. It meant that we were close enough to see the details of each lot of goods put up for bid. Alena sat between Ke‘oni and me so we could talk openly to each other. Our electronic toys allowed us to easily communicate with the Captain and John.

Alena had explained her personal system of shorthand which minimized the chance of other people being able to understand what she was writing. I had mentioned her shortcuts to Ke‘oni. As we were not the only ones using electronic gadgets, our communications with John would not seem unusual to the people surrounding us. Some of these people were working by proxy on behalf of mystery collectors who—like telephone bidders—wished to remain unknown throughout the proceedings.

I could not hear voices from anyone's telephones. Unless someone screamed in our ears, no one in the room would be aware of our exchange with the authorities. I received confirmation of my hopes regarding security when Alena's eyes became especially focused at one point. I could not hear a word of what was being transmitted to her and had to wait for her to input a note on her laptop to learn that John and Benny were positioned at the back of the room.

Shortly, the curtain behind the podium parted and the porter entered pushing a cart with the first lot of items up for bid. He arranged bejeweled hair ornaments and a wig once owned by Empress Sunjeong of the last dynasty of Korea on a small table to the side of the podium. The description in the catalogue said the Empress was the second wife of Emperor Yung-hui, the last monarch of Korea.

Research for an Asian travel video had informed me that this emperor had ruled for just three years after Japan forced the abdication of his father. Following the 1910 annexation of Korea by Japan, the Emperor and Empress lived together in captivity until his death in 1926. He must have loved her very much because I remembered that he abandoned the centuries-long custom of keeping concubines.

An unknown voice in my earpiece announced that the FBI believed the collection had been stolen by the Imperial Japanese Army during their occupation of Korea which lasted until the end of World War II. My mind turned to speculating on the journey the items had taken before arriving in Honolulu for this auction. Had someone stolen them from the closets of the Empress?

Perhaps a high-ranking Japanese officer had wanted a valuable keepsake from his overseas campaigns. Or maybe the thief had been a lowly Japanese soldier who was the son of a poor rice farmer. Such a man could never expect to experience the world the rare artifact represented. Of course, a poverty-stricken Korean who worked for a member of the royal court might have taken it in her search for a means to survival during the turmoil of war and its aftermath.

More importantly, how did these artifacts arrive in Japan? Was it in the trunk of the officer I imagined? Or in the lowly duffel bag of the enlisted soldier returning to his family in a country devastated by the end of the war?

Maybe they had been in the possession of a "comfort" woman pressed into service by the occupying Japanese forces. She might have given birth to a child of mixed parentage. I knew this was a curse born by such women in silence. Abhorred by both cultures, she would have been shunned by her society and lucky to find work as a cleaner or farm laborer. If that were not possible, she would have had to survive on handouts and scavenging. Had she and her child survived the Second World War, only to suffer in the conflict that resulted in the division of Korea?

My inner dialogue was interrupted by Ke'oni. "Are you ready for the fun to begin?" he asked.

"Yes, dear. Are you? Or are you just humoring me by feigning interest?" I responded.

"I'll admit I've had little experience with auctions—except for a couple of cases that required looking at a questionable auction house specializing in mid-eighteenth-century paintings. And one time I dealt with an art gallery playing games with unauthorized Salvador Dali lithographs. They turned up with an auctioneer who was less than diligent about verifying the provenance of the art he was peddling."

At that moment, our auctioneer entered the stage and moved to the podium. He was carrying a large binder and I wondered if it included notes about commission bids he would be handling for absentee bidders. There was no way to know for certain, but with high ticket items originating from many Asian countries, there might be a number of people relying on him to execute their wishes. Like telephone bids, Alena had explained auctioneers are happy to facilitate such sales, since they could earn up to three percent of the final "hammer" price. Clearly this man had several ways of earning money beyond the buyer's premium that was a percentage of each sale. Again, I wondered about his career plans. Perhaps he would move on to a position with Nippon Antiquities in Japan.

While the auctioneer organized his papers and adjusted his microphone, I continued reading. No wonder Alena was so excited about this event. Today would be quite an experience for someone whose only knowledge of the auction process came from a classroom. One of the tiny symbols that appeared beside the listings of a few lots indicated that the pieces had originated from somewhere requiring payment of the European Value Added Tax. I also noticed there were circumstances under which an auctioneer might withdraw an item from the sale—or reopen the bidding after the gavel had declared an end to the original bidding.

Now I understood why the man facing us is so respected. His name was listed as Tommy Kiyohara. He must be a member of the family that owns Nippon Antiquities. With the vital role he plays in the company's daily operations, it is likely that he is a partner or a member of the board of directors. I also suspected that "Tommy" was a nickname, or the anglicized version of a Japanese given name. He was fairly old, so it was unlikely he had been born in the United States.

Looking up, I saw a well-dressed Caucasian woman enter the stage and hand Tommy a folded note. He frowned momentarily and paused. While she waited for his response, Alena whispered a final piece of operational information.

"Like most movies you may have seen featuring an English style auction, this one is being conducted with bids ascending in price," she said. "They will open at or near the seller's reserve—that's the lowest amount that will be accepted by the seller. Then the auctioneer will call out escalating figures as the bidders indicate their acceptance of the amount he's named."

The auctioneer whispered something to the woman who had

brought him the note. He then offered a warm greeting to his audience and read a description of Lot One that offered little information beyond what was in the catalogue. This was the last calm moment I would observe that afternoon. The excitement in the room built considerably with each rise in bid. Some people sat with rapt attention focused on the stage. Like me, others tried to follow the action rippling across the room. To make sure that I was not perceived as participating, I kept my paddle firmly in my lap as I turned my head toward each successive bidder.

It was fascinating to note the variations in their behavior. After a few moments, I could spot the professionals. They were the people who kept bland smiles on their faces, with no indication of the depth of their interest. Those who were new to auctions seemed enthralled with the process, as well as the magnificence of the items in each lot. Ever the professional observer, Ke'oni controlled his demeanor as he absorbed the nuances of the action around us. I could look as animated as I wanted since I was known to be a newcomer to the auction scene.

I was so busy taking in everything around me that I barely heard the last bid of forty-nine hundred dollars for the first lot. I was sure there was a tremendous contrast between that figure and what the original seller had been paid. I just hoped that whatever they received had helped them survive the challenges that forced them to sell such personal pieces of dynastic history.

The next several lots continued the theme of women's personal items. They featured combs, brushes and grand hairpins inlaid with gold and silver, as well as gems and jades. There seemed to be many Korean artifacts, including a Korean head covering of woven raw silk adorned with a bejeweled peacock pin and a round fan with bamboo ribs, red silk, and tiny animals many colors of jade.

I noticed a clear escalation of value of the items being offered. The final small lots included a collection of china and ivory marks, seals, and signatures. Then came Asian silk wedding attire that caught the eye and spirit of Alena and the costly Japanese Samurai armaments Ke'oni had admired. There were also collections of silver, and furniture we had seen at the preview, and statuary from many religions and sects. It seemed that the themes of war and peace were interwoven on our journey back through the centuries.

The moment we had awaited finally arrived. The statue of the Buddha that had brought us to the auction was being wheeled to the side of the podium. As the auctioneer began to deliver another canned description, a voice called out.

"Halt!"

Tommy Kiyohara stopped speaking and looked around the room.

The voice called out again. "You cannot auction that which has been stolen."

A murmur spread across the room. Without turning in her chair,

Alena stiffened and caught her breath. Whispering intensely, she said, "Oh my God. It's my father. What do I do?"

I did not know whether she was asking the Captain for directions, or support from Ke'oni and me. In my ear I heard the voice of Captain Makani.

"Don't do anything, Alena. Don't even look around. And don't say anything. John and Benny are behind you, and they'll size up the situation. Ke'oni, if there's a break in the proceedings, I want you to get up and move to the back of the room...but away from John and Benny. All audio channels are open so you can hear each other."

Ke'oni quietly confirmed that he had received the instruction. Glancing at me, he put his arm across Alena's shoulder and bent over to whisper in her ear. Seated between us, she was facing away from the aisle down which her father was walking. She rubbed her forehead for a moment, then exhaled deeply and removed her eyeglasses with communication devices. Quickly she replaced them with a pair of sunglasses from her pocket. She might not be able to talk with Captain Makani, but at least she was not so recognizable. There was little I could do except to be a calming influence, so I squeezed her hand once.

Alena shrank into her seat. I turned my head and tried to read the lips of the auctioneer who seemed to be looking for clues from a younger Japanese man who had risen from the audience. By then, Alena's father had reached the stage. Allowing space for the other audience member to approach him, Professor Horita stepped to the left. The man then pulled an envelope from his pocket. As he unfolded a small sheaf of papers, I saw a red seal on a form that appeared to be written in Japanese. All three men bowed slightly. Despite the angst of the moment, the auctioneer and the man I assumed was the head of the Kiyohara family were trying to follow the gracious etiquette of Japanese society.

While the men conferred, the people surrounding us began to stir and the level of murmured voices rose as bidders speculated about the significance of the interruption. After a couple of minutes, the auctioneer returned to his microphone. He smiled broadly and, in a calm voice, announced a short intermission. He then rejoined Professor Horita and the other man.

After a brief silence, people rose and began moving toward the doors at the back of the room. Ke'oni signaled for Alena and me to remain where we were as he joined the exodus. I was torn about what to do and simply sat there watching the stage. Shortly, a couple of men came out from behind the back curtain and removed the trolley with the statue of the Buddha. In a sickening way, the scene reminded me of my visions of the heinous crime that had led to this moment.

Makani's voice abruptly crackled in my ears. "Alena. Natalie. Get out—now. Take the center aisle and exit the room immediately. Alena, I think you'd better come up to the ops room. Natalie, I want you safely out of the way, but nearby so you can watch what happens."

By this point, the rows of people in front of us were moving steadily up the center aisle. I whispered Makani's instructions to Alena and noticed that John and Benny were now walking down the left side of the room toward the stage. Alena and I joined the line of people vacating the auction room. As she rushed out, I noticed Ke'oni standing by himself just inside the doors. I sauntered over to stand by him as he looked down at the catalogue.

"That's good, Ke'oni and Natalie. Just stand there, out of the way," urged the Captain from his vantage point upstairs.

He then gave further orders to John and Benny, who joined the trio in front of the stage. I watched John reach out to Alena's father and was certain he was showing his badge. The professor looked slightly confused for a moment. Apparently assured that his concerns were going to be addressed, Professor Horita nodded once and began speaking in a voice so soft that no one beyond the tight circle of men would be able to hear what was being said. After a moment, all five men exited to the anteroom behind the stage.

We spent a few minutes maintaining our assigned roles as we innocuously observed the auction room. Perceiving the depth of the uncertainties surrounding us, Ke'oni continued to remain watchful for anything that might be pertinent to solving his old case. Finally, we heard the voice of Captain Makani. He calmly directed us to join the other bidders who were filtering into the foyer. I could only imagine the conversations he was having with his superiors.

CHAPTER 10

We must ask where we are and whither we are tending.
Abraham Lincoln [1809 - 1865]

Stepping into the foyer, we found that a coffee bar had been opened. There was also a refreshment station that included afternoon delight in the form of California's interpretation of Champagne. Ke'oni judged it prudent to stay with an influx of caffeine, but there was no reason for me to abstain from a stronger drink to fortify me for any new surprises that might materialize next.

As I approached the display of cold beverages, I was joined by Evelyn Souza. "What a surprise to see you here again," joked Evelyn. We were quickly served glasses of bubbly and moved toward our men, who were already deep in conversation.

"What do you think of all the excitement?" asked Jim.

"Being new to the auction process, everything's a little mysterious," I replied, glancing at Ke'oni for approval of my non-engaging response. He just smiled nonchalantly, and I knew I was on the right track for this interaction.

"Well, I think it's more than mysterious. It really puts the entire event up to scrutiny," Evelyn declared. "I wouldn't want to spend an arm and a leg on something the police later decide I didn't really own."

"I don't think you have to worry about that, Evelyn" said Ke'oni. "The police will halt the event if they feel there's a question of legality. Things like this occur all the time in the world of art and antiquities. The authorities are probably looking through the paperwork on everything up for auction right now. We'll soon know if the bidding is going to resume."

A rather bland announcement came over the public-address system. Without any comment on what had caused the interruption, we were informed that the next round of the auction would begin in fifteen minutes. We were encouraged to revisit our bids in the silent auction room before retaking our seats. Evelyn quickly departed for that room. With a woeful sigh, Jim followed her.

Ke'oni and I paused for a couple of moments to let the crowd dissipate. I then expressed my speculations about what was taking place upstairs.

"There's no point in guessing, Natalie. Let's just wander into the silent auction room. While I wait for further instructions, you can decide whether you want to up your bids."

When we entered the room, I found there was a crowd gathered around the table with the enameled eggs that had no gems. I immediately decided to pass on that offering. I was glad to see there was not as much interest in the pillboxes I had been coveting for so long. It only took a couple of minutes to accomplish what I hoped would be my final bid, and we quickly moved to the live auction room.

When Tommy Kiyohara resumed his position at the podium, he made no reference to the startling reason for the break in the auction. However, he did begin the bidding with a lot that had been scheduled for much later in the program. It was an ornate pair of *cloisonné* vases that had once adorned an elegant piece of furniture in a Japanese statesman's home.

The second lot offered a lovely collection of Georgian sterling silver. It included a huge platter with tea and coffee services as well as a boxed flatware service for twenty-four with matching serving pieces. Next there was a pair of *bodhisattvas*. Featuring rare yellow-brown crystalline accents on their edges. They strongly resembled the white jade pieces owned by Pearl Wong.

Alena looked as interested as I was. She whispered, "These figurines might have flanked a statue of Quan Yin on the altar of a temple, the home of royalty or possibly a highly placed priest. The white Hetian Jade has what geologists call *sucrosic* crystals or sugar crusts. The statuettes could have been commissioned by anyone. Asian artists of the past did not usually identify their personal work—or even the studios from which a piece of art originated. The background material I read says it's believed that these pieces with hollowed *Lou* carving were created in the South of China during the Song Dynasty."

Those details were especially interesting to me, since they paralleled what I knew about Pearl Wong's artifacts. The bidding on the statuettes quickly escalated. This was partially due to telephone bids. I wondered whether they came from a single person or a group of people who had pooled their funds for this once-in-a-lifetime purchase. Then there was the man sitting in front of me. From his demeanor and the deference shown him by auction house staff, I suspected he was a broker representing either a wealthy collector, or an institution.

When the bid hit $100,000, my fellow audience member reached into his breast pocket and brought out a smart phone. I was right. The man was definitely a broker seeking direction from his buyer. After two more increases of $10,000, I saw a slight shake of his head. Clearly, he had backed away from the deal. Clearly Pearl's jade pieces were of comparable value!

By the time the auction concluded with the last major furniture lot, I was drained by the intensity of the afternoon's events. Ke'oni and I returned to the silent auction keeping within the parameters of our public roles. There I learned I had won the art déco silver pillboxes for which I had yearned. I completed the transaction and tucked my prizes firmly under my arm. In view of everything that had happened, it was no surprise to hear an announcement that the party scheduled to follow the live auction had been cancelled.

We then moved into the hallway where Ke'oni gave me a kiss before going up a back stairway to check on the progress of the investigation. Meanwhile, I visited the restroom to dab my face with cool water before our trek home. My phone buzzed while I was drying my hands. It rang a second time before I could see who had called. As I suspected, the caller was Nathan, wondering how the auction had gone. I was pondering the answer to that question myself. I assured him that we were all okay, but that I was in a quandary about what would occur next. I promised to call back as soon as I had something tangible to report.

When I re-entered the hallway, I saw that Ke'oni had not yet returned from the ops center. I was attempting to identify a flower a gardener was adding to the tropical garden in the nearby courtyard when he tapped on my shoulder.

"Hi, honey."

"How did the meeting go?" I asked, turning to walk with him out to the parking lot.

"As you can imagine, it was pretty awkward watching Alena trying to calm her dad. Finally, the Captain gently inserted himself into the conversation. He had confirmed that HPD was already investigating both the theft of the Buddha and the murder of Minister Fujimoto."

I clicked the doors of my Optima open and tossed the keys to Ke'oni. "I hope that reassured him," I said, sinking into my seat and immediately turning on the cool cushion feature.

"On the one hand, yes. But it also motivated the man to volunteer in any way he could to bring the guilty party or parties to justice."

"Well, he *was* involved in the original case. I can see where he might have something to offer," I said.

"That may be true. But considering the way he burst into the live auction, I think Captain Makani is reluctant to involve him publicly. Given the professor's language and cultural expertise, the Captain does want him to join JD in re-examining the original case file. There is one other positive aspect to the man's unexpected appearance. It certainly opens the door for JD to insert himself into the affairs of the Nippon Antiquities—if not the Kiyohara family itself."

"What about Alena? Was Dr. Horita pleased that his daughter's made detective?"

"Definitely. But I had the impression he's worried about her working undercover."

"I wouldn't think he has to be concerned about her safety. It's not like this is a current murder case. The killers of the minister could be dead, as well as the person or persons responsible for ordering the theft of the statue."

Ke'oni glanced over at me as he steered us up the Pali Highway. "I agree that she should be safe. And we should all be happy to have her help in uncovering whatever facts may emerge. Turning to Arthur Conan Doyle, *the little things are infinitely the most important.* I have a feeling we're about to discover a lot of details that will prove invaluable in our investigation."

Knowing the many tasks I would have to address upon arriving home, I decided to call Nathan while we were in transit. He quickly picked up the phone and I could hear Kūlia barking in the background.

"What's going on?" I asked, putting the phone on speaker.

"My little buddy feels that three doggie treats are simply inadequate to cover the stress of the day. You see, we had an invasion of both birds and cats this afternoon. Kūlia was quite put out when I refused to let him participate in the mêlée that was unfolding outside the *lānai* doors."

I joined him in laughing about such antics and affirmed the joy our animal companions bring into our lives. "So, what's the outcome of today?" he asked.

"Personally, I can tell you that I am the very proud owner of some art déco silver pill boxes," I boasted.

"That's nice. But have you learned anything about Ke'oni's old case?" inquired my brother.

"I think we're back to our unending waiting game," I said. I then let Ke'oni provide a rundown of the day's events on speaker phone. It had been exciting for all of us at the auction. It was great to hear the finer details of the police operation I had not observed.

"It sounds like you two have had quite a day! By the way, I have some news that might prove relevant to your inquiries," Nathan announced. "I was reading the Sunday newspaper while you two were prowling through treasures and crimes of the past. For fun, I went through the announcements of estate sales. I discovered a little item that might be of professional and personal interest to you, Ke'oni."

"I'm all ears. What did you find?"

"You know it's been some time since we started talking about buying a boat. Today I may have found the ideal one."

"That's great. But how does finding a recreational boat play into the professional realm of my life?" questioned Ke'oni.

"I thought that would get your attention. You see, the thirty-two-foot motorsailer I've discovered just happens to be part of the Kiyohara estate that's being liquidated next weekend. I'm hoping *we* might get a wonderful new toy, while *you* learn something to help solve your old case."

By the time we arrived home, Ke'oni and I had relived the noteworthy points of our adventures in the world of antique auctions. We had also speculated on what might develop that week. Ke'oni was enthralled with the prospect of finally getting a boat. I was intrigued about the conversations Alena might be having with her father. And there was no way of knowing what investigative opportunities the upcoming estate sale might offer. I was sure that if we got involved, Alena would need to maintain her cover as my fledgling interior designer.

At home, Ke'oni rushed to the office to call John about the estate sale. I followed up on a few voice mails. Most important was one from my publisher wanting to know when we could move forward on the 'Iolani Palace article, to whom I sent a quick text message. There was also a breezy message from Izzy saying that all of Miriam's Ladies wanted the rundown on the auction I had been discussing for several days.

They knew Alena from her involvement in the solving of Miriam's murder and had seen her dashing in and out of my cottage recently. Therefore, I had mentioned her completing a college degree and working as my interior designer. That provided an excuse for her involvement in the auction we were attending, without revealing the undercover nature of her work as a detective. Suspecting we would be exhausted after our fulsome days in Waikīkī, Izzy had prepared a casserole of barbecued chicken and rice for us.

"What are you doing dear?" asked Ke'oni opening the refrigerator. At the sound of that door opening, Miss Una materialized from parts unknown.

"Reassuring Harry that I'm moving forward with the 'Iolani Palace article. And resupplying Miss Una. There was plenty of water in her bowl but only a few crumbs of her dry food. Right, my little darling? I suspect you've been emptying 'Ilima's plates with the blessing of Izzy. I think we need to start chipping in on the cat food bill next door!" With that declaration, I set out a plate of feline shrimp casserole.

We laughed with gratitude that we never had to worry about our housemate when we were gone for a prolonged period of time.

"Selfishly, I'm glad to say we also benefit from the kitchen next door. Izzy guessed that we might be tired today and fixed some dinner for us. That'll make gearing up for our next undercover assignment easier."

"That's actually on hold for now. John said he won't have any information on the Kiyohara estate sale for a couple of days."

"Then let's have some fun tonight. I'll call The Ladies and suggest they come for a soak in the hot tub followed by a potluck supper. We've got plenty of cold wine and your latest tea creation, as well as some leftover broccoli salad in the refrigerator and ciabatta rolls in the freezer."

Joanne quickly accepted my invitation on behalf of her two housemates—with the *proviso* that Samantha needed an hour to complete a paper she was editing for class the next day.

Shortly before sunset, Izzy, Joanne, and Samantha paraded through the back gate with arms laden with food. They were escorted by 'Ilima, who clearly anticipated another romp with Miss Una. Soon everyone's towels and swimsuit covers were draped over chairs, and we were immersed in the warm water. I definitely needed the pulsating jets to soothe my aching hips and legs. Somehow Ke'oni showed no effects from our days involved with the auction.

After promising to display the silver pillboxes I had bought later, I let him take the lead in telling the tale of our auction adventures. I wondered how detailed his descriptions would be. Knowing the thoroughness of today's media, I assumed that reports of the disruption caused by Alena's father would probably appear on the nightly news broadcasts. Ke'oni must have had the same thoughts. He concluded his playback of that tidbit of information without mentioning the detective's connection to the professor.

"How exciting," exclaimed Izzy.

"How fortunate that the event continued, so you were able to get the pill boxes you wanted," observed Joanne.

"That's true. I would have been very disappointed if the authorities had decided that the auction had to stop," I concurred.

"Did you finish your paper, Samantha?" inquired Ke'oni. "I hope our lesson at the range and tour of clients didn't interrupt your schoolwork too much."

"Not at all. It's giving me just the break I need. I've spent the whole day researching the political and social changes on the Iberian Peninsula following the 1469 marriage of Ferdinand of Aragon and Isabella of Castile. Did you know they were cousins?"

"I may not know much about history, but I know where some of that story leads. That's when the inquisition took over Spain and banished Jews and Muslims," said Izzy.

"Kind of reminds you of the current interaction between religion and politics," remarked Ke'oni wryly.

"How did your family fare in those years, Izzy?" asked Samantha.

"My ancestors were already living in what became Portugal. It was another country that was pretty much ruled by the Catholic Church. As long as you were a true believer, you were fine," she answered.

"You forgot one little issue," countered Joanne. "Are you sure your family didn't have any women accused of being witches?"

"Not a whisper of that in my family. I think a story that big would have been carried down through the generations."

"One fact that's often overlooked is the emergence of the *Marranos* or crypto-Jews at that time," said Samantha. "They were Jews who converted to Christianity...at least on the surface. However, many of them continued to practice their true faith in private. Even with a supposed conversion, they were subjected to discrimination both legally and so-cially."

"Weren't they despised by both Christians and Jews?" I asked.

"You're right," responded Samantha. "They were called *tornadizos* or *renagades*."

"Do you think we'll ever get beyond name calling and other signs of religious bigotry?" I wondered.

"Don't hold your breath," said Ke'oni.

"I wish I could say you're wrong, but the historical tales I've been studying don't offer much hope," concluded Samantha.

After that depressing conversation, we finished our time in the spa by sharing tales of favorite adventures in shopping—a topic that may have been boring for Ke'oni. Once The Ladies had changed out of their swimsuits, I showed them my stunning prizes of the weekend. We then turned to the pleasure of our meal, accompanied by both sun tea and a sangria Samantha had made. We finished the night with Izzy's lemon scones topped with a fresh compote made of strawberries from Joanne's garden.

It was lovely to end our fast-paced weekend by relaxing with such wonderful friends. But after the excitement of the auction, normal life the next week seemed rather dull. We would be playing another wait-ing game until local, national, and international agencies assembled in-depth reports on Nippon Antiquities,

Ke'oni turned to his clients on Monday while I concentrated on pull-ing together the threads of my article on the retired chefs of Kapi'olani Community College's culinary program. During my call to the head of the department I learned that her staff members were already consid-ering a celebration of their predecessors' accomplishments. The woman responded positively to my idea of holding the affair at 'Iolani Palace during one of the Royal Hawaiian Band's Friday concerts.

The next day, I did some fact checking with the management of both the palace and the band. I was able to verify that the event I was trying to coordinate was acceptable to both organizations. Next, I checked local calendars of events and found we could schedule our event in a couple of weeks. We did not want to delay very long because of the health chal-lenges facing a couple of our star interviewees.

Once the game plan was in place, I called a couple of contacts I had with local television stations to see if we could get coverage of the picnic we were planning. My magazine article would not be appearing until a couple of weeks after the concert. Therefore, it would be nice for the men and women we were featuring to have the pleasure of being on the nightly news the day of the concert.

When Ke'oni returned home that Monday night, he delivered some news that made me glad my field work for the article would not occur for another week or so.

"John gave me a call today. It seems that we're making some headway on the investigation and plans for participating in the estate sale."

"What does that mean for us?" I asked.

"Well, you might want to check the freezer for any tidbits that can be turned into a meal on Wednesday."

"Mm. And who, beyond our favorite policeman, will we be entertaining?" I asked. I was grateful that he did not say we would need to have guests on Thursday afternoon, when I attend my culinary classes.

"We're keeping Alena under the radar until everything is worked out. But given the source of our info on the upcoming estate sale in Hawai'i Kai, the Captain thinks we should include Nathan in our speculative planning."

"I'm always glad to see Nathan. He can bring Kūlia with him to play with Miss Una and 'Ilima."

"I'll have to admit that's one of the funniest sights I've ever seen—a small dog frolicking with a grown cat and a kitten, without any of them getting hurt."

"Maybe it's because he's a mixed breed dog, with the best qualities of his ancestors coming forward," I proposed.

"And maybe it's just because he's a sweet animal who loves to play with everyone," concluded Ke'oni.

"Or it's because Miss Una taught him the rules of the house," I countered.

Wednesday night we had Nathan and John over for dinner. It was one of the few evenings that John could join us, since he has become increasingly involved with Lori Mitchum. After all the times Ke'oni has been the only male in the room, it was my turn to be the hostess to three men. Since much of the conversation would focus on the boat the Kiyohara family was selling, we decided it was safe to have a barbecued dinner on the *lānai*. That way we could also supervise the play session between Kūlia and the cats. We would move inside for the more serious aspects of the upcoming estate sale.

There was not a lot of preparation to be accomplished before our guests' arrival. Ke'oni had parboiled the beef short ribs in advance; I had made a carrot and raisin salad. Shortly before the dinner hour, Ke'oni cleaned off the patio furniture and I prepared trays with flatware, dishes, and beer steins. I completed our meal by making garlic butter for soft Italian bread sticks and then added chopped steamed potatoes and dressing to stretch a leftover bowl of Izzy's delicious salad.

Some people might consider that our meals with John were a presumption on his part. There are several reasons why I do not. First, the information we pass back and forth could hardly be delivered at his office. Second, I think our countryside lunches provide a valuable break in his otherwise hectic schedule—something he and Ke'oni did not enjoy when they were officially partnered. Third, I am delighted to have the opportunity to practice my expanding skills in the kitchen without my dear one being aware.

Nathan and John arrived at the same time and joined me in carrying things out to the patio table.

"I feel so honored to be included in this little *tete-a-tete*. Usually *you* get all the fun, Natalie. It feels great to join in your derring-do adventures," said Nathan, reaching down to release Kūlia from his lead.

"Indeed. I now officially make you the third musketeer in my unofficial team of collateral investigators," declared John with bravado. "I just ask that you stick to the same rules I've set out for Natalie. You follow all instructions from me and the Department precisely. You never reveal your involvement in a case. You never get involved in any physical action and absolutely never carry any weapons. Do you think you can do that?"

"I hereby swear to honor those rules and will obey any and all instructions you give me in the future," Nathan responded with a lop-sided grin and mock salute.

With that, the men gathered at the grill and I prepared the table. As to Kūlia, he had already been greeted by Miss Una and 'Ilima who seemed to know they were playing the role of hostesses to a special guest.

I did not follow the finer points of the men's discussion about the boat Ke'oni and Nathan were hoping to acquire at the estate sale. Nathan seemed to have memorized the details that had caught his attention. Despite the men's obvious interest in the topic, I found my mind wandering to other issues that might arise...and items that might be delightful additions to our own home.

There were some snippets of their conversation that floated into my hearing. The yacht was a thirty-two-foot motorsailer designed and built by Lars Halvorsen and Sons of Sydney, Australia, in 1964...before the Japanese boat industry took off. It had had a total refit in 2010, with new main and storm jib sails...as well as a headsail on the furler...and a new 40 horse power Volvo diesel engine.

I doubted that I would remember these few technical details. However, there were a few items I found interesting. New satellite equipment for navigation and monitoring weather conditions meant that less cabinet space was taken up and the galley and lounge area offered greater storage. Also, refurbishing the mahogany interior had included combining two of the five bedrooms and expanding the *en suite*. Even if I never put to sea on the vessel, I would be able to use the bathroom if we had a pier-side cocktail party.

With the true reason for our meeting awaiting our attention, we did not linger outside. After a long bout of racing around the yard—and a couple of tasty tidbits—it did not take much encouragement for Kūlia to willingly enter the house. Meanwhile, his playmates returned to The Ladies garden for a *postprandial* session of shared face washing.

It only took one trip to clear the *lānai* with four pairs of hands, As the men settled around kitchen table, Kūlia plopped down beneath its center. I joined them with servings of Keʻoni's latest homemade ice cream—green tea with pistachios. While we finished dessert, John and Keʻoni continued regaling Nathan with highlights from our weekend. I doubt that it was intentional, but their recap drew to an end as I was wiping down the kitchen counters.

CHAPTER 11

There is nothing like first-hand evidence.
Sir Arthur Conan Doyle [1859 - 1930]

As I sat down, Ke'oni rose to pour fresh glasses of tea for all of us. John walked out to the living room and returned with his very worn briefcase. He opened it and pulled out a narrow lined yellow notepad and several stapled sheets of paper.

"I guess it's time we get down to the business of prepping you for a little field work, Nathan. I've always felt there's something to be said for beginning at the start of a cold case, so let's open the evening's main event with a review. I'll let you do the honors, Ke'oni, since it was one of your cases."

"I knew transcribing my old hardcopy notes would come in handy one day."

After turning on his tablet and scrolling through several folders, the man of my life launched a smooth delivery of the observations he had made a decade ago. I knew that some facts might materialize that would be new to me. I opened one of my half-sheet spiral notebooks and started jotting down a mixture of contracted words and shorthand.

"And now, despite her frequent disclaimers, Natalie Seachrist will provide a summary of the prescient visions she has had about this sad and drawn-out affair," said the Lieutenant.

"It started with our looking for a few furnishings after we finished our remodel of the cottage...by subscribing to antique and auction catalogues," I began. I then recounted the progression from a brief vision of Minister Fujimoto's murder to the subsequent two containing increasing detail.

Gradually, Nathan's face changed from open curiosity to cool withdrawal. It did not take much imagination for me to realize that he was thinking about my visions through the years and those I had had of his granddaughter's death. I was probably the only one who noticed the shift in Nathan's mood. I was glad that John quickly redirected the conversation to the motorsailer that had captured Nathan's attention in Sunday's newspaper. Even though the attractions of the boat had been covered at great length during dinner, the men managed to prolong their discussion for another quarter of an hour. Eventually John moved on to the estate sale and auction of the boat.

"I had Alena do some checking. Like the Waikīkī auction, you two need to be prepared to finalize the sale immediately if you win the bid on the *Marimu* on Saturday. It's on a weekend. You should have forty-eight hours to obtain a cashier's check to cover your purchase. Since it's a private transaction rather than a public auction, there's no way of knowing if they'll remove any items from the list of things being offered for sale... or *how* they'll execute each transaction."

"Nathan and I have been thinking about purchasing a boat for a while. I'm sure that some of the dealers we've been talking to will show up at the Kiyohara home," responded Ke'oni.

"That's good. You and Nathan have the perfect cover for being there as soon as the gates open. Your new contacts in the boating world can confirm your desire to check out the motorsailer."

"Hey, we're ready to do a lot more than look at the boat. If it's everything that's been advertised, the only question about our purchasing her will be the price," declared Nathan.

I thought about the complexities of a large estate sale. "That and the little matter of the competitive bidding. Alena told me that the Kiyohara's are tough negotiators. Even if there's a set price, it's likely there will be several prospective buyers that day. Companies like this love a bidding war. If a couple of people offer the same all-cash price, the owners, or the managers of the event, will have the final decision about who gets the prize."

At that point John jumped in with a suggestion. "It's too bad you don't have the benefit of my real estate agent. She gave me a major lesson in closing a deal when I was buying my condo: Submit a letter stating why you deserve to make the purchase. Of course, writing a letter while standing pier-side might be a little awkward."

"Writing a letter of intent is a great idea," said Nathan enthusiastically. "As a mature and respected professional, I just happen to have some serious letterhead stationery. And I'm certain that between one personal story and the other, Ke'oni and I can dream up a really good case for why we should win the day. What do you think, Ke'oni?"

"Hmm. I guess we don't want to emphasize my being a retired police detective. But we could add a sentence about my having taken early retirement because of an injury."

"And I can honestly mention that being out on the water brings me closer to my deceased granddaughter who greatly loved the ocean."

"Not only is all that true, but it's easily checked...if anyone wanted to bother," added John.

Regarding another concern, John noted, "I think we're covered regarding everyone's reason for being at the estate sale. I'm sure there will be a lot of people attending both the live auction and the estate sale in order to obtain belongings from one of the Island's wealthiest families."

He then turned the conversation back to the mechanics of the upcoming weekend. "I guess the first issue is timing your arrival. You two guys should probably be there all day. Given the value of the boat—and it's being offered in a silent auction—I don't think anyone will be surprised that you're there for the long haul. I can always text you with updates regarding officers and agents who may be present. You'll just have to pace yourselves to remain on site."

"That means bringing a sizable number of snacks and beverages," I piped up.

"You're right," agreed my brother. "By the way, I'm guessing Ke'oni and I should arrive together?"

"Well, there are a couple of ways of looking at that. If I need to take off, it would be good to have a second vehicle," countered Ke'oni.

John then joined in the debate. "It's true that something could happen that would require you to leave unexpectedly, Ke'oni. However, I was going to suggest that Nathan leave his car at the observation post we're setting up at a nearby home. Then the two of you could arrive together in your truck. Likewise, Alena can team up with Natalie, since she's now driving a Crown Vic. Otherwise, it might be rather obvious that she's a cop. It's unlikely that more than two of you would need to leave at the same time. It shouldn't be that hard to run to the other house for whatever vehicles might be needed. How's that sound?"

"Fine by me, boss," replied Nathan smiling broadly.

"That's a wonderful idea," I said. "If I'm not going with Ke'oni, I can sleep in an extra hour—or squeeze in a walk before departing for another fun day of playing among priceless antiquities."

"The former sounds like the better part of valor. You know how your hip felt after this last weekend," Ke'oni gently reminded me.

"I think that brings us to the overall plan of the day," continued John. "Ke'oni, I want you to make the most of your opportunity to check out the property. Most of the house and grounds will be open to the public. It shouldn't be too awkward for you to roam around. And you should be able to get away with taking pictures of what you see and transmitting those images to the ops center periodically.

"The Feds and International teams involved with this operation will be interested in anything that may have been obtained illegally. That means they'll have people in place throughout the day. But if you recognize someone, I think it's best that you men ignore them, unless to do so would look odd. You know, like someone you graduated from the Academy with, Ke'oni. Or a colleague with whom you've worked, Nathan. With all the electronics that'll be in play, we should be able to alert you if there are any changes in the playbook. Any questions so far?"

"Well, I have one. A major one. The excuse for Alena and me being there is to buy furnishings for the cottage. I wonder if we're going to expected to haul away any purchase that's too tempting to pass up immediately?"

"She has a point," said Nathan.

"Mmhm. Serious on two levels. First there's the issue of what counts as *tempting*. And then there's the matter of my truck, which she's never driven," mused Ke'oni glancing toward the door to the garage.

"I'll agree that I don't want to begin a career as a truck driver on such short notice," I admitted.

"I think we've already solved that dilemma by leaving Nathan's car at the observation post and taking Ke'oni's truck to the Kiyohara estate. If there's something that needs to be removed from the property, Alena's licensed to drive most anything on the road."

I thought for a moment. "The only catch would be that if we have to drop something off at the Lanikai cottage, it's going to eat up at least two hours of our time."

"That's really not a problem," Ke'oni responded thoughtfully. "Nathan and I will be hanging around to see if our bid on the boat is accepted. Even if you and Alena take the truck, I'll be fine."

"Good thinking, ole buddy," said John smiling. After glancing at his notes, he continued sharing his thoughts.

"Next...the main issue of the day...any evidence of the presence or theft of the Buddha. We're curious as hell about where it's been for the last umpteen years. There are plenty of rooms in the home that can be ruled out. Given its size, there are few pieces of furniture that could have supported the weight of the statue."

"You can bet it hasn't been in the foyer or poolside," I responded.

That concluded our speculations and planning. The next couple of days passed quickly. In preparation for a day on my feet, I refrained from doing much walking. Instead, I spent time stretching at the beginning and end of each day and doing a few exercises in the spa. Whether it was because of the gentle movement—or absence of memorable dreams and visions—I was sleeping quite well. In fact, I never heard Ke'oni get up on Saturday.

"Good morning, Natalie," said Ke'oni, trying to woo me into consciousness. Even when his smooth baritone voice fails to rouse me, the scent of his daily presentation of Earl Grey tea does.

"Uh, thank you," I croaked, sitting up. "You'd better set it down. I'll run to the bathroom and try to open my eyes before raising a cup to my lips."

"No rush, honey. But I'm leaving before you. I thought we should review a couple of things before I take off. I'll put the small cooler in the truck while you get going."

He kissed my shoulder and helped me to my feet. By the time I had pulled on an old swimsuit, Ke'oni had completed loading everything he would need for the day.

"You remembered your new hat?" I inquired as I entered the kitchen.

"If you'll look at the hat rack, you'll see there's an empty hook," he said with a broad smile.

"After all those stories we're hearing about the rise in skin cancer, I just want to make sure you're safe."

"Mmhm. And don't forget to take that advice yourself," he said. "Now, let's do a quick review. Kalaniana'ole Highway to Hawai'i Kai is the simplest route. With single lanes, it's easy to hit slow traffic, even without a tour bus. So be sure to allow a little extra travel time."

"Yes, Papa," I nodded.

He kissed me and left after a few more words to synchronize our perceptions of how the day would unfold. Given my slow start, I decided to forego any beach time. I did manage to do a little weeding in the back yard under the ever-watchful Miss Una after I enjoyed a breakfast of fruit and cereal.

Although everything was pre-staged, it took several trips to the garage before I could depart. Ke'oni and Nathan had each taken their preferred beverages with them. I was bringing a cooler with fruit, snack foods, and sandwiches. I was also carrying a large handbag that could accommodate a bottle of tea, a notebook, and the full-page display ad the Kiyoharas had run in the Wednesday paper. Not knowing what items might catch my eye, I was taking two additional coolers in case there was something temperature sensitive that I wanted to buy. I could hardly change clothes during the day, but I packed a couple of pairs of shoes and sandals in case my feet started to ache.

The men had been at the estate for an hour by the time Ke'oni called me. He was enthralled with the boat for which he and Nathan had longed. He was less enthusiastic regarding items that would be of interest to me. Most of the furniture was gargantuan in size and wholly inappropriate for White Sands Cottage. Of the smaller items, most were beyond my budget and so classically Asian in material and design that I would only consider purchasing a couple of them.

How would I be able to prolong *my* stay at the Kiyohara home? I could, of course, feign interest in the boat. But that choice was problematic in nature. Once I had walked up and down the pier a couple of times, I would be expected to go on board. How much could I *ooh* and *ah* over the nooks and crannies for storing goods and the fabulous electronics that had won the attention of my sweetheart and twin?

Hmm. I would have to decide what to do about the reality of my lack of interest in anything seafaring. Knowing the level of research she would have performed, I knew that Alena could probably provide more than one excuse for us to remain on the property. I decided to set that issue aside and just enjoy my drive through Waimanalo.

I thought about the adventures I have enjoyed in this beach community that remains unseen by many Island visitors. That reminded me

I needed to write an article on the Ono Steaks & Shrimp Shack. It might seem like a hole in the wall, but its tiny kitchen produced some of Oʻahu's best farm- and ocean-to-table food. Another item to put on my list of topics for Samantha Turner to research...as soon as I had access to a pen and notebook.

As I passed Sea Life Park, I was reminded of the scavenger hunt Keʻoni and I had participated in while immersed in two eerily similar murders. When the road became more winding, I realized I was nearing Mokapuʻu Point. I would have stopped at the lookout if I had nothing scheduled for the day. The view to Maui is lovely on a clear day like this. But it would soon be time to look for the turnoff to the home serving as HPD's observation post. I wondered if Captain Makani would be heading up today's contingent of officials, or whether a Federal officer might have taken over.

Regardless of who was in charge, I knew that authorities of one category or another had been on site for a couple of weeks. Fortunately, the owners of the house were on a Mediterranean cruise and would not be home for another month. Their only concern was that the property be returned to them in relatively good condition. Given the probable tax bracket of property owners in the ocean-side neighborhood, I could imagine the elegant items that might be on view.

Even if their home was not filled with antiques of the quality and quantity of the Kiyohara's, there were bound to be many unique things of value. I have always enjoyed viewing properties of the well-heeled. I was hoping to be allowed to roam around for a bit before moving on to the official focus of the day.

I was glad I was able to synchronize my arrival with completion of Alena's briefing for the day. She answered the gate's intercom and directed me to park in front of the four-door garage at the far right of the house. The gates quickly opened, and I slipped onto a short but winding roadway bordered by a hedge of oleander full of bright red blossoms. I was impressed by the obvious care of professional landscapers for there were no flowers lying around to endanger the health of pets, children, or Federal agents. I wondered if there was a Federal team of yards-men maintaining the premises to preclude the weekly arrival of non-vetted staff.

At the end of a circular driveway, I joined a row of cars and vans parked diagonally in front of the house and garage. Their angles were so perfect that I almost expected to see a valet signaling me to leave my car running with the keys in the ignition. I recognized this could be especially useful if a speedy exit by a large number of people was required.

Although the house was a single-level masonry structure, there was a peaked portico at the center of the home that extended over the driveway. I found the usual Island array of shoes and sandals beside the double-doored entry. Guests of this home were treated to the benefit of a chair to sit on and there was a beautifully waxed *koa* wood shoe rack on which to place one's footgear. There was also a basket with pristine blue booties for those choosing to keep their shoes on.

I opted to take off my gel slippers knowing I would be departing soon. Upon entering the house, I saw Alena standing in front of a gas fireplace. She was deep in conversation with a man whose back was to me. As she walked forward to greet me, he turned and I saw that it was her father.

"Dad, this is the woman I was telling you about, Natalie Seachrist."

He crossed the room to shake my hand. "Yes, of course. I've seen your picture beside some of your delightful travel articles over the years. One time, when my wife and I were returning from a visit to family in Fukuoka, I saw a short piece you had written for Singapore Airlines. It was too bad we hadn't read it before one of our trips overseas. It featured some wonderful travel tips on electronic gadgets that require adapters to convert from U.S. and Canadian 110 voltage to the 220-voltage used by most of the rest of the world. We ended up having to replace several items before we returned home."

We all laughed about the funny things that occur in international travel. Even a well-educated and traveled man like the professor can be presented with challenges.

"My difficulties in travel can extend far beyond mere technical issues. Despite my being a supposed expert in Japanese culture and language, my family's origins can be problematic. If I don't watch my pronunciation and word usage, a speaker of modern Japanese will recognize that my use of the language harkens back to farmers emigrating from Kyūshū over a century ago."

"That's rather like have a Parisian conversing with a French-speaking person from Louisiana," I remarked. "But I've found that if you act humble and ask for assistance, you get a better response from native speakers than if you come across as being defensive."

With a twinkle in his eye, the professor commented, "That is not the experience of many visitors to Paris."

At that point, Captain Makani entered the expansive living room. He greeted all of us warmly and then asked John and Professor Horita to join him in the office. That gave Alena the opportunity to take me on a short tour of the beautiful home. I am not overly fond of the lines of mid-twentieth century modernism. But I did appreciate the quality of woodwork in the Danish solid teak furnishings sprinkled among English Tudor pieces in rich walnut.

Seeing my gaze moving back and forth over the contrasting designs, Alena offered a reason for what I was seeing. "I saw the profiles of the owners. They're an older couple. Both married before. I'll bet that when they bought the house, they simply combined everything they had. The quality of both the Tudor and Danish cabinetry is quite lovely. Just think how awful it would have been if they were mixing ornate French provincial pieces with the Danish."

The time allotted to window shopping at the observation post was short-lived. Before I could admire the ocean-side garden, it was time for a briefing by the Captain. Soon we were issued cell phones from HPD, plus Alena's see- and hear-all glasses. We were then ready to move on to our real destination.

I checked in with Ke'oni as we walked out the door. He informed me that he had previewed the estate sale with my personal desires in mind. My love of romantic candlelight could be rewarded by purchasing one or more of the altar candlesticks that still held candles in rich colors. Thank goodness I had brought those extra coolers with me!

We were able to park my car next to Ke'oni's truck. It seemed perfectly natural for our foursome to have a short teatime at the trunk of my car. We stood sipping cinnamon sun tea and nibbling raisin oatmeal cookies while the men discussed the sale items they found most interesting. Given the constant number of people coming and going from the parking area allotted to visitors, it was unlikely that anyone would pay much attention to our conversation. I brought out the estate sale ad to keep up our cover story. Almost on cue, Alena reminded us of why her father was available to us.

"Even my dad has remarked on the significant pieces from Japan's cultural history being offered today. I'm sure the family's *butsudan*, or shrine, with its scrolls and icons has been removed. But it will be wonderful to see the other sacred religious items, like figurines and bowls for holding flowers and incense. I've noted that there are many candlesticks that may come from Buddhist temples. There are a couple of tables that could have been used as altars for sacred statues," she said with emphasis.

I looked at Ke'oni at the mention of the candlesticks. The men smiled knowingly at each other and then returned to the focus of their day. In the midst of more seafaring technicalities, Ke'oni made an interesting observation.

"You know, boats of this size—and even smaller—have been used for trans-oceanic voyages."

Alena immediately picked up on the ramifications of his remark. "Yes. A boat like the Kiyohara's has an amazing capacity for holding all kinds of things. I can see why you're really serious about acquiring this one professionally as well as personally, Ke'oni."

"I'm glad you two have a new interest in life. But if my eyes glaze over, it's from information overload, I pronounced."

"I doubt that they'll take a personal check for something that costly, so I hope you've figured out how you're going to pay for your new toy," said Alena.

"We have that covered," replied Nathan. "I have a high-limit American Express card for the deposit."

"We have forty-eight hours to produce a cashier's check for the remaining amount," added Ke'oni.

I took a final look at the ad. Concurrently, Alena turned on her tablet and brought up exterior and interior pictures featured on the website of the real estate firm selling the house. Aside from some chairs the men had found extremely comfortable, there were no items of interest in the gardens. Alena announced that we would concentrate on the home itself...both the interior and the exterior. The men, of course, would return to the boat dock to see if they needed to increase their bid.

I knew the day would present challenges on many levels. Agents from myriad national and international organizations would be at the Kiyohara estate. But there was no guarantee they would notice the anomalies local law enforcement might discover. It was also true that most of the family's high-value possessions had been sold at the live auction, where they had been carefully scrutinized by a variety of specialists in antique appraisal and *provenance*.

Our team had to appear like the casual shoppers we claimed to be. Alena and I were using the phrase, "I think Auntie Carrie would have found it interesting" to indicate a piece needed to be examined closely by the experts behind the scenes. Also, Alena could tap her father's knowledge when she wanted confirmation of anything suspicious. If anyone were passing while he was speaking into her ear, it would look like I was merely deliberating on purchases for my home.

CHAPTER 12

...Go and search diligently ...
The King James Version of The Bible: Matthew 2:8 [circa 70]

O ur little group may not include globe-trotting investigators or noteworthy antiquarians, but our viewpoint and role in the inquiry was different. We were present to observe the estate sale from a local perspective, in order to glean insight into the inner dynamics of the Kiyohara dynasty...at least their operations in Honolulu. We would also be able to look for evidence of where the Shākyamuni Buddha may have been kept for the last decade. With the statue being in nearly pristine condition, it would have been tended carefully.

It is not a massive or water-proof figure that could stand on its own in any environment. Even if it were, I knew it would be sacrilegious to set it on the ground. Ke'oni told me that he had examined the gardens. He had found no sign of a boulder large enough, or appropriately shaped, to hold the statue. Nor was there a structure that could have served as an outside altar. That meant the Buddha must have been placed on a substantial piece of stone, a table, or an altar within one of the structures on the property...the home, the guest house, or the tea house.

Old or new, anything appropriate to serving as the base for the Buddha would not have been overlooked by our monitors at the Nippon Antiquities auction. Our team's analysis of the extensive inventory of the family's belongings had yielded few items that fit the necessary requirements of size and stability. As Alena had observed, there was no way to know who had determined today's dispersal of the estate's household items. It was possible that anything that remained in the home after the estate sale would be left to tempt potential buyers of the property. I wondered if there was a separate list of pieces being retained for the upcoming sale of the house.

There was one other possibility, which Alena was busily investigating: Was there a space that was unaccounted for in the real estate pictures and descriptions we have seen? Perhaps a hidden cabinet had been built into the structure of the dwelling. My speculations faded as we entered through massive etched glass and wrought iron doors.

We found a large foyer that was relatively empty when we entered the home. To the left, was a beautiful mahogany desk staffed by a man completing a transaction for an elderly woman escorted by a representative of the auction house. Beside the desk was a luncheon table covered with a padded dark blue linen tablecloth to protect the valuables. Behind it sat a woman facing a large monitor and keyboard. Conversation between the staff indicated that she was accessing the inventory of items included in the estate sale.

I glanced at the customer's two-tiered cart. It held a pair of Limoges lamps and porcelain vases and figurines by Dorothy Okumoto that featured her signature accent of delicate plumeria flowers. Among the woman's selections was a small standing Buddha with a beatific smile. I tried to act casual but could not. The cart was too reminiscent of the one that had been used to carry the stolen Buddha past the crumpled body of the Reverend...and out the door to an unknown location, which might have been the house in which I now stood.

I exhaled the breath that I realized I had been holding. Alena and I then began a comprehensive tour of the property. As we moved into a hallway behind the foyer, we found a happy line of people accompanied by auction staff *en route* to finalizing their purchases. Clearly, there were many attendees who had been waiting for the gates to open, including unidentified authorities, as well as early shoppers.

We walked through formal rooms intended for entertaining the most important of guests. We were both impressed by the detailed finish work on the ceilings, walls, and doors. This was especially evident now that the majority of its furnishings had been removed. The workforce at the house must be superb. Even the empty spaces were immaculately maintained. I could just imagine being there for a magnificent gathering of twenty-four guests in the dining room that featured *koa* wood wainscoting and a coffered bronze ceiling. The only thing remaining in that room was a huge Italian marquetry chest of drawers that made my small Italian marquetry tea cart seem insignificant in comparison.

Alena approached the piece as though it were ideal for my humble bungalow. She turned over a large tag that was dangling from an ornate carving. "What a shame, Natalie. It's sold. To a Mr. and Mrs. Gerald Bishop. I wonder which branch of the old missionary family they're related to?" she questioned. I watched her eyes and could tell that someone was whispering non-sweet things in her ear. Within a few minutes, the powers that be would probably know exactly who the purchasers were and whether they had any connections to the Kiyohara family.

"I think it may actually be the work of Giuseppe Maggiolini, an *intarsiatore*. He was a marquetry cabinet maker from Milan," she observed. "His work is neoclassical in style. With his repetitive designs featuring ornate borders, authentication is fairly easy. That makes his work highly collectible."

We continued to admire one room after another that shone with pride of ownership. No attempt had been to follow specific themes. There was simply a flow of furniture that blended priceless architectural details with décor from around the globe. I noted an emphasis on comfortable Western style chairs and sofas that were being removed. Perhaps this was because the immediate family had lived outside of Japan for a prolonged period.

Moving through swinging double doors leading from the dining room, we entered a butler's pantry. We were alone for the moment. Alena pulled a laser measuring device from her pocket and began checking the cupboards that lined both sides of the space. She opened and closed several doors. When she nodded to me, we continued on to the kitchen.

I was amazed by what I saw. It looked like a kitchen from a five-star restaurant had married its luxurious residential cousin. The room was ringed with custom floor-to-ceiling *koa* cabinetry that included sections with open shelving and glass-fronted cupboards. Along one wall was a pair of SubZero stainless-steel refrigerators and two matching freezers.

In the middle of the room was a stainless-steel center island with an eight-burner gas stove featuring both a grill and flat griddle. To the side were two electric woks that could yield full meals themselves. There were also two massive dishwashers and several sinks, obviously dedicated to specific food preparation processes. On the far wall was a comfy-looking built-in sofa and coffee table that would provide a heavenly place from which to watch a master chef preparing a memorable dining experience.

In general, there was little left for sale in the room. At the back of most counters were raised roll-up doors for small appliance garages. Whatever items might have been within them were gone. A few mismatched items sat on one counter. Some, like stainless steel spoons in varying sizes were tied together with string. I browsed through the oddities that make food preparation a breeze for both accomplished chefs and novices. I grabbed an old blue and white ceramic platter and began filling it with items I have never considered vital to my kitchen gadgetry. Aside from the appliance garages, the only other unexpected spaces I found were a narrow floor-to-ceiling pull out spice rack and pop-open cabinets that held garbage and recycling bins.

While I occupied myself in my role as the happy homemaker on a lark, Alena continued her careful analysis. I watched her examine the room. I knew she was contemplating the possibility of hidden compartments. We were lucky that no one came in to question her work. At one point, Alena got so excited that I thought she'd made a spectacular find. I remembered reading that there was a wine compartment for which the sales sheet had boasted "rolling racks and spaces, but did not see it. When she opened a door hidden within a *koa* paneled wall, it merely led to a tiny temperature controlled room with a tall smoked glass compartmentalized wall with cubicles for storing one's most valuable bottles of wine.

"You look disappointed that you didn't find anything," I said in a stage whisper.

"We're just getting started. Who knows what remains to be found? Speaking of unexpected discoveries, what have you been gathering?"

"Oh, just a few gadgets for my own kitchen."

Alena grinned. "I can guess why those little items would be of interest to you. What's new in your culinary program?"

"Don't get too excited. I'm still a novice cook. Following that class on miso soup, we're going to make French onion, cream of mushroom, and chili-based soups. Then we'll be adding salads and sandwiches to complete luncheon and light supper menus. My current objective is to be able to prepare everything for a wine tasting party. You'll have to come to the party to see what edible delights I dream up."

"That sounds wonderful! You'll have to tell me what wine I can bring," offered Alena.

"I will. I'm so inspired by Chef Akira's classes. That's why I'm quietly adding to my kitchen toys."

"Isn't that a bit risky? Keʻoni's a superb detective. You've told me he often cooks. Don't you think he'll eventually notice what you've added to the drawers?"

"Too true. That's why I'm going to hide these in the car. When I get home, I'll conceal them until the next holiday. Then I can present them to Keʻoni as a gift. I'm hoping that by then I'll have gotten so far in my classes that we'll have had that party that will serve as my culinary debut."

Alena chuckled in response. She again focused on a distant point, and I knew she was receiving instructions from the powers that be.

She gave the kitchen a last hard look and said, "All right, Natalie, if you're finished here, we'll get on with our tour."

Hall by hall, room by room, we worked our way through the house. Alena continued her dimensional explorations but found no indication of nefarious activity. I enjoyed being immersed in the details of one of the most exquisite homes I had seen in quite a while. On a corner table in one hallway I found several candles in varying colors. There were also a pair of brass candlesticks and a set of tiny figurines that looked like a family of the Ainu people from the island of Hokkaidō. I picked them up as they seemed an appropriate memento of the last murders we had investigated.

Some of the spaces we moved through were crowded. I saw that several of the people walking through the house were accompanied by badge-wearing real estate agents. Perhaps excursions like this were good for introducing clients to high-end properties. I wondered if the technique yielded fat commissions.

From time to time, I got a call or text from Keʻoni. The cut off for the *Marimu's* silent auction was in a couple of hours so Nathan and Keʻoni were taking off —ostensibly for lunch. In reality they were meeting with John and the captain, as well some of the agents who had been monitoring the property for more than a month.

In each room we visited, Alena looked closely at any of the pieces of furniture that could have held the Buddha. Sometimes we were alone in a room. That allowed her to bend down and use a small but strong flashlight to examine the top surface for scratches and other signs of wear. She also continued checking walls and closets for hidden rooms or compartments.

In a near whisper, she said, "There's probably some space that's unaccounted for in a multi-million-dollar property of this size. Maybe there's a *safe room*. Given the home's age, they shouldn't be that hard to spot."

We completed our circuit of the home without her discovering anything remarkable. I told her I would return after I had paid for my purchases. In the foyer, I joined a few people waiting in line and quickly moved forward to pay for my kitchen gadgets, candles, small figurines, and a couple of candlesticks.

After stashing my acquisitions in my car, I walked through the house to meet Alena in one of the side *lānais*. I found her seated in a well-padded wrought iron chair. She looked asleep and I hesitated to disturb her. I was saved from my dilemma when a couple with three noisy children tromped past us moving toward the front of the property.

Abruptly aroused, Alena sat up and yawned. "The guys were right about these chairs. They were definitely chosen by people looking for comfort. What a shame they're not for sale."

The area was clear of shoppers, potential home buyers, and Nippon Antiquities staff. I sat down in a chair matching Alena's and settled into a rhythmic rocking motion that eased the rising pain in my hip. Assured that no one could hear us, Alena announced she needed to determine whether there was any difference between the dimensions of the outer walls of the main house and the inner spaces she had already measured. I waved her off to accomplish her task and sipped on a mango juice box I had stashed in my bag.

For a few moments I watched her tinker with a device in her palm. I then replaced my drink in my bag and sank more deeply into the chair. By the time my companion had rounded the corner of the building, I was enjoying the cooing of doves in the numerous trees on the property. There were many beautiful plantings around the small guest cottage on the side. Every once in a while, I caught an exotic floral note in the air. Eventually my curiosity overcame my desire to rest, and I got up to find the source of the fragrance.

Against the cottage's white stucco walls were the bright red blooms of heliconias sprinkled among split leaf monstera philodendrons. Low to the ground were several types of ferns and trailing coral shaded creeper.

There were also exotic orchid plants in *raku* pottery with glazes that matched the elegance of the flowers they held. I enjoyed inhaling the mix of orchid scents for a while and then walked around the building.

I saw no sign of Alena. Perhaps she was examining the teahouse or what appeared to be a tool shed situated beyond a delightful *koi* pond with waterfall. Near me was a wrought iron bench at the base of a *neem* tree. With its curved back and thick cushion, it looked like an ideal resting spot for me. While admiring the tranquility of the Island garden with its classic Japanese accents, I was struck by the contrast to my reason for being there.

If Hitomu Kiyohara had not died, would Ke'oni and I have seen the image of the Buddha in an auction catalogue? My guess was no. If I was right, the man may have been a devotee who had enjoyed the sacred piece for a very long time...without anyone else in his family having a similar sentiment for the statue.

The question was whether the patriarch's desires were behind the theft. If he had been a devout Buddhist, it was unlikely that he would have permitted the murder of a revered minister. Was her death merely collateral damage? If such a powerful man had initiated the theft, he would have known about her demise. But surely that would have affected his spiritual well-being. And if he were merely a money-grubbing thief seeking a high-value item for profit, he would have converted the piece into cash long ago.

Maybe I was looking at the wrong scenario. Had the statue been a gift from a well-meaning employee or family or staff member seeking to curry favor with the head of the Kiyohara dynasty? Had Hitomu Kiyohara even known about the path the iconic piece travelled prior to arriving on his doorstep? If not, what had he been told about its history? With his professional background, he would have realized a number of things.

Despite the limited vision I had been told he had, he should have been able to discern the date range of its creation. By the sense of smell and the feel of the materials that were used, he may even have been able to guess the Buddhist sect to which it originally belonged. And with all the news coverage that surrounded the statue's disappearance from the temple and the death of one of its ministers, how could he not connect the dots and realize he was involved in murder as well as grand larceny?

The only facts I knew about the statue's provenance was that it had been a gift from a temple in Japan to the one in Honolulu from which it had been stolen. Again, if the owner of this home had been spiritually minded, how could he justify receiving and holding the piece? I could not wait to see the results of the research currently being conducted on Hitomu. Were there any circumstances to account for an otherwise honest man ending up with such a tainted antiquity?

Sighing, I leaned back and focused on the irony that a family that might have been caught up in such horrible crimes would have created the veritable heaven in which I sat. Slowly the beauty of flowers and birdsong soothed my angst. As often happens when I sink into a state of idyllic rest, my breathing deepened, and awareness of my surroundings faded. Perhaps it was the penetration of the fragrances surrounding me that nudged me into a visionary state.

Again, the images within my visionary eye present themselves in hazy sepia tones. I am standing beneath a tree. It is not the neem tree of the Kiyohara family's Hawaiian estate. Overhead are the short-lived blossoms of an elegant Japanese cherry blossom tree. Ahead in a low-lying mist I see a small kidney shaped lake. Across its span is an arched bridge. In the distance on the right, I view a compound of aged wooden buildings fronted by a tori, *the traditional gateway to a sacred space.*

Seated beside me sleeps an elderly man on a stone bench. He wears a black cotton yukata *and* obi. *On his bare feet are soiled* getas, *probably from walking across the damp ground. Despite the lack of adornment, I know that he is a Buddhist priest. At his feet a small girl is perched on a flat rock. She also wears a* yukata *of summer weight cotton, but hers is a bright floral pattern. Her shoes, a smaller version of the man's, sit neatly on the ground beside her. She softly sings a rhyming song while playing with two small branches of jewel-toned Shidarezakura cherry blossoms that have fallen from the tree above.*

I feel, rather than see or hear, the dreamt thoughts of the man. He is pleased to have given a revered statue of the Shākyamuni Buddha *to his son who is leaving his home and faith to pursue a monastic life within a new school of Buddhism. The gifting is one of goodwill toward the young man's dedication to his recently found faith. While he will miss his son, he is glad that his granddaughter will remain at his side.*

Upon the sharp and prolonged scream of a male peacock, the child rises and looks across the landscape. My eyes follow hers across the mist to the lake. At the sight of a young man crossing the bridge, the child hastens toward the lakeside. I hear her small cries caught on the wind, but the distant man clearly does not. Realizing she may not be able to catch up with him, she looks around for an alternative means to reach him.

Sprinkled across the lake are dark stones of irregular shape and placement. The girl's head turns from one to another. I feel her sudden determination. Quickly, she pulls up the hem of her yukata *and runs into the water. It is shallow and she easily reaches the first of the stones. Springing from its edge, she manages to obtain a toehold on the second. This one is somewhat larger. Realizing she will need momentum to widen the span of her next leap, she breathes deeply and runs forward. I hold my own breath as the scene devolves into slow motion.*

I sadly watch as the small girl falls headfirst into the water. She flings out her arms in hopes of capturing her goal. But it is not to be. Falling short by several inches, her hands smack the water now agitated by her splashing body. I see rather than hear her choking gulps but can do nothing to alter her dire situation. I glance frantically at her grandfather, who continues his deadened sleep. I look ahead at the fading image of the man who has crossed the bridge and continues his journey into the distance. At last, I take a breath. Upon the wind, I hear notes from the child's song played softly upon a wooden flute, as the scene is replaced by a curtain of black.

I jolted into full consciousness with a profound sense of sorrow. How had the girl's father and grandfather lived out their lives without the pleasure of watching such a sweet child grow into adulthood? For a few moments I stood up and stretched my back and joints and then bent forward to touch my toes. I tried to shift my mind from the disturbing image of the child and looked across the peaceful yard to the *koi* pond, whose water fountain had switched on while I was viewing an almost operatic tragedy. I exhaled and inhaled deeply, wondering why I had experienced the sorrowful vision.

I looked around but there was no sign of Alena. I checked my phone. No new messages. Searching for distraction, I thought about how Ke'oni and I might augment the landscaping at Auntie Carrie's home. Through my life, I have usually viewed grounds-keeping like food preparation—an element of daily life that must be dealt with despite my desire to ignore it. That was why I enjoyed condo living for so long. There were no responsibilities—as long as I was willing to pay for whatever upkeep needed to be performed.

Aside from the little matter of our undercover work, today centered on playing house. Being a newbie homeowner, I was happiest with plants that took care of themselves, unlike the perennially falling blossoms of the plumeria trees at neighboring Mokulua Hale. I took another look at the lovely plantings in which I stood, wondering what might be duplicated in the moister environs of Lanikai. Perhaps I should add edgings of Mondo grass to a few areas of our yard. If we chose perennial plants of varying height and color, Ke'oni and I could brighten the property without committing ourselves to inordinate hours of labor.

Looking at the edge of the pond in front of me, I tried to block the image of the little girl I had just watched die. I sighed and returned to the reality surrounding me. Still no sign of Alena. I got up and strolled toward the back of the guest house to see if there was anything else of interest. I heard two male voices floating out of an open window. One sounded like he might be a native speaker of Japanese. The other voice resembled that of broadcaster Jon Stewart—which is to say, he had no definable accent. There was no fractured grammar, no use of *ain't*, and no regionally identifiable terms"

I avoided attracting attention to my eavesdropping by grabbing a couple of flowers that were laying on the ground. Looking intently at my hands, I cocked my ear to better hear the conversation that was floating out from an open window in the back bedroom.

"What do you mean?" spoke the man who sounded like a native Japanese speaker.

"You know what I'm saying. This should never have happened."

"I agree. But why are you challenging *me*? It is not like I caused my brother to die. And I had no way of knowing that his death would trigger liquidation of the estate. The last time I saw Hitomu's will, everything was in order for a smooth transition. You should remember that at the time he died, I was on a buying trip in Mongolia where communication was not ideal. The changes in his will were made without my knowing. I doubt that my being here would have made any difference in what followed."

At that point I was pretty sure I was listening to Tommy Kiyohara. But *who* was his companion? I thought about trying to look into the window. I was probably too short to see much. Even if I achieved my goal, the occupants of the room would be able to see me.

"That may be true. But when you heard about his death, you should have alerted his son to keep a few items under wraps. You know, act like you were interested in them for yourself."

"It is not my fault that they, especially *it*, ended up at auction. Did you expect me to reveal details previously unknown to the rest of the family in an open telephone conversation? Everything had been set in motion by the time I arrived in Honolulu. All I could do was perform my usual role as auctioneer."

CHAPTER 13

Do what you can, with what you have, where you are.
Theodore Roosevelt Jr. [1858 - 1919]

Well, that solved one issue. I was right in identifying speaker number one as Tommy Kiyohara.

The second man then said, "Okay. We can't change what happened. We're where we are."

"I did tell you NOT to show up today! All we need is for someone to connect you to my family...that could re-open the initial investigation."

"Today is a big event and there're people from all segments of the community. I just bought a new condo. No one would suspect my checking out an estate sale. If anyone expresses any doubt about us, we haven't seen each other since the original case. What have you told the authorities about the acquisition of our special *item*?"

"That it came from our family's household in Japan, arriving here after the Second World War. I emphasized that that is true for many antiquities connected to Japanese families and businesses that have moved to the United States."

It was a shame I did not have a recording device with me. But even if I had, there was nothing in the conversation that would ensure the men could be brought up on a charge of grand larceny, let alone murder.

"Sounds good. Stay with that short explanation. You'd better listen to me on this. If you don't want this house of cards to come tumbling down."

There was a pause in their conversation. Then I heard a cabinet shut.

"There isn't anything left for *you* to worry about—assuming nothing materializes to discredit you."

"There's nothing that could show up, no matter how deep they dig."

"Hmm. Not even a household inventory?"

"It hasn't been that long since Koji took the reins of daily operations. He digitized all records, including everything in the household. We checked it carefully. There's no mention of where the pieces came from, or their purchase prices."

"All right. Just don't muddy the waters. Leave everything alone."

A snort was the only response I heard. Then there was silence. I heard a slight rustling of paper and took a chance and stood on tiptoe to peer in the window. In the center of the small bedroom, I saw both men turning toward the open doorway.

Nothing incriminating had been revealed in the words I overheard. Nevertheless, I was certain we were on the right path to finding out who was behind both the theft and the attendant murder. The biggest question was whether I would be able to identify the voice of the second man in the future?

Pondering that thought, I quickly walked to the small front porch. It was too bad that I arrived a moment too late. As I glanced to the left side of the cottage, I saw the ramrod straight back of a tall man in gray slacks, a rust-colored aloha shirt, and the heels of highly polished black leather shoes.

My initial impulse had been to dash after the departing figure, but knowing that Tommy Kiyohara could arrive momentarily, I picked up a couple of flowers from the ground. In another minute, Tommy was coming out the front door. This meant that the man who had exited the cottage first was the mainland *haole*. Keeping my cover intact, I smiled and continued feigning interest in the blossoms in my hand. Tommy stared at my hands for a moment...probably contemplating whether he should call me out for the theft of a few flowers. He looked up at my face briefly and sauntered off toward the front of the main house.

At least I had pinpointed part of the cast of characters involved in the crimes that had remained unsolved since Keʻoni's time with HPD. Hearing my name called, I pivoted to see Alena approaching from the right side of the guest house. I quickly relayed my recent experience to her, and we speculated on the involvement of auctioneer Tommy Kiyohara's companion in the original investigation.

"If only you'd been walking on the opposite side of the house! You would have been able to identify the man who was with Kiyohara," I said tossing my tiny bouquet under a shrub.

"At this point, I think we should be grateful you observed what you did," Alena replied. "It means we can be fairly certain that Tommy Kiyohara was part of the grand larceny—if not the murder at the temple."

Alena was quiet for a moment while she received some feedback from whomever was monitoring the microphones mounted on her glasses. When she next spoke, Alena was careful to keep her voice low.

"I've checked out the teahouse and the tool shed. The construction of both is really flimsy. There's no way either one could have supported a compartment or even a piece of furniture sturdy enough to hold the Buddha. As to those two guys who were in the guest house, it sounds like they were there for more than a couple of minutes. There's no telling what remainders of their presence we might find."

Once we were inside, she verified that no one was within hearing and asked, "Which room were they in? There's always a chance I might be able to lift a fingerprint."

I showed Alena to the bedroom on the right. It was unfortunate that there were no furnishings with which she could work.

"I heard a rustling of papers. But as you can see, there's no dresser or other piece of furniture from which anything could have been removed."

"There are a couple of rooms with closets. I guess it's back to my measuring in case there's a space we've missed."

She then began her round of spatial analysis in the living room. Meanwhile, I wandered around seeking anything today's bargain hunters might have overlooked. I found a striped orange tiger lily orchid in the bathroom. There was also a large basket with assorted brands of shampoos, body washes, and creams. I guess even the rich and mighty stoop to coveting the personal care products of finer hotels and resorts.

In my youth, cruise lines, and manufacturers of high-end personal care products were thrilled to provide samples to travel and leisure journalists like me—undoubtedly in hopes of getting free verbal or written promotion. It was true that such an endorsement might not reach the level of success of an entertainment celebrity or product placement in a block buster movie, but word-of-mouth promotion has always been popular with marketing departments.

I continued wandering around the small cottage since Alena did not need my help. It was like a suite in a hotel for the elite. In the small kitchen, I found a stove top with two burners, a grill, and an electric wok. Below were a wine cooler and compact refrigerator. There were also a combination microwave-convection oven, blender, and espresso machine. Shiny and strategically aligned, the small appliances seemed poised for inclusion in the eventual sale of the property. Ever curious, I began opening the few cabinets and drawers. I discovered small silver spoons and lace-edged linen cocktail napkins in one, and small jars of honey and jam, plus assorted packets of sweeteners in another.

Eventually I found Alena in the second bedroom examining a sleek built-in dresser of *koa* within the closet. To the left was a chrome rod with several heavy, padded satin hangers. Alena carefully pulled out each of the surprisingly shallow drawers. In the bottom one I noticed a curious item. It was a small wooden lap desk. She lifted it out and opened compartments sized to hold paper and miscellaneous writing items.

"Nothing here of interest," she sighed.

"Except for that desk. It may be rather small for hiding anything but a scrap of paper or a picture. However, it would be ideal for writing great epistles in my wingback chair. There's no price tag, but it doesn't look terribly old and it's clearly nothing a home buyer would seek."

"That's true. I'll bet you could talk one of the Nippon Antiquities staff into selling it to you! I think I'll check the wall between this kitchen and the living room and then we'll be through here," she said moving away.

I set the small desk on the floor and turned back to close the closet doors. Although I am short, I am slightly taller than Alena. I took a final look at the dresser and noticed that the corner of a hanger on top. There was probably nothing else. Nevertheless, I strained to reach it. The only way I could do so was to jump up and flip it outward. I managed to dislodge it, but when the hanger fell toward me, I slipped and fell against the dresser.

Just then I heard a click and the right edge of the dresser moved slightly outward. I gasped and softly called to Alena. I was glad there was no one else around to hear my distressed plea. When she did not come to join me immediately, I wondered if I needed to go and look for her. Before I could act upon my concern, she appeared.

"What's up? Ohh. I see," said Alena with a widening grin unseen by any remote listeners. She softly observed, "A hidden compartment I missed."

Together we pivoted the right side of the dresser and stared at the cavity that was revealed. At the back of the relatively narrow space was a small but sturdy altar table in ornately carved rosewood. In the center of it was an unusual space free of dust. It approximated the circular dimensions of the base of the *Sh*ākyamuni Buddha which had been kept from public view for a long period of time.

A pause punctuated our amazement.

"Isn't this interesting, Natalie. What you might call a niche with a sturdy table ideal for holding a valuable article of antiquity."

"Indeed."

Again, my designer seemed lost in thought. I wondered about the details of the conversation she was hearing among the members of national and international investigators at the listening post. I could not wait for the debriefing at the end of this lengthening day!

I clutched the nearly forgotten lap desk to my chest while serving as lookout for our clandestine undertaking. Meanwhile, Alena took several pictures of the hidden space and altar table. She then knelt down and captured images of the underside of the table.

"Anything memorable?" I asked pointing to the table.

She shook her head and signaled that we should push the dresser back into its normal position. Finally, she took pictures of the closet and all of the walls of the bedroom.

Waving her index finger toward the door, she indicated that I should continue to keep watch in case someone entered the guest house. I stood in the doorway of the bedroom, where I could glance down the short hallway while watching Alena continue her analysis. With precision and speed, she reached into her shoulder bag and brought out a finger-printing kit. After a few moments she stood and replaced her paraphernalia in her bag.

"Nothing here but a few overlooked dust bunnies," she said in a relatively normal voice.

We returned to the comfort of the chairs on the *lānai*. While Alena emailed her pictures to Captain Makani, I checked in with Ke'oni regarding the motorsailer of his dreams.

"I was just about to call you," he announced. "Nathan and I've been invited to take a short cruise on the *Marimu*...along with a couple of other bidders. We shouldn't be too long. It'll give us a chance to see all of the boat's equipment in action!"

I turned back to my designer for the day and told her about Ke'oni's news. There was no way of knowing how long the seagoing adventure would take—or when the auction would end. That meant that Alena and I needed to remain in the area for some time.

Another realtor entered the *lānai* with a client, cooing over the condition of the estate and the future prospects for its profitability. Alena casually pointed to her glasses. I got the message that the powers-that-be were giving her instructions.

"Gee, Natalie, I think we've seen most everything we can. I didn't notice anything in the teahouse that isn't too Asian for the style of your cottage," said my partner in property analysis. I interpreted that to mean that we were supposed to report back to the command post ASAP.

"I guess you're right. I'll see if I can negotiate a deal on this lap desk. Then we can go to lunch and consider how today's acquisitions fit into your design for my living room."

I was soon the proud owner of an elegant means for capturing my thoughts. When Alena joined me in the entry way, she announced that we needed to go to the observation post for a summary of the up-to-the-moment activities of the day. I was glad that we were taking my car, since it would allow me to examine my purchases if Alena needed to speak privately with the men and women in charge of the day.

When we arrived, it appeared that some of the team had been dispatched elsewhere, because parking was not a problem. When we walked in the door, we were greeted with friendly nods from both those who knew us and complete strangers. Clearly, our descriptions had preceded us. There were wonderful aromas in the air. I realized that I was quite hungry after our active morning. One perk of being part of a multi-agency action is that mealtimes are often planned to maximize efficiency and minimize downtime.

During this lunch break, I was delighted to enjoy a buffet featuring an enormous salad bar and barbecued chicken and fish—plus a local favorite, sweet rolls from King's Bakery. The varied skills of everyone present had been tapped for food preparation rather than bring in caterers who could impair the high level of security. Even Alena's father had volunteered his talents, performing as our barbecue master of the day. Planning ahead, he had even raided his family's pantry to provide a few specialties for the benefit of locals, as well as visitors to the Islands.

"Check out the salad bar," said Alena. "You'll find my mother's pickled heirloom Japanese eggplant and her cousin's *kimchi* made with Napa cabbage and a touch of fermented chili paste. And along with the usual pots of steamed white rice, there's stir-fried brown rice with fresh vegetables from our garden."

The large supply of varied foods was appreciated by everyone. Although some of the mainlanders might have been uncertain about whether they would enjoy everything on the menu, they were delighted to see several recognizable appetizers and desserts.

I was glad to be able to visit with the professor while he grilled a second piece of *'ahi* for me. He glowed with pride as I complimented the dual role Alena was serving. She was clearly a key player on the investigative team. She was also a gifted designer who was ensuring Auntie Carrie's cottage would be a unique home for our family through continuing generations.

Our casual setting allowed me to ask him about his life and work on several levels. In the midst of talking about his lifetime of travel, I learned he had written academic papers about the evolving nuances of Asian languages in today's rapidly changing electronic age. More importantly, I gained an appreciation for the years that the Reverend Fujimoto had served families like his.

"With her background in musical performance, the *sensei* offered input to creative programs for every generation at the temple—especially those in the after-school curriculum in which I sometimes worked. Alena was young when Reverend Fujimoto died, but she continued to speak of her for several years."

At no point in his sharing did I hear anything that might have contributed to the murder of the minister. From everything I had observed in the current investigation, it truly seemed she had been killed simply because she was in the wrong place. What a shame that she had decided to seek a few moments of prayer in the temple just when two violent criminals were implementing a scheme to steal a sacred object.

The smoothness with which he remained open yet discreet would be a lesson to anyone in a politically sensitive position. In addition to the personal insights I gained regarding the victim, I learned a lot about the work Dr. Horita had performed for local, national, and international agencies. His tasks had ranged from simple translation to in-depth cultural explanations. I admired the way he was careful to avoid specific details that might impact ongoing cases.

It gave me pause to consider how I handle revelation of my visions. I suspected that by now there was an awareness of my little "gift" in more than one office at HPD Headquarters. But since no one made any comments regarding that topic, it might mean a decision had been made to leave John Dias as the official link to that aspect of my life. This suited me for several reasons. It meant I could continue to act on the premise that almost no one knew my secret beyond family, Ke'oni, the good Lieutenant, and perhaps his boss.

As I had foreseen, Alena needed to confer with numerous officials after lunch. This gave me time to rearrange my recent acquisitions in the car. With food removed from one cooler in the morning, I was able to pack the candles I had purchased. How wonderful that they would arrive home intact despite the heat of the day. I wedged everything else between the jacket I had worn in the morning and the lap desk. With my organizational tasks concluded, I returned to the house.

The meetings among the personnel of the various agencies had concluded so I could present the photos Ke'oni had sent me during the morning. No one seemed especially interested in the people or objects that were featured, but I knew they would be added to a database that might prove useful in cases that were not currently on the horizon.

The pace of the afternoon seemed slow after my momentary sighting of one of the men I suspected of having committed the crimes we were investigating. I rested for a while in a comfortable lounger on the back *lānai*, surrounded by huge pots filled with a variety of plants and fragrant flowers. The plantings ranged from the bright white flowers of the *natal plum* and baby blue *plumbago* to *bromeliads* that displayed miniature pineapples.

Periodically, Ke'oni and Nathan sent me pictures of their cruise. My twin focused on structural features of the *Marimu*, while Ke'oni zeroed in on her technical equipment. It was good that no one aboard the boat could see my facial responses, which fluctuated between boredom and nausea at the thought of going to sea. My only concern was keeping my voice bubbly and sounding as if I were really interested in oceanic adventures. This was important since I might be overheard by the boat's captain, on-board representatives of Nippon Antiquities, or other men seeking the winning bid.

Thank goodness for my experience in making videos in the travel industry! That allowed me to minimize expressing my true feelings. It also provided some vocabulary appropriate to the needs of the day...*Oh, Honey, how many berths are there? Can we accommodate the Ho Family? Is there enough space to hold our catch on a really good day? How many days can we stay at sea without putting into port for fuel or provisions?*

At the conclusion of each of our communications, I went inside to pass my phone to a tech who transferred the images and texts I had saved in an electronic image folder. I was certain that if Ke'oni were here, he would have been included in the discussion of these processes.

With so many federal and international agents floating around, it might seem there was no need for our little group to continue to be involved. But Ke'oni was one of the first detectives on the scene to examine both the minister's murder and the theft of the Buddha. There was the chance that he would observe someone, or something, connected to the original case. Therefore, all of our "performances" at the Kiyohara estate had to look and sound appropriate to the roles we were playing.

As I continued waiting for Alena to complete her rounds among the on-site agents and officers, I reflected upon the various results the day might yield. Personally, the most important was Ke'oni and Nathan potentially becoming the owners of the *Marimu.* Beyond liking each other and loving me, the beauty of their relationship is being able to pool their funds to purchase a vessel neither could afford on their own. My greatest concern was their safety. Fortunately, neither of them seemed attracted to racing or other major ocean-going events. Aside from sharing this new hobby with each other, they could plan sea-going events with friends and colleagues possessing a similar interest.

Perhaps having a special focus in our later years is what allows us to live vitally until our end on this plane. It looks like I will be able to test this theory with the yachting life Nathan and Ke'oni anticipate experiencing. As for me, I do not think my new column on food and entertainment counts as a hobby. And while detecting may not be a hobby, it has become an ongoing but hidden feature of my life.

This involves learning everything possible about Nippon Antiquities and the Kiyohara family. Presently, the first item has been accomplished as much as possible by our little team. As to the second, I cannot say how much we will contribute. Of course, we are hoping the *Marimu* will end up in our hands and that something will materialize from examination of her by Ke'oni and the team of CSIs that will be assigned to the task.

The auction of the boat was still ongoing. The men aboard the boat are not the only people competing against my brother and Ke'oni. Nathan texted me periodically about the bids being reported by the representatives of Nippon Antiquities who were aboard. My stalwart men remained focused and have upped their bid three times. I wondered how high they can go without emptying their retirement funds. Despite my personal distaste for life on the open seas, I found myself becoming increasingly excited for them.

Eventually, I got the text I had been awaiting: The boat would be arriving at the dock shortly. Win or lose, it was time for Alena and me to return to the Kiyohara estate. As we were about to leave, Captain Makani pulled us aside.

"I just heard from our inside man. It looks like the estate sale is closing up this afternoon. Nearly everything has been sold. Some of what's left will be used to stage the house for its sale. The rest will end up in the gallery."

As my designer in chief and I walked toward the pier a few minutes past four p.m., Ke'oni called to announce that the auction had been officially concluded.

"We did it! The *Marimu* is ours!" said Ke'oni excitedly.

"That's it? It's all over?"

"Yes, dear. Or maybe I should say it's now starting. The *Marimu, Sea Dream,* really is becoming a feature in our lives…if you'll have her."

I laughed while watching two men stomp off the boat. They were probably other bidders who had been vying for ownership of the vessel.

"Now don't get too carried away. You know how I feel about small objects on water carrying humans. It's worse than Miss Una viewing bubbles in the spa."

"Well, at least agree to come aboard occasionally for drinks!"

"Sometime. Maybe. Eventually."

"What about Tuesday? Nathan and I have to move the boat over to the Kāne'ohe Yacht Club and we'll need a ride home."

"Let's see how the day develops," I replied, with hope that Nathan's girlfriend Adriana could serve as a backup. I couldn't help but envision the lovely Indian Portuguese woman who helps out whenever she can pitches in she can. With her exotic shining black hair and deep brown eyes, it is no wonder that my twin has fallen in love with her. Of course, it does not hurt that she is also a physician and they share many aspects of their professional challenges!

When Alena and I arrived at the edge boat a few minutes later, we were welcomed aboard with glasses of Dom Perignon champagne. I could hardly turn that down despite my trepidation about boarding the boat and exhaustion after the hours I had spent calling and emailing in the guise of a supporter of all things nautical. Thank God I had the right footwear for this unexpected challenge. I was grateful that Alena played the role of a youngster eager to learn more about the life of a driver of boats while I remained anchored to the rail claiming to admire the ocean view.

With the men's plans set to move the *Marimu* in a couple of days, our group departed. There had been no new developments since the last transmission of photos. Only Alena needed to return to the lookout post for a final summation of the day. Aside from failing to see the second man at the guest cottage, my one regret was that we had several vehicles to drive to a single location and I was already wiped out.

CHAPTER 14

One thing at a time and all things in succession.
J. G. Holland [1819 – 1881]

We had known the day would be unpredictable and were grateful that Adriana had volunteered to drop in at Nathan's home to take Kūlia for a walk. After a morning of performing a round of physicals for the children at Hale Malolo, she decided to remain at the house and prepare a little surprise for us.

When we pulled up at my brother's home at sunset we saw that Adriana had lit the palm trees and lights around the garden. Another surprise was finding two pitchers of margaritas and several platters of *pūpūs* on the *lānai* table. Vegetables, cheese, bread, and teriyaki chicken strips. What a woman...and what a chef! I had better step up my game and start learning to prepare a few delectables for moments like this.

Adriana had proven herself an ideal addition to our family. She was able to share many aspects of the healthcare profession with Nathan. And, as the survivor of a terrorist attack in France, she related to the violence that had invaded our family with Ariel's murder.

She knows that Nathan sometimes consults on HPD cases. As a doctor, she is accustomed to dealing with issues of privacy. While we were publicly celebrating the acquisition of the boat, she knew we were concurrently involved in the investigation of an open case—about which none of us could discuss the specifics.

Ke'oni and I enjoyed a drink with Adriana, while Nathan disappeared inside the house for a short while. He returned wearing a fresh aloha shirt and carrying another in his hand.

"You're more than welcome to wash up and switch to this shirt, if you like, Ke'oni."

"Thanks. I was just longing for the shower I'm going to take as soon as we get home."

Ke'oni changed shirts and soon the men settled into a review of the *Marimu's* many features, and their experiences in qualifying as certified drivers of motorized boats.

"I was glad we could take the courses online," said Ke'oni. "I appreciate the State's rules after watching the chaos of a boat running amuck near a beach. It gives you a personal perspective on the requisite skills for driving any boat."

"They certainly were thorough in the process to register us as certified vessel operators—gender, birthdate, eye color, hair color, and especially which certified classes we'd taken," commented Nathan.

I could tell their conversation would continue for a while. I signaled for Adriana to follow me to my car. We spent a short while looking at my prized possessions from the estate sale. I could tell she would enjoy a similar outing in the future. I promised to let her know when I would next be venturing forth for an antique sale of any kind.

"So how much time do you think we'll need to move the boat?" Nathan asked as we re-entered the *lānai*.

"Well, a Kāneʻohe Yacht Club staff member estimated four to five hours. Evidently the water around Mokapuʻu Point can get a bit rough. Other than that, it's pretty much a smooth ride—since we'll be using the motor rather than the sails."

"Being new to all this, maybe the bigger question is do we need an escort or experienced crew?"

"I've asked a couple of people about that. We could hire someone. But I had a chat with John Dias. He told me he has a friend who might like to come out with us. Quite a sailor, I guess."

Keʻoni (and Nathan) had been very smooth in how they handled this part of their conversation in front of Adriana. Reading between the lines, I was sure Keʻoni meant that one of the growing team of investigators on the case would be joining in their first boating adventure.

We kept the evening short and tag-teamed our way home. I think Keʻoni was grateful that I had not purchased any furniture at the sale. Not only was he able to avoid further exertion that night, but we would not be facing rearrangement of an already well-furnished home. The few accessories I had purchased could be absorbed into the current décor. As he helped me empty the car, I managed to avoid opening the compartment where I had squirreled away my purchases for the kitchen.

We were greeted by Miss Una as soon as we entered the house. I guessed she may have had too many hours of playing mentor to ʻIlima.

"Yes, my love, I know it's been a long day. You always seem so content in The Ladies' garden that I guess I've been neglecting you," I confessed.

She stared up at me, as though she understood and concurred with every word I had uttered. After a quick rub and a circling around my legs, she led me to her bowls. When I saw water in one and a full portion of dry food in the other, I questioned her complaint. But after setting my armful of candles on the counter, I opened the refrigerator.

"My, aren't you lucky. There seems to be a perfect portion of ʻahi for you." A couple of lengthy meows and a small jump toward my hand pronounced her approval of the menu. Given the length of our day and the food we had consumed at Nathan's, I was glad there was no need to make another meal—or even popcorn for the movie I planned to turn on after bathing.

I heard the shower running when I entered the bedroom.

"Couldn't wait for me?" I called out as I peeled off my clothes.

"Be grateful. After the hours I spent on the boat, I thought you'd appreciate my taking a pre-shower," said Ke'oni, welcoming me into the steamy enclosure.

That night I fell to sleep during *Sleepless in Seattle*, one of my favorite romantic comedies. The last thing I remember is the boy on his way to New York. Ke'oni must have made it to the final scene, because I found the DVD had been returned to its case in the morning. The fragrance of coffee beckoned me, but I was uncertain whether I would make the effort to go for a walk or swim. I was glad that Ke'oni saved me from my dilemma.

"You're up," he said, entering the bedroom with a couple of mugs in hand.

"I guess so. But I'm tempted to forego our usual Sunday morning outing," I said.

"After everything we did yesterday, I think we should both take a complete break today. Let's make an omelet with cheese and anything else that looks good. Then we'll just watch movies and end the day with a delivered pizza and whatever wine is lurking in the cooler.

"Tomorrow you can turn to putting your new goodies away. I'll catch up on emails and calls, then finalize whatever must be done before moving the *Marimu* on Tuesday."

I sighed and felt less guilty about taking a day of leisure. By eight thirty on Monday we launched into a day of organization. As I emptied the waste baskets in our office, Ke'oni filled me in on his latest news.

"I've already had a call from JD. Our day may not remain entirely empty. He's hinted that he may have a reason to join us later. I'm supposed to wait until ten o'clock to call him back. He expects to have a report on a couple of fingerprint tests Alena ran on the guest cottage by then—plus initial analysis of your photos, and those Nathan and I took of the *Marimu*."

Light work around the house was the perfect start to what might be another busy week. Ke'oni ensconced himself in the office while I wandered around the house like a bored maid with a duster. After a while, I had a sense of where I wanted to position my new purchases. The first item to find a home was the laptop desk. I set it on my new oversized computer workstation for easy access. Seeing Ke'oni immersed in a spreadsheet, I continued playing house.

In the dining room, I put a green altar candle in one of the brass candlesticks and placed it on my Italian marquetry tea cart. It might not be worth thousands of dollars, but the cart added an international flare to the room. The rest of the candles and the set of Ainu looking figurines wound up in the credenza. With Keʻoni's help, I would eventually implement Alena's idea of creating shelved shadow boxes for items like the figurines.

I continued dusting my way through the house. When I heard my significant other on the telephone, I realized it was a perfect time to dash into the garage for my kitchen gadgets. I quickly secured them in the niche to which I had been assigning their fellows. It was shortly after ten and I realized that Keʻoni must be speaking to John. I had not checked into the prospects for arranging some lunch if he were going to drop in, but I knew we had plenty of frozen leftovers.

"Hey, Natalie," called out Keʻoni.

"I'm in the kitchen," I responded. "I've looked our supplies over. I think I can make a variation on a cobb salad, whether or not John is joining us."

"I just spoke to him, and he does have a few details on the investigation to go over with us. I hope one o'clock is okay. That gives me long enough to pick up some hardware and woodworking supplies."

"Sounds perfect, honey."

We hugged and he took off for a shopping trip that I knew would include more than one stop. With a couple of hours to myself, I decided to squeeze in a bit of serious work. I began by checking my calendar and making a call to the Waimānalo poultry farm that would provide me with organic eggs as well as information for the article I am planning.

When I entered the office, I found Miss Una sprawled across my new laptop desk.

"A new toy to explore?" I asked.

The only response I got was a flick of her tail. Obviously, my recent absences had been resented. I stepped forward and extended my arms to swoop up my darling girl into my arms. As she turned abruptly to avoid me, her collar caught on a corner of the desk. Fortunately, the quick release mechanism on the collar sprang open and she sprinted from the room. Obviously, I'd have to catch her to replace the collar with her name and phone number printed on it.

I considered whether to start assembling my article on the teaching chefs at Kapiʻolani Community College. There was no deadline chasing me. But it might be a good time to initiate use of the laptop desk. It only took a couple of minutes to fill its compartments with writing implements and lined notepads.

Next, I pulled a few folders from my file cabinet and sat down at the small table beside it. Glancing through the preliminary information on the Kapiʻolani Community College's culinary arts program instructors, the Royal Hawaiian Band, and a history of the concerts themselves, I soon had a working outline for my article. I would ask Samantha to research any remaining gaps.

A repeating sound of tapping interrupted my concentration. Looking down, I saw Miss Una had returned to the room and was lying in front of the laptop desk. There's something about that cat of mine: she's quite the little detective. Whether she's spying on elements in her surroundings or physically uncovering a clue, she has helped to discover important aspects of more than one crime.

"What are you up to now, my Noble Beast?" I asked.

As usual, she ignored my query and focused on playing with the desk's glass drawer knobs. She may not have fingers on her furry little paws, but I know when her claws need trimming. When they are long, they work remarkably well for prying objects loose. After a couple of moments, she had eased a drawer forward and was perusing the contents at its front. I was intrigued by her growing dexterity and watched her wriggle out a small gum eraser.

I moved over to my workstation and picked up her hard-won trophy. "I am proud of your growing tactile skills. But I don't think we want to explore the effects this might have on your intestines."

Clearly miffed, she again exited the room. I replaced the eraser in the drawer. Then I stacked my folders on top of the desk and picked it up. I enjoy varying my writing environment and chose the living room for a comprehensive work session. I turned on NPR for a little melodic inspiration and sat down in my reclining wingback. I thought that hearing a cantata by Mozart might inspire my erstwhile companion to join in today's creative adventure. But she did not appear.

With my preliminary outline to the side, I picked up a pen and began jotting down the essentials of my new piece in a fresh notebook. I soon filled several pages with fragments of text and my outline was punctuated with arrows indicating changes in sequence and ideas for images I wanted to include with the article on a concert at 'Iolani Palace. I finished my labors with a list of people I needed to contact.

Glancing at the clock above the bookcase to the right of the fireplace, I saw that I had more than an hour before John would arrive. That was enough to doze for a few minutes before starting on lunch. I enjoy my mini naps and have found they leave me as refreshed as when I sleep in bed for a couple of hours. I then set the desk on the floor beside me. With the sense of accomplishment I often feel when completing the first phase of a new project, I leaned back in my recliner for a brief nap.

A repetitive sound of crinkling paper awoke me. What a ruination of a lovely dream about Mount Haleakalā at sunrise. The receding shadows on the largely barren soil always reminds me of pictures I have seen of Mars—except for the majesty of periodically blooming silverswords. I remember a Hawaiian auntie telling me about a relative of hers who had painstakingly built small circles of stones around the distinctive plants to encourage their survival.

I tried to keep my eyes closed and ignore the irritating noise. If it would just stop, I might be able to get a few more minutes of rest. But that was not to be. I reopened my eyes to behold Miss Una playing with my new desk. She was pawing at a drawer, trying to open it further than the crack she had accomplished already. It was not difficult to see the source of her focus and the resulting sound. I spotted the corner of a piece of what initially looked like onion skin stationery paper from another age.

"All right. That's enough torture of both my ears and *my* new toy."

For once, the cat looked at me without frustration at my interrupting her fun. Her expression was almost a plea for me to pay heed to her discovery.

"Well, girlfriend, I guess this calls for my attention."

I got up and she jumped onto the back of my chair to get a clear view of whatever I might do. Carefully, I picked up the small desk and set it on the coffee table. Whatever Miss Una had found was situated between the drawer and the walls of the desk. I sat down on the sofa directly in front of my new writing surface. It was clear that the right drawer was out of alignment. I jiggled it slightly, thinking it would slide back into place. It did not.

Considering the amount of money I had paid for it, I did not want to mar the finish of the antique by forcing the wood with a sharp instrument. I opened the center drawer and eyed my tray of office miscellany. I then selected a slim plastic ruler to aid me. I inserted it below the drawer and eased it back and forth, while pulling gently on its knob. The drawer popped out after a couple of moments. I could now see what was preventing it from opening and closing properly. Gingerly, I slid the ruler into the space and carefully extracted a small, folded sheet of rice paper.

My latest find was an Asian scroll with calligraphy. Today's discovery was not classic, but it brought back memories of purchasing the mahogany desk in the living room. It was at a time when Ke'oni and I were searching for an antique jade artifact while investigating the murders of two men in China town. As I spread out the delicate sheet now in my hand, I saw a few lines of what I thought was Japanese text presented in superbly uniform brush strokes. It might not be an old piece, but it demonstrated the writer's pride in the quality of their work.

I noted slight creases that had been smoothed, as though the sheet had been thrown away and then retrieved from a waste can. I have seen similar pieces of classic Asian calligraphy. It has always made me feel guilty about my own poor penmanship. With the symmetry of the layout, I guessed this might be a mantra or chant. I was tempted to try and translate the text with the app on my phone, but I knew they often gave inaccurate results. I was glad that I would be able to ask Professor Horita to translate the text. He might even comment on the possible writer, if not the intended recipient of it. Our good lieutenant would be pleased to see this little item!

I quickly put my find into one of the clear archival sheet protectors Ke'oni keeps in his computer station for such moments just as he arrived from his errands. I set it on top of my lovely new desk, where it would remain until I was ready to share my discovery. Then it was time to shift gears. I went into the kitchen to prepare a light lunch as Ke'oni cleaned up. I mixed a salad of greens topped with sliced teriyaki chicken, heated a loaf of Italian bread, and set out a pitcher of Ke'oni's latest sun tea with fresh mint leaves.

As I was busy in the kitchen John arrived. It was lovely to be sharing our weekday leftovers with a friend like John. When these meetings occur on a golfing day, we serve as a staging point and sometimes a dressing room during a busy day. The latter is especially true now that Lori Mitchum has entered the picture. Largely due to her influence (or at least her inspiration), we are seeing a new man: better wardrobe; slimmer body; sleek appointments in his new condo. He even has a weekly housekeeper to maintain the premises for their occasional romantic rendezvous.

In a short while, our kitchen "cabinet" was assembled around Mom's old table. The simple meal I had prepared was quickly consumed and we were ready for work.

"I've got to confess there are no major developments in the case—or cases—depending on how you look at it. There are a lot of little pieces that I'm sure will come together eventually. Let's start with the few concrete things that have come to light.

"Alena's fingerprint hunting at the Kiyohara estate didn't yield many useful results. Throughout the property we found the expected fingerprints of family and staff. But some areas of the main house had too many layers to be clearly identifiable.

"There were also a lot of smudges that didn't yield enough markers to be identified in the guest house. The big news on that front is that there were a few partials that may be from a couple of Yakuza lieutenants known to frequent the Islands occasionally.

"Even if these prints can't be used in court, they show a pattern that indicates we're on the right track. Someone within the Kiyohara circle is definitely involved with criminal activity that extends beyond Hawai'i. Of course, we have to consider that those folks may not have anything to do with our investigation. But I'd say the embers are building to produce quite a fire.

"As to the re-examination of the autopsy of Minister Fujimoto, there's not a lot to report. Marty said that the gun that was used to kill her was unremarkable. It was probably a .38 Smith and Wesson Model 10 type revolver with a four-inch barrel. That was the typical service issue weapon for military, police, and anyone who liked to look official. That was also about the time a lot of public safety organizations were switching to Rugers. There were increasing numbers of S&Ws that entered the resale market, as public safety officers and the general public upgraded their weaponry.

"If we get our hands on the gun that actually killed her, there's a chance we'll get a serial number from which we can identify its history. Criminals think they'll be safe from prosecution if they file off a gun's serial number. But with today's chemical forensic analysis, we can often raise an image despite the perp's best efforts."

"How could a team of crooks—even acting without direction from a boss—be dumb enough to keep a weapon after committing a murder?" I queried.

John shrugged. "We've seen it all. The guy who actually committed the murder might have put the gun away for a long time. Years later he thinks he's safe and brings his little playmate back out for some new action."

"What else did you find? On the grounds of the estate? The main house? Or the guest cottage and tea house?" I asked.

"The Feds have the inventory list from the auctions and estate sale… and what looks like the rest of Nippon Antiquities' records. They are also questioning a few items that have come in from Japan and elsewhere."

"What about the dock? I didn't see anything while we were there. But if you can get some CSIs in for a look—say tomorrow when we're moving the *Marimu*—maybe something will emerge," suggested Ke'oni.

"That's a good idea. But, there's a lot of other things to be considered. As you know, several teams, including a few with local real estate accreditation went through the property during the sale. Nothing unusual came from that. Of course, some of the items put up for sale are being closely reviewed by our foreign cousins. They've indicated there are a couple of pieces that align with their lists of things that went missing in World War II—surprisingly in Europe.

"The big news of the day concerns your adventures with Alena at the guest cottage. The one thing we were looking for was a hint of where the Buddha has been. Your discovery of that altar table in the bedroom closet has paid off big time. The lab has compared the base of the statue with the outline of dust in Alena's photograph and they match!"

Ke'oni and I simultaneously shouted, "That's great!"

"In fact, I have to say the pictures Alena took were excellent. There are so many that it's going to take several days to process the contents of all of them."

Ke'oni nodded and asked, "What about the ones Nathan and I took?"

"Same thing. You guys were pretty thorough in your own image transmissions. But until we get our hands on the *Marimu* for a complete investigation, we can only guess what might be significant."

"I know you're right, JD. The story isn't finished. In some respects, it's barely begun. Who knows who or what will come to light? Maybe Nathan and I will find a packet of white powder beneath the floorboards of our little motorsailer."

"I'll admit I like the direction of that narrative," responded our favorite detective. "But without fingerprints or catching a deal going down, there's nothing we can take to the Prosecuting Attorney or a judge. Of course, something could show up during your little journey from the Kiyohara estate to the Kāneʻohe Yacht Club. That's one of the reasons I wanted to stop by today. We've put together a good team for that. You'll enjoy getting to know Captain Ibrahim Williams whose seafaring experience includes sailing single handed around the world. While Ibrahim is busy at the helm, his buddies will be making the most of the opportunity to scout out the boat. They'll be getting a general feel for her—measuring every part of the vessel as well as picking up whatever evidence they can. And before they start on the boat, they can follow up on your idea about the dock.

"Finally, we've been looking into Uncle Tommy Kiyohara and his elder brother, the family patriarch. Seems old Hitomu was a straight shooter. As to his son, he hasn't been in control long enough for us to have caught any whiff of malfeasance. Regarding the others, the conversation you overheard between the mysterious *haole* and Tommy fits with some tidbits that international bodies have collected over the years. But again, nothing actionable has been revealed. So, we just keep on keepin' on. By the way, I've been wondering if you ever ran across Tommy in the past."

"I've been going through some of my old case notes on the few antique heists I dealt with. I found a couple of references to Nippon Antiquities, but nothing on Tommy. I have a feeling that he has kept his distance from anything that might catch the attention of the authorities. Totally innocent staff members always handled day-to-day operations, and anything criminal was committed by select persons who have remained out of sight.

"That's about all the news from my end. Anything else occur to you two?"

CHAPTER 15

What has puzzled us before seems less mysterious,
and the crooked paths look straighter.
Jean Paul Richter [1763 - 1825]

I have a surprise for both of you since you didn't get here early, Ke'oni. As you know, I bought a few odds and ends at the estate sale. My prize from the day is a small laptop desk."

John looked curious. Ke'oni nodded slowly.

"Miss Una has again proven to be rather dexterous in discovering oddities on her own. This time she found a piece of rice paper that might prove to have some bearing on the case."

The men glanced at each other as I hurried out to the living room. When I returned, they were discussing the removal of the *Marimu* from the Kiyohara estate. I set my prized discovery on the table like a cat presenting a mouse.

"Great. A potential clue in a language I can't read," said the lieutenant. But from his broad smile, I knew he was happy to have something new to explore.

"I'm pretty sure it's *hiragana* Japanese," I observed. "That's a phonetic lettering system that's simpler than *kanji* which comes from Chinese characters. There's also *romaji*, which is Japanese written in Latin script, like English. That allows non-speakers of Japanese to take a stab at pronouncing it. That's how I could chant Buddhist prayers at the temple."

John moaned and looked pained. "And I thought *one* form of a foreign language was a challenge. Okay. We've got another hidden scrap of paper. Whatever you've just discovered, we need to get it translated before we'll know if it's related to the case."

I quickly responded. "Alena's father is the perfect one to perform the task. With his being a member of the temple and having knowledge of the stolen statue's history, he'll be able to do far more than merely translate it. He'll be able to explain how it might have been used in conversation if not ritually. I can scan the sheet and I'll give him a call this afternoon to get his email and send it to him."

"How about you scan it and I'll take the original off your hands. I can get the lab analyzing the paper, ink, and any fingerprints that may be on it. But as Keʻoni knows, we can't lose any more time. Paper is not a hard surface. This doesn't look like it was written yesterday. After seven or eight years, amino acids vaporize, degrading most evidence that might have been there.

"You can forget all the hoopla in crime scenes shown in films and on television. We probably couldn't lift a partial print without causing the water-based ink to flake off or run. On the positive side, if we manage to learn something that links it directly to the Kiyoharas, maybe someone in the family or their firm will open up about what they know."

"You know, JD, that brings up something I might be able to help with," said Keʻoni. "I know the official local, national, and international teams are looking into Nippon Antiquities. Maybe I can do a little unofficial nosing around. I can see if anyone in the community has any knowledge about the company's daily operations and employees. We could learn whether any of them have any connections to local gangs that interact with the Yakuza. There could be any number of details that don't appear in the public record."

"Good idea."

"And after I talk with Professor Horita, I'll do a bit more research on the interaction among Buddhist sects, JD—I mean John," I offered.

"No problem. If fact, I've been meaning to tell you to call me JD, too, Natalie."

"Well, I didn't want to be presumptive about your friendship, guys."

Keʻoni smiled and explained. "The reason for the nickname is that at one time there were a lot of Johns in the game—and I don't mean those with the ladies of the evening down on Hotel Street."

I ignored the direction of his joke and quickly scanned the rice paper clue through its protective sleeve. Before John left, he gave Keʻoni a note with the contact information for the three-man CSI team helping to move the *Marimu* the next day.

After checking in with the man, Keʻoni called Nathan to confirm their plans. I heard a hoot from the *lānai*, when my twin informed him that all of the financial details were in order and the boat was theirs. My men had secured their dream toy! I knew our lives would be evolving in more than one way. Soon Keʻoni's voice became a buzz punctuated by technical terms I did not recognize, so I turned to contacting Dr. Horita.

I was glad that the professor answered my call immediately. I was uncertain of the message I would have left if he had been unavailable. He soon verified his interest in my little project and gave me his email address. We then settled in for a comprehensive conversation about the case in general. I managed to avoid any mention of my visions and kept any discussion of my role in the affair minimal. I shifted topics as soon as I could.

I began by talking about the valuable suggestions Alena had made regarding improvements to Auntie Carrie's home. "Your daughter is very gifted. She's even mentioned ways in which we might enhance the *lānai* and yard."

"She doesn't have much free time now, but she loved to work in the garden with me when she was a young girl."

"Speaking of that, I have to tell you I really loved the pickled eggplant you brought to the buffet at the estate sale."

"That's a recipe from my wife's family. There's some secret ingredient one of her aunties passed to her. That's why she only makes it when there's no one at home."

"I think every family has its little secrets. It's a miracle if they only deal with food."

We laughed, and I moved back to our current project. "I have enjoyed visiting your temple for many years. Whether for a wedding, funeral, or a personal moment of meditation, the atmosphere has always been uplifting."

"That is something that unifies our visitors as well as our regular congregants. Sometimes I am amazed at the ease with which our ministers handle the many aspects of life at the temple."

"I assume that's why they enter the priesthood...to help people in every way they can."

"You are right, Natalie. I know I could not address the numerous tasks they perform with such ease."

"We all have unique talents. Look at how you help the police. I'm so grateful for your aiding me in the analysis of this short passage. It may add to our understanding the household in which the stolen Buddha is believed to have resided since its theft. Speaking of which, there's a question that has come up in discussions of the case. The statue that was stolen is of the *Shākyamuni* Buddha. But I've been told the altars of Jōdo shin temples usually have *Amida* Buddha. I thought there was just one Buddha, presented in different poses by artists from different cultures."

"Ah. I see your confusion. It is not the *pose* that is relevant. I think I mentioned that the *Shākyamuni* Buddha is the image of the *historic man*, Siddhartha Gautama who was the Nepalese sage who would *become* the Buddha. The *Amida* Buddha displays his image *after* he has become enlightened."

"So different sects of Buddhism are linked to different images of Buddhas. But that makes it even harder to understand why a *Tendai* temple in Japan would have sent your *Jōdo shin* temple such a gift."

"It may seem confusing, but all images of the Buddha are revered by Buddhists regardless of their school, what you call sect. I do not know the details of the gift of the statue that was stolen, but most temples have multiple statues of Buddhas and *Bodhisattvas*, what you might call saints."

With that summary philosophical lesson, we concluded our visit and I emailed the text that I needed to have translated. I then returned to outlining research topics for the event at ʻIolani Palace. Primarily, I needed to know the backgrounds and specialties of each of the chefs to be honored. Samantha could easily check the public records for their basic bios. To understand their unique skills and teaching methodologies, I would conduct brief phone interviews with other staff at Kapiʻolani Community College. I could also rely on those sources to coordinate our menu.

Knowing the next day would prove challenging in many ways, I checked in with Keʻoni about dinner. Our lunch had been light, so I thought we could splurge with some specialties from Whole Foods Market and Kalapawai Café. The first would supply two roasted chickens from which there would be wonderful leftovers. An Italian salad minus the olives would be great from the second.

The next morning began very early. The alarm rang at an excruciating 3:30 a.m. While Keʻoni showered, I fixed pre-cooked waffles and sausage links that would provide a good foundation for Keʻoni and Nathan's strenuous day. Just the smell of the heavy meal at such an early hour was a bit much for me.

I handed Keʻoni a cup of strong coffee when he arrived in the kitchen. "Did you start work this early when you went on surveillance assignments and undercover?"

"More likely, this is when I'd be getting off such duty," he responded. "It wasn't that hard. You learn to sleep and eat when you can. It's not something I miss about the job. Of course, today is special. Not only do I get to follow up on my last unsolved crime, but Nathan and I are entering a whole new phase of recreation...and exercise."

"What do you mean by exercise? It isn't as if you're going to sail around the world in some itty-bitty sailboat by yourself."

"You have no idea what it takes to put a vessel to sea, with or without a motor. And the *Marimu* has both a motor and sails. If you'd like to join us, you'll quickly discover just how much goes into those little nautical jaunts from point A to point B."

"Thanks for the offer. I think I'll continue to pass on that form of adventure. But I will keep my promise to join you for happy hour at the end of some of those days."

"Speaking of which, we don't know just how long this day is going to be. What's on your agenda?"

"There's no way you're going to be through before noon. I thought I'd do a bit of research and confer with Samantha about the background work I'd like her to do on the Kapiʻolani Chefs. She's really becoming a great asset."

"Yes. She's going to be very beneficial with Nathan and me wanting to spend some quality time with the boat. I'm looking forward to setting Samantha up as my backup receptionist. I think I'll have her update my client and financial records whenever she can take time from her studies."

"That sounds like a good plan. How nice that we can trade her services between us...depending on who's facing a deadline."

"You know, Natalie, there's one little item on our personal schedule that may have to be delayed for a while."

"I know where you're going with that...a trip to Japan. I have a feeling Stan Carrington is going to be taking in the next Sapporo Ice Festival without our scintillating company."

"Maybe by the time we're able to join him, he and Tamiko will have tied the knot. I just hope they'll get married here so we can welcome her to the HPD alum family."

At that point, I heard the doorbell chime and a moment later Nathan walked in escorted by Miss Una.

"I see our feline pal is undisturbed by the likely scent of your canine companion," said Ke'oni with a chuckle.

"Hey, I'm a loveable guy," retorted Nathan.

While the men enjoyed the end of the pressed coffee with their meal, I prepared one cooler with a variety of sandwiches. In another, I put several whole fruits and a container of vegetable sticks. A small duffle bag held almonds, macadamia nuts, and a variety of chips. There was no need to bother with beverages, as each of the men was supposed to bring his preferred drinks. Nevertheless, for good measure, I tossed in a few cans of orange passion fruit juice.

As I puttered around, I caught snatches of their conversation. They had plans to take their new boat beyond the waters surrounding O'ahu and had elected to join the Kāne'ohe Yacht Club...with memberships as Seniors. They were already anticipating Sunday brunches, games of cribbage, and regular stops at the bar for both food and drink. I also heard reference to KYC being the state's oldest continuously operating yacht club. I could not decipher the finer details of their boat safety certification—or the procedure if their vessel were ever stopped by a State of Hawai'i law enforcement officer.

Within a few minutes my favorite men were off to set sail. All I had to do was pick them up once the boat had arrived at its new home. Until then, I had several free hours since it was unlikely that they would call me before late afternoon. I chose to use part of the time for a leisurely walk along our beautiful white sands beach. Miss Una had departed for destinations unknown, so I strolled alone in my search for shells and coral.

Upon my return, I decided to prolong my laziness with a soak in the hot tub. I threw on an old swimsuit and pinned up my hair. With a fresh bowl of water for any cats who might appear, I was ready to settle down for a while. I positioned my spa pillow behind my head and began taking measured breaths in alternate nostrils. The practice is calming and simultaneously energizing and about the only activity that I retained from the yoga classes I have abandoned since moving to the cottage.

Within a few minutes, Miss Una and little 'Ilima showed up. Although she was the titular mentor of her young companion, Miss Una followed the kitten across the *lānai* and up onto the towels stacked behind me. They remained perched there despite the occasional water spray that found its way onto their fur. Eventually they realized my interpretation of water therapy was not very exciting and turned to intensely grooming each other. Soon the movement of the water worked its magic and I fell into a peaceful sleep for a while. Then I slipped again into something darker.

Again, I face the altar of the Buddhist temple I have come to know more intimately than I desire. Unlike the most recent vision, this is not an expansion of details of the death of Minister Fujimoto. Rather it is a return to the initial one—presenting a surreal interpretation of the real temple. Again, I see myriad sacred statues of Asian deities sitting on pedestals from varied types of architecture. They are both fluted and smooth. Some are covered in Egyptian hieroglyphs, Celtic symbols, or Viking runes.

A tinkling of bells and the intonation of "OM" pull me deeper into my experience of the vision. When I open my eyes within the vision, the statues have disappeared, and a large screen has been lowered in front of the altar. I tour ancient temples and megalithic structures from across the world in rapid succession. The last is a stone altar I recognize from an ancient Hawaiian heiau in Kāne'ohe.

In another moment, I am floating above the temple compound. I see that the front parking lot is crowded with senior citizens of many backgrounds. They are moving toward two tour buses, following one another like lines of school children in my youth. Soon they depart, turning right onto the Pali Highway toward Windward O'ahu.

My chest reverberates as a Bonshō bell sounds. I am sitting in lotus position on a cloud over the temple. The layout of the grounds below is quite symmetrical. Although I am out of doors, I hear the sound of OM chanted by many voices in harmonic tones and smell a rich blend of incense.

At the back of the temple is another parking lot. Between that and the street beyond, is a narrow strip of garden with fragrant flowering plants. Among them walks a petite gray-haired woman with a small dog on a leash. Eventually she takes a seat on one of four circular stone benches facing a sundial.

The scene shifts again. I am even higher in the sky. To my left is old Fort Ruger. On my right is distinctive Diamond Head. Such a beautiful and tranquil scene. Abruptly, I am pulled from my reverie by the sound of brakes applied by a speeding car. I look down and see the elderly woman who was walking in the Temple's garden. She is clearly shaken and dazed, standing in the street that features mostly homes. I watch as the driver's side door of a dark brown sedan opens. A tall man steps out. I do not hear him speak but know that he is soothing the woman as he takes her arm and escorts her and her dog to the curb.

Reopening his car door, I watch him slide back into his seat and pull his left leg inside. I see gray slacks and black shoes with tassels. I do not see the soles, but somehow know they are the soft composites that Ke'oni and many police officers wear. The car speeds away before I think to look at the license plate. But the blurred image of the back plate reminds me of those at the time of the crimes we are investigating.

I feel a light touch on my head and hear a soft mewing in my ear. Pulling myself back from scenes of an unrecorded past, I am surprised by the nuzzling of my beloved feline friend. It appears that she is becoming accustomed to water—at least when one of her humans is near. It would be nice to have her beside me whenever I experience a vision. I am glad to easily return to my own life and time. But I wish I had seen more of the scenario that had evaporated.

It seems as if the closer I get to the perpetrators of the crimes in the Buddhist temple, the more gaps I find in the crime story and its timeline. Maybe I need to re-examine the famous Ws of Who, What, When, Where, and most importantly, Why. The When and Where are clear, for both the date and place of the joint crimes are fixed.

As to the *Who*, the victim is clearly identified. The number of perpetrators appears to be at least three—the two criminals I saw in the temple, plus Tommy Kiyohara. But who instigated the theft? Tommy? I do not think the men in the temple were Japanese...or Buddhist. That means their only connection to Tommy or any other members of his family must be financial. In other words, they were merely the hands by which the evil deeds were done.

And the *What*? There are really two matters under consideration. The most important is the murder. But it does not stand alone. The killing of the minister happened during the commission of grand larceny. I simply cannot believe that the wonderful woman I had initially known as Ayameko Fujimoto was targeted for murder. Surely, she was an unfortunate consequence. There is also the matter of time. The occurrence of the crimes might be defined, but there are the subsequent years to consider. I am certain the Buddha was concealed in the bedroom closet of the Kiyohara estate guest house for a significant period. But there is no indication of when it was installed. If it was not immediately following the theft, where had it been kept? By whom? Had such a person, or persons, committed secondary crimes during their possession of it?

One or more people may have felt blessed by their access to the statue. Again, I question how anyone could feel that the proximity of a sacred artifact compensated for the high crime of murder. That simply did not fit the profile of a religious person.

I have seen displays of sacred relics from several religions during my worldly travels. Regardless of whether the featured pieces were modern or ancient, I found the reverence they engendered to be genuine. It was the powerful belief of many attendees that was awe inspiring to me.

Surely anyone who had revered the statue of the *Shākyamuni* Buddha through the successive years could not have known its origins. In all probability, he, she, or they, had simply performed their devotional acts believing they were progressing in their spiritual journey. Who within the Kiyohara family or the auction house was likely to have sought the treasured statue, or benefitted from someone else's acquisition of it?

There did not appear to be any women in the Kiyohara family or Nippon Antiquities who were likely candidates. Hitomu Kiyohara, the patriarch, had been a widower for many years. His son Koji had been born late in his life. That man did not display any signs of either criminality or religiosity. The life and demeanor of Hitomo's younger brother Tommy—or Yasuhiro, which is his given Japanese name—appeared at odds with a devotee of any religious belief.

Who was left? Why not start with the patriarch himself? We knew little about the newly deceased leader of the Kiyohara family. But since he was prominent in the art and antiques markets of both the Hawaiian Islands and Japan, there should be a lot of information about him on the internet. I might not speak or read Japanese, but I knew who could assist me with publications in Japan. In fact, Professor Horita may already have knowledge of the man, wholly unconnected to the crime we are studying.

As to the *Why*? I had a feeling that that would remain unknown until the case was solved...and there was no indication of how long the duration of the investigation would be. Well, at least I had narrowed the focus of my next inquiries to Hitomu Kiyohara.

As I looked across the yard, I caught sight of two tails dashing toward The Ladies cottage. It was likely that Izzy was offering something more tempting than a bowl of water. At the moment I needed to shower and prepare for whatever else the day might bring. Soon I was dressed and enjoying a cup of tea and bagel with *lehua* honey from the Big Island. I just hoped it would sustain me until Nathan and Ke'oni were ready for dinner—or cocktails with heavy *pūpūs*.

Contemplating my options, I decided I should survey the yacht club's menu which might be available online. Perhaps my twin had sent me a mental note because I had barely pulled up the club's website when Nathan called to announce that my services as a chauffeur were needed. I could tell he was surrounded by a number of people. I inquired about the agenda for the evening, and he quietly emphasized that the *captain* and *his crew* were being picked up separately. That alerted me that the CSI team was on the move...perhaps with coolers of evidence rather than leftovers from lunch.

I made a quick call to ask The Ladies to keep watch over Miss Una. Then I hopped in my car and began the relatively short trip to the Kāneʻohe Yacht Club. It was earlier than I had expected to be summoned. The weather was so lovely that I rolled the windows down to enjoy fresh instead of processed air.

Nathan had provided minimal information. I wondered if we would be enjoying a simple libation, or a meal before heading to his home. I met Nathan at the club's bar as he had requested. He was waiting for Keʻoni to finish his farewell to their *crew*. His phrasing conveyed the idea that the men were probably transporting the evidence they had gathered to a lab for testing. My twin also announced they wanted to celebrate their first day at sea with a round of drinks. Knowing we'd be there for a while, I went to the ladies room to comb my windblown hair.

I returned to find that Nathan had gone back to the yacht for something he'd forgotten. As usual Keʻoni was happily chatting with the bartender. From their conversation, I realized the man was a retired sheriff from Maui. A few years earlier he had worked at the Moana Hotel in Waikīkī where he was accustomed to pouring my sweetheart's favorite faux cocktail, a virgin tonic with two slices of lime. He was clearly delighted that today's order was for two tall gin and tonics for the men in addition to my call for a glass of Chardonnay.

As Keʻoni handed me my wine I informed him of the vision I had while soaking in the hot tub. Since Nathan was absent I was able to reveal to Keʻoni that I had seen a dark brown vehicle nearly strike an elderly woman walking her dog, then speed away. I had to cut my explanation short as Nathan returned carrying the Aloha shirt Adriana had given him.

There was a surprising lack of discussion of the day's events beyond cursory remarks on moving the *Marimu* to her new home. The men seemed more interested in teasing me. I rose to the occasion and was on my best behavior. I feigned curiosity about their new hobby... until they asked if I would like to check out the boat in her new slip.

Keʻoni cajoled me by saying, "Honey, we won't be going to sea. You only have to step over one side of the boat."

"That's what you say. But you know that old Finnish proverb, 'The water is the same on both sides of the boat...'"

CHAPTER 16

Tis an ill cook that cannot lick his own fingers.
William Shakespeare [1564 – 1616]

I volunteered to be a true chauffeur that afternoon since I had been relaxing most of the day. As we approached Nathan's driveway, I could hear him softly snoring in the back seat. Ke'oni roused Nathan who shuffled into the kitchen where we found Kūlia lying in his woven basket. He must have had a good time with Adriana because he barely raised his head. For a moment, I felt guilty that again we would be late in returning to Miss Una. At least I knew she was happy romping with 'Ilima and enjoying delicacies from Izzy's kitchen.

Adriana was enjoying a monthly evening out with girlfriends. She had left a fresh baguette of French bread and a local whipped butter on the counter. When I opened the refrigerator, I found a beautiful salad of mixed fruit from the yard. There was also a platter of chicken thighs and drumsticks in my parents' go-to dry rub of kosher salt, cayenne pepper, garlic and onion powders, cumin, brown sugar, and a kick of smoked paprika.

Our households were becoming intertwined because of planned seagoing activities. Fortunately, Ke'oni had been accumulating double sets of tools and Nathan had outfitted the captain's desk aboard the *Marimu*. The men are not perfect clones size-wise, so I had brought a suitcase with wardrobe changes for Ke'oni. We would refill it with items from Nathan's closet to store at our house.

It was good that Nathan's new solar water heating system provided the renovated guest bathroom with an abundance of hot water. While both of my men cleaned up from the rigors of their day, I laid out beer and Maui potato chips. As we visited, I soon realized that Nathan and Ke'oni were not being overly polite in avoiding nautical topics. They were simply tired of the subject after so many hours of being immersed in it. With lagers in their hands and a glass of Pinot Grigio in mine, we sat on the ocean-facing *lānai* watching the changing sky as the chicken slowly cooked on the barbecue.

In response to my look of inquiry, Ke'oni said, "There's not a lot to report. The journey was pretty straight forward..."

"Except for the excitement of some rough water between Makapuʻu Point and Waimānalo," cut in Nathan.

"It wasn't that bad," responded Keʻoni. "Except for a little surge, it was pretty much like we'd been told might happen."

"Now that really gives this girl a lot of confidence about this new phase of play time for you guys," I observed. "Maybe you'll take today as a sign that small boats should remain near land."

"I'll have you know that the *Marimu* has actually traversed the Pacific Ocean. We saw it in the Captains' logs," retorted Keʻoni.

"I hope that's not something you plan on repeating," I said fervently. My comment went unanswered.

The darkening evening was particularly beautiful, with cirrus clouds across the sky.

"Looks like there might be rain tomorrow," observed Nathan.

Keʻoni laughed, "maybe that's just as well. My ankle is telling me I've been on my feet too long today. But I think I'll be getting a bit of rest since our *crew* will be initiating a few rounds of lab tests for the next couple of days."

"I take it that means they wouldn't want you two contaminating the boat in the meantime?"

"You nailed that, Natalie," replied Keʻoni waving a raised spatula. "We'd love to be launching our new *hobby*, as you call it. But I doubt that will happen immediately."

In a few minutes we were seated at the table. The rub for the chicken had worked its magic and we enjoyed a sumptuous dinner. With the scent of roasting fowl in the air, Kūlia roused himself for a few tasty bites on top of his kibble—minus the skin and seasoning.

"For the most part, it *was* an easy trip," commented Nathan to calm my fears. "And the techs got everything they needed...and more."

The investigation of the *Marimu* was one area of interest to all of us. "What did they do?" I asked.

"Well, they had begun their work even before we put to sea by taking photos of the boat," said Keʻoni. "They were very subtle about it. They took the general shots any tourist might take. That included a video of the Kiyohara estate. Who knows what *that* will reveal?"

"And they shot some from the boat to the shore," continued Nathan. "I think that we should frame some of them. They'll make great additions to both of our art collections."

"They're quite a team. One of the CSIs—Akita Okumura—is with HPD. He's a deep-sea diver and an award-winning photographer," Keʻoni explained. "Joe Swan is an evidence specialist with the CIA. Along with Captain Ibrahim Williams of the Coast Guard, all three of them have considerable seafaring experience.

"While we were at sea, Akita and Joe continued their work while'Keʻoni and I remained at the helm with Captain Williams. You'd be amazed at how thorough the examination of the boat was. They shot every space they could access. Periodically they sprayed luminal, but there was no sign of blood. At the end, they announced they didn't find any obvious signs of substances of questionable natures...of course, you never know what the lab tests might reveal.

"Samples of water from the bilges, plus the holding and freshwater tanks, were collected. That was in case someone flushed drugs or something else down the toilet. There were also a number of bags of who knows what vacuumed from the floors and several surfaces.

With a broad grin, Nathan announced, "The big news of the day emerged when the guys were examining the owners' cabin. A hidden compartment materialized behind the detailed paneling that serves as a headboard behind the bed.

"It wasn't obvious because there was a classic bas-relief of an intertwined Phoenix and Dragon...representing the female *yīn* and masculine *yáng*," explained Ke'oni. "It was really intricate. Joe was tracing the pattern with his finger when I called out to see if he was ready for lunch. Startled, he leaned against the wall to get his footing and the panel popped open to reveal a narrow space. Joe said it would be the ideal location for art, jewelry, gems, gold..."

"Or drugs," chimed in Nathan.

"Ooh that sounds exciting. What's next?" I asked.

"Even though there was no *gotcha moment*, the team took away quite a few samples. It's going to take them several days to organize everything and run preliminary tests.

"The bottom line is that we won't be putting to sea for any fishing or other recreational boating for a while," my twin said rather sadly.

"Well, you knew this purchase was part of an investigation from the start. You'll have the rest of your lives to indulge in your new hobby," I rejoined. "What about the bottom of the boat?"

"You mean below the waterline?" asked Nathan.

I nodded.

"A survey had already been done before we closed the sale," said Ke'oni. "When we arrived at a calm area about two thirds of the way, Akita went over the side for a look below the waterline. He didn't find anything unusual. Just the expected fasteners for sonar and other sensing devices like a diving platform...OR, something more nefarious."

Nathan added, "The captain asked if I would bring Kūlia the next time we have an outing. He said they'd be bringing a sniffer dog to check for explosive residue or drugs. It will look more natural if there are a couple of man's best friends."

"But what if they don't like each other...get in a fight?" I wondered aloud.

"Kūlia?" asked Nathan. "When has he ever picked a fight? He's not aggressive, just misunderstood sometimes."

"You mean like when he and Miss Una were getting acquainted?" Ke'oni remembered with a chuckle.

The image of Miss Una declaring supremacy in her territory brought smiles to all of us.

"Besides that, a sniffer dog is trained to only respond to the commands of his handler," said Ke'oni, dismissing the subject.

"To sum up," I began, "The HPD lab is working on the samples from the boat. The multiple task forces are doing their research and cross-referencing everything past and present. Meanwhile, Dr. Horita is analyzing my latest find. The bottom line is that we're all stuck at anchor unless I have another vision, or someone in authority notifies us otherwise."

The men nodded, and we all sat back to watch the sky become a display of stars against a velvet black background. It was such a beautiful night that I suggested that Ke'oni and I should camp out on our bedroom *lānai* when we returned home. But clouds were streaking across the sky by the time we pulled into the driveway. We concurred that it was too much work to blow up an air mattress and opted for a comfortable night's rest in our bed.

The next morning, Ke'oni began his day by repositioning the equipment he had taken on board the *Marimu*. He and Nathan would be leaving very few things on the boat until they were informed that they could consider the motorsailer wholly theirs. Their next visit to their new acquisition might be to provide access to additional specialists who needed to examine her.

It was clear that he would be busy for the time being. I decided to take Miss Una for a short stroll to the beach. She concurred with my idea for once. We sat for a while, watching a mixture of elders taking their constitutional walks and young mothers introducing their offspring to the joys of sand and surf.

"When my dear, are you going to familiarize your bitty buddy with this activity? Don't you think 'Ilima would enjoy our outings?"

She graced me with a twitch of her ear at the name of her friend and continued observing her surroundings, in case something untoward invaded her space. Luckily, there were no dogs—large or small—to incite her to fight or flight. She remained by my side until I decided to resume our walk.

When I returned from my brief sojourn, I found a message from my contact in the culinary program of Kapi'olani Community College. Evidently the health of one of the chefs to be highlighted in my article had received a disappointing verdict from his physician. The upshot was that if I wanted to feature him, we had to schedule our attendance of the Friday 'Iolani Palace concert immediately.

I was glad that the research on the chefs was complete. Samantha had given me a summation of her review of past college brochures, menus, and recipes. There was no way of knowing how the space in a publication like *Windward Oʻahu Journeys* would be allocated. The piece I was writing could be held if there were no immediate space available... or shortened to accommodate everything else that had to go into an edition. But when I checked in with my publisher, I was assured there would be ample room in the next issue. I could even have the immediate services of chief photographer Andy Berger.

Kapiʻolani Community College students were in charge of menus for the Chefs: tempera battered chicken fingers kissed with fresh tarragon, yakitori beef skewers with grilled pearl onions, and a kimchee inspired coleslaw. There will also be sweet Hawaiian rolls from King's Bakery, tea infused with raspberry lemonade, or Holsten alcohol-free Pilsner, and finally, miniature malasadas." The school was responsible for contacting the chefs—and arranging their transportation. I would address the challenge of involving our local media. The stars were again aligned. I was able to schedule both a reporter from the *Honolulu Star-Advertiser* and a newscaster from KGMB TV to interview the chefs at this Friday's concert. Thank heavens for careful planning and having good relations with media outlets, including competitors in today's tight magazine market!

I had everything set for Friday by the time Keʻoni and I met in the kitchen for lunch. He was free to attend the concert with me. Samantha would join our team as my Gal Friday for any problems that might arise. Attending school had really boosted her organizational skills, and she had a satchel full of office and electronic tools to meet the needs of any public event.

With an empty nautical calendar for the foreseeable future, Keʻoni was continuing with diverse projects. The first was sorting a large stack of photos and then placing them in archival quality albums.

"I haven't been able to face the images from my birthday party," he stated. "You worked so hard to give me the perfect celebration. But that was the night Miriam died and I just haven't been in the mood to look at the pictures of the event."

"I know, honey. It seems almost disrespectful of us to think of that occasion with much joy. But it was an event she really enjoyed. I'm sure she would want us to remember her greeting everyone dressed in that pretty *muʻumuʻu.*"

I returned to a much-needed round of re-organization of my desk and background files for upcoming assignments. When I was through, I joined Keʻoni in the living room, where I found him continuing to sort pictures under the watchful eye of Miss Una who was sitting on the arm of the sofa.

"This looks like more than your birthday pics," I observed.

"You're right. I didn't realize it, but I never got around to dealing with the ones from my retirement party. Look, here *you* are. At the punchbowl with John Dias. Remember?"

"I was surprised when you invited me. Although we'd known each other for a while, Except for some research I needed your help on, we weren't all that chummy. I don't even remember John, or anyone besides you from that night."

I sat down. He then shared more photos and stories about his colleagues. Many pictures showed HPD officers and members of other public safety organizations—and even a couple of politicians. I doubted that I would remember many of the details except for the few men I had invited to his birthday bash.

Neither of us have children, but it is possible that someone might appreciate seeing such images in the future. By the time we pass on, there is no telling where some of these people might have ended their careers. I could imagine Brianna looking through these albums and contacting relatives who might appreciate learning about their loved one's past activities.

At sunset, I raided the freezer and defrosted a package of fettucine Alfredo and a bag of chicken thighs Ke'oni had grilled a couple of weeks earlier. I chopped a sweet Maui onion and the meat and stirred the relatively uniform pieces into the fettucine. The microwave would perform the rest of the cooking. With a few slices of tomatoes from Joanne's garden on the side, we had a great mid-week meal!

I did not experience any visions that night but could not stay asleep for more than an hour at a time. Rather than bother Ke'oni with my restless movements, I got up and went into the living room. I was hoping to fall asleep in my favorite wingback recliner. However, Miss Una's interpretation of house beautiful halted that idea. Her preferred taste in paper normally ranges from the edge of lined yellow pads to expensive linen stationery. On this evening she had decided to play among the carefully segregated stacks of Ke'oni's pictures. The little rascal was nowhere in sight, so I could not express my displeasure to her personally.

I tried to segregate the images as Ke'oni had. The only ones I recognized were of the celebration of his birthday. Although it was obvious that some had been taken at his retirement, others portrayed men and women whose relationships to Ke'oni was not easily ascertained. Not even their wardrobes indicated the dates of the photos as there were no major shifts in the style of the Hawaiian shirts and dresses shown. But it was clear that some people had considerable flair in their selection of shoes and accessories.

After a while, I was tired enough to return to bed. We arrived at Friday in a blink, with the eager support of our corner of the world. Even The Ladies had been excited to plan another outing. Although Joanne declares her amateur status as a photographer, she would be snapping a couple of shots that would be contenders to accompany the text of my article. Izzy was bringing her niece's children and Larry and Lulu Smith were joining them as well.

Ke'oni, Nathan, and I arrived at 'Iolani Palace early to ensure everything had been arranged as I planned. A representative of the Royal Hawaiian Band had already set up folding chairs in an area assigned to the former chefs and their companions. There was also space for attendees in wheelchairs. The designated section was to the side of the bandstand to ensure good viewing by the general audience. As we did not want to tire our star guests, we had scheduled their arrival for as late as possible.

Ke'oni and I spread out a couple of large blankets for those of us who could sit on the ground. As expected, Izzy brought snacks for everyone and Nathan arrived with a cooler of assorted beverages for anyone who might be thirsty before our catered meals arrived.

"I can't believe how many people are here today," I said. "It feels like Lei Day or King Kamehameha Day." I could not help wondering if the killers of Reverend Fujimoto might be in the park.

I patted Keoni's hand and moved to welcome the chefs with what I hoped was a sincere smile. The men in my recent visions had been going about their normal lives for many years. Had they been married at the time of their heinous crimes and returned home to kiss their wives and play with their children? Had they been reciting prayers of peace and harmony at religious services while burying their horrid deeds within their hearts?

Those men were not Japanese. But not all attendees of services in a Buddhist temple are Japanese, or even Buddhist. And what about Tommy Kiyohara? How involved had he been in the crimes of grand theft... and murder? Had he ordered the theft of the *Shākyamuni* Buddha? How could he look at the men who had murdered the gentle minister and claim to be a devout seeker of spiritual purity? Most of all, how could a follower of any representation of Buddhism knowingly look at the stolen statue and chant sincere words of devotion?

Just then, a child's balloon burst, sounding almost like a gun. I flinched and nervously looked around. Ke'oni took my hand and turned my face toward him, as we shared a moment of unwelcome memories of violence we had each experienced during our working years.

I pulled my thoughts back to the park and patted Ke'oni's hand before moving to welcome the chefs with what I hoped was a sincere smile. Addressing several of our guests, I said, "You're all getting boxed lunches—but have no fear. They feature some of your favorite recipes.

Our guests smiled broadly. In the past, my writing assignments seldom included benefits for friends or family. That makes my new column especially enjoyable for all of us. I slipped Nathan into my party for this event, and he enjoined sampling everything that would be mentioned in my article. The food was delectable, and we enjoyed watching it being delivered with love by Kapi'olani culinary students who were pleased to serve their mentors.

The setting was ideal, with a leafy canopy above us to filter the hot rays of the sun. Who needs a formal dining room when you can sit under banyan trees surrounded by the laughter of caring people bonded by the pleasure of consuming such a feast? I just tried to forget about the recurring infestation of termites that threatens to shorten the lives of the trees.

I surveyed the happy faces of the people who filled the grounds of 'Iolani Palace and declared the day a success. The photos that had been taken previously of the Palace as well as from the kitchens at Kapi'olani Community College were beautiful. Being gifted at shooting bodies in motion, I was certain that Andy Berger's images of band members, the general audience, and our featured emeritus educators would be equally stunning. And there was no telling what Joanne might contribute to the cause. With varied subjects in both text and images, there should be something for every reader.

I could already envision the positive response the column would bring. I wondered if future pieces should include surveys for post-article analysis of increases in patronage at the venues I cover. We might also insert side bars with recipes. For this piece, we could offer a basic cupcake recipe, one for the vegetable vinaigrette, and another for the yakitori sauce. Surely this would invite a little snipping of pages to be added to our readers' own recipe collections.

I glanced over at a blanket where several generations of a Japanese family were eating classic barbecue dishes from bento boxes. The apparent father of two young girls looked familiar. He turned to engage an elderly man who looked deep in thought.

"I know you are still deeply saddened by the loss of your friend, grandfather. But Hitomu would want you to enjoy the music and your grandchildren today."

"You are right. He would have enjoyed this concert very much. It was one of the few things he could still appreciate," he said.

Did I just hear the name *Hitomu*? It's not that common a name in the Islands, perhaps not even in Japan.

"It was so sad to walk through his home and see all of his treasures being dispersed to people who could have no appreciation for the years it took him to gather such beauty. Even with his eyesight nearly gone, he could still enjoy the textures beneath his fingers."

The younger man passed his elder a plate of what looked like sliced mango. "He had lived so long in near darkness. I still don't understand why he took such a trip."

"He told his relatives that he had not visited the temple on Mt. Hiei for some time. And remember, he did not travel alone. His granddaughter and her husband accompanied him. They have assured me that he had days of great pleasure in that journey to his homeland. He died where and how he wished."

If only I had my recorder with me! Unfortunately, I had passed it to our guests of honor so they could record their reflections on the day.

The concert was especially appropriate to our theme of honoring our elders. It was comprised of classic Hawaiian music written by *Na Lani 'Ehā*, the Royal Four: King Kalākaua, Princess Likelike, Prince Leleiohoku, and Queen Lili'uokalani. The performance began with the state song "Hawai'i Pono'ī" with lyrics written by King Kalākaua, known as the Merry Monarch. The program concluded, as always, with the beloved piece, "Aloha 'Oe" composed by Queen Lili'uokalani, the last reigning monarch of the Kingdom of Hawai'i.

I caught a wholly unexpected sight as I focused on the conclusion of the successful affair. It was of Tommy Kiyohara standing beyond the bandstand facing toward the Hawai'i Archives. He was speaking to someone behind a banyan tree, so I could not tell who it was. However, the man's right hand was resting on the tree trunk and I could see that his skin tone was lighter than Tommy's. I also noticed that he was wearing a ring. It had a blue stone, like the perpetrator I envisioned in the temple. And there was something that sparkled at the top. Unfortunately, the KGMB newscaster approached me to verify which chef he was to interview. By the time I looked back, both Tommy Kiyohara and his mystery companion had departed for parts unknown. If only I had gotten a better look at the ring!

Being on the man's right hand, I could assume that the ring was not indicative of marriage. That suggested the jewelry might be linked to a school or sports team. Class and championship rings are very important in Hawai'i. For although conviviality among rivals is a universal aspect of life in the Islands, school loyalty is of paramount importance. Even if I could not identify the man, learning his *alma mater* and approximate age could narrow the field of suspects.

Therefore, it would be helpful if the ring I had seen commemorated a sports championship. While there are a lot of high schools in the islands, it is likely that a person who is no longer young might feel a greater sense of pride in an event from his college days. As I thought about it, wearing such a ring fits in with the quality dress shoes and slacks that I had seen. They clearly spoke to the man's sense of style and pride in what he wore!

I looked at the phone in my lap with its camera. Had I not been seated, I would have sprinted across the lawn to try taking a picture of the man with whom Tommy had just had a semi-private tête-à-tête. I've come so close to seeing his face in both visions and real time. In my mind, this was the most important piece in the puzzle of who killed Minister Fujimoto and stole the Buddha. But was this the countenance of an underling? Or was it the face of a kingpin of crime who had authorized the theft and overlooked the murder?

There are several groups of men in the case under investigation. Two or three men (not Japanese and presumably not practitioners of Buddhism) were directly involved in the killing of a Buddhist minister while stealing a valuable antique sacred statue. Then there is the Kiyohara family that operates an antiquities and auction business in both the U. S. and Japan. And there are the two men I have observed at both the Kiyohara family's estate and the concert at 'Iolani Palace. A single man is connected to these two locales. Tommy Kiyohara. While he is not one of the two men who committed the murder, nor likely to have been the potential driver of the getaway vehicle, he is part of the Kiyohara family. And he is one of two men I have observed at both his family's estate and the palace.

Was the same man involved in both of my sightings of Tommy? If so, was he directly involved in the Temple crimes? Is he connected to Nippon Antiquities? Is this mystery man the one I overheard talking secretively with Tommy in the guest cottage on the Kiyohara family estate? It is just too bad that I missed getting a clear view of this man with whom I believe Tommy rendezvous regularly. I am convinced of it.

At least I could take satisfaction in having verified a few facts today. The man I have observed is a *haole* with light skin tone. That means he must not be out of doors very often. I did not notice any wrinkles, so he could not be as old as Tommy. The most important find is that he does wear a distinctive silver-colored ring...on his right hand. And that ring has a blue stone and silver lettering at the bottom of a design that is carved into the stone.

CHAPTER 17

*Could a greater miracle take place than for us
to look through each other's eyes for an instant?*
The Tao Te Ching, Chapter 54 [Third Century BCE]

My work at the Palace was finished. There was no way I could go back in time and run to the tree and wrestle Tommy and his companion to the ground. It was time to get home to organize my notes before watching televised news reports of the successful event I should be celebrating. Of course, there was no guarantee that all of the interviews with the chefs would be featured that night. The Ladies had volunteered to set up recordings of news programs before they departed to attend the post-picnic dinner at the Ka 'Ikena Restaurant on Diamond Head. That occasion had been hastily scheduled as a scholarship fundraiser for the culinary program at Kapi'olani Community College. I was hoping it would provide a variety of potential quotes for my article and that Joanne might get a few more pictures of the elderly chefs being honored that evening.

I provided Ke'oni with a brief summary of my missed appointment with destiny, but we did not have much time to discuss it since we had arranged a potluck with Nathan and Adriana. We were all disappointed that his sweetheart could not join us for the concert, but she had had to vaccinate a number of residents at the Hale Malolo Shelter. By the time she and Nathan arrived at White Sands Cottage, Ke'oni and I had picked up the odds and ends that had spread across the house during our preparations that morning. I was glad our culinary efforts were minimal since our guests were providing pork ribs. They also brought a couple of chilled bottles of Korbel Natural Champagne to celebrate my first major public event since retiring from the world of leisure and travel.

While Ke'oni and Nathan checked the status of the recordings we had set in the living room and office, Adriana and I monitored the small TV in the kitchen. In between news items we organized supper. We began by starting the rice cooker and heating the foil-wrapped ribs in the oven at low temperature. Next, we prepared a variety of fresh vegetables crudités to serve with fresh ranch dressing from the Kalapawai Market. Finally, we filled a *koa* tray with an assortment of nuts, crackers, and cheese, plus another with a bottle of champagne and Auntie Carrie's leaded Czech crystal flute glasses.

When Adriana and I entered the living room with the tasty hors d'oeuvres, Ke'oni stopped discussing his photo album project. Stepping forward to take one of the platters I was holding, he said there had been only one interesting news item on the concern—an interview with the oldest chef in attendance.

Nathan set the album he had been examining on a side table. I was surprised when he commented on recognizing many of the police officers featured in Ke'oni's pictures. I assumed his knowledge must come from his periodic assistance to public safety entities during his career.

My brother soon observed, "Many of the party shots go back quite a while. I know that some of the guys have been retired for several years and one of the couples is deceased."

He looked down at the glasses Adriana was setting on the coffee table. "I see you're continuing to honor Auntie Carrie's tradition." he said in greeting.

"Absolutely. No occasion should be celebrated without good wine and the finest of crystal in which to present it," I replied.

"These glasses may not be from the royal courts of Bohemia, but I have a feeling they'd fetch quite a price at auction," he commented.

After pouring the bottle of the Korbel, Adriana passed a glass to each of us. "Allow me to offer the first toast. To Natalie, whose personal and professional activities have brought joy to so many people. Thank you for welcoming me so warmly into your family!"

"It has been a pleasure to see the smile return to my dear twin's face! It's so wonderful that you even share your professional lives."

This was the first time the four of us had been so involved with one another. I learned that Adriana was equally disinterested in things nautical. It was likely that we would enjoy a lot of girl-time when the men put to sea. Nathan revealed that he would be easing back on his practice and referring several patients to former colleagues. He and Ke'oni could not pass up another chance to talk about their dreams for voyaging across the waters of the state. At least I did not hear any plans for farther-flung adventures!

We wandered from room to room throughout the evening, checking on various electronic recordings to see how the picnic was being reported. We were surprised to find a short piece on a national cable TV channel refencing the European and Asian specialties of a couple of our most senior chefs. What a trove of material to draw on for my article! The only challenge might be in keeping within the requisite word limit.

Balancing Carrie's old *koa luau* plates on our laps, we gathered in front of the living room's large wall-mounted television. Thank goodness for generously sized paper napkins and a large waste basket. I was also pleased that the barbecue sauce on the ribs was not to the liking of Miss Una. After verifying that no one had a treat she could not by-pass, she exited the house. I assumed there would be a surveilling of the offerings Izzy was serving 'Ilima. My darling kitty may have departed too soon, because Ke'oni served a dessert of creamy macadamia nut ice cream, topped with Amaretto. It was the perfect conclusion to an active day.

Ke'oni escorted Nathan and Adriana out while I verified that we had a wide variety of recordings I could review the next day. The night passed without incident, and I awoke with a desire to blend relaxation with organization. We left Miss Una to play in Joanne's garden with 'Ili-ma and took a brisk walk to the beach. After a brief soak in the hot tub, we turned to our individual responsibilities.

Happy or sad, there is always a sense of let-down after a special event. Of course, I had important follow-up work. This would include choosing the images that would accompany the text of my article. Ac-cordingly, Andy was already working on tweaking the photos he had taken at the culinary school and palace. Although we could not use them all in this article, having a file with high-quality pictures meant that the magazine would be ready for future news stories that might feature them.

Several of the chefs might not be with us much longer. It would ben-efit their legacies if *Windward O'ahu Journeys* could provide great por-traits to other media at the time of their passing. I was glad that some of Joanne's images would be added to this collection, since her images were particularly moving. Her work truly reflects our Island culture with her inclusion of varied settings and people of every age and ethnicity!

It was good that I had sufficient lead time to adjust the layout I envisioned. There were so many elements to include in this feature: A couple of recipes from the boxed lunches; quotes from the chefs; plans for expanding the college's culinary program; and anything that might materialize from the evening at Ka 'Ikena Restaurant. With the school using the old Ft. Ruger Officers Club as a venue for refining their stu-dents' skills, the menu offerings were always unique. I hoped the dinner following the picnic had yielded close-ups of the college's staff, students, and other guests conversing.

Midway through the afternoon, Joanne called to invite me for tea and to view her edits of the photographs she had taken at the picnic and dinner. Of course, Miss Una joined me for the visit to her favorite neighbors. She immediately perched herself on the kitchen stool. After glancing at the table filled with photos, she turned to supervising the late lunch Izzy was serving 'Ilima.

I laughed. "It would seem Miss Una's lost interest in photography since destroying Ke'oni's organization of vintage pictures for his al-bums."

I accepted a cup of wild mint tea and turned to the matter at hand.

"Oh, Joanne. These are superb. I like them all. It's going to be very difficult to select which go into the current article and which will be reserved for future pieces."

"Whatever you choose is fine with me, honey. I'm just honored that you feel they're worthy of being included in a magazine."

"You must stop seeing yourself as an amateur. I've been in this game for a long time. Your work is equal to nearly every photographer I've known."

At that point, Samantha walked into the kitchen and pulled a soda from the refrigerator. "I've told her that repeatedly. I think the only way we're going to get her to appreciate her work is to secretly enter it in a contest or two. Maybe a few blue, or even red ribbons, will settle the issue! I especially liked the shots of the band setting up, with musicians warming up in the distance."

Seldom one to miss out on a social gathering, Izzy popped into the house with a couple of grocery bags. Looking over the pictures moving in rotation across Joanne's laptop, she declared, "My favorites are of the park filling up with families...with the youngest *keikis* and their elderly *tūtūs*, and the service animals accompanying a couple of the older chefs."

"That's an excellent observation!" I said. "I want copies of everything you've taken Joanne. I hope you won't mind signing a publishing release agreement so the magazine can print some of your work in the future. I promise you'll get credit as the photographer and hopefully a stipend upon their use."

"Of course. I'm thrilled that anyone wants to see my pictures!" the humble artist replied. "Give me a minute and I'll download the files to a memory stick. The only thing I ask is that I'd prefer to do any editing that's needed."

"I'm sure my publisher will agree to that. There's no way Andy can provide all the images the magazine needs, and he's always said that he wouldn't want someone touching his work, so he avoids editing anyone else's."

That evening I experienced another restless night. I carefully left the side of the man I love and walked through the house counting my blessings. The patterns of daily life may seem repetitive. But who could ask for more than to abide in a lovely cottage in one of the most picturesque beach communities on Oʻahu? While I would miss Ariel each day, her twin Brianna, Nathan, Keʻoni, Miss Una, and good friends provide wonderful companions with whom to share my life. Also, there is the joy of a twilight career into which I have glided with little thought.

In the kitchen, I checked to see that Miss Una's nutritional needs had been met. I had truly enjoyed my tea at The Ladies' home and brewed myself a cup of tea from the fresh mint Joanne had provided from a hanging pot under the eaves of the back *lānai*. I wandered into the living room, where I found my cat curled up below the coffee table.

Fortunately, nearly all of Ke'oni's photos had been put into the albums that lay in a stack. Cradling my cup and saucer in my lap, I minimized the chances of ruining the many hours that had gone into that project.

"Well, my little binky, it looks like your photographic days are over," I said, nudging her with my toes. She must have had a draining day, because she did not open even one eye. After finishing my tea, I casually glanced at the few remaining images that lay loosely before me. The majority displayed men midway through life. Their haircuts made it likely that all of them worked for government agencies of one type or another. Moving on to the albums, I soon realized that the photos I had just reviewed were duplicates or poor-quality shots of similar subjects already in albums.

I was now fully awake despite drinking a caffeine-free beverage. Inspired by Ke'oni's organization of pictures of his life, I quietly entered the office and inserted Joanne's thumb drive into my computer. As her exquisite work came into view, I was glad that I had purchased an ultra-wide monitor when we moved into the cottage. It allowed me to view several images at once and easily create thematic panoramas.

I perused Joanne's work without noticing the passing of time. I could only guess at the images she might be holding for further refinement. The ones I was now enjoying were sequenced in reverse order from that in which they had been shot. With a thud, Miss Una suddenly jumped onto my desk. We had arrived at an accommodation recently that allowed me to work under her close supervision. To the left of the monitor, I had positioned a small soft cat bed with rolled edges where she could rest her chin while watching cursors and vibrant images dance across the screen.

After a momentary ear rub to confirm my awareness of her presence, I returned to strolling visually through the parade of our adventures at the concert. When several pictures of dogs appeared, my companion sat up and stretched a paw toward the keyboard.

"No, you don't. We've discussed this behavior before. You look. I type. Okay?" While withdrawing her paw, she repositioned herself to study my work more closely.

I then turned to grouping images by theme in folders named for easy recognition. Scrolling through the last pictures requiring organization, I noticed something beyond the heartwarming foreground of an elderly woman caressing the head of a beagle wearing the coat and harness of a service animal. In the background was someone who looked familiar.

On the left side of a banyan tree stood Tommy Kiyohara. It was good that I had seen him often enough to recognize him in profile. To his right was a male figure in tan slacks and a peach-colored short-sleeved aloha shirt. Again, I could not see his face. However, I clearly saw him as a lightly tanned *haole* with little hair on his hand and arm. The small amount that was visible was reddish blonde. As I noted before, his right hand bore a ring in silver or white gold. This shot clearly showed a square blue stone with a carved emblem in the center. It displayed what might be a date in silver toned lettering at the bottom...and a diamond at the top!

I might not be a specialist in digital image enhancement. But between the resources of John Dias at HPD and *Windward Oʻahu Journeys*, I was sure I could easily find someone who was! This was a great note on which to end the night. I picked up Miss Una and returned to bed. In some ways, I wish I could say that I returned to sleep. But that was not to be. The night still had another gift to offer. At the end of our current round of untimely and unwelcome deaths, I welcomed it.

I positioned Miss Una on the headboard. Then I snuggled under the covers and kissed Keʻoni's shoulder. Soon I could feel myself slipping into what I hoped would be several hours of deep sleeping. But at some point, I moved beyond dreaming of floating on the gentle waves at our nearby beach to a violent view of another body of water.

Framed like the sepia edges of an old photo, I see turbulent waves rolling below a murky cloud-filled night sky. I realize I am looking down on a scene of total devastation. I wondered if it has been caused by man or nature.

From the edge of the wharf along the shoreline to the unseen reach of land are crushed and fragmented warehouses and other buildings. Despite this, some of their windows, doors, and roofs are amazingly intact. My eyes pan across to the right. On the outer edge of land are heavily damaged boats ranging in size from what appear to have been small recreational watercraft to large commercial fishing and freight vessels. Framing much of this tableau is lumber, often resembling huge toothpicks tossed about by a giant. Glimmers of colored metal (perhaps from cars, trucks, or metal warehouse roofs) periodically rise and fall with what might be an incoming tide.

The destruction is beyond anything I have ever seen personally. It reminds me of what I know occurs during an earthquake, hurricane, or tsunami. As I glimpse the top beam of what might have been a tori, *I realize I am probably viewing the aftereffects something terrible that happened in Japan. I then see the side of a battered U.S. jeep dating from around the Second World War...So this event must have taken place during the Allied Occupation of Japan between 1945 and 1952.*

This is a new experience, for I find myself alternating between experiencing the vision and analyzing what I am viewing. I think of the times I have researched historical occurrences of tragedy across the globe in order to report on modern natural disasters. I survey the shifting wreckage before me with sorrow. This must be a large city. Given the time frame, I think of *Kitii Taifu* (Typhoon Kitty) in September of 1949. I remember being surprised to learn that the damage was caused less by gusting winds than by torrential rains. I know too well that the survivors of such disasters face long-term shortages of food and water, followed by outbreaks of communicable diseases.

Despite huge depressions filled with murky water, I feel as though the winds that carry debris are blowing dust toward me. I blink and close my eyes. When I fully reopen them, I view a different location. This one is inland. It is away from the turbulent oceanside spectacle but displays parallel sights of wholesale destruction.

Now I stand in front of mounds of the same giant matchsticks of lumber, with roofing sitting atop or imbedded at odd angles in a sodden morass. Everything surrounding me appears in shades ranging from light grey to black. I hear the cries of the injured and entrapped. As within all of my visions, I know there is nothing I can do to alleviate the suffering I am observing. I pray I might witness some measure of relief arrive. Soon the force of the wind dies down. The calls of those who are suffering soften, sometimes to barely audible whispers.

I see a movement to my right. A boy around ten years in age stands in front of one of the remaining edifices. It has two stories. Its grid-work of window frames are largely empty of their glass panes. Some roof tiles remain on the structure. Most lie on the mound of crisscrossed wooden debris like elements from an immense children's building set. Across the landscape are indications of what once existed. In the foreground is a rectangle of interwoven bamboo that might have been a fence. Interspersed in the pile are what seem to be desks, chairs, and shelving. In the distance, a small blue baseball cap perches on a wood beam. It is surprisingly undamaged and nearly as clean as the day its wearer first donned it. To the back and right sits a roof on poles. It frames the entry to what could have been a school, warehouse, or office building.

Bewildered, the boy looks around searching for anyone or anything that might alleviate his plight. His torn clothing does not look like a school uniform. Rather, it reflects what might have been a special occasion for a distinguished young visitor. On top of slacks of a light hue, he wears a dark blazer and at his neck hangs a loosened and skewed kerchief-like tie. Whatever the purpose for his presence, this is clearly not the end of the day he had foreseen happening.

Seeing his lips move, I draw nearer. I wonder if he is consciously speaking to himself or to someone nearby. I scan the view before me, seeking further indication of where the boy and I are. On the far side of the building's entry is a bent metal pole sticking out from the rubble. Barely attached, I glimpse part of a dark circle on a background of white fabric. I am definitely in Japan, Land of the Rising Sun. What I am looking at is a flag with the Nisshōki or Hinomaru, "the circle of the sun." I remember that this symbol of the Japanese state was disallowed by the Allied Occupation from 1945 to 1949. That means the vignette I am viewing could not have occurred earlier than 1949, which does correspond to the time of Typhoon Kitty.

There is no way I can alter the unfolding scene. I hear three Japanese sentences formally intoned. I ken the essence of the vocalization of these words, if not their precise translation.

"Namu Amida. Namu Kanzeon. Namu ichijo Myōhō Renge Kyō."

From my visits to the Buddhist temple and explanations by friends, I recognize the first phrase as a statement of the speaker taking refuge in the Amida Buddha...which indicates no particular sect of Buddhism. The third sentence is part of the Lotus Sutra that Buddhists of many sects recite. The middle passage is unusual. It does not hail a Buddha, but a Bodhisattva...an enlightened person who chooses to remain on earth to help others. This reference could distinguish the boy as a follower of Tendai Buddhism!

His choked pauses demonstrate the boy's suffering. Sometimes his words shift to three simple statements I have heard recited before. I ken, rather than translate, the meanings of his words.

I put my faith in Buddha...

I...my brother and I, put our faith in Dharma...

We put our faith in Sangha, to...to join together in harmony.

His words continue, shifting in sequence and emphasis. Occasionally, there is a pause as the boy leans in toward the large beam laying across the wooden wreckage. There is no way he can move the obstacle. Even if he could, doing so might worsen the chances of survival for anyone lying beneath it.

I cannot tell the passage of time. Suddenly, I hear shouts from an arriving throng of people. Men and women, of all ages, dressed in everything from a traditional kimono to Western suit, rush onto the scene. Some move toward the doors. Others move beyond the covered entryway and go toward the rear of the damaged building. A few men move directly to the now smiling boy. The swirl of sound is beyond my ability to hear individual words, let alone gain any sense of their meaning.

One thing is clear: These are the rescuers the boy has sought. He excitedly points to the beam as he is pulled to the side by gentle hands. The final words I hear are, "Yasuhiro and I sought refuge in the Buddha and we have been saved."

As the scene fades, I hear a tinkling of small temple bells.

CHAPTER 18

*...sectarian bigotry...dwarfs the soul by shutting out truths
from other continents of thought...*
Edwin Hubbel Chapin [1814 – 1880]

I awoke drenched in a cold sweat, feeling as though I had been swimming in the ocean for a very long time. I looked up as a furry appendage came down to pat my forehead. The paw was quickly withdrawn, as Miss Una jumped to my side and then onto the floor. Looking up, she clearly called for me to get up and follow her. Since her usual desires tend to be in the line of culinary delights, I was surprised when she walked through the bedroom toward the bathroom and sat down. Maybe she had finally learned that I need to visit that room before I can meet her needs in the kitchen.

Despite my efforts to remain quiet, Keʻoni stirred and faced me. "What's up, Natalie? You don't look very good." He reached out to stroke my damp arm and then wiped the moisture off on the top of the sheet. "I take it this has been another one of your dream-filled nights?"

"Well, it was definitely a vision. But it was different than usual. It was like I was watching a movie—and analyzing it's many elements and parts. I now understand why Tommy Kiyohara has spent his life caring for his brother...and honoring that man's devotion to Buddhism. Tendai Buddhism, that is."

Keʻoni looked at the clock on his nightstand. "It's a bit early to launch a new day fully, but why don't we brew some chai tea. Then we can talk about what has shaken you so deeply."Drinking one of Keʻoni's special teas is always soothing. His interpretation of chai tea fits my taste perfectly with the right balance of cinnamon and cardamom. Pairing that with some chocolate biscotti Izzy had recently mastered was the perfect middle-of-the-night snack. Of course, that did not occur until Miss Una had received a treat of her own—thinly sliced fresh ʻahi. I breathed in slowly as I sat savoring both of my taste treats. The clear concern Keʻoni displayed made me think about how important the support of one's loved ones is in life.

"As I started to explain, I think I now understand Tommy Kiyohara's life-long care of his brother. It wasn't just as the younger brother who adored his older sibling. He truly owes his life to Hitomu. What I envisioned was the Kiyohara brothers caught up in a dreadful storm in Kyōto. I'm pretty sure it was Typhoon Kitty in 1949."

"How much of the storm did you experience...or watch?"

"Not much personally...except for feeling like the blowing dust was about to fill my eyes. What I saw was the aftermath. At first, I saw a harbor with buildings smashed into huge toothpicks. There were boats and ships destroyed beyond repair and a wharf that didn't look like anyone would be able to use it for a long time. After that, I blinked because of the dust swirling around me...even though I knew it could not affect me. Next, I saw something totally different. The waterfront scene was gone. I was somewhere beyond the harbor. I was looking at..."

I shuddered at the image of Tommy, in front of the damaged building that I decided could have been a school. Ke'oni patted my hand and poured fresh tea from Auntie Carol's Patricia pattern Spode teapot. Its delicate but colorful intertwining of flowers seemed almost Asian in design. It reminded me of why we were sitting around this table that seemed to be at the heart of so many of my deeply emotional conversations.

"I know we're looking at Tommy as the kingpin in terms of stealing the statue, even if he did not approve the accompanying murder. But what I saw was the result of a young boy being saved against all odds by the prayers of his older brother. You see, the brothers were in the midst of the debris left by the storm. I've no idea how long Tommy was trapped beneath a huge mound of rubble of concrete and large wooden beams. It surely would have affected a child who had just gone through a world war...and would grow into a man who would serve loyally at the side of his family's patriarch throughout both of their lives.

"He must have felt indebted to his brother throughout his life. For Hitomu had remained near him, fighting with the only tool he had—the repeated chanting of prayers for hours. When help finally arrived to lift the heavy beam that entrapped Tommy, Hitomu must have felt it was the strength of sacred prayers that had saved them. So, I wonder why he didn't become a monk, instead of a business tycoon. And from what I've just envisioned, I'm surprised the experience didn't push Tommy toward similar beliefs and practices."

Ke'oni thought for a moment. "There's no telling what moves a person toward serious faith. Maybe he just felt that that was his brother's path. Although he may have accepted that the prayers helped him, they didn't really touch him internally. You know my family, like that of a lot of Islanders, includes people from many faiths. The Portuguese side is Roman Catholic. The Hawaiian is Congregational. And, like a lot of my cousins, my Dad didn't have any religious affiliation. He just went to whatever services his wives wanted to attend. He was gone so much of the time, that religion never became a sore point. Then, with everything

I saw in my years with the military and HPD, I've just snoozed through a variety of ceremonies without giving the subject much thought."

"You're probably right. I haven't sensed that Tommy has any kind of spiritual connection. But based on his respect for his brother Hitomu who was a devout Buddhist, I don't see why he would get caught up in such a theft. I heard Hitomu crying out to the Buddha for help. It was in a non-sectarian way, except that one of the words he used referred to the *Kanzeon bodhisattva* not the *Amida Buddha*, which makes me think that the Kiyohara family practices *Tendai* not *Jōdo Shin* Buddhism."

Ke'oni sighed. "That makes me join JD in finding the issue of religion completely confusing. How would that make any of the family interested in a *Shākyamuni* Buddha?"

I cocked my head to the side and opened my palms upward.

With that question remaining unanswered, we returned to bed. When I finally awoke at a quarter past ten, I found myself alone. I knew that Ke'oni would have fed Miss Una, who had probably departed for a morning session of frolicking with 'Ilima. In the bathroom I found a note, apologizing for his leaving without speaking to me. His neighbor Ben had called to report that a freak overnight windstorm toppled trees on both of their properties and he had gone to help with the cleanup.

Heavy winds over the island might explain some of the sounds I heard in my vision. Speaking of which, I needed to call John Dias with the impressions I had gained regarding the depth of the Kiyohara brothers' bond. And from my viewing of Joanne's photos, I could provide new details about Tommy's mysterious companion. The clothing I saw may have been consistent with my previous glimpses of the man; seeing the color of his hair and skin should check a few more boxes for identifying him. Then there was the matter of his ring. With a bit of enhancement, we might be able to connect it to a school, class, or big sporting event. And that could narrow the cast of potential suspects even further.

After a shower to clear my head from my nocturnal experience with the turmoil of a Japanese typhoon, I went into the kitchen seeking nutritional sustenance. Seeing the land-line phone blinking, I knew we had received at least one call. I dialed the number to get my voice messages while coffee was brewing. The only call was from Professor Horita confirming compilation of his translation.

Before dialing him, I thought I should touch base with John to see if there had been any new developments in the case...especially any that might impact the professor's analysis of the Japanese text he was translating. But before I could follow through with either man, Ke'oni called to check on how I was feeling.

"You didn't seem to be getting much rest, even after our little chat in the kitchen."

"You're right. I haven't been up all that long, and I still feel tired. I'm still trying to fit the pieces of my vision together. Did I say anything in my sleep that might help?"

"Nothing that I recall, but you tossed and turned quite a bit. For once, *I* was thinking of getting up for a stroll around the house."

"Sorry, dear. How early did Ben call?"

"He was very considerate. He waited until after seven. I don't think he was expecting me to hop in my truck. But once I was fully awake, and saw you were finally getting some peace, I decided to take care of the tree clearing."

"So, how's it going?"

"What came down were a few *albazio* trees. They are really a headache since they're so quick growing and pretty invasive. But I remembered the University has an experimental project going to utilize them for building low-income housing. I figured we could use the trunks and bigger limbs to build a couple of gazebos. And we can use the smaller branches as kindling for the few times when we actually light a fire."

"That seems like a great way to complete the gardenscape. But it doesn't sound like you're going to be able to come home for to hear what Alena's dad has to report."

"You're right. We might as well keep going over here. Besides, you know I'm not a lot of help when it comes to the finer points of antiques— let alone what could be a philosophical thought for the day."

"Don't mock what you don't understand. It could be those age-old prayers that kept Hitomu Kiyohara alive for so long. By the way, I was thinking of giving John a call to tell him about my latest vision and to see if anything's come up that might relate to the translation exercise being performed by Alena's dad."

"That's probably a good idea. You can tell me what you learn at dinner. I'll pick up a pizza and salad on my way home."

On that note we parted. I was lucky to catch John as he came out of court after testifying on a case that had gone to trial after two years of investigation.

"I'm glad you called. I've learned a bit more about the family's history in Kyōto, as well as Sapporo."

"That sounds interesting. I just had another nocturnal trip and have a new perspective on the Kiyohara brothers to share with you."

We compared notes a bit further and determined that it would be good for both of us to meet with Professor Horita. After a couple of additional calls, I was able to schedule a lunch for the three of us at the Spalding House Café at the Honolulu Art Academy that afternoon. It was ideal for the professor since he would be giving a lecture on the history of Japanese silk manufacturing during a tour of the museum's *kimono* collection which included some fine examples of garments worn during religious ceremonies.

After verifying that The Ladies would keep Miss Una out of mischief, I changed clothes and drove into town. No one in the Horita family knows of my visions and I was glad that John was able to meet me a few minutes ahead of our luncheon appointment.

"You can see why I think Tommy Kiyohara believes his brother saved him during the Kyōto storm of 1949," I said concluding the report on my vision.

John's perspective was parallel to that of Ke'oni. "If Tommy isn't religious, and his brother was nearly blind, why steal an antique statue? Wouldn't any kind of statue have served the purpose of inspiring the man's prayer time?"

"I'll admit I can't answer that question. Even if his eyesight was failing, Hitomu's other senses would have been working. By touch and even smell, the man should have known the difference between a modern piece and an antique. But without clear vision, I'm torn about whether he would have been aware of the statue's origin. Earlier, I thought he would've been able to discern a lot about the statue, and that he would been aware of the news stories on the theft and murder. But we don't really know the range of his abilities or what he was doing at the time of the crimes we're investigating."

"Well, maybe the professor will give us a new perspective."

At that moment our companion arrived. We were quickly seated and provided with menus offering the Sunday delights from Chef Robert Paik. Our delicious meal was served in a lovely garden environment complete with a waterfall and sculptural ceramics by Jun Kaneko.

I knew that everything would be fresh, with tomatoes from nearby Hau'ula and greens from Waipoli on the island of Kauai. I opted for a salad with the pepper-crusted 'ahi, topped with papaya, avocado, and papaya seed dressing. Professor Horita was keeping to his nearly vegetarian diet, with greens, faro, slivers of local vegetables, sourdough croutons, and a balsamic vinaigrette kissed with Hawaiian honey. John was John. He had a barbecued kalua pulled pork sandwich. At least the bun was made in-house and he got the benefit of vegetables with the celery seed coleslaw.

Since it was a working day for the gentlemen, we all bypassed the alcoholic offerings and chose the delicious signature blend of coffee (mine iced). Of course, there were some items none of us could resist. Although Dr. Horita remained circumspect and ordered a mango sorbet, both John and I splurged with pineapple upside down cake and caramel sauce.

"I'm delighted that you have a speaking engagement here today, Professor. Otherwise, I doubt that we would have enjoyed such a great lunch," declared John with a broad smile.

"With all the times we've crossed paths, I think it's time you both started calling me Nori."

"If you call me John. So, Nori, what did you learn from Miss Una's latest discovery?" asked the lieutenant.

For a moment our translator looked confused. "Oh, let me clarify," I said. "The scrap of rice paper you translated was found in a laptop desk that I bought at the Kiyohara estate sale. It was my cat Miss Una who pulled it out of a crevice on the side of a drawer."

"I see," said Nori, smiling as he passed out copies of the text he had translated. "Let me begin by saying that you were correct in a couple of your guesses. First, the text *is* written in *hiragana*. Second, even though it is well-worn—as though from constant reference by a reader—I could tell it was recently written. Perhaps it is a new copy of something written long ago. The good news is that there was enough writing on the fragment for me to recognize that the words come from a mantra honoring the Lotus Sutra. Since I'm providing you with a copy of my translation, I won't recite it. I should caution you that like many philosophical writings, there are multiple definitions of each of the words the writer used."

I watched John nod his head and accept the paper he was handed with a blank look on his face. I knew he was trying to appear involved. Unfortunately, we were moving into an area of which he has little understanding and even less interest.

"I know this is sacred Buddhist text. But I don't remember it being part of the chanting in your temple," I said.

"You're correct. Our temple is of the Jōdo Shin tradition. As to the Lotus Sutra, it is primarily associated with Tendai and Nichiren Buddhism."

Nori paused to look at John and me. "Let me clarify. I believe the Kiyohara family member who owned this worn piece of rice paper is unlikely to be of the Jōdo Shin tradition."

"Different Buddhas and prayers for different sects... It's all beyond me," said John. "But I've gotten some reports from Japanese prefecture police departments and our State Department." John looked down at his notes for a moment. "I can confirm that the Kiyohara family are Tendai Buddhists and until about a century ago, they lived in Kyōto. Looks like their money has always come from peddling art and antiquities. Originally, they operated through markets and private sales.

"One researcher dug up an interesting document. It referred to the Japanese government seeking the family's help in the late nineteenth century when there was expansion to the northern island of Hokkaidō. It kind of reminded me of the spread of the U.S. across North America. There were the native people, the *Ainu*, only a few towns, and no modern roads or railways.

"Anyway, the Kiyoharas moved some of their family north to the coastal Hokkaidō town of Otaru and helped with the shipping of building supplies and constructing a railroad to the new city of Sapporo. Then they returned to selling art and antiques through stores in Sapporo and Kyōto...and after WWII, here in Honolulu."

"Well, that covers their business side of life," I noted. "What about the religious side of things?"

"There's not much *I* can say about that, except that the family still identifies themselves as Buddhist. And they've continued donating to the Enryakuji Temple—which is where Hitomu Kiyohara died. Beyond that, I'll have to defer to Nori."

The professor looked hesitant. "Again, I don't want to bore you with details you don't need."

"I'll appreciate learning anything that helps us figure out *how* and *why* these crimes happened...and *who* caused them to occur," responded John.

Nori looked at both John and me. "Well, going back to the thirteenth century, Jōdo Shin Buddhism was founded by the monk Shinran Shonin who abandoned the rigid rules of Tendai Buddhism. Shinran was declared a traitor and sent into exile with other independent thinkers prior to civil war erupting among political factions, the *samurai,* and even warrior monks. This eventually led to a new government—the Kamakura Shogunate."

"Isn't that when the *samurai* sword was invented?" questioned John with greater interest.

Nori chuckled. "I'm not sure that 'invented' is a term the *samurai* or *bushi,* would use. The long curved Japanese sword to which you refer is the *katana* which evolved over hundreds of years from earlier Chinese weapons.

"I do not know how the family you are investigating fits into all of this. I *can* say their surname is prominent among those who lost wealth and influence. By the time they were asked to help the Meiji Emperor's government, they must have accumulated a new fortune and were continuing to donate artistic icons to temples on Mt. Hiei—even paying commissions for sacred art, probably including the statue that came to Honolulu!"

A few seconds of silence followed as John and I tried to absorb the significance of that last statement.

"I know these details of philosophy, history, and politics are complicated. I'm trying to show you how the Jōdo Shin tradition of our temple exists beside the Tendai tradition supported by the Kiyohara family. Again, I cannot say why the *Shākyamuni* Buddha statue was given to our temple. But Buddhists of all traditions honor sacred art.

"There is another aspect of Japanese history that could have a bearing on your case. We know that the stolen statue of the *Shākyamuni* Buddha is quite old. This image is one of the first artistic expressions of Buddhism to enter Japan. It is likely that *early* Kiyohara family ancestors would have donated such a statue to the original Enryakuji Temple where it would have been added to a growing numbers of artifacts. Through the centuries such items would have been moved repeatedly to save them from periodic fires, warfare, and construction on Mt. Hiei."

John's face lit up. "I don't mean to jump in. But if the Kiyohara family donated something like that, so long ago, they might have been outraged when their ancient gift was sent to a Honolulu Jōdo Shin temple. Wrong sect and definitely the wrong place."

"I can understand the family feeling slighted if that was the case. But could their outrage lead to a murder as well as a theft? And why wasn't the statue stolen when it first arrived?" I wondered aloud.

Nori thought for a moment. "Again, the answer is probably complicated. The criminals who perpetrated these crimes may not have been aware of its arrival in Honolulu. Maybe someone in the family accidently learned about it on a trip to the Enryakuji temple. Specialists in antiquities, let alone sacred treasures, often compare notes. I can easily picture an important visitor from America being given a tour of storerooms closed to the general public. Maybe a casual comment about the location of the family's gift led to the revelation that it had been given to our temple.

"Subsequently, the criminals could have been motivated by both rivalry and revulsion. This would make sense if members of the modern Kiyohara family adhere to the tradition's original precepts. You see, Tendai Buddhism is not historically linked to the island of Hokkaidō where you say members of the family moved a century ago. If there was no temple in which to observe their traditions, they may have maintained their religious practices at home. This would have separated them from the modernization of Tendai."

We sat drinking our beverages for a few moments. What a revelation! I had rejected the idea that a devout Buddhist could have ordered the theft of a revered object. I would have thought that regardless of sect, the murder of a Buddhist minister would taint the object. Instead, their view could have been that the gift of the statue was a betrayal. In fact, their beliefs may have decried the legitimacy of a female priest. Perhaps a man raised with such precepts—religious or not—might not feel remorse for her death. In fact, retrieving a valuable symbol of his family's heritage may have seemed a worthy act.

"I appreciate all you've told us Nori, but I'm sure glad there won't be an exam on the finer details!" said John. "My final news concerns what we've learned about Hitomu Kiyohara. As a pre-teen, his health took a downturn. It began when he and Tommy were caught in the aftermath of a storm while visiting cousins in Kyōto. Even though the boys were rescued, Hitomu took it upon himself to help with rescue operations for several days.

"The release of dust and chemicals in the air took their toll on his lungs and eyes. That could have limited his educational opportunities. As Tommy began to move through school faster, there must have been discussion about the line of succession. Eventually, Hitomu decided not to become a monk. He became the patriarch of his family and their business empire—all made possible with Tommy at his side."

Our lesson of history and philosophy had concluded. Nori began sorting papers in his briefcase while John pulled out his phone to check a couple of text messages.

"It seems my day is not complete. Hitomu Kiyohara's autopsy report has just arrived from the Kyōto Medical Examiner's Office."

John and I thanked Nori for his assistance as he departed to prepare for his lecture and tour at the museum.

"In case I learn anything exciting, what's on your agenda this evening?" John asked me.

We parted company with the understanding that Ke'oni and I would be delighted for him to join us for pizza and salad...and a bit of hopefully non-depressing morgue humor.

On the way home I checked in with Ke'oni. He said not to expect him before sunset as he still needed to organize a pick-up by Waste Management. That was fine with me since I needed some down-time before plunging into more investigative details. I let him know we were likely to have a guest for dinner that night. We decided he would bring home an additional pizza pie, since that entrée makes a great leftover after a few minutes in a covered frying pan.

After such a lovely luncheon, I knew it was a bit decadent to crave another carb-laden meal. However, I love Prima restaurant's mission to support local farmers and ranchers—not to mention the results of a pizza baked in their kiawe wood fired brick oven! Our menu would begin with grilled Caesar salad with tangy freshly made dressing. That would be followed by a signature thin crusted pizza with tomato, mozzarella, arugula, and San Daniele prosciutto di Parma. In case that wasn't enough, there would also be a second pie featuring spicy meatballs and chilies.

CHAPTER 19

...always picking up odds and ends for our patchwork mind.
Charles Dickens [1812 - 1870]

At home I changed into one of my old swimsuits and wandered outside to look for Miss Una. I glanced across the back fence and saw Joanne weeding a row of lettuce plants while 'Ilima and Miss Una were playing under a plumeria tree.

"It looks like you're having a wonderful time," I called out.

"You're right. I dropped Izzy and her niece off at the airport at noon for a trip to Maui. Since Samantha isn't home from school yet, I thought I'd put in a little time in the garden."

"Would you like some help? I'll bring my tools and a couple of bottles of sun tea."

"I'd love the company, and a drink would be great."

The next hour passed quickly, as we caught up on The Ladies' activities and my writing. "My article on the chefs at 'Iolani Palace is nearly wrapped up. I have just one complaint. Your photos are so wonderful that I've had trouble finalizing my top two. But as I promised, all of the others will eventually be the highlight of one article or another!"

Later, I took a shower, did some laundry, and mixed a pitcher of lemonade with Meyers lemons from our yard. Ke'oni arrived home a bit earlier than he had expected. We were enjoying the rainbow light show in our front fountain when John arrived. After an infusion of gin in our drinks, we enjoyed our simple meal in the growing dusk framed by the windows of the dining room.

"What a day! Two great meals and a double whammy in evidence," declared John. "The reason I say I've had an evidentiary doubling is that when I met with Lori—who's on duty for the weekend—I found a translation of the Kyōto prefecture police officers' incident report as well as the autopsy of Hitomu Kiyohara."

We each grabbed several dishes and moved inside. Since I did not need to look over crime scene images or reports, we decided to sit in the living room. Ke'oni went into the office for his laptop and a pen and lined pad of paper for me. I moved the photo project to one corner of the coffee table and John opened his briefcase.

After passing a few sheets of paper to Ke'oni, John said, "I guess the Kiyoharas wanted the full story about Hitomu's demise. That was probably because he fell to his death while visiting the temples at Enryakuji. His granddaughter and her husband had accompanied the old man on most of his trip. At some point, they left him in the care of relatives at the Kyōto gallery. When he expressed a desire to smell the cool air up at Mount Hiei, a young woman staff member volunteered to take him.

"Evidently the man was very moved by his visit to Tenporindo, the oldest structure at Enryakuji. They paused at a small shrine while walking back down the mountain. The woman needed to use the restroom. Said she was gone only five minutes. He had disappeared when she returned to the stone lantern on the path where she'd left him. She rushed down the trail to the next lookout point, where she found his cane leaning against a wall. She peered over and saw his body lying sprawled below.

"Her testimony stated there was no one in sight. She couldn't see any way to get to Hitomu by herself and called for help. When the medics arrived, he was clearly beyond help. The police arrived at about the same time as the EMTs. Their report's very formal, but I can read between the lines. My bet is that the police personnel were shaken by whatever orders the high mucky mucks issued. Here's my summary of their findings:

"The body of the victim was located 23.4 meters—that's 76.8 feet—down an embankment from the low stone wall that runs along the edge of a stone pathway. He was lying at a forty-degree angle from the wall above. The body lay on moss, fern, and rock covered ground. The right side of his skull showed a small fracture, and his limbs were unnaturally splayed. Surprisingly, the thick antique kimono he was wearing was not torn, although it did display stains from the greenery on which it had rolled. Same for the trainers on his feet. After looking this over, my guess is that he stayed on the paved paths until his fall—which I'd say must have been pretty gentle—until he cracked his head.

"It looks like the forensic folks were quite thorough. They measured everything and took both video and still shots. There was no evidence of a struggle and not much blood in evidence: A small amount of expiratory blood was found on the rock on which his head landed; a few drops of castoff spatters were found on the surrounding ground and two nearby rocks. There was no evidence of transfer stains, as would have been found if the body had been moved. No footprints were discovered. The only disturbance to the ground was the impact and rolling of the victim's body."

Ke'oni observed, "If his body rolled or was dragged over the ground, it could have obscured adjacent footprints."

"Maybe. But the report says the hillside was damp. If someone walked around the body, and back up the slope, some evidence of their footprints should have remained evident."

"The victim's wallet, cane, trainers, and glasses found above the victim's head were bagged and tagged...not quite the authorities' terms. Given the abundance of moss on the area's rough granite stonework, there was no hope of getting fingerprints. They tried, nevertheless. The cane was analyzed, but there were no signs of unusual use...and just Hitomu's fingerprints. Same thing for his clothing. And there was nothing remarkable found on the woman's attire, which the authorities collected."

Ke'oni looked up from his laptop. "I've worked with the Japanese Public Security Intelligence Agency on a couple of cases. You're right about that country's security personnel strictly following protocol."

John agreed. "There's nothing of further significance in the incident report. The authorities checked the registry most people sign when entering Enryakuji. They interviewed anyone who was near the Tenporindo temple during the relevant time frame. No one reported seeing or hearing anything unusual...the old man and the woman weren't even noticed. There was some kind of special event taking place at a lower point on the mountain, so I guess most visitors were caught up in that. In short, there were no signs of foul play and no obvious indication of suicide. Maybe with his minimal eyesight, a bird flew by and startled him, and he just fell over the wall."

"A couple of things have caught my attention," I said. "He was wearing an antique *kimono*. That must be very valuable, and it was clearly at risk of damage on such an excursion. Also, his cane was found standing against the wall; that means he set it there. And don't forget that he made a point of going to the oldest temple in the complex. It was rather like he was paying respect to his ancient relatives."

"Hmm," replied John, nodding. "I'll move on to the autopsy situation. Japan has a couple of kinds of autopsies. Given his age and health— and that there was no sign of his death resulting from a crime—multiple procedures would not be required normally. However, he'd lived outside the country for several decades and only returned to Japan for business and periodic visits to the Mount Hiei temples. So, when the wealthy and prestigious Kiyohara family expressed concerns, alarms were sounded in officialdom."

"Therefore, a "pathological" autopsy was called for. And since the cause of death was not obvious, an "administrative" autopsy was also indicated. Given the international complications, the postmortems were performed by the former head of Kyōto University's Department of Forensic Medicine."

"If you're nervous about the response of outsiders, pick someone at the highest level to execute a procedure," I joked.

John waved some papers. "We received both the original Japanese autopsy reports and English translations. Since it seems there's no question of murder here, I'll just go through the highlights."

After that, he handed Ke'oni copies of the English versions of the reports and commenced with the findings. I could tell our Lieutenant was self-editing, so I forced myself to pick up the main points. I found the details of the man's attire and accessories interesting.

"Case number, name, location, date, time, personnel, titles...The body is that of an adult Japanese male, age, measuring 167.64 centimeters [5 feet 6 inches] and weighing 63.526 kilograms [140.05 pounds]...normally developed and consistent with the given age of 79 years. Overall, the victim was of unremarkable health, except for considerable thickening of the corneas...

"The victim was received wearing a black antique rinzu kimono *with* obi *over a white silk under-kimono...a pair of black Giorgio Armani suit pants...boxer shorts... The back of the hand-sewn kimono features the falling wisteria crest of the ancient Fujiwara clan in detailed hand-embroidery in couched gold thread. Date of manufacture is estimated to be mid-Edo period [late 1700s]...None of the items of clothing were bloodstained, but the kimono, obi, and pant legs were streaked with greenery and mud... pair of black Kizik trainers...gold wedding band...antique double strand of 108 round ojuzu [prayer beads] in white jadeite, with one gold oyadama [mother bead] found in the victim's left pants pocket."*

I thought about the significance of those items as John looked over another page in the report.

"...scalp hair is silver, straight, and short...Fingernails, medium in length...the only signs of struggle are on the right palm and anterior forearm, consistent with the photograph of the scene showing the patient's right arm extended above his head...no surgical scars...Pre-mortem minor abrasions are present on his face and hands, evidently sustained during his fall. On his left anterior forearm there were numerous residual scars being horizontal in orientation and varying in length from 0.8 centimeters and 1 centimeter and a central one being five centimeters...no tattoos or other visible marks.

"...a 3.01625 centimeter wound on the right temple, at 6.35 centimeters below the top of the head and 10.16 centimeters left of the anterior midline...open depressed skull fracture...hemorrhage...stroke due to dissection of the right internal carotid artery due to blunt force trauma to the head.

"Beyond that, there were a postmortem CT scan and MRI. Then there's the usual organ analysis, indication of partially digested food, negative urine screen and an order for routine toxicologic studies. Aside from personal effects, there was a video of the incident scene and eleven autopsy photographs. The death certificate states death from unintentional injury, resulting from trauma to the head sustained during a fall, causing fracture of skull, hemorrhage, and stroke.

"Any questions boys and girls?" concluded John.

"I've already expressed my concerns…except the prayer beads made of white jadeite," I said. "As you know, I've done a fair amount of research on jade and related stones. If the jadeite came from Japan, dating to the Kamakura period—about 700 years ago—it would be pretty rare. You see, probably from over-mining, Japanese jadeite seems to have disappeared from then until new sources were found in the early twentieth century. Combined with the other issues I've raised, Hitomu's trip to the mountain sounds like a ritual to me. And that points toward suicide."

"You could be right. Anything tug at you, Ke'oni?" asked our fearless leader.

"I've been following along with the written report. I think you're right in suggesting that everyone involved with investigating Hitomu Kiyohara's death was operating under fear. Fear that any failure on their parts could result in A) one or more persons losing their job, and B) the potential for triggering a financial, if not political, scandal."

JD shrugged his shoulders. "Moving on to issues closer to home, I have some info on Tommy Kiyohara. With Nippon Antiquities closing its Ala Moana gallery, we've been wondering if Tommy would retire. After all, he's not so young. If he were to retire, would it be here? Or in Japan? Obviously, he won't be inheriting the Hawai'i Kai home that's being sold. But that hardly matters, since he's got enough money to live anywhere he'd choose.

"Evidently the family's been buying properties across the Islands for decades. Some of the homes have been used as rentals; others have served as vacation destinations for staff in the two galleries in Japan. I'm guessing that the long-term plan was to divvy everything up among family members whenever the time was right. I'd say that time has arrived with the death of their patriarch.

"As you can tell, we're moving ahead full throttle. We've got multiple task forces involved, and there's no telling what they'll turn up. One report I'm waiting for is the team reviewing everything about the *Marimu*. The only hint of wrong-doing is that the Coast Guard boarded the boat about ten years ago. Nothing came from that incident. At least nothing beyond a sniff of blood diamonds that disappeared from a Tōkyō gem merchant at the time the *Marimu* was making the return voyage to Hawai'i. We're also awaiting the results of a few more tests—toxicology, DNA from some skin cells, and a couple of drops of blood found aboard the boat."

"With everything I've envisioned, you should be able to uncover information on the Kiyohara family's activities since World War II," I said.

"You mean aside from collecting awesome commissions and fees from the sales of other people's valuables?" Ke'oni added.

"I concur with your dim view of their business," John nodded. "This is one of the hottest cold cases I've ever touched. As you've both observed, there can't be all these pieces without one hell of a picture materializing in the end! In the meantime, I think I owe you more than one dinner at Buzz's. Or maybe that restaurant up on Diamond Head."

With that he began shifting some paperwork back into his briefcase. "So, what are all these photos? I think I recognize some of the groupings of folks, but I can't quite place them."

"Those shots were taken over the last twenty years or so...more than half of them occurred at parties you attended," Ke'oni said with a laugh.

As I entered the office to drop my notes on my desk, the men were beginning a trip down memory lane. I then went into the kitchen to prepare a pitcher of iced tea with lemon slices. When I returned to the living room, I found them joking about widening waists and receding hairlines.

JD was in a teasing mood. "Hey Natalie, Ke'oni says you don't remember many people at his retirement party. Is that because you'd been having too much fun, or just hadn't made it to our gatherings before?"

With that, he passed me an album and pointed to a picture in which I was standing by a punch bowl. "Now that's not fair. I remember that aspect of the party. I didn't even like the punch. It had too much mango juice in it."

"As opposed to the amount of rum," joked my honey. "The man you're standing next to liked it quite a bit. In fact, he liked it so much, that I had to offer him my couch that night."

I glanced at the man whose face he was tapping. Good looking. Well dressed. Top of the line aloha shirt and, and, despite the late hour, a sharp crease in his cuffed gray slacks. Completing his ensemble were highly polished black Italian loafers with tassels. Obviously, the man had rolling accounts at the dry cleaners and shoe repair. As I was about to close the album, I looked across the picture one more time.

While I had been pouring soda into my plastic cup at the party, the man I now stared at seriously was passing a cup to someone out of camera range. What was in view was his hand. His right hand. On his ring finger was a silver-colored ring with a dark blue stone in the center. It featured a carving of the logo of Chaminade University—with a brilliant white diamond at the tip of its upraised sword. To complete the image that reflected my memories, was the sleek silver-colored metal lettering for a year beginning with one nine!

I sat back, stunned. I licked my lips and swallowed. Then I took a sip of my tea. Both of my companions remained silent but glanced at one another significantly. I knew I needed to say something about my prolonged pause.

"Mmm, did this man have shoe soles like you guys? Was he in law enforcement?"

"I think we could give a qualified 'yes' to the second question, right Ke'oni?" nodded JD.

"And I can say 'yes' to the first. He spent a fortune having some cobbler on the mainland customize those already expensive Italian shoes with composite soles," added Ke'oni.

"I get the sense that Natalie needs to take a closer look at a few more of the pics in these albums of yours," affirmed John. "Want to take a guess at who you're looking at. Give up? It's Ke'oni's old partner, the one and only Tony Brennan."

"Isn't he the one you hinted at being slightly dirty?"

"With the amount of bling the guy wore, there were more than a few whispers going around," agreed John.

"No one could ever pin anything to him officially. But he was one of Internal Affairs repeated persons of interest," announced Ke'oni.

"Well, I can tell you he is definitely *my* person of interest," I declared firmly.

"I think this turn in our conversation moves us to a whole new level of analysis. Before I go to Makani, I think we need to go back over the key points of our investigation—beginning with you, Natalie. How about you go and recline in your favorite chair. Close your eyes and take us back through the sequence of your sightings of the tall *haole* man you've seen with Tommy Kiyohara. And it wouldn't hurt to include the other guy with him at the scenes of the crime. How about you take notes on that little toy of yours, Ke'oni, while I lead Natalie through the memories of her adventures…envisioned and in real time."

As I positioned myself, my furry friend arrived to lie across the back of my chair.

"It appears that our trio, plus one, is ready to go," I commented.

"Okay then. Take a few of those deep breaths you've learned in yoga and open your mind. Let's start with you taking us back to that first vision of the temple."

"I think that was the one with the funny statues and pedestals," offered Ke'oni.

Sinking back in space and time, I settled in for what I knew would be a long session of directed visioning. "You're right. In the first, it wasn't the real temple I saw. It had many pedestals with Asian deities from various religions, although the sounds of bells and chanting were realistic. I just thought I was having a funny dream…for a few moments at least. There wasn't very much to this segment. Next, viewing the real temple, I see a Buddhist minister in a beautiful black silk robe and plum-colored surplice. She is praying in front of the Buddha on the central altar. Then, suddenly, she is shot... That's all there was to that vision.

"In the next one, the temple looks normal. I now recognize the statue on the left as the *Shākyamuni* Buddha. I hear bells ringing and chanting. The minister enters the sanctuary. She again prays in front of the *Amida* Buddha. Then she's shot and slips to the floor. This time I watch as two men in blue coveralls from that defunct moving company enter.

"They're pushing a metal cart, or trolley, with bars on all four sides.

With barely a glance, they move past the minister's body to the *Shākya-muni* Buddha. The one at the front walks sideways—which is why I can't see his face. The second man is pushing from behind. The first man—who is probably your buddy Tony—pulls out what looks like a folding ladder from one of two shelves on the cart. Together they position it on the top edge of the altar. The first man reaches down again, and I see there are several blankets on the lower shelf. He lifts one and places it over the ladder. Together the men carefully move the Buddha forward onto the padded ladder. Then they pull the statue and blanket onto the trolley. Once the statue is positioned, they cover it with a second blanket.

"I watch the second man pick up a strap hanging from the bar on the back of the trolley. He wraps it over and around the draped statue and buckles it underneath the trolley. They both check to see that the Buddha is firmly in place. The first man refolds the ladder and puts it back on the shelf he took it from. Then the men push it back out the door."

"You say they push the cart back out of the room. Did they turn it around?" asked JD.

"No. There are bars on all sides of the cart. The first man stayed where he was with his back to me, holding the side bar of the cart. And the man who was at the back of the trolley when they entered, is again pushing from the back as the trolley retraces its movement to the exit."

"What can you tell me about the men? Age? Heigh? Weight? Ethnicity?" asks John.

"Not much. I didn't notice anything other than the coveralls during their first appearance. But my third vision developed somewhat differently. Unlike the other times I saw her, Reverend Fujimoto stands in the front parking lot of the temple. She's visiting with an older Japanese gentleman. They're mutually respectful, but I can't hear their words. After a few moments, the man gets in a car and departs. That scene closes. Next, I'm back in the sanctuary. I hear a soft drumming, the chiming of finger bells, and chanting. Silence descends. The sound of a shot slices the air, and everything freezes.

"The crime continues as before, except at a slower pace. I study everything closely. The man at the front of the trolley is fairly tall and slim, displaying charcoal gray slacks beneath the coveralls that are too short for him. The man at the back is shorter, burly, and walks with a slight limp. They're talking, but I cannot understand their words. The lead man sounds like a mid-Westerner. The second guy speaks in short phrases voiced in a local rhythm.

"Their actions are the same as before. As they prepare to exit, I watch them assume their positions at the cart, in reverse. This time I notice that the slim man's shoes, black, with the same composite soles as Ke'oni's. The gold watch on his right wrist looks valuable. As he re-adjusts his hands on the bar of the cart, I catch sight of that heavy ring with a dark blue stone.

"That's it for the visions that touch on the crimes and/or the man I think is Tommy Kiyohara's cohort. My next dream, or vision, was totally different. It was sort of a short film from ancient Japan. It's really a tragic tale in a beautiful traditional Japanese setting. It begins with a girl sitting with her grandfather—an old Buddhist priest—under a cherry tree overlooking a lake. I read his thoughts as he dreamed of giving his son a revered statue of the Shākyamuni Buddha upon his departure for life within a new Buddhist order. When the little girl sees a man in the distance crossing an arched bridge over the lake, she cries out and runs toward the lake. While jumping from stone to stone, she slips and drowns."

That was how I was now feeling. Like I too was drowning...in the details of lives past and present that have been filled with sorrow and halted before they could achieve their full potential. I rubbed my forehead for a moment and closed my eyes to regain my sense of equilibrium.

I felt the tapping of a paw on the top of my head and opened my eyes. "The next vision is where I get more detail about the man I suspect of being Tommy's accomplice. But there's nothing further about the murder scene."

"You look like you need a break, honey," hinted my ever-concerned human housemate.

When we regrouped, Miss Una was nowhere in sight. Ke'oni and JD were enjoying their latest find, Mehana Mauna Kea Pale Ale, and nibbling on smoky chipotle macadamia nuts. Ke'oni had refreshed my cup of tea and added a glass of cool water to the table beside my chair.

"Hey, where's my treat. I'm the one who's been working."

Ke'oni dropped a handful of nuts onto a napkin beside his bottle and brought his dish over to me.

"That's more like it. I need some sustenance before returning to viewing unpleasant things," I declared.

"Are you sure you're up to more tonight?" questioned John.

"Yes. I'm definitely making some progress in connecting a few dots that could prove pertinent to the official investigation."

CHAPTER 20

The question is not what you look at, but what you see.
Henry David Thoreau [1817 - 1862]

We joked for a few more minutes, and then I settled back in the recliner.

"Where were you when you had that vision while in the hot tub? Ke'oni gave me the overview but I'd like to have the full picture." JD said.

"I'm in the temple at the beginning of it. There is no expansion in the revelation of the murder and theft. I hear the tinkling of bells and the chanting of the word *OM*. My eyes close as I absorb the peace of the room. When I reopen them, I face a movie screen that is pulled down over the altar. I am given a tour of ancient temples from cultures across the world—including an ancient Hawaiian *heiau* in Kāne'ohe. Next, I am floating above the entire property the temple sits on. I see a group of senior citizens board two buses that turn onto the Pali Highway and go toward Windward O'ahu.

"I hear the heavy sound of a *bonshō* bell and many voices again intoning *OM*. I inhale the richness from a layering of incense. I'm sitting on a cloud looking down at a strip of flowering garden plantings between the back parking lot and the street at the upper end of the temple grounds. A petite gray-haired Asian woman is walking a small dog. She sits for a few moments on one of four circular stone benches facing a sundial.

"I blink and find myself positioned with a view from above. To my left is old Fort Ruger. To my right is Diamond Head. Suddenly, I hear a speeding car brake. Looking down, I see the woman who was walking in the garden. She is dazed, standing in the street of a block comprised mostly of homes. I see the driver's side door of a dark brown sedan open. A tall man emerges. His back is to me as he moves toward the woman and her dog. I do not hear him speak, but he calms her and escorts the dog and her to the curb.

"As he gets back in his car, I watch him pull his left leg inside. He's wearing gray slacks and black shoes with tassels. I don't see the soles, but I'm sure they have the soft composites you and Ke'oni wear. The design of the back license plate is reminiscent of the era of the crimes we're investigating."

I paused to sit up and stretch my arms outward. I moved my neck from side to side. Then I took a large drink from my glass of water. "As for anything else I've tapped into, you already know about the last vision I had. The one about the Kiyohara brothers when they were little boys trapped in a typhoon in what I think was 1949. The vocabulary that Hitomu used helped to validate that they're Buddhists—Tendai Buddhists. It also demonstrated why Tommy was so committed to aiding Hitomu throughout his life." I swallowed a sigh and Ke'oni gave me a look that confirmed he knew the toll that remembering each vision had extracted from me.

"This has been great, Natalie. Between my notes and Ke'oni's electronic record, I think we've captured the key points of what you've been *dreaming* about lately. If you're up to a little more, how about we conclude tonight's reminiscing with a recap of the times you think you've caught sight of the mystery man in person."

I took another sip of my tea and licked my lips before speaking. "We all saw Tommy in his role of auctioneer at the live auction. When I was at the estate sale, I think I saw the man who has been his accomplice. At the time, I was walking toward the back of the guest house when I heard two men speaking within one of the two bedrooms. As I heard in the temple, the one who may be Tony sounded like a national broadcaster with no regional accent. The other man had a soft Japanese accent. To cover my eavesdropping at an open window, I picked up some flowers from the ground and played at arranging a bouquet.

"The first man was complaining that something shouldn't have happened. The man I would soon confirm to be Tommy Kiyohara responded by saying that he didn't cause his brother's death. And he didn't know about the changes to the will that triggered the sale of all of Hitomu's properties and possessions. He huffily stated that at the time his brother died, *he* was on a buying trip in Mongolia, where the means of international communication are minimal. The other man accepted everything Tommy said, but pointed out that he should have told Koji (his brother's son) to keep a certain little item under wraps.

"At one point, I tiptoed up to the window and peeked in. But by then, they were leaving the house. When I reached the front porch, all I could see of the unknown man was his back as he moved down the side of the house. When Tommy came out, I was acting like an innocent estate sale customer and continued to play with the flowers my hand. He gave me a short look and moved away.

"The concert at 'Iolani Palace was the next occasion that I saw Tommy and his mysterious friend. I was looking at the bandstand when I saw the younger Kiyohara brother speaking to someone standing behind a banyan tree. I couldn't tell who it was, but I saw the man's right hand resting on the tree trunk. He was fairly tall and wearing a ring, like the perpetrator I envisioned in the temple. At that moment, a reporter came up to me with a question, and by the time I looked back, Tommy and his buddy were gone.

"I've thought a lot about that ring. It was on the man's right hand, so it was not a wedding ring. With its carved insignia on a blue stone at the center and something sparkling at the top, I doubt that it's an ordinary school class ring. Maybe it was designed to commemorate a sporting event. If it was a custom order, that would fit in with the high-quality shoes and slacks I saw him wearing at the estate sale."

Just then Ke'oni raised his index finger as though to break into my recitation. When John quickly shook his head, he sat back and I continued.

"The only other time I glimpsed the man, was last night when I was looking at a photo Joanne took at the concert. It was shot at nearly the same angle as what I personally saw. The longer I stared, the more details I noticed. He had rather fine hair on his hand and arm. It was reddish blonde in color. There were no wrinkles, so I was pretty sure he wasn't very old.

"In Joanne's picture, I clearly saw a diamond at the top of the heavily carved design in the man's ring...and what looked like a date in silver toned metal at the bottom. I've been thinking that maybe Andy Berger at *Windward O'ahu Journeys* could enhance and enlarge the picture."

John came toward me smiling. "Well, except for the lack of evidence that will stand up at trial, it looks like we have found the man of your dreams!"

"That's wonderful. But we still don't have a motive for the crime... and no clue as to why the statue was stolen in the first place," added Ke'oni.

"Or which of the men I saw actually killed the minister from outside the door to the sanctuary," I said with a sigh.

"That's really not an issue," said John looking through his papers on the coffee table. "Regardless of who pulled the trigger, both men will be charged with murder...whenever we can catch one, or both of them." He then paused for a sip of his drink before continuing.

"Of course, we do need to be able to identify both of them and prove their link to one another and the crimes. To wrap up tonight, let's review where we stand. At the direction of someone (possibly Tommy Kiyohara), we've got two men entering the temple, one of whom you've tentatively ID'd as Tony Brennan. After the killing of the minister, they steal the *Shākyamuni* Buddha statue and depart the same way they came in.

"One thing we haven't discussed very much is the Menehune Transfer Company. With their having been out of business for a while, we can't assume the perps had access to one of the company's old vehicles. Whatever they drove had to have a lift tailgate. Beyond that issue, we have no idea if there was a third perp driving it. I can't picture Tommy stooping that low, even if he had the time. Again, we have to wonder whether this was a one-time activity, or if these guys made a habit of working together on high-end heists. If so, it would sure explain Tony's lifestyle.

"Now, let's get back to our timeline. At an undetermined point, the Buddha was concealed in a hidden compartment in a bedroom of the Kiyohara guest house at their Hawai'i Kai estate. It seems logical to assume it remained there until the death of patriarch of the Kiyohara family. That occurred in a fall during a visit to the mountainside Tendai temple that his family's been connected to for hundreds of years. After Hitomu's death, the statue was placed in one of Nippon Antiquities' live auctions. Then, the home's other furnishings were sold in an estate sale where the family yacht was sold to you and Nathan in a silent auction. That leaves the house, which is now up for sale."

At that moment, John set his papers aside and stood up. He began pacing back and forth, pausing to point his right index finger from side to side to emphasize key points in his summation.

"It was at the guest house that you heard the voice of a *haole* man you've suggested is from the mainland. Although you heard him speak, it was only a few words that were not incriminating. So, there's not enough concrete info to identify him. You did catch sight of the man as he moved down the side of the cottage. But again, you couldn't ID him from his backside. But there are a couple of consistent characteristics you have pinned down. Height, fairly tall; ethnicity, reddish blonde haired *haole*; age, mid-range; and, a *great* wardrobe.

"As far as current threads of the ongoing investigation are concerned, we're waiting for more test results from our initial examination of the boat. So far it doesn't seem likely that anything will link to the heist or murder. But we can, and probably should, gain access to both the house and the boat again.

"Next, let's consider the patriarch of the family. He's had poor sight since the typhoon of 1949 and legally blind for a couple of decades. I think we can conclude it's unlikely he would have been involved directly with the transport of stolen goods aboard the *Marimu*. That brings us back to his helpful little brother. I can't picture Tommy being directly involved in seafaring crimes either. But whoever put out the contract for the heist of the statue was certainly capable of directing a job or two from a distance.

"We've also got to consider the man's death. I'd say that if there was evidence of a murder, the forensic experts in his homeland would have found it—given the pressure being put on them. Although neither the incident report nor Hitomu's autopsy provide any evidence of suicide, your non-scientific analysis leaves that issue on the table. To follow up, I guess we can look into his medical records. But I think that all we'll find is confirmation of what we already know: And, although he's been called the head of the family, he's had to rely on Tommy personally and professionally every day of his adult life."

"It's a matter of honor," I observed. "If Tommy had become the titular head of Nippon Antiquities, it would have brought shame to his brother. As long as the work has been done, it hasn't mattered whose name is on the stationery."

"The bottom line is that we've got no way to prove Tommy ordered the theft. And, there's no obvious link between Tony and any of the evidence we've discovered so far," concluded John with a frown.

"But look on the bright side. While you're waiting for those tests to come back, we can begin looking into my infamous former partner," suggested Ke'oni. "How *has* he lived such a grand lifestyle? And I do mean that, because I've heard that since his retirement, he's been able to buy a great condo, an expensive car not provided by HPD, and take some fabulous international cruises."

"How about you start checking out the man's financial profile. I'll ask Andy Berger to enhance that photo, so we can confirm the lettering on the bottom of his ring," I offered.

"That might prove useful," concurred Ke'oni. "But as I was about to say earlier, I can fill you in on that ring. Yes, there are numbers at the bottom of the Silver Sword logo. They are 1 9 8 2; and they *do* commemorate a sports event. In 1982, Chaminade University achieved an unlikely basketball victory over the top-ranked University of Virginia. As you know, Chaminade is where a lot of the public safety officers in Hawai'i get their BA degree if not their MA. Tony was so proud of that win that he ordered a custom ring."

"I'd forgotten about that fact...if I ever knew it. So that unique ring could provide a link between Tony and Tommy, who is clearly visible in the photo that Joanne took and can now be considered part of the public record," said JD with a smile.

"Should I still have the photo enhanced?" I asked.

"Absolutely!" JD affirmed. "And I'm glad that being the great PI you are, Ke'oni, you've undoubtedly got the connections to look into the man's credit activity. That leaves me, and the department, out of the picture until we can establish a clear cause for making an investigation of him official. So, I think that's it for tonight? Any overlooked areas of concern?"

I looked down at my hands for a moment. "Well, now that I have Tony in mind, I'm thinking more about the physical appearances of the men I saw in the temple. I've already described the one as a slim and fairly tall *haole*—now pegged as Tony. The other one was a shorter and broader local man," I said, sorting through my memories of several visions. "I think we can add another characteristic—the local man was older. I mean, even though I didn't see Tony's face, I did see his companion...and he was not young. If we consider today's date, he's got to be pretty far up in age."

"Let's think about another angle for identifying those two men," proposed John. "With all the battles and wars this country has seen, either or both of the men could have been in the military. What about Tony? Did he put in any active duty for his country?"

"I don't remember what reason he's given for never wearing any uniform except for that of HPD. I can say the only things that man's ever served are the security of his own body and his personal financial interests," said Ke'oni with a snort.

"Speaking of uniforms, what about the moving company's uniforms," I wondered. "Although the company's been out of business for a decade, they were in existence at the time of the crimes. That makes it likely that the local man had a connection to the company."

"That's a good point," said Ke'oni thoughtfully. "Back then, we didn't have your visions to draw on for details dealing with two uniformed men moving a trolley out of the sanctuary. It was good ole Tony who was tasked with looking into external aspects of the case. That included vehicles—like tourist and school buses, as well as utility companies, waste management, and other municipal departments that might have been on site.

"Then there's the matter of disposing of the statue. Tony was also in charge of looking into all of the Island antique stores and auction houses. Moving beyond the local market, he supposedly reached out to international sales venues, Interpol, Europol, and other public safety related agencies. That was a lot of paperwork I was glad to avoid, especially knowing I'd soon be leaving for a stint at the FBI's National Academy.

"I remember Tony complaining about the uncooperative personnel at U.S. and international airlines and shipping companies. They made it clear that without the proper search warrants obtained through customs sources, there was no way they would allow the examining of crates being shipped out of the Islands. I can't even imagine what it would be like to individually check all items being shipped through here."

"Your mentioning antiques and auction houses brings us back to Nippon Antiquities. Your partner must have been in touch with them," suggested JD.

"They've been one of the largest international auction houses in the Islands for several decades. Whether or not he was one of the perpetrators, Tony would have had to contact them in the normal investigation of the case."

"That means he may have interviewed Tommy Kiyohara personally. His notes should be in the case files, which I'll be checking out tomorrow" said John with a hopeful gleam in his eyes.

"What were *you* investigating originally?" I asked Ke'oni.

"In addition to going over the forensic reports, I handled aspects of the temple's campus—like their events and personnel. I even looked at the temple's calendar of activities for a couple of weeks before and the week after the heist. To be honest, I was busy running background checks on everyone involved with the temple. I didn't pay much attention to what Tony was doing. Again, this all happened just before my stint at the FBI's National Academy. When I left, I just assumed he'd continue to follow through on anything that was left undone.

"I was gone six months. By the time I returned, the case was cold. Nothing had emerged to help locate the statue. While our inquiries provided a sense of the minister's life before and after coming to Hawai'i, nothing had emerged to link her to the theft or her murder. Everything indicated that she died merely because she was on the premises at the time the job was pulled."

"Well, you've both got your homework assignments and I'll have a look into that moving company," said John. "Do either of you remember how large it was? Or, how many men might have worked for them?"

"You may laugh, but I was going to mention that I think we have a link to Menehune Transfer Company. Izzy's late husband worked for them for a while. Knowing her family's connections, she's probably acquainted with someone who has knowledge of the firm's day-to-day operations."

"Great! Could you give her a call tomorrow?"

"Sure John. But how do you want me to explain why we're looking into it?"

"I think that old line about a cold case plays well here. It's the truth and it doesn't reveal much. Okay?"

"Yes, sir!" I replied.

Picking up his briefcase, John said, "On that note, I shall leave you two to contemplate our progress tonight. Meanwhile I'll consider how we're going to bring the scattered pieces of this puzzle together."

What a night! I was both exhausted and exhilarated as I let Ke'oni walk John to the door. While I drained my cup of tea, I wondered if I should live it up and have a brandy Alexander and hope for a full night's sleep without any dreams.

When Ke'oni re-entered the room, he made the decision for me. "How about you light a couple of small candles on the back *lānai*, turn on the spa, and slip into a robe. I'll join you in our favorite bath as soon as I make you a wee potion of sleepy time magic."

I could not argue with that idea. Soon I was sipping a white Russian, while he enjoyed another glass of tea. After a few minutes of peaceful soaking—and having my feet rubbed—I turned the tables and returned the favor by massaging Ke'oni's shoulders.

That night I enjoyed the first deep and peaceful sleep I had experienced in a long time. By silent agreement, we did not discuss the case the next morning. We simply enjoyed fruit smoothies and went for a walk. As we approached the road fronting the pathway to the beach, I glanced back at our neighbors' yard and saw Miss Una watching us from their back wall.

"I think we've been given the feline equivalent of a blessing. I just wish I'd brought a towel and we could go for a swim."

"What do you think is around my neck," responded Ke'oni.

In a couple of hours, we were sitting at Mom's old kitchen table enjoying Kona coffee fortified with cinnamon and cocoa sugar. That, plus a couple of Izzy's biscotti would keep us sustained until we had a late lunch. We continued to watch for blinking lights or beeps from our phones and email notifications from the computers in our shared office. Since no one seemed to require our attention, I was able to complete my final edit of the article on the chefs. As I began closing my files on that project, I tried to reach Izzy on her cellphone. I got a recording stating that her voicemail was full. I feared it might be a while before I would be able to speak with her about the infamous transfer company. My primary questions focused on uniforms that had been centerstage in the outrageous events at a temple that is normally associated with universal peace and understanding.

In the meantime, Ke'oni reviewed and highlighted portions of his lengthy notes from the previous evening. Then he began reexamining his records of the original investigation...with special attention paid to anything regarding Tony. Periodically, he shared snippets of information with me.

"Once he took a vacation at the peak of an investigation. I've no idea where he went, but he came in one morning and said he needed to reconnect with an aunt who could die at any moment. Then there were the times Tony bought expensive boy toys like motorcycles, boats, and cars that should have been out of the price range expected for a single man living on a detective's salary. He always had a way of claiming he had found someone in dire straits, needing to unload the very item he was longing to pick up at a bargain basement price. I think the best Tony tale is the time Internal Affairs took a close look at his State and Federal income tax returns. Did I ever tell you about that?"

"No. But I'm eager to hear more about this golden child of good fortune," I said sarcastically.

"It was the year he bought a condo in a prestigious building in Waikīkī. It was not only large and on a high floor, but it had a great view of the bay. As always, he managed to sail through that examination of his personal affairs. Somehow, he just happened to have an uncle living in Australia who bequeathed him a tidy little sum in stocks, bonds, and cash. I've always wondered how closely that detail was researched. Probably not beyond the filing of a will and whatever form of probate system that country has."

On that note, we returned to our individual projects. I attempted to reach Izzy periodically. After completing my filing, I arranged for Andy Berger to enhance and enlarge some photos for me. I assured him that in addition to paying him for his time, I would compensate the magazine for any supplies he used. Within a short while, I sent him Joanne's picture of Tommy Kiyohara and the man I thought was Tony Brennan at 'Iolani Palace...plus a couple of Ke'oni's pictures that also featured our newest person of interest.

The morning passed without new assignments for either of us. We were soon seated in the kitchen enjoying a Panzanella salad with sour dough croutons and a variety of leftovers. A few sprigs of crushed peppermint leaves from a hanging pot on the *lānai* turned Ke'oni's last batch of sun tea into a classic drink we would enjoy throughout the afternoon.

"Do you think that tracking down the possible criminal activities of Tony Brennan will solve the case?" I asked.

"There's no way of knowing where the connection to Tony will take us, but I doubt that it will pinpoint a motive—other than financial gain. I think it would be premature and conceited to assume we can accomplish what Internal Affairs failed to do. I'm truly grateful for your visions...and the times you've seen Tony by chance. We wouldn't be anywhere near solving either the murder or the heist without your input. We have to remember that a lot of cases go unresolved, no matter what agencies are involved, let alone someone like you."

"I know you're right, but don't you feel hopeful about the prospects for solving the case, Ke'oni?"

"Sure. As of this moment. But I felt just as optimistic about solving the case that ended my career."

CHAPTER 21

Mysteries are due to secrecy.
Francis Bacon [1561 - 1626]

You've never fully explained the circumstances that led to your leaving HPD. I only know you were injured at work. And that when you were told you'd have to take a desk job, you opted to take early retirement."

"Like a lot of days, there was nothing special about my schedule leading up to the event that completely changed my life. I wasn't involved with a major crime case or undercover investigation. It was just a matter of following up on a warrant that came across the wires and a tip from an unidentified caller. A woman who was a con-game pro and occasional person of interest in international scams had arrived in the Islands for her brother's funeral. Unlike his older sister, he'd been a straight arrow guy. Arsenio Couto was a Marine who'd done three tours in Iraq and caught an IED on a street in Baghdad on the day he was supposed to ship home. He shipped home all right—in a body bag.

"Anyway, he was to be buried at the National Memorial Cemetery of the Pacific. A police officer assigned to CrimeStoppers was reading notices of upcoming burials at Punch Bowl. He remembered seeing a notice about a woman with a similar surname being sought by Interpol. I should say he recognized the similarity to the Portuguese surname, *Coutinho*. Although the officer noted the coincidence, he didn't think about it further until a call came in on the tip line. A waiter at Top of Waikīkī revolving restaurant called in to report hearing a Martina Coutinho make a suspicious cellphone call. He recognized her as a high school classmate who'd been on the run from the authorities for years. She was complaining about her awful boat trip from the mainland and saying how thrilled she was to be recovering at the luxurious Moana Hotel prior to attending her brother's funeral at Punch Bowl. The waiter wouldn't have called in except that she'd been very rude and didn't even leave a decent tip.

"That provided enough information for HPD to track her to the hotel. But a day had passed and they discovered she'd checked out a couple of hours earlier. Luckily, she'd talked to enough people that we were able to backtrack her to the boat she arrived on. Again, she wasn't there. But with the CrimeStoppers lead about the burial notice, the department was able to connect her to the deceased marine. So I was sent out with a female officer to pick her up at the cemetery.

"We did it that way because as a couple, we'd look less like we were there to arrest her. We arrived in the middle of quite a turnout. We noticed an honor guard off to the side of the grave, and a couple of families with children standing beneath a nearby tree. It seemed logical to join them since it gave us a good view of everything taking place."

"That makes sense. But how did you end up permanently injured if it was just a simple arrest?"

"That's a good question. There was nothing in Martina's past to indicate she'd be a physical threat to anyone. In trying to be polite about the funeral, we let everything unfold normally. The six-person guard brought the casket from the hearse to the gravesite. Family members and what I assume were close friends were seated. A Roman Catholic priest gave the service. Everyone stood for the three-volley salute and the playing of taps. Then the flag was folded and presented to the widow.

"Our perp had been standing at the end of a row of chairs. She then started to walk away casually. That was our clue to literally spring into action. We separated to try and pin her between us, but by then the woman was flying. We quickly realized that she wasn't moving toward the distant parking lots, but toward the hearse which had remained near the gravesite. Back in the day, I was quite a sprinter. I was pulling closer to her than my partner Ali. But just when I was thinking I'd be able to stop Martina, she reached into a pocket in her sundress and pulled out a handgun I later learned was a Smith and Wesson Model 637 pistol. And that my dear, is how I took two shots and ended my career in public safety."

"What happened to her? Marina Coutinho?"

"She and her little Lady Smith pistol sailed into the sunset. While Ali paused to stop the bleeding in my leg, Martina hopped in the hearse and took off. The driver claimed he had nothing to do with her. The reason he'd left the hearse on the roadway was that the widow had asked him to move the floral décor to the site of the post-funeral reception. Where the disappearing scam artist went has remained a mystery. My guess would be that Martina has continued to change her name and maybe the type of jobs she's pulling, since she's now guilty of shooting a public safety officer."

"What about the boat she sailed in on?"

"The Feds were very happy to hook up with the owner and captain of that vessel. It seems they'd been profiting from running high profile persons from place to place for a decade or more. I think their crew got off by helping to send their bosses to prison. In the end, that lovely Romsdal yacht was sold at auction."

Just then both of our cellphones chimed in unison. While Ke'oni checked a text message, I took a call from Izzy. She had seen my number appear as a missed call but couldn't understand why her voice messaging system was not working. Within a few minutes I had the information we needed on the Menehune Transfer company. The firm had gone into bankruptcy and that's why her husband was without work the last few years of his life. She said she'd check with a relative who had worked in the office to see if anyone knew the location of the Menehune Company's records.

After enjoying a quiet morning, our afternoon quickly became a time of action. John soon called with news on two fronts. First, an evidence bag from the *Marimu* had been misplaced. When it was located and opened, there was the welcome discovery of a good portion of a Menehune Transfer Company badge. It showed about half of a *menehune* shouldering an oversized moving box with the letters "transfer" at the bottom. The second item was more intriguing. The team of forensic investigators in Japan has sent Hitomu Kiyohara's belongings to HPD's forensic team.

John paused for a moment. "I know we've been seeing one another rather frequently, Natalie, but you know there are certain issues I don't like to discuss over the phone...or in an email. What have you two got planned for late afternoon? I've broken so many dates with Lori that I'd better keep tonight's. She works until five and it takes her about an hour to clean up for an evening among the living."

"I understand that concern. And I doubt you were planning to bring her to the windward side of the island. What if we meet you at the yacht club for a drink? We'll remain there for dinner. You can continue with any plans you've already made—or join us for whatever the club is offering."

With my phone on speaker, Ke'oni had heard the conversation. He nodded that he was fine with my proposal. Knowing JD's fondness for most everything on the club's menu and buffet, I had a feeling we'd be enjoying a festive foursome that night. Miss Una was not in sight when we departed for our four thirty rendezvous, but I left her an exciting plate of chicken pâté in case The Ladies failed to meet her high standards as a gourmand.

When we arrived at the yacht club, we found John standing at the side of the entrance. He was talking quietly on his cellphone. He disconnected and turned to us saying, "It's settled, Lori will join us here between five thirty and six."

"I don't know if you checked out tonight's menu board. I was doing some last-minute research on the Internet and tonight's specialty should please you. It's prime rib with Yorkshire pudding," announced Ke'oni. ""

That brought a smile to John's face as we entered the club. "Before I launch into my reasons for our meeting, is there anything you'll be add-ing to the dynamics of our meeting?"

"I think you'll agree that what I have to say puts another marker beside the name of my former partner."

"That's good, because I haven't found anything of particular note in the IA files."

The club's wait staff knows that Ke'oni is a private investigator and that our repeat guest is a lieutenant with HPD. They always manage to seat us in a corner where we can have some privacy. Since we had made reservations for dinner, our waiter was not surprised when we all ordered iced coffee initially. The men were satisfied with plain brew to accompany the club's signature mixed nuts toasted with a sweet and spicy seasoning blend. I topped my glass with a heavy sprinkling of cinnamon and cocoa powder.

"So, what unexpected piece of evidence have you uncovered for me?" queried John.

"As you requested, I've been reviewing my notes of the original in-vestigation. I'm hoping you'll eventually get more from the IA records than I have from my personal notes. Nevertheless, the process has refreshed my memory about a few things. I was glancing through my albums before shelving them and recalled that Tony threw a party for his sister soon after I returned from Virginia. She was visiting from the mainland. It was her birthday and Tony was playing the ever-generous big brother. He gave her a beautiful coral necklace from Ming's jewelry store. Men like that usually pride themselves in returning to the same sources for the bling they purchase.

"Although Ming's is out of business, one of their former jewelry designers is a gentleman I still have contact with. Charlie Chang's knowledge has been useful in more than one case, before and since my retirement. I took a chance and called to see if he remembered the ring we're looking into. Sure enough, he knew the piece. Intimately. It was one that he'd designed...for Tony.

"The reason he remembers the ring is that it features a Jager white diamond. It was the one Tony gave him to work into the Chaminade logo on his ring.

"These gems are highly transparent—except when exposed to florescent light, which reveals a bluish tint. They come from the Jagersfontein Mine in South Africa which closed down in 1971. Their value is not just from their unique properties. It is also because they're quite rare since they're not being mined anymore. The question is to determine how and where our boy may have obtained that diamond."

"What about the blue stone? I was thinking it might be lapis lazuli," I suggested.

"You're right about that. We may not think about it being a pri-cy stone. But its value can vary depending on several things: Where it comes from; if it has any visible calcite which depreciates it; or, flecks of gold-colored pyrite which increases its value. As usual, only the finest quality was ever good enough for Tony. The blue stone in his ring has all the right features. It's the deepest blue color, shows no calcite and has tiny flecks of gold pyrite around its edges. Best of all, Charlie was sure it had been mined in the Badakhshan district of Afghanistan. According to its designer, these features make this ring unique and therefore highly identifiable.

"Did your friend Charlie give any indication about how Tony obtained the lapis lazuli and diamond?" I wondered.

"According to Charlie, Tony laughed when asked. He said the stones had taken carefully guarded journeys along modern silk roads of high peaks and oceanic depths to reach him. I can make a case for the mountains of Afghanistan being the source of the lapis lazuli. Jagersfontein is an arid farming area, with one of the deepest man-made holes for mining diamonds. I don't see how both types of stones would have travelled together on a contiguous journey, with or without the reference to an ocean.

"There's one thing I should mention. Tony did a trade for the design and manufacture of his ring. You see, he had several pieces of unpolished lapis lazuli with which to barter. Although Charlie's designs are truly valuable, the white gold was the only material he had to contribute to the project. The pieces he could create from the rest of the lapis lazuli would more than pay him for his investment of time, talent, and a bit of gold. In fact, another bonus for us is that he still has a couple of the stones in his safe!"

"That's good to know, if we should need to verify the source of the ring," said John.

"I was careful to avoid saying anything about Tony's possible involvement in the heist and murder. I simply told Charlie that I was looking into a cold case and that the ring might play a role in its resolution. Since he's been out of the jewelry business for some time, I doubt he's had any contact with Tony. I concluded by confirming that he can identify the piece...and by saying I'd appreciate his keeping our conversation to himself, as he's always done."

"The photos of this one-of-a-kind ring provide the link between Tony and Tommy," declared John. "Now all we need to determine is a motive for Tommy's involvement. And we have to prove that Tony was one of the thieves and a participant, if not the trigger man, in the murder. It would also help to demonstrate how all the other parts of the story join together.

"I've just learned something that may provide an indication of Hitomu's state of mind at the time of his passing—although there's no indication of his having played a part in the crimes. He had a small digital recorder concealed in the shaving kit found in his hotel suite. Although he was legally blind, it seems he had no trouble in using an electric razor...or in recording a final message for his brother."

"About his eyes," I said. "I don't remember what the autopsy said was wrong with them."

"Thickened corneas; designated as Fuchs Corneal Dystrophy," answered John. "A lot of older people have the condition. It's not something an ME generally comments on because it's so common. But I continue to think the Japanese were being especially cautious about how they discussed the man's death.

"Someone with such a condition has shadowy areas in their vision...a kind of fuzziness, a blurring, sometimes with wavy lines. I haven't read his local medical records yet, but the Japanese ME remarked that his vision problems probably go back to the cleanup he performed after Typhoon Kitty...which I guess because of his family and age received some media coverage at the time. The ME specified that the results wouldn't have taken effect immediately. That over time, the chemicals he was exposed to in the blowing winds took their toll.

"As I was saying, Hitomu's recorder was in a hidden compartment in his shaving kit. That would make me wonder about the guy's overall lifestyle. But the Japanese forensic folks seemed more curious about why he was staying at a hotel rather than with family members. My thinking is that it was because he'd lived in the U.S. for a long time and was used to having his privacy. As a courtesy, the Japanese forensic team provided us with an English translation of Hitomu's message to Tommy."

He then laid a copy of the transcript between us. It appeared to be a well-written script of what Hitomu had said.

My Dearest Yasuhiro--Thank you for taking care of me and supporting me since we were young. I have very much appreciated the sacrifices you must have made to do so. When we went through the aftereffects of Kitii Taifu, neither of us could predict that we would move far beyond our homeland and have to rely on foreigners for our daily living. The days I spent helping with recovery from the storm taught me that there is no way we can plan for all the possibilities we will encounter in life. At that point, I thought I would become a monk. That changed in the midst of my studies. I heard many explanations of the differences in Buddhist schools of thought and realized that each has points of relevance. Therefore, there was no way I could dedicate myself to promoting only our family's practice of ancient Tendai principles. Each man or woman comes into life bearing karma. How can we know what has caused a person to act as they do in this life, let alone in a past existence? And so dear brother, I cast no judgment at you for what you may have done in your life. I cannot know what I have not seen. Even if I had, I cannot judge what I have not done personally. So, my dear little brother, live each of the rest of your days as best you can with thought to the end of your

journey. Thank you for everything. I apologize for leaving before you,
Hitomu

"I'm pretty sure this sums up Hitomu's state of mind. I don't think
we're going to learn anything else about the man. He had been relying
increasingly on his younger brother. If we read between the lines, I don't
think he was ever involved in anything nefarious. But it looks like he had
his own suspicions about his younger brother. Combine this message
to Tommy with his staying in a hotel—plus his wardrobe the day of his
death—and I think this brings us back to your feeling that Hitomu may
have committed suicide."

"So, what are you going to do with this final epistle of Hitomu's?"
asked Ke'oni.

"This is when I really wish you were back on the job. I think it's time
for a little good cop vs. bad cop. What I want to do is present Tommy —
Yasuhiro—with his brother's farewell message and see how he reacts."

"Even if I were still your partner, I don't think you need me. What I
do think you need is for a select group of people to be standing behind
the mirror he'll face when you present this evidence to him," suggested
Ke'oni.

"If you don't mind my saying it, I think he needs to hear his brother's voice. That will produce the deepest response," I said.

"As usual, you have a keen sense of human interactions, Natalie,"
John replied. "Maybe the best tact is a two-fold maneuver. I begin by
having him read the printout. Then I have someone come in with the
recording. We'll monitor everything throughout the interview. As one
of the original case officers, I can justify your being present Ke'oni. Maybe there should also be a psychological consultant present. And, I don't
think Captain Makani will want to be left out."

John then turned to me. "The only person I can't justify right now
is you, Natalie. However, I really do want your response to anything the
man says or does. A little bird hinted that the man upstairs may actually have an awareness that you've been contributing more than your
research ability on a couple of our cases. Let me see what I can set up."

"That still leaves the issue of my former partner. How are we going
to connect him to all this?" asked Ke'oni rubbing his temple.

"Good question. But I think it's time to stop the clock for tonight,"
said John, entering a few notes in his small notebook. "You keep checking on good 'ole Tony, while I put out a couple of calls about those out-
standing tests. I have a funny feeling that the torn Menehune patch may
prove as useful as that beautiful ring. You let me know as soon as you get
some more info from Izzy on that front, Natalie?"

On that note, our meeting concluded with the arrival of the delightful auburn-haired Lori. John got up and gave her a warm hug and kiss.
I could tell their relationship was moving forward nicely since she was

now involved with evidence relating to the case. The only issue we had to be cautious about was the depth of my involvement.

With that, I moved into a romantic mood myself. There are few moments that compare with watching a beautiful sunset over the waters of Waikīkī while holding hands with the man I love. As I enjoyed a delightful glass of St. Michelle's Indian Wells Reserve Chardonnay, I spent only a moment wondering about the modern silk road journey of blue and white gemstones.

It was beginning to feel like the border of our current puzzle was coalescing from separated pieces into a cohesive image we would soon recognize. Even Miss Una seemed to know that her human companions were in a good mood when we arrived home. I knew she was truly glad to greet us when she was sitting at the door to the garage with a couple of mouthfuls of food remaining on her plate. I swept her up in my arms and I suggested we all take in the moon glow from the covered lounge swing on the back lānai.

"I really don't want to write out any more lists, sweetheart. I'm feeling as though a lot of things are coming together," I enthused while positioning our little bundle of fur on the back of the cushion.

"I agree," said Ke'oni, pulling the coffee table toward us to serve as a footstool. "But I think a little of your list writing might be useful tomorrow...along with a few rounds of phone calls. For tonight, let's enjoy the sweet fragrances of our garden and that of The Ladies."

"And the presence of Miss Una. For once she seems more interested in us than her little playmate," I added.

It's amazing how much rest a person can get when stress is lifted from their shoulders. My stress had centered on uncertainty. The uncertainty of which aspects of my visions had been true, and which were embellishments of my creative mind. That made it so wonderful to awake with a sense of renewal and a confidence that the answers we sought would soon be presented! I even managed to start a pot of coffee before Ke'oni was out of bed. Soon he arrived in the kitchen with our buddy on his shoulder. I had not seen that since she was barely more than a kitten.

"Besides the coffee, what smells so good in here?" he asked, setting Miss Una on a chair.

"A little surprise I had sent in from Noah's in San Francisco—apple cinnamon bagels. I've been saving them for a special occasion."

"Aren't you getting ahead of yourself?"

"No. I think we need fortification for the home stretch!"

"I can't argue with that. I think we deserve a bit of gluttony. Then we can go into the office and begin writing that great list you suggested we make. At least, *you* can write out a master list of everything that you think needs to be examined. I'll cruise through my notes from your lengthy testimony last night."

Within twenty minutes Miss Una had enjoyed some crab tidbits and departed for a day at play. We cleaned the remains of our own breakfast and moved into high gear in the office.

"I can already see a division in labor," I said. "There are the things we're hoping JD is able to resolve. So far, that includes the contents of that evidence bag that was mislaid from the *Marimu*. Then there's his analysis of Tony's old case notes and anything new from Hitomu Kiyohara's medical records. And there's also the matter of the undercover officer who was placed with Nippon Antiquities. As for me, I guess my focus is on learning what Izzy's contact can provide about the former Menehune Company's daily operations."

Ke'oni nodded, opening his laptop. "Regarding my end of things, I put out a couple of feelers on Tony's accounts and licenses. He's never worked at it, but he does maintain a license as a PI. That means he has access to the same resources I do. But since my contacts are already in the know about his questionable profile over the years, I think I'm safe."

"What you're saying is that Tony could learn you're, well, spying on him, on his affairs?"

"Um, yeah. And I still question what he really did at the crime scene and later when I was gone. Depending on how this all goes down, I'm wondering what impact this case may have on other ones he investigated during his career. We still have no idea who his cohorts may have been in this case, let alone anything else.

"You know, Natalie, I've been looking over my notes on your recollections. There's another item you noticed that hooks him to all this. You identified a dark brown sedan on the street above the temple. That's exactly what he was driving when the crime went down. I didn't think much about it at the time, but Tony said he was on Lusitana Street when a car came speeding out of the temple's back parking lot. That's who you saw helping the lady and her dog...with one minor deviation from the truth. *He* was the one who nearly hit her as he was trying to get away from the crime scene."

CHAPTER 22

*We are the children of many sires, and every drop of blood in us
in its turn... betrays its ancestor.*
Ralph Waldo Emerson [1803 – 1882]

The day was barely half over when Keʻoni got a text from John wanting to set up a time for a conference call with both of us. Shortly we were soon speaking about some results from his work.

"Sorry I couldn't talk earlier. I was going through some evidence files in a very public space and didn't want to be overheard."

"Not a problem. But I do have high security on all of our devices," replied Keʻoni.

"That's good. As we planned, I've been tiptoeing through your old notes on the case. In addition to that, Lori and Marty have me on alert for some interesting news later today. Would you like to drop in for some of his fine brew later? At say, four o'clock. I can already tell you that there's been one interesting development regarding our mutual friend. It pinpoints some aspects of what we might call the timetable of his availability for a certain activity."

On the hour, Keʻoni and I walked into the ME's office and were greeted with a fresh pot of Marty's private stash of Bolivian coffee. It was a bit strong for me, but after I added milk and sugar, the jolt of caffeine was quite palatable.

"It's good to see you, Natalie," welcomed Marty.

"And I you."

"How's Nathan doing?" asked Marty.

"Quite well, considering everything that changed in his life with the passing of Ariel," I said truthfully about the impact of the death of my twin's granddaughter.

In a few minutes we were settled in the conference room looking at several stacks of forms and files.

"I guess I'll begin since I don't have much to say," John said. "I've looked over Tony Brennan's reports from the initial case. There's nothing irregular about them...except that there isn't much there. It's like it was a rookie's first time off the leash. Or, someone didn't want there to be much to look at in the future."

At that point, Ke'oni recounted the fact that Tony was the first detective on the scene. And that the man had a weak alibi for why he was in the area.

"By the way, since Lori had a class at the University Med School, Marty will do the full report on everything the ME's Office has been doing."

"The first thing I'll share with you is our review of a couple of new details from our forensic team. You know how technology keeps changing; even our microscopic tools are better today. So, we thought it would be a good idea to recheck her clothing for anything that might have been missed. Sure enough, a single strand of hair was found in the seam of her surplice. The DNA was not that difficult to find. It's already in the system. You know the Caucasian male to whom it belongs—Anthony Brennan, formerly of the Honolulu Police Department."

"There it is! Nicely tied with a bow," stated John. "That man was never involved with the victim's body during the crime scene investigation. In fact, Ke'oni, you told me that you and Tony were checking out the temple and its campus at the time the forensic folks were examining the crime scene and the body was removed. Next item, Marty has verified that Tony's name is not linked to any work performed in this office."

"Well, that last point moves us down the road toward an indictment," affirmed Ke'oni.

"I guess I should report my news," I said. "While Ke'oni was going through his notes, I had a conversation with Izzy's cousin who used to work for the Menehune Transfer Company. He was able to confirm a couple of links to this and maybe other cases as well. It seems that Nippon Antiquities has used that firm on a regular basis. When the original transfer company went out of business, one of the owner's sons acquired a truck and launched his own moving operation. Except for being older, that man matches my, um, *image* of the second perpetrator to a T."

John looked at me and absorbed my nervousness. "Ah, Natalie, I think you should know that Marty is fully aware of the special ways in which you've been helping me and the Department. So you can relax, Okay?"

I glanced at Marty, but he was too busy reading a report in front of him to pay attention to what was being said.

After a few moments, Marty began his report. "We've also gone back over the data on the bullet that was removed from the victim," he announced. "We have no records on potential shooters and the info on that bullet was rather vague. It's believed to have come from a .38 service revolver...type and manufacturer unspecified. However, Lori is somewhat of a specialist on European semi-automatic pistols. It's her opinion that the probable weapon was a 9x18mm Russian Makarov semi-automatic pistol.

John interjected, "We've seen quite a few of these weapons arrive in the baggage of soldiers returning from the Middle East—anywhere from Iraq to Afghanistan. There's quite a trade among collectors. Until recently, it wasn't that difficult to bring the weapons into the country. If we get our hands on the gun that killed the minister, there's a chance we'll get a serial number that could allow us to trace its history. With today's chemical forensic analysis, we can often raise an image that a perpetrator may have thought they'd removed."

"You said Afghanistan could be the source of the gun? That's where the lapis lazuli came from that's in Tony's ring," I volunteered.

"Whoa, Natalie. You're getting ahead of the man's presentation," said John with a chuckle.

Marty smiled and continued. "When John told me about that ring, I checked with the forensic team to ask about any other Afghan connections there might be."

"That brings us back to the evidence bag from the *Marimu* that went missing," added John. "Several things came to light once its contents were analyzed, including a few particles of lapis lazuli dust. Charlie Chang the jeweler confirmed that the stones from which it came were mined in the exact area of Afghanistan as the stone in Tony's ring. We've actually got a lot of evidence we can lay at the feet of Tony. We've got Charlie's testimony, a couple of the lapis lazuli stones he's got in his safe, and the ring itself.

"And, that portion of a Menehune uniform patch we found on the *Marimu* finishes the link between Tony, the boat, and the Kiyohara family. Luckily, our ability to lift DNA from fabric has come a long way. We've got a fingerprint on that specimen that belongs to our boy Tony, and it doesn't matter that we don't know how long the patch was tucked into the hidden compartment in the owner's stateroom. Also, we found slivers of Indian and Nepalese ivory embedded in that headboard.

"I'm beginning to think Tony, Tommy, and their friends have been conducting lucrative and nefarious seafaring activities through the years. There's no telling what goods the *Marimu* may have moved across the waters under the cover of Nippon Antiquities. The other detail that helps prove the link to Tommy Kiyohara is that he fancies himself quite the yachtsman. We have proof of his membership in yacht clubs across the Pacific. We're now cruising through the captains' logs to note dates and ports when he was aboard.

"Next, we'll ask our foreign colleagues to compare their records of relevant crimes they've been tracking to the dates and destinations we hope to uncover. If we're lucky, we'll find Tommy's itinerary in sync with those records."

"Wow. You've certainly had a profitable day so far," said Ke'oni with admiration. "Has any other evidence emerged?"

"Nothing that matters. The statue of the Buddha was carefully checked for possible prints and exposure to illegal substances. Nothing materialized. But there are partial fingerprints of Tommy all over the boat. Of course, he's got reasons for being aboard the *Marimu*. Now that we have enough evidence to bring Tony in for a little chat, I don't think we'll have any problem getting a judge to sign a search warrant for *his* property.

"That's where I'm thinking we might find the *Mother Lode*—prints from Tommy *and* a man, or men, connected to Menehune Transfer Company. And, don't forget those partial fingerprints at the Kiyohara estate that came from a couple of Yakuza lieutenants known to several international public safety agencies. Wouldn't it be lovely to find that Tony was busily mixing with those guys as well as the Kiyoharas."

I quickly responded. "It's funny that you should mention the Yakuza. When I was researching Japanese Buddhism, I ran across an interesting news item. In 2006, the principals of the Enryakuji priesthood—Tendai that is—performed a ceremony for former Yakuza leaders in Japan. It was quite a scandal because the temple was said to have received crime-related money. With subsequent media reports and criticism by the Japan Buddhist Temple Association, all of the directors of Enryakuji resigned."

"That may have nothing to do with our case, but it's amazing that religion continues to pop up in this investigation," observed John with a shake of his head.

"So, what's next?" I asked, looking from Marty to John.

The Assistant Medical Examiner smiled as he began bundling his files and evidence bags. "I will be putting my records to bed, very carefully...and adding to them when the last of the toxicology reports arrive. At this point, I'm not expecting anything that will alter the trajectory of the case in a major way."

"As to what could arise," began John, "there's one thread left to be pulled. And that is my undercover man at Nippon Antiquities. Manny Salazar is married to a distant cousin of the Kiyohara family. That made it pretty easy to move him into place. He'd announced he was finishing an MA in Asian studies and was looking for a part-time job. That suited the company's needs perfectly, since they really are liquidating everything in the Ala Moana gallery. Manny's checked in with us periodically, but so far he hasn't found anything of note. I'll next be concentrating on setting up a little visit to headquarters for both Tony and Tommy."

It took a couple of days for John to confer with Captain Makani and set everything in place for interviewing our persons of interest. The planning centered on creating an environment in which the final evidentiary details would emerge. The challenge was minimizing the appearance that either man had been revealed as a perpetrator of murder and grand larceny.

One of the strategies was to have Ke'oni make a non-threatening appearance as the second detective originally assigned to the case. That should reassure Tony that he had nothing to fear. If the retired detectives crossed paths with Tommy, he would undoubtedly say he was there to see his brother's effects which had just been returned from Japan.

On the day of the interviews, John greeted us at the doors of HPD headquarters. "Tony and Tommy will arrive soon ...separately, of course."

"And who will enjoy the pleasure of your company first?" inquired Ke'oni with a smile.

"Who do you think? Tommy is most likely to yield evidence without realizing what he's doing. Here's what's planned. Tony is supposed to arrive first and be held in the waiting room with you, Ke'oni. Tommy will be greeted as he enters and taken immediately to an interrogation room. That way they'll see each other but have no opportunity to pass words or signals. We're hoping that by following our pre-set program, Tommy (or should I say Yasuhiro), will feel motivated to shine a light on his partner in crime.

"I'll begin by expressing our sorrow for his loss. Then I'll present him with the transcript of the message his brother left him. After that, Nori Horita will enter the room with Hitomu's recording. I'll introduce him as a consultant. He'll sit beside me to watch Tommy's responses. The final nail in the coffin of reality will be Manny's arrival with Hitomu's clothing and personal effects in evidence bags. If recognition of his employee doesn't bring Tommy to the bargaining table, nothing will.

"Where will we be during this?" I asked.

"As I've said, for a few minutes, Tony will be cooling his heels with you, Ke'oni. That way he should continue to believe you've both been called in for an interview regarding your original investigation. Hopefully, he'll also be speculating on what Tommy might be unveiling. Once the "T's" are both in place behind closed doors, Ke'oni will join you, Alena, and the Captain in that famous large room with two-way mirrors spanning both of the rooms with our persons of interest."

"I get to watch the interviews?" I asked hopefully.

"Yes, indeed. You're Makani's guest of honor. With all you've done to bring this case to conclusion, he feels that you and Alena deserve to see all of the case come together."

Everything went as planned. John was very smooth in his handling of Tommy Kiyohara. He began by expressing the usual phrase of, "The department joins me in saying we're sorry for your loss." He even embellished it by adding that Hitomu had been a great asset to our city and the community of antiquity specialists.

"As I mentioned, we've received your brother's effects from the Kiyōto Prefecture's forensic folks. We'll be returning them to you shortly. I thought you might like to know that Hitomu left you a special message."

At this point, Tommy's face revealed a look of surprise. His eyes widened more when John laid the transcript of Hitomu's recording in front of him. As the man slowly read the text, John began spreading out pictures of his brother's body on Mount Hiei. Then he added crime scene photos taken in the temple sanctuary.

Since the activity in the room was being monitored, it was easy to time the arrival of Nori Horita with a recorder.

"Ah, here is Professor Horita. He sometimes aids us in international affairs. We thought you might wish to hear your brother's words as they were spoken."

Nori Horita said nothing. He merely set up the recorder in front of Tommy and sat down beside John. We, like the professor, were positioned to watch Tommy throughout the interview. At John's cue, Nori turned on the recording. The soft voice of Hitomu immediately impacted his younger brother. We watched Tommy's gaze move from the recorder to the photos displayed before him. His crestfallen face demonstrated that the plan was working.

Space may have been added to the back of the recording because a lengthy emptiness followed the words of the deceased.

"Very interesting. Don't you think Mr. Kiyohara? As you will note from the photos in front of you, we are also looking into this cold case related to the heist of the statue of the *Shākyamuni* Buddha that your firm recently tried to sell at auction."

Tommy looked from the photos to Nori, perhaps remembering him from the auction. Nori performed as desired. His face revealed nothing as he calmly returned Tommy's look.

John continued. "You know, we had a noteworthy visit to your family home in Hawai'i Kai recently. You wouldn't believe what we found in a closet in the guest cottage. A little pattern of dust that just happens to match the base of this statue," said John, tapping the image of the stolen artifact.

Before Tommy could respond, the door opened. Manny Salazar entered with several clear evidence bags. He stood at the head of the table while John methodically gathered most of the photographs into a stack...leaving the images of the deceased minister and the Buddha at the sides. Manny carefully laid out the bags with Hitomu's clothing between them. He then set smaller bags with his watch, wedding ring, and prayer beads on top.

Tommy looked up long enough to register his recognition of Manny as Nippon Antiquities' latest hire. Then he froze as John laid one final photograph on top of the evidence bags. It was the enhanced and enlarged image of him standing with Tony at the side of the banyan tree at 'Iolani Palace. And that was that...as the old saying goes. The man simply crumpled downward, resting his head in the palm of his left hand.

John nodded to Nori and Manny. They picked up the materials with which they had entered and quietly departed. John methodically straightened the three remaining photos and softly asked, "Is there anything you'd like to share with me?" The audio system of the room picked up Yasuhiro Kiyohara's full confession.

A short while later, elements of the preceding scene were repeated with Tony. He, of course, knew when to request an attorney... a person who was not long in arriving. My favorite part of the scene occurred when John announced that a forensic team was going through Tony's car and homes at that moment. Then he laid out the picture of Tony's right hand on the banyan tree at 'Iolani Palace.

"You know, that's quite a lovely ring, Tony. Very distinctive. According to Charlie Chang, there isn't another one like it in the world."

What did we learn in the end? A few days after our rendezvous with destiny at HPD headquarters, a group of persons intimately involved in the case met at the yacht club. There Ke'oni and I hosted a round of drinks and a final summation from Lieutenant John Dias. Also present were medical examiners Marty Soli and Lori Mitchum, Detective Manny Salazar, Detective Alena Horita and her father, professor Nori Horita.

"I think I'll turn to Manny for our first clarification," declared John.

Manny Salazar said, "In my work as an undercover officer, I obtained a temporary position as employee of Nippon Antiquities through a relative of mine. In that role, I had several opportunities to view records of both the company and the Kiyohara family. I feel comfortable in confirming my report that the Kiyohara family is comprised of some great people. As far as we can tell, none of them—except for Tommy Kiyohara—were involved in anything criminal.

"Once we apprised Hitomu's son Koji and the staff of Nippon Antiquities of the situation, they were most forthcoming about their operations over the years. None of them had any awareness that the *Shāk-yamuni* Buddha was on the family's estate until it showed up on the auction block. As long as Hitomu was alive, they accepted his brother Tommy serving as the virtual captain of their corporate ship. But once that was no longer the case, a lot of oddities came to light." At that point, Manny turned the floor back to JD.

"One of those oddities is the *Marimu*. Hitomu didn't like water in any form, so the purchase of the boat made little sense. His aversion to water might harken back to that typhoon which initiated his health challenges. His brother Tommy, however, seemed to love anything nautical. He had a standard line he used whenever someone questioned him about his periodic seafaring jaunts. It was something about flying the corporate flag in places where the company obtained the goods they sold in their galleries and at auction. That may be true, but with the minute amounts of gem dust and slivers of ivory found aboard, we're pretty sure that Tommy and his partners were running a few other games.

"That brings us to the matter of the Menehune Transfer Company. Hitomu's son Koji said that their company has always patronized family businesses like theirs. As long as he could remember, the folks at Menehune handled the moving of goods for Nippon Antiquities. When that firm went under, the son of its owner (Sammy Māhoe) took over the company name, filing taxes as a sole proprietorship. We think he's tapped into his circle of buddies whenever he's needed help. And we're pretty sure that he was Tony's cohort in our case. What we're not certain of is whether he drove the truck himself or had someone along for the ride. The catch is that he's quite a bit older than Tony and not in very good health. In the last couple of years, Nippon Antiquities has been handing out their transfer jobs on a piece-meal basis to other firms.

"As far as wrapping the case goes, Tony's lawyered up. But we've got his fingerprint on that Menehune patch we found on the *Marimu*. We've also got a direct link to Tommy Kiyohara. That's the picture of Tony's hand with his custom ring prominently displayed on a tree trunk beside Tommy on the grounds of 'Iolani Palace. The confirmation of that ring's origin is an affidavit from jeweler Charlie Chang. In it, Charlie details Tony's custom order and offers a technical description of all the lapis lazuli stones Tony traded for his design services.

"I've saved the best for last: The gun that killed Minister Fujimot! We found it in a small safe under a false bottom in Tony's bathroom sink cabinet."

John looked at Marty and Lori, who merely nodded in reply. "Lori's guess about that gun was right on the money. It *is* a 9x18mm Russian Makarov semi-automatic pistol, brought into this country from Afghanistan by a soldier who ended up on the street as a homeless vet. The man initially used it in a break-in at a pawn shop. Guess who handled that crime scene?"

"My old partner, good ole Tony!" Ke'oni said.

John nodded. "That gun appears to have become his backup piece. By the time we're through, we may find it's connected to a couple of other cold cases."

"What about Tommy?" I asked.

"As to Tommy, we've got his comprehensive confession. He's confirmed that he ordered the theft of the Buddha...and a few other items in the Islands...from Tony and whoever else he may have needed to help him. Tommy did not know about the minister's murder initially. But he didn't seem overly disturbed by it. We know he's not religious himself, but very respectful of his brother and by extension, somewhat honors the family's religious connections. When asked about his motive in ordering the theft of the Buddha, we didn't get a clear answer. All he said was that he always looked for ways to please his brother. He was babbling so much by then that I don't know how to classify that part of his confession. Maybe there's something you can add, Nori."

The Japanese linguist and cultural specialist nodded and paused before speaking. "This has been a complicated matter from the beginning. Tommy Kiyohara is not a practicing Buddhist. But he's lived among Buddhists throughout his life. Indebted to his brother for saving him as a child, Tommy may have wondered if Hitomu's prayers *did* play a role in his rescue. Desiring to bring light to his brother's darkening world, the statue represented something he may have perceived as being capable of enhancing Hitomu's spiritual experience. Even though the nearly blind man could not fully know the reality of the statue, he would have touched and even smelled its composition. Therefore, he would have known that it was an old and revered piece of Buddhist iconography.

"I should probably say something else about the history of this statue. As I have noted before, I do not know how this *Shākyamuni* image of the Buddha came to be given to our Honolulu Jōdo Shin temple by a Tendai temple in Japan. Over time, the origins of such a sacred object can become obscured. I do not think that anyone today would care to reargue the ancient rivalries between these two Buddhist traditions. It is possible that the leaders of the Tendai temple in Japan had some historic connection with members of our temple and reached out in this way as a means to laying aside past strife.

"John, you said Tommy Kiyohara told you his ancestors commissioned an artist to create the statue for his family's temple on Mount Hiei. Maybe he felt that giving the statue to another Buddhist sect in a foreign country was disrespectful to his family. I think that was the motive for the theft. Tommy thought he was retrieving a valuable symbol of his heritage…as well as bringing new significance to his brother's religious practice."

"But surely the murder of any Buddhist minister would have tainted that revered object," I suggested.

Nori shook his head. "I believe that neither the *sensei's* presence in the temple, nor her death, were considerations in the theft. It was sad, but not intentional. To Buddhists, the cycles of birth and death, with their attendant joys and sorrows, continue throughout humankind's experience of life on this plane. Think of the two images of the Buddha, as they have been in the temple and will be again: these are the faces of the Shaka man of Nepal and Amida, the one who has risen to Buddhahood. As has been said for centuries, the teachings of the Shaka enlightens you in this world and Amida, the Buddha of Infinite Light and Life saves you in the next."

Such thoughts have been expressed by many philosophies in our world. Perhaps that is why the Buddhist minister I observed at her altar had shown the world such a serene countenance even in death.

EPILOGUE

When I hear music, I fear no danger.
Henry David Thoreau [1817 - 1862]

Today's happy assemblage at White Sands Cottage was gathered to celebrate my leap forward in all things culinary...and the closure of a cold case of a murder that has touched me in many ways. Of course, only a few of our guests know about those matters. The party was quite lively, so I thought I could take a break for a few minutes and walked outside to the hexagonal gazebo Ke'oni was building for us in the backyard. Looking back through the dining windows, I saw that everyone seemed to be enjoying the buffet I was providing.

With Izzy flitting in and out of the backdoor with wonderfully smelling dishes, it was initially assumed that her kitchen was the source of these delectable treats. Of itself, that is true. However, I am the newbie chef whose hands have prepared these items. If that were known initially, the bowls and platters might still be full, for I have had a reputation for producing food that is noted for being less than fresh, let alone palatable.

Thanks to the produce from Joanne's garden and close supervision under Izzy's watchful eyes, I had shaped a menu I was proud to serve. I had begun by making and freezing cheese cracker dough. I also froze logs of Auntie Carrie's famous sugar cookie dough, which I baked yesterday and finished with vanilla paste icing and cinnamon sugar sprinkles. Likewise, the Maui onion soup was prepared yesterday and served today in pots de crème cups topped with crostinis oozing with a gruyere cheese from Maui. Earlier this week, I had made a compote of apples with whole cranberries, as well as one with strawberries and rhubarb. Those would be offered beside Ke'oni's latest ice cream of macadamia nut praline. Beyond that, the buffet offered Island wines and beer, plus:

~ Slices of ham kissed with local honey

~ Skewers of teriyaki Big Island beef strips, and plump shrimp from a nearby farm

~ Steamed brown rice with almond and onion slivers and a sprinkle of olive oil

~ Carrot salad with Mandarin orange segments, yellow raisins, and

chunks of fresh pineapple

~ A vegetable crudités platter with yogurt-based rémoulade

~ Crostini with garlic, basil, and cherry tomatoes, tofu, green onions, and minced shrimp

Earlier, as I was debating how to unveil the truth of my labors, I was honored by Chef Akira Duncan's announcement that he was proud to have me as his latest protégé. I then made my grand pronouncement to the friends, neighbors, and public safety officials who were serving as the unknowing tasters of my first culinary endeavor. At that point, my twin Nathan gave me the high sign that he and Adriana were impressed with my endeavors.

It has been a few weeks since the resolution of the Reverend Ayameko Kōha Fujimoto's murder. It amazes me about today's gathering being a rite of passage for me as well as the celebration of the life of a wonderful woman whom I never met on this plane.

Enjoying the sights and scents of my surroundings, I thought about how I view my place in life. My conscious mind knows that the past is behind us and that I must live in the present if I wish to enjoy the future. But somehow, for today at least, my creative spirit is savoring the joining of people whose lives have transcended time and culture for me.

I have returned to the misty scene of ancient Japan with a few variations. As before, I view the grandfather in his black cotton yukata *and* obi. *He nods peacefully, enjoying the presence of the womanhood he so loves. On the stone bench alongside him sits his beautiful daughter, playing a wooden flute he carved for her in childhood. Seated on a long flat rock at the base of the trunk of the blooming* shidarezakura *cherry tree, sits the happy girl child from my earlier vision. Dressed in her floral-patterned* yukata, *she plays rhythmically with two fallen branches of the jewel-toned blossoms. Beside her sits the Reverend Ayameko Kōha Fujimoto wearing her black silk* okesa *overlaid with plum-colored* hangesa. *Now without the eyeglasses of her maturity, she plays the haunting* koto *of her youth. On the far side of the bench I see a row of* getas, *large and small.*

At the distant call of a peacock, I look across the landscape to the compound of aged wooden buildings fronted by a tori. *On the left is the graceful bridge that arches across the small kidney-shaped pond. Sprinkled in the placid waters are the irregular stones that now appear harmless, with sporadic lotus flowers growing at their edges.*

Seated at the center of the bridge is a man in monk's robes, dangling his feet like a young boy. I know him to be the father of the girl child. He glances across time and space to his family. Inspired by the idyllic scene, he chants words from the beloved Lotus Sutra.

And each of these Buddhas
Settled under a jeweled tree—

As lotus blossoms
Adorn a limpid, cool pond.
   A gathering mist obscures my view, but I continue to hear the har-
monious weaving of the music upon the winds blowing through my vision.

NOTES AND ACKNOWLEDGMENTS

In writing this fourth book in the Natalie Seachrist Hawaiian mysteries, I have drawn again on my years as a long-term resident of Hawai'i. As other authors have observed about their work, the characters in this series have grown beyond my original conception. Most of mine have been created without connection to any person, living or deceased. A few do share characteristics with people who have impacted my life in one way or another, and a few of their names.

Where possible, I present factual information about the historical individuals and incidents I describe. I do not identify the temple in which my fictional murder takes place, but I have looked to the Honpa Hongwanji Jōdo Shin temple on the Pali Highway on the island of O'ahu for inspiration. The origin of the story of the love of an insect for its mate was taken from a *dharma* message I heard during a Sunday service at that temple. As on other occasions, I found the spirit of love and respect for all of life both inspiring and challenging.

As with many topics, I have sought accuracy in describing elements of Jōdo Shin Buddhism. However, there are aspects of the temple I describe that are drawn with the creative license of an author. Some of these adjustments were made in order to facilitate the solving of the crime I explore. The inspiration for this story rests on a violent incident that occurred at a Buddhist temple in Waddwell, Arizona in 1991. Nine victims were murdered, including a nun and her nephew, a novice monk.

As with aspects of Chinese regional dialects offered in *Murders of Conveyance*, this book has challenged me linguistically. While I have strived to present sufficient data to help readers without previous knowledge of Asian languages and philosophies, I cannot claim there are no errors in the information I share. I hope that you will find the brief summary of aspects of the Hawaiian language useful. The reader should note that there is no "s" in the Hawaiian or Japanese languages. Since the book is written for an English reading audience, I have applied English grammar rules for possessives and pluralization, as in the words *leis* and *getas*. I should also mention that although Chinese, Japanese, and other Asian languages place the surname (family name) before a person's given name, I have usually followed the norms of English and placed given names prior to surnames.

The expressions of Buddhism I touch upon developed over many centuries in their movement across the Asian continent to Japan. This led to many variations existing in the spelling, pronunciation, and even the precise meaning and usage of terms I include. Similarly, local, regional, and national artistic schools developed singular and conjoined interpretations of philosophical iconography. In short, many of the personages and terms I mention have been discussed in innumerable essays, treatises, and books by worthy scholars throughout recorded time. I hope that while I may barely scratch the surface of many topics, you will find your own path to exploring those you wish to pursue further.

Hawai'i has embraced cultural elements from the myriad peoples who have immigrated there. Beyond food and philosophy, architecture has added a richness to Island living. The last home I lived in on O'ahu was a townhome in Kāne'ohe. It was located in Temple Valley on the windward side of the island. The community's name is drawn from the stunning non-denominational Buddhist Byōdō-in Temple situated in an area cemetery. To enhance relations with its neighbors, the temple provides free access to its property through a small gate on a side street. Unfortunately, I did not learn of its existence until the last year of my residence, when I became a frequent visitor to the beautiful edifice.

The bright red temple is a perfect scale model of a temple in Uji, Japan. Its distinctive features include parklike grounds with a beautiful pond, a large *bonshō* bell that visitors can ring, and a golden statue of the *Amida Buddha*. Also prominent are magnificent peacocks, ancient symbols of Asian royalty. Their stirring cries often call one's attention to perches on the temple's upturned eaves, lintels, railings, and other architectural elements.

The International Festival of the Pacific is now a multi-month event in Hilo, Hawai'i. It is sponsored by the Hilo Japanese Chamber of Commerce and Industry to honor the arrival of the Japanese to Hawai'i and the historic role of Japanese culture in the Islands. Appealing to both local residents and tourists, the event includes many of the elements I describe. The major performance of international music and dance is no longer a part of the Festival, although there is a desire to see it return.

Planning for the 150th anniversary celebration of Japanese immigrants in Hawai'i was conducted by the Gannenmono Committee with assistance from the Consulate-General of Japan in Honolulu. The festivities featured the Japanese Defense Force ship, *Nippon Maru* which returned to Hilo on Jan. 6, 2018. Built in 1930 the original sailing ship was named *Kaiwo Maru*. The barque trained 11,500 naval cadets over 54 years for the Japanese National Institute for Sea Training, until its decommissioning in 1984.

As I mention, the late *Kumu hula* Dorothy (Dottie) Mitamura Horita organized entertainers for the Hilo International Festival for many years. She was a superb performer herself, as a singer of many types of music, as well as a dancer of *hula*. I knew her from the early 1970s, when she hired me to perform Scottish Highland Dancing at the festival. After the show, off-island performers were treated to a lovely annual Japanese dinner at which attendees were encouraged to offer a capella songs. One year, when students of mine performed, I was honored when Dottie sang a beautiful arrangement of "Oh Danny Boy" to thank me for my participation.

Like Natalie Seachrist, I am not fond of boating—in any kind of water. For readers who may have an interest in pursuing that activity in the Islands, please be aware that there are licensing requirements in Hawai'i for the protection of boat drivers and their passengers, as well as the general public. Please visit the website of the State of Hawai'i Department of Land and Natural Resources, Division of Boating and Ocean Recreation for further information.

In 1949, Typhoon Kitty [*Kitii Taifū*] emerged from the area of Kwajalein and struck the island of Honshū, Japan, from the south. It hit the cities of Yokohama, Tōkyō, and Kyōto, before dissipating as it moved northward toward the island of Hokkaidō. In addition to damage to port facilities and hundreds of vessels, more than 200 people died, and additional thousands were injured and/or rendered homeless. Torrential rains caused more storm damage than the winds which gusted to eighty miles per hour. Occurring after WWII, the Supreme Command of Allied Powers (SCAP) was in charge of many aspects of daily life in Japan, including recovery from the event. As Japanese media were curtailed at the time, I am grateful that U.S. military journalism covered aspects of this tragedy.

The 2006 scandal at the Enryakuji Temple on Mount Hiei was an actual event. Senior members of the Tendaishū priesthood at Enryakuji performed a ceremony for former Yakuza leaders in Japan. It was a national scandal because the temple was said to have received crime-related money. With subsequent media reports and criticism by the Japan Buddhist Temple Association, all of the directors of the temple resigned.

Many people have assisted with verifying information included in this work and refining the storyline and text. I again wish to acknowledge Tim Littlejohn, a State of Hawai'i library manager. As this series has unfolded, Tim's input has been invaluable in encouraging my attention to cultural sensitivity and the harmonizing of numerous elements in my plotlines.

Additional thanks go to long-time colleagues and supporters who have provided myriad forms of input. I am sad to tell you that this is the last book for which the late geologist Keven C. Horstman, PhD, was able to share his knowledge with me. I trust that the generous and comprehensive assistance he provided to so many people will serve to guide many people in future research and analysis.

Fellow writers in a weekly literary salon have also provided unending support and inspiration for several years, including the late Larry Sakin, who was a political writer and radio host; Kay Lesh, psychologist, memoirist, and mystery writer, whose keen yet calming edits have soothed rough corners; and, poet and prosaist Bill Black, whose invaluable technical expertise has saved me from innumerable potential flaws.

I also thank readers of this series for their input including readers Bob Shrager, Jean and Frank Kaleba, Betty Soli, and Nelda Garza. As always, I am grateful to the intrepid staff of the Kirk-Bear Canyon branch of the Pima County Library System for their interest in and support of local authors. And, what can I say beyond "Thank you immensely" to my fabulous and sometimes challenged editor, Viki Gillespie, a perennial book lover and former book seller. Finally, I thank my husband John Burrows-Johnson for his patience and support through the decades.

Errors you find are wholly my fault. I hope they do not detract from my desire to communicate the humility and love of life that practitioners of Buddhism express in daily life. Please contact me about egregious flaws you find, as I would dislike repeating them. I also wish to hear your suggestions regarding historical and cultural themes that might be appropriate to the Natalie Seachrist series. You may contact me at info@JeanneBurrows-Johnson.com.

ANNOTATED GLOSSARY
NON-ENGLISH & SPECIALIZED VOCABULARY

This extensive glossary is provided for readers (especially students) who may wish to expand their understanding of the terms used in this book. Many Buddhist terms are derivations from Chinese and other Asian languages. Please note that many Hawaiian words have multiple spellings and (with or without diacritical marks) may have multiple meanings. Also be aware that Hawaiian words, especially names, have ambiguous, layered, and sometimes hidden meanings.

A

A cappella
Chapel like; in the manner of the chapel. [Italian] Performance by an individual or group without instrumental accompaniment.

Addendum
Give toward or that which is to be added. [Latin] Supplementary material added to a book, letter, report, etc. including omissions, postscripts, afterwords, appendixes.

Aficionado
Enthusiast. [Spanish] Person who is a knowledgeable admirer of a subject or activity.

'Ahi
Tuna. [Hawaiian] Often yellow fin tuna. [Scientific name, *Thunnus albacares*]

Ainu
Also Ainyu. *Human.* [Japanese] Indigenous people of northern Japan and eastern Russia. Today they inhabit the northern Japanese island of Hokkaidō and formerly northeastern Honshū. They also populate the Kamchatka Peninsula and the Sakhalin and Kuril Islands now controlled by Russia, despite a dispute with Japan since World War II.

Alma mater
Nourishing mother. [Latin] Academy, school, college, university, or other educational institution one has attended.

Aloha

Love, affection, compassion, loved one. [Hawaiian] Traditional greeting of salutation and farewell, expressing love, friendship, and mercy.

"Aloha 'Oe"

May you be loved or Farewell to Thee. [Hawaiian] Title of the iconic song written around 1878 by Princess Lili'u Loloku who would become Queen Lili'uokalani.

Amida Buddha

Infinite light. [Japanese] Also *Amitābah* or *Amita* [Sanskrit]. *The Buddha of Infinite Light and Life.* The Enlightened Buddha believed to provide guidance toward rebirth in *gokuraku* [Japanese, *heaven*].

B

Bento

Useful thing. [Japanese] Borrowed from Chinese *biàndang*, [Hanyu Pinyin Chinese transliteration]. Dating from the late twelfth century, originally single food portions for farmers, hunters, and warriors that is served in a container based on a farmer's seed box. Traditionally, accompanied by protein, vegetables, and rice or noodles.

Boat Day

Except for during World War II, the arrival of ocean liners at Honolulu's Aloha Tower between the 1920s and 1950s was a communal celebration and major factor in the local economy. Lei greetings and performances by hula dancers and the Royal Hawaiian Band welcomed passengers. Boys and young men often dove into the harbor for coins thrown overboard by the tourists.

Bodhisattva

Enlightened existence. [Sanskrit] One on the path to Buddhahood, who has attained the enlightened state, but remains outside of nirvana [*heaven*] to assist others in attaining enlightenment. Often likened to saints in other religious beliefs, one of the most sacred is Avalokiteśvara (other names include Guanyin or Kuan Shih Yīn and Kanzeon, the masculine expression of Kuan Yīn) of whom the Dalai Lamas are believed to be reincarnations.

Bonshō

A Buddhist bell [Japanese] Also called *tsurigane* [*hanging bells*] and *ōgane* [*great bells*]. The large, lotus-shaped bell [resembling a seated Buddha] is used at Buddhist temples to mark time and call monks and parishioners to prayer. Cast without a clapper, they require a *shumoku* [a wood beam hung on ropes] to ring it from the exterior.

Bravado   *Brave, courageous.* [Italian, Spanish] Now usually meaning overbearing, boldness, showiness.

Bromeliads   Thousands of varieties of this monocot flowering and foliage plant originate in tropical and subtropical regions of the Americas. They grow in environments with full sun to deep shade, often growing on trees. With short roots and stems, their leaves vary in color, shape and length. Rosettes are vibrantly colored, with some species featuring miniature pineapples. [Scientific name, *Bromeliaceae*]

Buddha   *One who is awakened; the Enlightened or Knowing one. One who has attained Buddhahood.*

Byōdō-in Temple   A non-denominational Buddhist temple in the Valley of the Temples Memorial Park in Kahuluʻu Valley at the foot of the Koʻolau Mountains on the island of Oʻahu. Finished in 1968, it commemorates the 100-year anniversary of the start of Japanese emigration to Hawaiʻi. It is a smaller scale replica of the United Nations World Heritage Site in Uji, Japan, Byōdō-in Temple built over a thousand. It features a wooden Amitabha Buddha, covered in gold and lacquer. Other characteristics include a five-foot tall, three-ton pound bōnshō bell, small waterfalls, bridges crossing a fishpond with koi carp, wild peacocks, and rippled designs in the site's gravel.

C

Cape Plumbago   Also *cape leadwort* This decorative evergreen climbing plant is from South Africa. Featuring five-petal blue to lavender flowers, it grows as tall as 6-10 feet and 8-10 feet wide. While growing well in hot regions and drought resistant, it is killed by very low temperatures. [Scientific name, *Plumbago auriculata*]

Carte blanche   *Blank Paper.* [French] Full discretionary power to act as desired.

Cloisonné   *Partitioned; enclosed.* [French] Artistic work featuring enamel, glass, and/or gemstones within cellular frameworks of flattened gold, silver, brass, copper, or other metal wire that has been soldered or welded.

Crudités   *Rawness.* [French] Appetizers of sliced or whole raw vegetables usually served with a dipping sauce.

D-G

Dénouement   *Untie.* [From French, *denoue*] The resolution of a story after its climax.

Dharma   *Universal law, order, principles, etc.* [originally from Hindi] A term derived from and utilized by several Asian schools of philosophy and religion. The Japanese Buddhist schools of thought referenced in this book apply the term to the teachings and doctrines of the Buddha and one's life path lived in accordance with them.

Entrée   [French] A meal course preceding or between main courses. In the United States, it is the main course of a meal.

Etiquette   *Ticket; attach, stick.* [from French, *estique*]. Protocol for appropriate behavior and procedure required by norms of society.

Geta   *Clogs.* [Japanese]

H

Haku lei   [Hawaiian] A braided lei.

Hale   *House.* [Hawaiian]

Haleakalā   *House of the Sun.* [Hawaiian] The house used by the demi-god Māui. Name of a volcano and national park on the island of Maui.

Haleʻiwa   *House of the frigate bird.* [Hawaiian] A surfing beach and town on the north shore of the island of Oʻahu.

Hangesa   *Surplice.* [Japanese] Japanese Buddhist clerical garment.

Haole   *Foreigner, of foreign origin.* [Hawaiian] Current usage, an American, Englishman, and/or Caucasian.

Hapa   *Part, mixed, portion, fragment, fraction, percentage.* [Hawaiian] A term frequently used to indicate someone of mixed ethnicity.

Hau   *Red hau.* [Hawaiian] A flowering mallow tree. [Scientific name, *Hibiscus tiliaceus*]

Hau'ula	*Red hau tree.* [Hawaiian] A rural community on the northeast side of O'ahu named for a flowering mallow tree.
Hawai'i	*Place of the Gods.* [Hawaiian] Fiftieth state of the United States of America; name of the largest Hawaiian island (known as the Orchid Isle or the Big Island); the largest island in the United States. The Kingdom of Hawai'i was established by King Kamehameha I between 1795 and 1810. In a coup d'état between 1893 and 1894, the Kingdom was overthrown by resident foreigners (largely United States sugar industry businessmen) who established the Provisional Government of Hawai'i which lasted for a few months. The Republic of Hawai'i was then founded and existed until the United States annexation of Hawai'i in 1898 through passage of the Newlands Resolution. The Organic Act of 1900 authorized the election of a single non-voting delegate to the Congress of the United States. That year, Col. Robert William Kalanihiapo Wilcox became the first delegate to the United States Congress. Statehood was granted by Congress in 1959.
"Hawai'i Pono'ī"	*Hawai'i's Own True Sons.* [Hawaiian] The Hawai'i State song that was originally the Hawaiian Kingdom's national anthem. The music was composed by Captain Henri Berger, the royal bandmaster of King Kalākaua (known as the Merry Monarch) who wrote the lyrics.
Heiau	*Temple.* [Hawaiian] Ancient Hawaiian temples were built of varied materials and designs. They were sacred sites at which priests, royalty, and sometimes commoners could give offerings of fruit, fish, and other foods in gratitude for harvests and fortunate occurrences. Heiau were also used by individuals seeking blessings of good health and success, as well as for communal undertakings, such as war. They continue to be revered and used ceremonially today. Those with massive stone platforms are sometimes attributed to the menehune.
Heliconia	This monotypic plant herbaceous perennial plant is native to the forests of the tropical Americas, some islands of the western Pacific and Maluku,

Indonesia. It is named for Mount Helicon, home of the nine Greek goddesses who are muses of the arts and sciences. They feature paddle-shaped leaves and flowers, (waxy bracts), ranging from green to bright yellow, orange and red; their nectar attracts hummingbirds and butterflies. [Scientific name, *Heliconia*]

Hiragana *Ordinary* or *simple kana.* [Japanese] A syllabic and phonetic system for writing Japanese. Other forms of Japanese lettering include *katakana, kanji,* and *rōmaji* (a Latin-based script).

Hoi polloi *The masses; the common people.* [Greek]

Hokkaidō *Northern Sea Circuit.* [Japanese] Second largest Japanese island, it is the northernmost of the nation's main islands. Previously known as *Ezo* [also *Eso* or *Yeso*], the indigenous Ainu people remain a distinctive element in its population.

Homage *Respect, esteem.* [Latin and French] Vassal's oath of loyal service.

Honolulu *Sheltered Bay* or *harbor.* [Hawaiian] Located on the island of O'ahu, it is the largest city in and capital of the state of Hawai'i.

Hors d'oeuvres *Outside of work.* [French] Originally food partaken after working hours. It now refers to appetizers served before a meal, usually with wine or cocktails.

Hula [Hawaiian] Traditional dance of Hawai'i

Hula halau *Hula long house* or *workshed.* [Hawaiian] A school in which hula, the traditional dance form of Hawai'i, is taught.

I-J
'Ilima *See* Pua 'Ilima

In situ *In position.* [Latin]

Intarsiatore *Marquetry cabinet maker.* [Italian]

'Iolani, Palace *Royal hawk.* [Hawaiian] Home of the monarchy of the Kingdom of Hawai'i. Originally named *Hale Ali'i,* [*House of Royalty*], it was built in 1845 for King Kamehameha III [1813-1854]. The palace was renamed in 1863 by King Kamehameha V [1830-1872] in honor of his deceased brother, King Kamehameha IV [1934-1863].

Jōdo Shinshū   *The True Essence of the Pure Land Teaching.* [Japanese] A school or sect of Buddhism also known as Pure Land Buddhism. It focuses on the chanting of the Nembutsu affirmation of placing one's trust in the Amida Buddha, rather than on rituals to achieve salvation. Images of the Amida Buddha are prominent on the altars of this form of Buddhism. Believed to be the largest Buddhist school in Japan, its founding is credited to Shinran Shonin.

Joss stick   *Xiāng* [Pinyin]. A type of incense used in Asian temples.

K

Kahakō   *Macron.* [Hawaiian] A diacritical mark [a dash] placed over a vowel to extend pronunciation of the vowel's sound.

Kailua   *Two seas.* [Hawaiian] Bay, beach and town on the northeast end of the Windward side of Oʻahu.

Kaʻiulani, Princess

The royal or sacred one. [Hawaiian] A niece of Queen Liliʻuokalani, she was the last princess of Hawaiʻi. [1875-1899] Also the name of a Waikīkī hotel and upscale clothing line.

Kalanianaʻole   *The royal chief without measure.* [Hawaiian] Highway and beach park on east Oʻahu, named for Hawaiian Prince Jonah Kūhiō Kalanianaʻole.

Kalanianaʻole, Jonah Kūhiō (Prince, 1871-1922)

The royal chief without measure. [Hawaiian] When the Kingdom of Hawaiʻi was overthrown in a coup d'état between 1893 and 1894, Prince Kūhiō lost the opportunity of being king. He served a year's imprisonment for his participation in the Wilcox Rebellion in January of 1895 that aimed to restore the sovereignty of the Hawaiian Kingdom. During an extended honeymoon after marrying Chiefess Elizabeth Kahanu Kaʻauwai, he briefly joined the British Army and fought in the Second Boer War in

South Africa. Called *Ke Ali'i Maka'ainana* (*"Prince of the People"*), he was elected as a non-voting representative to the U.S. Congress for ten terms following the term served by Robert William Kalanihiapo Wilcox who was elected in 1900.

Kamehameha   *Hushed Silence, The Quiet One, The Lonely One,* or *Placed in the dark clouds.* [Hawaiian] Dynasty of Hawaiian Kings, founded by King Kamehameha the First [1758-1819] of the island of Hawai'i who fully unified the kingdom by 1810.

Kāne'ohe   *Bamboo man* or *husband.* [Hawaiian] Town in Windward O'ahu, west of Kailua.

Kanji   *Han characters* [Japanese]. *Hanzi*, classic Chinese logographic characters that are used for writing parallel words or phrases in Japanese. Other Japanese character writing systems based on phonics include *Hiragana, Katakana*, and *Rōmaji*.

Kanshō   *Calling bell.* Also *Gyojishō*, or *ritual bell.* [Japanese] A small hanging bell rung with a mallet.

Katana   From *"kata"* (*one-sided*) and *"na"* (*blade*). From the Chinese word *dāo* for a Chinese saber used for slashing and chopping. The Japanese katana sword has a long curved, single edged blade with two-handed hilt and a squared or circular guard. Dating to the late 13th century, the official term for this sword in Japan is *uchigatana.*

Kanzeon   *See* Bodhisattva

Keiki   *Child, offspring.* [Hawaiian]

Ke'oni   Diminutive form of "John." [Hawaiian]

Kiku shidare zakura   *Chrysanthemum weeping cherry blossom.* [Japanese] The deciduous tree may be named for biannual Japanese Buddhist memorial services. With semi-double ten-petal flowers, the tree blooms with light to deep pink buds and then nearly white flowers. The weeping Higan cherry tree has low susceptibility to heat and stress and has been recorded to live many hundreds of years. Such is the Miharu Takizakura [*waterfall*] cherry tree located in Fukushima Prefecture. This National Treasure of Japan is believed to be over 1,000 years old. [Scientific name, *Prunus subhirtella*]

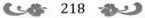

Kimchi	A traditional Korean side dish of pickled and fermented cabbage.

Kimono	*Wearing thing.* [Japanese] a traditional Japanese sleeved wrapped robe that has developed into a T-shaped garment worn with an *obi* [*sash*] tied at the back.

Koa	Acacia tree [Hawaiian] An endangered species known for its fine-grained wood, favored for building canoes, furniture, accessories, jewelry, bowls, plates, and other utensils. [Scientific name, *Acacia koa*]

Koto	Six-by-one-foot Japanese stringed musical instrument traditionally made from paulownia wood [Scientific name, *Paulownia tomentosa*] featuring thirteen silk strings and movable ivory bridges. A base *koto* has seventeen strings. First played by musicians seated on the floor.

Kuan Shih Yīn	Also *Guānshìyīn* or *Guānyīn* [Pinyin]. Adapted from the Indian male bodhisattva [*demi-god*] *Avalokiteśvara* [Sanskrit], it was introduced to China's Tang Dynasty [618-907] by Buddhist priests via the Silk Road. Associated with feminine characteristics [yīn] of compassion and kindness, by the Song Dynasty [960–1279], the figure fully integrated into Chinese culture as the female *Kuan Shih Yīn*, the demi-goddess of mercy who hears all of humankind's sufferings. She is revered especially by women in many Asian philosophies including Buddhism, Daoism, and Jainism. In Japan, the name *Kannon* or *Kanzeon* refers to both the female demi-god of mercy and the male demi-god of compassion. Their images are often featured on Tendaishū altars.

Kūlia	*Stand upright or strive; lucky.* [Hawaiian]

Kyōto	Located in the central plane of the Japanese island of Honshū, the city was the capitol of Japan for over 1,000 years. Because of its artistic, religious, and historical value, Allied Forces in World War II spared it from strategic firebombing and an atomic bomb.

Kyūshū	*Nine provinces.* [Japanese] Located to the southwest of Honshu, it is the third largest island in Japan. It is from this slightly tropical island that

148 field hands known as *gannenmono* [*first year men*] were contracted to work on Hawaiian sugar plantations in 1868.

L

Lānai Porch, balcony, deck, veranda. [Hawaiian]

Lanikai Community on the southern edge of Kailua in Windward Oʻahu.

Lapis lazuli Blue stone. Lazuli is derived from the Persian word lazhward for blue. It is also the root of the word, azure. The stone has been mined in the Saresang deposit of Afghanistan's Badakhshan district for over 7000 years.

Liliko ʻi Passion Fruit. [Hawaiian] A vine native to South America. The aromatic citrus fruit has many seeds and is sweet-tart in flavor. Yellow passion fruit [Scientific name, Passiflora edulis forma flavicarpa] is predominant in Hawaiʻi. Its juice is often used in food and beverages.

Lei Garland. [Hawaiian] or wreath of flowers, leaves, shells, candy, or other decorations.

Lóngnü Dragon girl or jade maiden. One of two acolytes traditionally shown with Kuan Shi Yīn. She represents sudden enlightenment. In a temple, she should be placed to the left of Kuan Shih Yīn.

M

Maître d' *Master of.* [French] Term usually referring to a restaurant's headwaiter. A *maître* d'*hôtel* is a hotel manager.

Makiki *To peck.* [Hawaiian] Type of volcanic stone used as a fishing weight or adze. Neighborhood northeast of downtown Honolulu.

Malasada [Portuguese] A deep-fried doughnut.

Mandala *Disk* or *circle.* [Sanskrit] A symbolic geometric design especially associated with Buddhism, Hinduism, and Jainism. Representing balance and harmony within the universe, they are often used ritually to focus a person's attention in searching for completeness.

Mānoa *Thick, solid, vast, deep.* [Hawaiian] Valley and neighborhood northeast of downtown Honolulu.

Location of the main campus of the University of Hawai'i.

Marimu — *Sea dream.* [Japanese]

Marquetry — Also *marqueterie. Inlaid work* [French, derived from the verb marqueter, *to variegate*]. Dating from the eighteenth century in England, France, Germany, and Italy, an artistic application of smooth surfaced veneers to furniture, pictorial panels, and decorative accessories. Materials vary, often in wood, mother of pearl, horn, gilt metals, or pictures.

Maui — [Hawaiian] Located northwest of the island of Hawai'i, Maui is the second largest Hawaiian Island. Legend says that it may have been named by the ocean-going navigator Hawai'i Loa. Described as coming from a land identified as Ka'aina kai melemele a kane (*land of the orange-yellow handsome sea of kane*), Hawai'i Loa is believed to have discovered the Hawaiian Islands. In this origin story, it is said that after naming the island of Hawai'i for himself, Hawai'i Loa named the island of Maui for his eldest son, believed to have been named for the demi-god Māui, a trickster who captured the sun. Maui is also the name of a star near the Pleiades cluster of stars in the Taurus constellation.

Medinilla — A tropical flowering perennial plant found from Africa east to southern Asia and the western Pacific. Offering flowers from soft to vibrant pinks, the plant grows as bushes, vines, and small trees. [Scientific name, *Medinilla*]

Mêlée — *Mixed.* [derived from French] A rowdy scuffle or brawl.

Menehune — [Hawaiian] A people of small stature whose legendary presence in the Hawaiian Islands may predate the arrival of the Polynesians. Noted for their exceptional craftsmanship, they are credited with building temples and other sacred sites as well as common objects of daily living (including fishponds, roads, canoes, and houses). Tales of the nocturnal menehune center on their fabricating massive objects within a single night.

Mokapu'u Point — *Bulging eye.* [Hawaiian] Ridge remnant on eastern edge of O'ahu which features a lighthouse and stunning beach view.

Mokulua [Hawaiian] Two adjacent islets, as those off the Lanikai shoreline.

Monkey pod Also known as *parota*, the exotic hardwood is native to Central and South America. Easily grown, it is now found throughout the tropics [including Hawai'i and the Philippines], and in some parts of the United States. The tree can grow to 50 or 80 feet. Resistant to decay and insects, it is popular for woodworking. [Scientific name, *Albizia saman*]

Mother lode Reference to the underground main vein of an ore or mineral. Now used colloquially to refer to the real or imagined origin of something of value.

Mu'umu'u *Cut short, maimed, amputated.* [Hawaiian] Dress adapted from garb of nineteenth-century Protestant Christian missionary women. It often has no yoke and is short sleeved.

N
Nā Mokulua *The two islands.* [Hawaiian] Two adjacent islets off the Lanikai shoreline. Viewed from the shore, the larger island is *Moku Nui* [*large island*] and the smaller is *Moku Iki* [*small island*].

Natal Plum A flowering drought tolerant perennial shrub native to Southern Africa. The plant features spiny broad-leafed green leaves, oval green, red, or purple fruits that are edible when ripe, and fragrant star-shaped white flowers. [Scientific name, *Carissa macrocarpa*]

Neem A tree in the mahogany family. The bitter antiseptic resin is used in medical and personal care products, and as an insect repellent. It was introduced to Hawai'i in the nineteenth century. [Scientific name, *Azadirachta indica*].

Nembutsu Also, *Nenbutsu* or *Nianfo*. [Japanese] Name of a Buddhist chant of a single phrase that recites the name of the Amida Buddha: *Namu Amida Butsu* [*I follow/return to/take refuge in the Amida Buddha*].

Niello *Blackish.* [Italian and Latin] Powder or paste used as a blackened inlay in etched or engraved metal objects. Dating from the Bronze Age [from 3300 to 300 BCE, depending on locale], it is comprised of copper, silver, lead, and sulfur.

Nisshōki *sun-mark flag.* [Japanese] The flag of Japan is colloquially called *Nisshōki* (Circle of the sun). It features a crimson disc on a white background. The name "Japan" was conferred by foreigners. Its people refer to the nation as *Nihon* or *Nippon* (origin of the sun), hence its description as the land of the rising sun.

Nuʻuanu *Cool heights.* [Hawaiian] Valley, stream and neighborhood north of downtown Honolulu.

O

Oʻahu *The Gathering place.* [Hawaiian] The third largest Hawaiian island. Location of the City and County of Honolulu. The capital of the state of Hawaiʻi.

Obi *Sash.* [Japanese] A sash worn by both men and women with a traditional kimono.

Objets d'art *Objects of art.* [French] Small, decorative items that are usually collectible.

Ojuzu *Counting beads.* Sometimes used interchangeably with *onenju*, *thought beads*, they are used in Japanese prayer bead rosaries in bracelet form, along with *oyadama* [*mother beads*].

Okesa Or *kesa*. [Japanese] *Surplice.* A religious vestment.

ʻOkina *Glottal stop.* [Hawaiian] A diacritical mark [ʻ] used to indicate a vocal break in sounding consonantal sounds, like that separating an interjection's syllables, like "oh-oh."

OM Or *ahum*. *I am.* A spiritual symbol and chant. Signifying ultimate reality, it is significant in Asian philosophies including Hinduism, Buddhism, and Jainism. When chanted, the vibration of the sound *ahum* is said to parallel the "cosmic hum." It can vibrate at a frequency of 432 hertz, which is found throughout nature.

Onaijin *Shrine area.* [Japanese]

P

Pali *Cliff or craggy hill.* [Hawaiian] Cliff in the Koʻolau Mountains at the head of Nuʻuanu Valley on Oʻahu. On its windward side, it offers a panoramic view.

Paulownia Named after Anna Pavlovna daughter of Tsar Paul I of Russia, the small fast-growing Asian tree of the bignonia family features heart-shaped leaves and fragrant lilac flowers. Its fine grained, light and warp-resistant wood was historically used to make Japanese clogs [*geta*] and samurai sword storage boxes [*shirasaya*]. It is now used to construct low-cost housing units. [Scientific name, *Paulownia tomentosa*]

Pīkake   *Peacock.* [Hawaiian] The Arabian jasmine is a fragrant shrub or climbing plant that is native to India and tropical Asia. It has rounded dark-green leaves and small white flowers that are frequently used to make a *lei*. Princess Ka'iulani was fond of these elegant flowers and her peacocks. [Scientific name, *Jasminum sambac*]

Plumeria   Also *frangipani.* Flowering and fragrant tropical tree in the dogbane family. Its flowers are often used for making a lei. [*plumeria*]

Postprandial   *After eating a meal.* [Latin root, *prandium*, referring a late breakfast or a lunch].

Provenance   *The point of origin.* [from the French *provenir*, *to come from*] The record of ownership for an antique item or piece of art used to authenticate its nature, origin and history.

Proviso   *Foresee* or *provide* [from the Lain *providere*] A provisionary stipulation or clause, often inserted in a legal document.

Pua 'ilima   *Flower or blossom of the 'ilima.* [Hawaiian] A species of the hibiscus family native to some Pacific islands, it grows upright or horizontally in sandy soil near the ocean. The herbaceous shrub has blossoms with five petals, usually in colors ranging from yellow to orange. The official flower of O'ahu. [Scientific name, *Sida fallax*]

Pūpū   *Marine* or *land shell; circular motif.* [Hawaiian] Today, an appetizer.

R
Raku   *Enjoyment.* [Japanese] Glazed pottery dating from the sixteenth century when Zen Buddhist masters sought natural ware for the classic Tea Ceremony. Alternating extremes in manufacturing temperature symbolizes completion of the cycle of earth, fire, air, and water, and the spirit of the artisan re-

siding in the ceramic art.

Rémoulade

From *remolas* [*horseradish* in the French Picard dialect]. A pungent condiment originating in France. Originally served with meals, it is now used as a dipping sauce with appetizers.

S

Saichō

A Buddhist monk [767-822] who is credited with founding the Tendaishū Buddhist school. Posthumus title *Dengyō daishi*. After serving as an envoy to China's Tang Dynasty 803-804, he gained support of the imperial court and established the Enryakuji Temple on Mount Hiei overlooking Kyōtō. Saichō adhered to a strict monastic life, eschewing "robbers, alcohol, and women." He went out into the world to uplift all people, including women like Eshin Ni, the woman he married. He an originator of chanting the mantra, *Namu Ichijo Myoho Renge Kyo* [*Glory to the Sutra of the Lotus of the Supreme Law*]. He may have introduced tea to Japan.

Samovar

Self boiler/brewer. [Russian] A metal urn with spigot, traditionally featuring superb ornamentation and heated with coal or charcoal.

Sans

Without. [Middle English and French]

Sapporo

Fifth largest city of Japan, it is the capital of the northern island of Hokkaidō. Its construction began in 1868 during the nation's expansion and modernization under the direction of Emperor Meiji. Aside from production of beer, it is noted for the annual Sapporo Snow Festival featuring massive ice sculptures.

Sashimi

Pierced body. [Japanese] Thinly sliced raw saltwater fish, served with varied garnishes and sauces.

Shākyamuni

Sage of the Shākya clan. Additional names include *Śākyamuni, Shakuson, Shaka Nyorai.* [Japanese] This is the name of the historical man Siddhartha Gotama (or Gautama), who was born in Lumbini, Nepal, circa 500 BCE. He is revered for discovering the Dharma (*Universal Law*) and revealing it to sentient beings to teach them about the elements of the path to spiritual awakening. After his spiritual awakening, he was called the Buddha or *awakened one.*

Shancai

Known as the *Golden Youth*, this acolyte of Kuan Shi Yīn (*the goddess of mercy*) is believed to bring gradual enlightenment. In a temple, he is placed to the right of Kuan Shi Yīn.

Shànghǎi

City at the mouth of the Yangtze River in the center of the coast of the PRC. Having the largest population of any city in China, or the world, it is classified as a province.

Shidarezakura

See Kiku shidare zakura

Shinran Shonin

[1173-1262] A Japanese monk who was originally a follower of Tendaishū Buddhism but later founded Jōdo Shinshū Buddhism. Like the rebellious monk Hōnen he followed, Shinran rejected established clerical practices and taught that all people can reach the Pure Land [heaven] by simply chanting the *Nembutsu*. Such undermining of prevailing religious norms by emerging expressions of Buddhism led to a lengthy holy war. Shinran is noted for spreading egalitarian principles by refusing to identify himself as a monk and rejecting prohibitions against eating meat and gender equality. Beyond rejecting celibacy, women clerics were featured in his practices, beginning with his wife Eshin Ni.

Shumoku musume

[Japanese] A wooden beam hung with ropes that is used to toll a large Bonshō bell from the outside.

Shōtoku, Prince

[574-622] From *sho* [*sacred*] and *toku* [*virtue*]. A leading Japanese politician and lay Buddhist scholar who built numerous Buddhist shrines in the Asuka period. Additionally, he wrote the first historical Japanese chronicle and initiated many irrigation and highway projects, welfare programs, and helped to import the Chinese lunar calendar and artistic styles.

T

Tabi

Foot pouch [Japanese] Dating from the fifteenth century, these divided-toe ankle socks are worn by men and women with thonged footwear such as flip-flop sandals, clogs, getas, and zoris.

Tendaishū Buddhism

Derived from mid-eighth century *T'ien T'ai* Chinese Buddhism, it is the oldest continuing school of Japanese Buddhism. It was established by the monk Saichō who served as an envoy to the Tang Dynasty of China. With the support of The Japanese nobility and imperial court, the Enryakuji Temple was established on Mount Hiei as the headquarters of the sect Established in the ninth century CE. The chanting of the mantra, *Namu Ichijo Myoho Renge Kyo* [*glory to the Sutra of the Lotus of the Supreme Law*] lies at the core of Tendaishū teachings. Conflicts with previously established sects of Buddhism and strife between the imperial court and leading clans led to the Genpei Civil War. With diminished prominence, Tendaishū warred with newer Buddhist sects such as Jōdo shinshū and Nichirenshū.

Tête-à-tête   *Head-to-head.* [French] Private conversation, often between two people.

Tori   *Pass through and enter; Bird perch.* [Japanese] Traditional Japanese gate normally found in front of a shrine and structures related to the Imperial Japanese family.

Tūtū   *Grandfather or grandmother, auntie, uncle* [Hawaiian] The term is used often as a title of respect for an older unrelated person. There is no "T" in the Hawaiian language, so *kūkū*, is the correct spelling in Hawaiian, although it is seldom used.

U

Ukupalu   *Blue-green Snapper.* [Hawaiian] This Hawaiian species has firm, translucent, pink, flesh that is moist with healthy oil. Its delicate flavor makes it ideal for being cooked and sashimi preparations. [Scientific name, *Aprion virescens*]

Una   *Tortoise shell.* [Hawaiian]

W

Waikīkī   *Spouting water.* [Hawaiian] The name of a chiefess; a famed Oʻahu beach.

Waimānalo   *Potable water.* [Hawaiian] Land division, bay, beach, and other features on the island of Oʻahu.

Y

Yakuza   *Eight, nine and three* (a reference to a game of chance) [Japanese] Transnational organized crime syndicates originating in Japan.

Yáng   *Masculine force in nature* [Chinese], expressed in sun, light white, gold, and strength. Chinese surname; clan and dynasty.

Yīn   *Feminine aspect of nature*, [Chinese] expressed in moon, darkness black, silver, and passivity. Chinese surname and dynasty.

Yukata   *Bathing clothes*. [Japanese] An unlined cotton summer kimono.

Yung-hui   Last Emperor of Korea. Installed on the throne as a puppet ruler by the Japanese.

About the Author

Jeanne Burrows-Johnson:
Author, Narrator, Motivational Speaker

Jeanne Burrows-Johnson is an author, narrator, consultant, and motivational speaker who writes both fiction and non-fiction. Academically, she became a member of Phi Beta Kappa while completing a Bachelor of Arts degree with distinction in history at the University of Hawai'i. During graduate studies and a teaching assistantship in the World Civilizations program of the University of Hawai'i, she was accepted for membership in Phi Alpha Theta. She is also a member of the National Writers Union, Arizona Authors Association, Sisters in Crime, Arizona Mystery Writers, and is a Lifetime Member of the British Association of Teachers of Dancing, Highland Division.

Drawing on experience in the performing arts, education, and marketing, Jeanne's authored and co-authored articles that have appeared in professional and general readership publications including: *Broker World,* the *Hawai'i Medical Journal*, *Newport This Week*, and *The Rotarian*. She was art director, indexer, and a co-author of the anthology *Under Sonoran Skies: Prose and Poetry from the High Desert*. Jeanne is the author of the award-winning Natalie Seachrist Hawaiian Mysteries which offer Island multiculturalism and pan-Pacific history in a classic literary style that is educational as well as entertaining.

After residing in Hawai'i for two decades, she now lives in Tucson, Arizona. As a consulting wordsmith, she draws on her interdisciplinary background to assist authors, artists, and other creative professionals achieve their desired potential at blog.JeanneBurrows-Johnson.com and

Imaginingswordpower.com. Samples of her writing and descriptions of her projects are available at her author website, JeanneBurrows-Johnson.com. You can share your comments and questions at Info@Jeanne-Burrows-Johnson.com.

DISCUSSION QUESTIONS FOR
YEN FOR MURDER

<u>ART & LAYOUT</u>

~ Did the book's cover provide a hint to the story?

~ Which aspects of the book did you find useful?
☐ Cast of Characters
☐ Pagination Art
☐ Chapter Quotes
☐ Prologue
☐ Epilogue
☐ Summary Guide to Hawaiian Pronunciation
☐ Annotated Glossary

<u>WHAT PARTS OF THE BOOK DID YOU FIND INVITING AND/OR USEFUL?</u>

<u>ASPECTS OF THE BOOK/SERIES</u>

~ Did you feel you were experiencing the settings?

~ Which of your senses were stirred? How?
☐ Sight
☐ Hearing
☐ Smell
☐ Prologue
☐ Prologue
☐ Epilogue
☐ Summary Guide to Hawaiian Pronunciation
☐ Annotated Glossary

~ Which places mentioned in the book [or series] would you like to visit?

<u>STORY</u>

~ Did anything in the plotline surprise you?

~ How did you relate to the expanding visions present through the book? Which one impacted you the most?

~ What relationships did you find most compelling?

CHARACTERS

~ Did you find the characters believable?

~ Did they remind you of anyone in your life, television, or films?

~ Which characters are you looking forward to meeting in future books in the series?

~ What are Natalie Seachrist's most endearing characteristics?

HISTORY

~ How would you evaluate the author's research?

~ Did the historical events and figures enliven the story?

~ What historical events would you like to explore further?

~ What historical people would you like to learn about in greater detail?

~ Was this book a good platform for introducing aspects of history and multi-culturalism?

ISLAND CULTURE

~ What have you learned about life in the Hawaiian Islands?

~ Which of the foods or recipes would you like to try?
[Some recipes are available on my author website]

What have you enjoyed the most about this book and/or series?

The First Three Murderous Volumes of the Natalie Seachrist Hawaiian Mysteries

Prospect For Murder

After a shattering vision of her grandniece's body draped over a vintage car, the protagonist moves into the Honolulu apartment the girl was to rent. Aided by retired police detective Ke'oni Hewitt and her feline companion Miss Una, the writer strives to learn the truth of Ariel's death before the police close their inquiries. But has she put herself in front of a murderer willing to kill again?

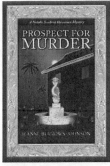

Murder On Mokulua Drive

Again featuring the lush environs, culture, and pan-Pacific history of Hawai'i, the trio pursues solving another unforeseen murder while settling into the seaside cottage of Natalie's Auntie. Does resolution of the gruesome murder lie in the deceased's transnational past? Or in the visible present among innocuous seeming companions?

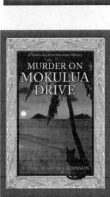

Murders of Conveyance

As Natalie and Ke'oni enjoy the Chinese New Year Aloha Scavenger Hunt, she dreams of a 1950's murder. When it parallels one in their Honolulu hotel, she volunteers to help Ke'oni's former partner, HPD detective John Dias. Expanding visions soon link the two deaths to a woman dressed in red and hints of a priceless white jade Kuan Yin figurine.

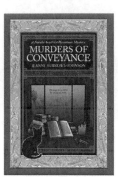

SNIPPET OF PROLOGUE TO *A SPINELESS MURDER*

THE NEXT BOOK IN THE NATALIE SEACHRIST
HAWAIIAN MYSTERY SERIES

BY JEANNE BURROWS-JOHNSON

PROLOGUE

I see my path, but I don't know where it leads.
Rosalia de Castro [1837 - 1885]

Sinking into that state between one of my visions and sleeping, I feel my body lighten as I float through a night-time sky filled with a hazy moon and stars that sparkle from behind wispy cirrus clouds. I sigh and wonder what may be revealed in this night.

Abruptly, the warmth of a bright sunrise forces me to open my eyes to find that I am standing on a palm tree lined walkway. I walk forward into ground-level fog until I find myself standing in the squarish foyer of a tall building. The floor beneath my sandals is worn linoleum. Ahead is a flight of stairs. Climbing upward, I pass floor after floor seeing nothing beyond periodic landings.

My fatigue increases with each step I take. Leaning against the hand-rail to catch my breath, I inhale deeply and then continue my journey. After climbing another flight of stairs, I reach the top. I know better than to look below me, which would only trigger dizziness. Instead, I focus on the scene before me.